Chapter 1

Footsteps approach. I'd know the sound a   ., the headmistress's skyscraper heels clattering closer and closer, the echoing corridor heralding her arrival and delivering the fatal blow to these last precious moments I have before squalling, unruly children burst into my classroom ready to start another tedious term. I'm at the piano trying to capture the fleeting fragments of melody flitting through my mind. This might be the composition, the masterpiece that earns me my way out of here.

The door grinds open. I don't look up, but fumble for the pencil perched behind my right ear to draw the notes onto my manuscript. Composing is getting harder. If I don't record a melody as it dances on tiptoe through my head, it goes twirling off into the fathomless hole gaping ever wider in the middle of my aging brain. But the sound of two chattering women stepping into my classroom startles the snippet, and it darts out of reach. Damn. C, A, A♯, G. Or was it C, A♯, G? I put down my pencil and reach under my glasses to squeeze the bridge of my nose. It's no good. I can't remember.

"Ewan," the headmistress says. "Hi."

Her theatrical smile shows bleached white teeth. My lips twitch, but I manage not to laugh aloud. She is never so friendly, but with a new member of staff at her side, she'll do anything to impress.

"And good morning once again, Mrs Phillips."

We have already drawn swords in our first bout of term, and I see no point in pretending otherwise. I raise my voice because I love the acoustics in here. The sound comes bounding back to me like an exuberant dog which jumps up and licks my face, reminding me that no matter how many years I've spent down here, exiled in the chocolate-box prettiness of Cambridgeshire, it still links me with a silvery granite umbilical cord to home, to Aberdeen. I stare at the lines and notes on the page in front of me without seeing, lost in nostalgia for my old life. If only I could go back. No, that's silly. I can't, even if it was all a long time ago.

The headmistress coughs to remind me there is a point to her visit.

"If you're not too busy Mr. Davies,"

I huff, brow raised, as she transforms her west-country yokel's voice into lion-taming mode, tired of being ordered around and I've only been back at work two days and, let's see now, forty-five minutes. This isn't how I thought my life would turn out; this isn't how I saw it. The younger 'me', my teenaged self, walked away a long time ago, shaking his head in disgust at just how much I've managed to screw things up. None of this is what he had in mind.

"This is your supply teacher, Mrs Cartwright. Mrs Cartwright, this is Ewan Davies, the Head of our Music Department."

I look up from my manuscript with a sigh. Behind the headmistress's cheap, chain store suit and dyed, ironed blonde hair, there lurks something flowery. Fantastic: another beaded, part-time do-gooder washes up in my department with nothing useful in hand but some fanciful idea of serving society by teaching its little darlings. I am about to turn back to my composition, when something startling sparks in my mind. It goes 'spark, spark', and 'whoosh' as recognition sets my memory alight. Oh god, no. Please, no. No.

"Rebecca!"

I stand up. My piano stool goes toppling across the linoleum floor and lands with a crash I don't hear. I am trembling, my face tingling, the skin prickling as though it were fizzing, while my heart tries to seize the initiative, punch its way out and run. What is she doing here? She shouldn't be here. My body runs hot and cold and cold and hot, my ordered life melting into chaos. I grab hold of the piano with unsteady hands, and my manuscript falls from its stand, its pages floating to the floor like ragged silken strands from the tapestry of time ripped apart by this most unexpected and unwelcome collision of past and present. Shockwaves ripple through my cells. My mouth opens and closes, hanging like an attic trapdoor, but I can't make a sound. Coherent speech is beyond me.

My ex-wife claps her hands together, and laughs, setting an assortment of silver bangles on her arms chinking with every move. She is almost dancing with delight, towering over the headmistress's diminutive form in flat, fair-trade sandals. Her colourful, patterned skirt, which I know will have been handcrafted by a peasant woman on some far-flung hillside, swirls around her ankles, while an embroidered white tunic highlights wholesome, freckled skin glowing with self-righteous vegan health and vitality. Her mouth settles into a wide smile as she looks at me, her fingers fiddling with a silver moon pendant around her neck. I am gawping, I know, but I don't have the nous to stop.

"Hello Ewan."

"You know each other?" The headmistress is bubbling with astonishment. I expect it amuses her to see me off-guard, and that's all the prompting I need to set about retrieving my shattered senses.

"Uh, yes." I step out from behind the piano. For a second I falter. What should I do? But then my body moves, as though possessed by a will of its own, and my legs cover the classroom in long, easy strides. Behavioural 'norms' are so ingrained, I reflect, we all do whatever it takes to act in what is deemed 'an appropriate manner.'

"How are you?" I hold out my arms. Rebecca gives a squeak of delight, and throws herself into my embrace. We hug each other tight, outwardly correct while inwardly my mind is lurching, staggering from side to side across the plain of rational thought, searching for clues as to how best to proceed.

She draws back to look up at me, her blue-grey eyes blurry with tears, her clutching fingers creasing my lilac shirt sleeves.

"It's been so long."

Nine and a half years, but I decide not to say this aloud. It might sound like I've been counting.

"So how do you know each other?" The headmistress's toothy smile has been downgraded to a frown, and I'm not surprised. After all, she's already let it be known this morning what she thinks of my 'contributory unpleasantness' that led to the resignation of mousey Miss Harris, my previous 'colleague'. Well, what did she expect? If I'd been allowed to interview Miss Harris in the first place, she would never have come to work here, fresh out of teaching college and wide-eyed with fear. She barely lasted a term. I need someone who can grasp my methods without the need for second explanations, someone who will work as hard as I do. Standards don't achieve themselves.

"You aren't some long-lost, feuding relatives, I hope."

Everything in me sinks. I go to speak. I open my mouth to shepherd out words, because this is the part where I speak up. This is my cue to say 'actually Mrs P, this is Rebecca my ex-wife and no, I can't work with her, I'd rather work with the, frankly, pathetic Miss Harris', but I don't. Instead, I honour the plea in Rebecca's eyes, and nod to the stirring in my soul whose seductive whispers are suggesting this is a twist of woolly, romantic fate, my beloved returned to my arms after all these years. I don't believe in fate, but it's a pretty story.

"We met at university," Rebecca obliges, her eyebrows arching, warning me not to contradict, but that part is true. I make myself smile and nod, hoping the headmistress will fall for Rebecca's nonchalant tone. I daren't look at Mrs Phillips for fear I see her reaching for the dial which will turn up the heat of her scrutiny, her terrier's eyes unearthing their own conclusions. Rebecca bites her lip. She's always done that. Doesn't she realise she might as well slap a neon sticker with the word 'guilty' onto her forehead?

"Haven't seen each other for years though, have we?" I say, trying to throw the scent.

"And look at you, you haven't changed a bit," Rebecca grins, clapping her hands together. "Well, apart from the grey hairs." Her hand reaches out to touch the silver I try to ignore snaking through the auburn, but she thinks better of it and recoils.

She draws her hand away, and steps back. I breathe out, realising I have been holding my breath, afraid of the impression we are creating. Rebecca turns to the headmistress who, I fear, isn't sure how to interpret what she's just witnessed, and mouths some platitude about how great it's going to be working alongside me. I say nothing. I say nothing because I have missed my chance. I missed my chance to speak, and now I am complicit in the lie. It's going to be great working alongside Rebecca. No, really, it is. Perhaps if I say it often enough it will be true.

Chapter 2

Mrs Rebecca Cartwright waits until the headmistress's heels have clattered out of earshot, then she lets out a whoop of delight, and throws herself back into my arms. We hug, we laugh, and I am wondering what would happen if I were to try and kiss her, when she steps back, her eyes wide and serious.

"Ewan, thank you."

"For what?" I shrug, sifting through my recollection of the last five minutes for what I have done that warrants thanks. It is a fruitless search.

"For not telling the headmistress."

Ah, that. She is wringing her hands together, threading her fingers over and over again, the silver bangles clinking and clunking.

"I've been qualified for six months now but it's been impossible to find a job. The agency said this might be permanent if I make the right impression, and with it being in Thatchington, it's so handy for home."

I smile to myself. No one has ever, or would ever, describe my ex-wife as 'laconic'. She burbles away letting anything and everything flow from her mouth. I wonder if it's occurred to her it might be harder for her to keep quiet about our past than me.

"Thank you for giving me a chance. If you'd told her we've been married, that would have been the end of that. You do think we'll be okay working together, don't you?"

She looks at me with her beautiful eyes sparkling beneath their long, luxurious lashes. I'm holding my breath again. In the last few years, the pain of missing her has been growing weaker. Today, it's as though we have never been apart. And when she looks at me through those eyes, not the hard eyes that accused and ridiculed, I will grant her anything. This, she knows.

"Oh please," I scoff, loving my own show. I'm such a performer. But then I've spent years polishing my routine. Lying comes as easy to me as breathing. There have been more times than I can remember when it's been almost as important.

"That was all such a long time ago. Of course we can work together. And nobody needs to know." I'm almost convincing myself.

"Nobody needs to know," she echoes, pondering my words. "Thank you Ewan. You've always been a kind soul. Thank you."

She reaches out and takes both my hands. Her eyes glisten, teary. I am thinking to myself that if this were a film, the music would be sweeping to a crescendo as the handsome, though somewhat misunderstood, hero leans in to kiss his lady. But I see something flit across Rebecca's face, and the bitter voice of experience asserts she isn't sharing in my fantasy.

"You know, I haven't asked."

"Asked what?"

Actually, I know what she's thinking. It's a gift, you see. I can hear other people's thoughts. Not just anyone's thoughts, you must understand, before you start pitying me for being privy to the hormonal meanderings of a class-full of bored teenagers, just special people; people who have something important to say to me. So I know she's going to ask if I'm married, and I'm going to feel embarrassed when I have to say no while she's probably ensconced in a perpetual game of 'happy-bloody-families' with some fabulous guy and a pack of starry-eyed kids. Great. Why does it always come down to this? If they don't want to know what amazing job you perform, then it's do you have a successful home life. Of course, she doesn't know about Marcia; that was after she left. I'm glad she doesn't know about Marcia, come to that. There would be no question of her being able to look at me, never mind talk to or work with me if she knew what I'd done.

"How are you?"

I misunderstand. On a subconscious level, this is probably intentional.

"Well I'm fine of course," I chuckle at her serious expression, her searching eyes, and the way she's holding onto my hands, refusing to let me pull away while she scans my face for the true answer. Ah, wait a minute, she wants the true answer. Damn. I had hoped she might have forgotten, but how could I ever expect her to forget about that? Unease starts knotting up the soft tissue deep down inside my belly, stiffening my body. I'm not safe any more. She knows too much about me.

"No, how 'are' you Ewan? You know what I mean."

This time I yank my hands away, afraid she might insist on finding out for herself, ripping back my sleeves to inspect my scars. But there's nothing to see she hasn't seen before. Marcia's death saw to that.

"Rebecca, I'm fine." But she's got that look on her face, her lips are pursed, her eyes narrowed as I take a step backwards. Both her eyebrows rise as she cocks her head, and I realise I've got my arms folded behind my back. You can almost hear a clank as her brain adds two and two, but makes it into a number she thinks she knows. Too late I let my arms dangle by my sides. She goes on looking through critical eyes.

"I'm telling you now; I can't do this any more. I can't go on like this. You need help. And if you don't make an appointment to see the doctor, then this marriage is over."

"Fine 'fine', or 'oh yes Rebecca, let's pretend everything's great'?"

So that's it: my ex-wife thinks she can breeze into my classroom, charm me into letting her stay, and then resurrect the most embittered argument of our married life. It's been nine and a half years. I don't have to do this. I don't have to pick up the gauntlet. And I do not have to explain myself to anyone.

I ponder my arsenal for a suitable response. There is the flat 'I'm fine, thank you' which could be delivered in a stern tone of reproach designed to deter further questioning. There is the spikier 'mind your own business' which I think I favour, but will heap fuel on her suspicions. And then there is the, frankly, explosive 'what concern is that of yours' which is almost wriggling to be let out of my mouth.

This is what I choose. I rather like it. A two-pronged defence, it's cutting yet evasive.

"You know, that's not a conversation I would have with any other member of staff in this school. And you're here to do a job, not nit-pick over things that may, or may not have happened in the past."

Oh, but I'm good. Her cocky, composed air crumples, and I congratulate myself. It isn't without reason I'm widely if not unanimously viewed as an awkward bastard amongst the staff. It's nothing to me if I leave people huffing and scowling in my wake. We're here to do a job. Standards don't achieve themselves, or by being all cosy and chummy drinking tea together in the staffroom, pretending we care about one another. But then she arches her left eyebrow, and I remember I've never won an argument with her yet.

"Well then, far be it for me to enquire after your state of health. But being unable to answer the question in a civil manner tells me as much as I want to know."

I flap and flail, my tongue stammering as I struggle for an answer, but, as usual, Rebecca is serene in her victory. She holds up both hands to silence me.

"Subject closed," she says. "Now, you'd better go through what do you want me to do this morning."

Outfoxed, out-manoeuvred: checkmate to my ex-wife. Why is she here? I stand staring, immobile while inwardly I am awash in a seething ocean, clinging to a life-raft, my sanity, which feels like it's dissolving in my hands. It had been flat calm up until now. In fact, I've been becalmed for years, bobbing along, contented with the numbness of nothing happening, safe in monotony. But now the sky has turned from soft grey to purplish-black, the water is boiling with a sudden violent swell, and I've been pitched overboard, all in the space of the last half-hour, the last half-hour in which I had expected to be happily composing, conjuring music around me as I floated in peace on my sea. I look at Rebecca, and she folds her arms, waiting.

I turn to my desk, and shiver.

Chapter 3

To my relief, and rather to my surprise, Rebecca proves to be a competent teacher, and so after its tumultuous start, my morning rumbles on without encountering any more potholes. I say 'to my surprise' not because I bear my ex-wife such an ill-will I cannot entertain the thought she might be good at her job, but for the simple reason that, when you think about it, teaching music to secondary school students isn't an obvious career move for an archaeologist.

The last I heard, she was in charge of a dig somewhere in Turkey, as far away as imaginable from the familiarity of a place like Thatchington with its bevy of blue plaques and over-documented history. This area isn't a frontier for those who like to scrabble through the earth with their bare hands seeking ambiguous clues to an uncertain past; there aren't any prizes to claim or theories left to devise. I must remember to ask what prompted such a dramatic change in her plans, and, as my memory goes on opening boxes stowed deep in the recesses of my mind, if she ever wrote that book she was planning. Hmm. I tap my pen against my cheek gazing across a landscape of empty desks. I wonder.

My grandfather's old watch tells me there's only a half hour left of lunch break. I stare at its dull gold face in the vain hope it might change its mind and move its hands back a bit so I won't have wasted so much time thinking about Rebecca. My stomach gurgles. It won't stop complaining. All the canteen had to offer today was a splurge of processed food, so I haven't eaten. I shift from side to side. Damn this uncomfortable chair, I should ask for a new one. I put down my pen, and stretch my arms above my head, flexing the tension from my shoulder, my spine stiff from sitting. A change of scenery, yes, that's a good idea. I push back my chair and get up stretching and yawning. What can I do with half an hour?

I know. There's something I need to look up on the internet. If I nip upstairs to my office, I will have time to look at the computer over a cup of tea before class, and, if my office companion is busy charming the ladies in the staffroom, the chance to listen to something soothing, a little Debussy perhaps, to smooth the nerves that would have been ruffled anyway today by being back at work, but are fluffed up, startled by the breeze of Rebecca's presence. I have one last stretch, and then I button up my waistcoat. This is my favourite suit, cut for me by the tailor here in Thatchington. It's too warm for this time of year, but its dark pinstripe lends an air of invincibility which helps me withstand the tedium of life in this establishment. I leave my jacket hanging on the back of my chair as I head off upstairs.

I share an office with my friend Alex Garvie, who runs the Art Department, and as I skulk round the corner to our lair on the first floor, I find the door wide open and his big voice booming out into the corridor. Much as it is good to spend time with an ally in this damned school, my heart sinks. I had been coveting my own company, and he isn't alone.

"Those idiots that run that summer club, all tree-hugging do-gooders the lot of them, they let the kids run riot. I ask you, Becks, what is the point of running a kids' club"

"If you're not going to supervise the little bastards properly?" I finish for him, having already heard the story of how the holiday club have trashed his darkroom at least three times, the first with him ranting, strutting up and down in my classroom like a demented cockerel. He folds his hands behind his wild mane of blonde hair as he laughs one of his wild, infectious guffaws and crosses one corduroy leg high over the other on his desk, a grudging nod towards smart attire undone by the splatters of paint adorning his bare arms.

"Exactly," he grins. "I couldn't have put it better myself. The tossers."

"Welcome to the wonderful world of Thatchington High," I say to Rebecca who's sitting giggling, her hands wrapped around a mug. She's laughing along, but her eyes dart from me to Alex as though she's ready to bolt at the first hint laughter isn't an appropriate reaction.

"And Mr. Garvie," I say, in a perfect mimic of the head's bucolic lilt. "How many times do I have to tell you to get your feet off your desk?" I'm very good. He actually takes his feet down and sits up as I pad over to investigate whether there is any water in the small plastic kettle we keep hidden down between a pair of filing cabinets in direct contravention of another of the head's edicts 'thou shalt not make hot drinks in thy offices.' "Fancy another cup of tea?"

"I'm fine, thanks" Rebecca's eyes are shining as she watches me, and she holds her mug against her cheek. "Ewan Davies, you haven't changed a bit. You've lost a lot of weight though."

"You know him?" Alex asks. "You never told me. See, all the more reason for you to go and tell our glorious leader you want to come and work in my department. That's all right with you, mate, isn't it?" He says to me. "I'll have my star pupil working for me, and you can have Nancy back. Sounds fair. I'll have another coffee, ta."

"Fair? I've only just got rid of him. He's your problem now."

'Nancy' is our moniker for the teaching assistant, Nathan James. He's supposed to be a trained teacher, although no one in the school would dream of letting him loose with a class. As he says in his booming rugger-boy tones, he just wants to give something back to society, and he's signed up to a government scheme designed to do just that, to enable bright young graduates to give two years of their time before turning into the corporate high-flyers and captains of industry most have been born to be. But the problem is quite simple: all the qualifications in the world, and he has plenty, can't make him any less of a buffoon. He's been a thorn in our sides for a year so far at Thatchington High, and I think the only reason he has a job here is because his father, a golfing buddy of the head of the school governors, does everything he can to delay the day his son gets the chance to ruin the family's wine business.

"Yeah, but Becks is one of my best students," he grins at her and she blushes, and, well I'd say she is 'simpering'. I shake my head, this frippetish Rebecca a disturbing caricature of the headstrong, no-nonsense woman I know. But Alex is the subject of many schoolgirl crushes, not to mention a certain frisson of feeling towards him from many of the female members of staff, particularly the younger ones. There is a visible hitching up of bra straps, and crescendo in girlish giggling whenever he saunters into the staffroom, along with a flurry of offers to make him cups of coffee. You've no idea how much it cheers me to see Rebecca, no, sorry, 'Becks' is in no way immune either.

"I'm just going to have to tell Fifi P," he says.

I sigh, and rummage for a clean mug amongst my collection of tea, and his collection of coffee. If the headmistress is anything like the rest of the women in this school, she'll be thrilled he has a nickname for her too.

"How does Rebecca come to be one of your best students? I mean, appearances can be deceptive, but I wouldn't have had you down as old enough to have taught her at school."

"Nah, evening class, mate," he says. "She's good. That's why she should be working for me, not you. Go on," he wheedles Rebecca and pushes his telephone across the desk. "Ring Fifi and tell her; go on."

"Leave Mrs Cartwright alone," I sigh, spooning coffee into his mug. "You are incorrigible. Poor Tessa." I can imagine his elegant wife sitting here, rolling her eyes at his performance. For a while I dated a girl called Jemima. She had long titian hair, and Alex was so excited about painting her, he invited us round for dinner, only to drag Jemima off into his studio while Tessa and I sat drinking wine in the kitchen. 'He's always like this around someone who inspires him,' Tessa had said, trying to soothe my glum demeanour. 'Take no notice, it'll wear off soon.' But it was me who bored Jemima first.

"How is Tessa?" Rebecca asks.

Her question hits me hard between the ribs, and I turn aside as I fish the teabag out of my mug, for fear she should see me wince. Until this morning I didn't know my ex-wife lived nearby, let alone that we shared friends. I scowl at the thought of her sitting with Alex's wife, chattering over a pot of tea, as I do when I pop round to swap seeds or cuttings with someone who shares my passion for gardening. And I imagine Rebecca gossiping, picture Tessa's pale eyes widening as Rebecca giggles over our past, as she divulges too many mortifying snippets. What if everyone finds out? This is no good. Never mind having her transferred to Art, I can't have her working here at all. I pass Alex his coffee, and wander over to my desk.

"Ta mate. Yeah, she's all right is Tessa. Expanding nicely, I suppose you could say. Mind you, she's had plenty of practice, though, hasn't she? Hey, don't tell anyone," he glances at me and leans in closer to Rebecca, dropping his voice. "She says I've got to go for," and he gestures with his fingers, "snippety-snip."

"I can't say I blame her," I sit down at my desk and sign in to the computer.

"Did you get away with the kids through the summer after all?" Rebecca asks. She is sitting with her back to me, and I'm beginning to feel as though this is some sort of contest in which we're flapping and displaying, trying to outdo one another with extravagant claims to our rights of the exclusive ownership of Alex's friendship.

"Yeah, spent three weeks camping in The New Forest," he says, oblivious to our tussling. "The nippers are getting quite keen on the whole outdoors lark."

"You made a pregnant woman go camping?" I look up from the keyboard, struggling both to push into the conversation, and picture Tessa as someone who willingly spends swathes of the summer roughing it in a tent. My finger hits 'enter' and the system sets off scouring its vast databases for anything it can find on dye added to meat. I read a series of newspaper articles during the summer about the safety of food being produced these days. No one I've spoken to since they were published either saw them, or seems to be aware of what's going on. I am beginning to think the articles only featured in my newspaper, and that they were put there on purpose.

"Aw, she loves it, mate. Yeah, but I'll tell you what though," he says, his joviality melting like summer snow. "If it wasn't for Garvie-number-four coming along, I'd tell Fiona-bloody-Phillips where to shove her job. What are my photography students supposed to do without a darkroom?"

He launches into another tirade, this time provoked by a suggestion of Nathan's the repairs become a class project, his anger re-igniting like pockets of wildfire on a ravaged heath despite the best efforts of firefighters to bring it under control.

"I tell you what mate," he says to me, red faced and panting now. "I'd like to punch Nancy so fucking hard he won't know what day it is for at least a week."

"As I said," I look up from sifting through the fruits of my internet search and project a glowing wide smile to Rebecca. "Welcome to the wonderful world of Thatchington High. I bet you're glad you're only here for the day."

Alex mutters something about 'this wretched place' into his coffee, smarting at Nathan's interference in his beloved department, and screws up a sheet of paper on his desk with the relish I imagine he'd employ in wringing the man's neck. A hazy smile crosses Rebecca's face as she studies his muscled arms, and her eyes light up with mischief.

"Why do you both work here if you don't like it then?"

"Oh, you know," he melts back into a grin. "Still trying to paint the masterpiece that'll make my fortune, while Tchaikovsky over there is still trying to finish his symphony. One of these days we'll be rich enough to retire, eh Ewan?"

"Just don't hold your breath," I say, trying to concentrate. I've found this website called 'fascinating facts they don't want you to know.' They have a forum discussing additives in food, but you have to sign up, enter your name and email address. I loosen my collar. If there is a conspiracy to cover up what's being done to food by the processing and manufacturing industries, I don't think it's prudent to advertise that I've discovered it. I've devoured enough espionage novels to be afraid of what might happen.

"Yeah, but between you and me, Becks," Alex leans across to Rebecca, grinning at me. He indicates me with a nod of his head. "He says he hates working here, but the truth is he loves it here so much he'll never leave. Sleeps in a cardboard box in his classroom, don't you mate? Course, that's 'cause he's a miserable old sod. Wait a minute," he sits up, eyes wide with inspiration, and claps his hands together in delight. "This is perfect, the solution to your woman drought."

Oh god no, not in front of Rebecca. I know what's coming next. My face fires with colour and I try to interrupt, but Alex is riding a wave nothing can deflect.

"Becks, I bet you've got a nice single mate he could go out with. Of course, that would have to be a nice desperate single mate, a-ha-ha-ha."

My humiliation is complete. First I'm forced to work with my ex-wife because I'm too much of a coward to refuse, and then one of my closest friends suggests enlisting her help to find me a girlfriend. Rebecca smiles, but she is kind enough to resist laughing along. She says something along the lines of she'll have to see what she can do, but I can't bring myself to look at her as I sip my tea, to acknowledge my failure on this front. I might have wanted to maintain certain appearances around my ex-wife, but my dignity has been revealed a sham by Alex's ongoing obsession with me being single. You'd think after all this time he'd have something more original to say, but he is too busy entertaining Rebecca, or 'Becks' as he calls her, to notice my chagrin. They laugh together, their chummy camaraderie like a spiky stone in my shoe jabbing deep into my sole.

Later, she gives a polite knock before opening the door to my classroom. I am busy trying not to think about her, gathering up sheet music from my last class as she pops her head around the door and, just as this morning, her sudden appearance sends me reeling. I trip over a metal music stand, and it goes skittering and clattering across the floor along with the pages of score I was holding. She grins, sidles around the door, and bends down to help me pick everything up. For the umpteenth time today, my face flares with hot, sweaty colour at being in her presence. Why is she here? I hope she doesn't have to be here tomorrow, I'm not sure my overstrung nerves can bear the strain.

"Thank you," I say as we both stand up, and she hands me the rest of the music. I glance up at the clock and see the time is heading towards a half past four. "You should get off home now. Thank you for everything you've done today. It's been busy, and I bet you're tired." And then, because I can't resist twisting the knife stuck deep in my gut, I add, "I expect you'll want to get home before your husband starts wondering where you've got to."

"Rick? Oh, Rick won't be home yet. And he'll be so pleased to find I'm working at last, I should think he'll be delighted to find I'm not there," she says with a wry smile. I don't know what to say to this, and the awkwardness between us grows soupier. The memory of me, the teenaged runaway, stood at her door without even so much as a suitcase or a change of clothes, bobs up to the surface, and I wonder if this time it's she asking me for help. And I would be obliged, I know.

She pulls on a long, plum coloured cardigan, and picks up her bag.

"Oh, I'd better give you these."

I watch as she rummages in a multicoloured bag, a hotchpotch of fabric remnants stitched together, I'm guessing, by some women's fair-trade cooperative she likes to support, waiting to see what it is she has to give.

She produces the folder of teaching plans I'd given her earlier in the day, and a trickle of disappointment it isn't something more exciting quivers down my spine.

"I think I'll be here tomorrow, but I don't know until I hear from the agency. Fiona did say she'd like me to carry on until you find a permanent teacher."

"She did?" My face flushes with fresh colour. The palms of my hands break out into a sweat, and I tuck them under my armpits just in case she should try to shake one. 'Fiona' should have discussed this with me.

"Okay, she says, swinging the bag up onto her shoulder. "I'll be off then. Unless I hear anything to the contrary, I guess I'll see you tomorrow."

I watch her walking to the door, her hands stuffed deep into the pockets of her cardigan. She lingers, one hand on the door handle, and I can see she's biting her lip. She turns. Her eyes meet mine, and she gives a tiny smile.

"Ewan, I just wanted to say, it's really nice to see you again."

Moments pass as hours as I stand gawping at her, struggling to find not so much the right thing to say, but the capacity to speak at all. And when I do manage to talk, the voice that comes out sounds strangled and squeaky, so far removed from my normal tones I would have denied it belonged to me at all.

"You too," the voice says. "It's good to see you too."

Chapter 4

Arriving home, I take out my key, and unlock the door to my home. I pause for a moment. The flower bed by the door is full of tall jaggedy eryngiums, and I love the way their thistly flowers and blue-green foliage contrasts with the pristine plain white painted walls of my house. It took me two or three years before I managed to grow the seedlings, and now they are healthy established plants, their prickles too much for even the most determined of the slugs in my garden. They are magnificent, but much more important to me this evening, they look exactly as they did when I left this morning. The house does too. Nothing has changed, everything is still in place and in order, no matter how unsettling my day. I sigh and feel my shoulders relax as I look up at the house, comforted by its misshapen walls and exposed crooked timbers being unremarkable.

I push open the heavy wooden door, and as I step inside, my wife's grinning face appears from inside the kitchen at the end of the hall.

"Ewan darling, did you have a good day?"

I don't know what Rebecca's cooking, but it smells good. As I slip my jacket from my shoulders, my mouth is watering, the juices in my stomach gurgling in anticipation, and I can't quite remember if I ate any lunch today. I was going to have something to eat, I think, after I showed the new supply teacher the way to the dining hall, but then I went to my office to find something, and I don't think I did ever make time for lunch. It's all a bit hazy, but it doesn't matter because here comes my wife. She's gliding towards me, her face radiant with a beautiful smile.

"Dinner smells good," I say, holding out my arms to her. "Have you missed me?"

As she steps into my embrace, there is a knock at the door. Damn. My fantasy Rebecca flees. I huff at being forced to relinquish the warmth of her imaginary arms, and go to answer.

It's Vi, my neighbour from across the street.

"Hello love."

Her generous mouth is cracked with a wide grin which both animates her various bobbing chins and displays a collection of twisty stained teeth enough to give her dentist nightmares. She is clutching a small, flat, brown paper wrapped package in her podgy hands, but as always, since she is resplendent in her uniform of vest, waterfalls of beads, raggedy skirt and faded pink flip-flops, it isn't the package I notice first, but the necklaces vanishing down into the depths of her generous cleavage. My neighbour cleans for half the street beside me, takes in parcels for us, and oversees our comings and goings, but in another life, she must have been the inspiration for those voluptuous figurines of fleshy earth goddesses you see displayed in the British museum. She sees where my eyes are looking, laughs, and holds out the packet.

"Got you a nice piece of salmon from the fish-man, I did. Beautiful it is. He'll like that, I said to the fish-man. I'll have some for me and Dave too, I said. And we've got little Cory staying with us tonight. Our Carol's gone off out with that Steve what she's seeing now. He works on the motorway, he does. Did I tell you?"

"Thank you Vi," I say as she hands me the fish. "And yes, I think you did tell me about Carol's new boyfriend." The problem with Vi being so accommodating when it comes to the postman, and in this case, the 'fish-man', is that she is a regular visitor to everyone's front doors and consequently, we are all experts on the intricacies of the relationships being played out by different members of her large extended family.

"Well he seems like a nice enough fella, but I was talking to that Marjorie who knows our Ella from when she worked at Neville's and she reckons her friend told her that he's already got three kids with three different women. Fancy that, eh love? I told our Carol that's the last thing she needs is to be landed with another kid, but you know what she's like; she don't listen."

I imagine the only way to survive if fate has placed you as a member of Vi's family is to cultivate the ability to 'not listen' as her prattling flow must only cease for the hours at night when she is asleep. Your ears would be worn out, I think, and I wonder if you could be driven mad simply by having to listen to her talking on and on, day after day, sentence after sentence, a sentence stretching on until the end of your days. Perhaps you would long for insanity to come and rescue your battered sense. Yes, the release of madness, or the mercy of short life; an interesting choice, and I wonder which I would choose.

"I've made him fish pie for his tea, little Cory. He'll eat it all you know. Not like what he does for his mother, mind you. Our Carol's always moaning about what he doesn't eat, but he's always an angel for me. Mind you, he's always behaved himself for me and Dave, he has. Never been a scrap of bother. But then, he's always known where he is with me and Dave. Always there for him, we are. Always there, and that's important, isn't it love?" I nod, and she is pleased with my verdict.

"Well you know about these things what with being a teacher and that. I said to Dave you'd understand, I did."

Heaven be praised, there is a muffled shout from across the street, from the swarthy mouth of 'our Dave', and I am released. Vi takes the note I offer from my wallet and sails back down my path, flipflops slapping against her gnarled heels. I shut the door in relief. Now, where was I? Oh yes, I remember, Rebecca; the one I married.

I carry the fish back through to the kitchen, and put it down on the side. She is standing at the cooker, stirring a saucepan. Ah, and it smells delicious, whatever it is she's cooking. I can't quite decide what she is cooking, because I'm not sure what, if you were to pop up and ask me, I want to eat right now. If I knew the answer to that, I'd be able to address the issue of my growling stomach. I remember now, I didn't have any lunch.

I put my arms around her, and snuggle against her warm neck. She giggles, her curly crimson hair shimmying over her shoulders. Her hair was always bright red when I knew her. I'm surprised I recognised her this morning with it restored to its natural light brown. It's so unlike her, it's as though it has changed her into a different person, and which is, I suppose, true.

The story always made me laugh, no matter how many times she told it, the memory of the day she'd stamped back into the kitchen at her childhood home in Deerbridge, in South Devon, steel-capped boots clattering against the stone floor, her presence quivering with the unwashed, untameable energy of having just survived her first weekend away at a music festival. Her mother had glanced up from cutting out rounds of pastry for a welcome home batch of jam tarts, and dropped the cutter with a shriek.

"Rebecca! What the bloody hell have you done?"

"What?" Rebecca had tossed her scarlet hair over her shoulder, and planted her hands on her hips. But she couldn't help biting her lip. She might well be high on youthful rebellion, but her mother never swore. She had known this would be a difficult scene, but at least her father was away all week. There would be time to fine-tune the strategy of presenting her radical make-over before he got home.

"Your hair, what have you done? Oh, Rebecca," she burst into dramatic sobs and buried her face in her floured hands. Rebecca rolled her eyes. This, she had predicted.

"You had such beautiful hair. What did you have to go and do this for?"

"I like this colour," she said, and congratulated herself. Her mother was so wound up over her hair that she'd failed to notice the tiny stud punctuating her nose. She flounced out and retreated to her room. I chuckle. Rebecca always says 'we had that battle later,' and I bet they did.

My mouth twists as I am remembering my in-laws, or 'ex' in-laws, if you like. They were kind, gentle-mannered people, Rebecca's father a high court judge, but they'd never met anyone like me before. I remember standing, shuffling from one foot to the other, sipping sherry in her father's study, the women excluded by long standing tradition, he struggling to find something to say to the shy Scottish boy who'd never had to speak to someone so important, it was as though the man wore invisible robes of office. They thought it was odd that I had no family, and they loathed our tiny wedding, such a far cry from the lavish occasion they'd spent Rebecca's life imagining. After she left me, I never heard from them again. There was no point.

I look down at the brown paper packet sitting on the worktop. A piece of salmon, Vi said. I wish she hadn't bought it, thinking back to one of the reports I read in the paper. It was all about the evils of farmed salmon. When I was a boy, salmon was something my mother cooked for my father, and he alone, on his birthday. It was too expensive for me and her, she said. But now it's everywhere, limp pink fillets sliced, smoked, poached and peppered on offer, in sandwiches, plastic wrapped pale flesh so full of goodness and now cheap enough so everyone can enjoy my father's yearly treat. But I read of a nightmare world, of polluted water, of mutated fish stuffed with chemicals and crammed into tiny enclosures, barely able to swim and surrounded by bloated, floating corpses of those who have already lost the struggle, or whom you could say nature has released from their manmade hell on earth. And people eat this stuff. The thought flips my stomach.

The queasiness spreads its sickly fingers upwards. My throat tightens. I stare at the packet, as though its tainted contents might suddenly spring to life, might sprout clawed tentacles and attack, one touch of its horrid flesh enough to contaminate me with its filth. Salmon is good for you: that's what everyone says. You see pictures everywhere showing sleek, healthy fish, captions saying 'eat eat eat', and 'it's ever so good for you'; 'good for your heart, good for your brain'; 'eat salmon and live well'. Would anyone eat it if they knew what I know, what that journalist knows? And here's Vi buying it for me, making it into a damned fish pie for her grandson. I loosen my collar. Perhaps I should go and tell her not to give it to him. But will she listen? I don't know. I don't know what to do.

I have to get rid of it. But I mustn't touch it; I don't want to be contaminated. No, wait a minute, I've already touched it. I stare at my hands in horror as if I can see a contagion erupting, nasty oozing pustules breaking out across my fingers. Wash them, I must wash them. I let the water run hot, grit my teeth, and plunge in my hands. The water scalds, but I don't relent. I must be clean.

I dry my scarlet hands, take a bin bag from the cupboard, and scoop the packet inside. There, that's better, and I tie it several times, just in case the fish tries to escape. The breath flows easier from my lungs now the packet is contained. My shoulders soften now I've averted the danger. You know, you'd think it would be against the law not only to fill our food with such poisons, but to use such blatant advertising propaganda to encourage us to eat them. 'Eat salmon, it's good for you': I've even seen this message in doctors' surgeries. It should be against the law to let us eat this stuff in our food, but if it isn't, then why is it allowed?

I haven't thought of this before, and the realisation hits me with a force that has me rigid and holding my breath once more. It's so obvious that I wonder why I've never thought of it before. There is only one possible reason they are getting us to eat all this stuff, and that must be to control us. Nobody is free, I realise. It's all part of a devious scheme which I have unwittingly uncovered. I grasp the sides of the sink as my world, the world I thought I knew, reels in flux around me. Wait a minute, that journalist must know. Maybe I should contact him. Perhaps I should go and have another look on the computer, register with that website I found at lunchtime. But if I sign up to a forum they'll be able to trace me. And if they find me, they'll be able to monitor my browsing. What will happen if they realise I'm on to them? I grip hold of the work surface, barely daring to breathe. I think over my computer options: home, the library, work. They will be able to trace me if I start asking too many questions. Now I've realised what's going on, I'm not safe.

Wide-eyed, I look round the confines of my kitchen and out of the window into the quiet garden, scanning my familiar surroundings for a hint, a suggestion I am being watched, monitored to make sure I eat up my salmon, to make sure I'm complying. I see nothing obvious, so I take the wrapped salmon and throw it in the bin. There, I'm safe. No, wait a minute. I can't have it in the house. It's not safe.

I unlock the back door, and pad to the dustbin, feeling as conspicuous as a giant, my tiptoes crunching on the gravel, but I've got to get the fish outside. I've got to get it as far away from me as possible. And as I reach my bin, another thought ices my blood. Vi. She buys fish for me every week. Perhaps she's part of this, the plot I mean. I think she might be an agent with the responsibility for making sure everyone in the street complies. In fact, every street in every part of the country probably has its own Vi watching, making sure everyone eats up. I pause, the dustbin lid in my hand. She puts my bin out for the dustmen if I forget. Oh my god, what if she checks my rubbish? If she finds the fish in here, she'll discover I've foiled their plans. She'll know I haven't eaten it.

My hand is shaking as I put the lid back down on the bin, darting glances down the side of my cottage to across the road to Vi's house. I bet she's watching me. I've been in their house only a couple of times. It's crammed full of junk, each room overflowing with stuff she never throws out. But all this is a cover. She probably has some sort of special room in which she keeps her files. And as I stand there, I realise I can hear her voice in my head. Damn, I don't want to be able to hear Vi. I hold my breath as I put down the bin lid and scuttle back indoors. But I can still hear her. She's on the phone making some sort of report.

"Monday 6th of September, 1835hrs, gave #12 a piece of salmon, but he tried to resist. Silly fool doesn't realise there is no escape."

I sink down on the step at the bottom of the stairs, my hands clamped over my ears, but it's no good. I can still hear her. Did I say my ability to hear other people's thoughts is a gift? Sometimes I'm not so sure. God, I need a drink.

Chapter 5

I am in school the next morning, collecting my post from the office and about to tiptoe past the Head's office for fear of waking the sleeping tiger, when the door flies open to reveal she is already awake, and waiting to pounce. "Ewan," she says, as though it were a surprise to her to find me in here, as though her office doesn't have a window down one side. "Just the person I need to see."

Why does she 'need' to see me? Fear stirs down deep in my gut and opens one liquid yellow eye. Is the Head too watching me, as Vi watches me? I shudder. As though she can smell my reluctance, Mrs Phillips opens the door wider, ushering me in. I give an inward groan, the time I'd earmarked for working on my composition before class dissolving in the ether of what triviality she has deemed important today. It was late last night before I resigned myself to being unable to recapture the bit of melody I'd been working on before Rebecca burst back into my life. As stubborn as its creator, it refused to reappear. Even whisky didn't tempt it out. I had been hoping to find it slouched against the piano this morning, arms folded, foot tapping: waiting.

"I just wanted to have a quick word with you," she says, her straight hair quivering as she speaks. "It's about your friend, Mrs Cartwright?"

I detest her habit of intoning every remark into a question. And what of my 'friend' Mrs Cartwright? I'd like to pretend I haven't given Rebecca another thought, only the fact I watched the glowing red display of my alarm clock count the seconds throughout the night will testify how much her reappearance has unsettled me. When I gave up trying to sleep at four this morning, I couldn't even summon the presence of mind to concentrate on a book, and it's only some trashy thriller I'm reading, nothing taxing. Rebecca Rebecca Rebecca.

"I wouldn't exactly describe her as a 'friend' as such," I say, frowning at the thought of just how far I should explain. It was easy practising my confession to the mirror. I can see myself, hear myself performing it now.

'Actually Mrs Phillips, I need to talk to you about that. It's a rather delicate matter, and I didn't know how to bring it up yesterday. You see, Rebecca is actually my ex-wife. I think you'd prefer it if we didn't work together.' And I see her brow furrow with horror at the thought, and she

says 'good heavens Mr. Davies, I can't have that in my school. Thank you for bringing it to my attention. I'll sort it out right away.'

"Oh?" She folds her arms tight across her chest, and tilts her head to one side, scrutinising my expression. "But I thought you both seemed rather pleased to see one another yesterday. Is there a problem then, Ewan?" And now it's her foot tapping, warning me not to resist being shoehorned into the plan she's concocted.

"No." Yes.

"Good," she says, but I don't like the way her eyes linger, unblinking. She'll attack if she senses even so much as a hairline crack in my composure. "Because I wouldn't want you to be unhappy with the issue of staffing your department, we've had that problem too many times to mention."

I bristle at how we always fall into this routine, she the disapproving matriarch, me the naughty boy who won't do as he's told. Damn, it's like trying to talk to a younger version of my mother. Thank heavens I don't have to do that any more.

"If you will make decisions without consulting me, what do you expect? Standards don't achieve themselves. I need to have a say in who works alongside me."

"Well, Mrs Cartwright made quite an impression yesterday, and since you are, or at least," she gives an eyebrow a sly tilt, "appeared to be old friends, I wondered what you'd think about offering her the permanent vacancy."

What do I think about offering her the permanent vacancy in my department? I suppose if you look at it from Mrs Phillips's position as chief bean-counter, given the trouble we've had finding a replacement for my colleague, old Vic Greene, who retired at Easter, Rebecca is the perfect choice. But Rebecca isn't Vic. I think on his weathered brown face, on the sight of him cruising along the road to school perched up high on an old Raleigh, his briefcase stuffed into a basket at the front, and his quiet, unflappable demeanour. He'd been a rock as I'd fumbled my way around the running of the department in the early days. "Relax man," he'd say. "The world isn't going to end just because FiFi P," he liked Alex's nickname for the Head, "hasn't ticked all her boxes." I miss

Vic. Next time I see him in the pub, I'm going to beg him to come back to work. On my knees if that's what it takes.

"Isn't it a bit soon? Don't we want to wait and see how she pans out? I mean, she might not want the job anyway." I am babbling, I know, and the Head unfolds her arms, and plants them on her hips, her head cocking to the other side, weighing me up. Stop talking, I tell myself. You're giving too much away.

"Is there something you aren't telling me?"

"No."

Think Ewan, think damnit. A brilliant idea breaks through the clouds smothering my wits.

"It's just a bit of a surprise to find Rebecca taking up teaching, that's all. Let's just say it was 'unexpected'," I add to water the seed of doubt I've just planted in Mrs. Phillips's mind. "I wouldn't have thought it was quite her 'thing'."

"Really? I found her very enthusiastic," Mrs. Phillips says, chewing over my words. "Still, I suppose you know her better. All right then, I'll wait until the end of the week and then we can meet to discuss things. Keep me posted with your thoughts."

Did she just say 'until the end of the week'? I have to put up with Rebecca being here until the end of the week? My mood hunkers down into dark, foreboding depths, but I try to distract it from its misery with the promise I have four whole days in which to come up with a cast iron reason why she is an unsuitable candidate to become a permanent fixture in my department. It shouldn't be too difficult; I am hard to please.

But as the week wears on, my opinion undergoes a seismic shift. Try as I might, researchers scanning the universe for intelligent life in distant solar systems have more chance of success than I do in finding a reason for opposing Rebecca's appointment. She is more than merely competent; I sit in on one of her lessons only to find I could take notes from how well the pupils respond to her methods. Everyone adores her; I can't walk down a corridor without someone stopping me to tell me how wonderful my new teacher is and did I know she'd volunteered to do this and that. To begin with, I have to clench my teeth and make myself smile and say 'oh really, how fascinating' and suppress the snarl of 'she's only temporary', but by the time Mrs Phillips collars me to say she thinks we should offer Rebecca the job, I don't mind. Rebecca hasn't just charmed the entire school, but me too. I had forgotten how much I loved her. She was great company, she is great company. I don't know what I've done all these years without her.

Actually, that's not true. I do know what I've done all these years without her, I've missed her. Everything, from the way she stuffs pens through the messy bun coming undone at the back of her head, to the way she nibbles her bottom lip when she's thinking, it's all coming back to me. I had forgotten the way she laughs with such abandon when something really tickles her, head thrown back, her shoulders shaking with delight. And the way she clasps her hands together when she's so pleased she can hardly keep still, I had forgotten that too. So I'm grinning from ear to ear, watching her delight as Mrs Phillips tells her we'd like her to accept our job offer. Rebecca is bubbling, effervescing with happiness. It is infectious.

"Ewan, thank you," she throws her arms around me once we're out of earshot of the Head and the radar listening abilities of her office staff. "I can't tell you how much this means to me. Thank you so much. I won't let you down, you know. I'll work hard."

"It wasn't just my decision," I chuckle, my hands hovering, unsure whether to reciprocate the hug no matter how much I am tempted. It would feel so good to pull her close, it's as though my cells are crying out to be pressed against hers.

"I know, let's celebrate. Are you in a hurry to get home tonight?" I shake my head. Her hands clasp together once more, and she twirls on her tiptoes, eyes alight with a brilliant idea. "Then let's go and have afternoon tea at that little café just off the High Street. Come on, it'll be just like old times."

Going out for afternoon tea in a little café down by the river was one of our little rituals whenever we had something to celebrate while we were studying in Cambridge. I'm not sure I'm comfortable with the idea of doing that now. It seems a little over-familiar, and, as I keep telling myself, we must be professional. All I've been able to think about this week, minute after feverish minute during the longest nights I've ever spent alone, is sweeping her back into my arms and pretending the cruel words, the break-up and the intervening years never happened, but she is married to someone else now, and I've unwittingly wound up as her boss. I must keep her at arm's length if for nothing else but the sake of my own sanity.

"Don't you need to get home? I mean, don't you think Rick might mind you having tea with me?" She has told me rather a lot about 'Rick', his export business and the long hours he works. I wonder how much she has told him.

"Why would Rick mind?" She peers at me, shaking her head as though I'm being especially stupid, and she's having to struggle to see through my dull mind.

"I just thought he might not like the idea of you spending time with me," I say, the colour rising once more in my face. She's still looking at me as though I'm being ridiculous. I stick my hands in my pockets, and shuffle my feet.

"It's only a cup of tea, Ewan. I'm not inviting you away for a wild weekend."

"Thank goodness for that," I jabber. And then, because I'm frightened she might give up the whole idea and I want to spend a bit longer in her company before we have to go our separate ways for the weekend, I blurt, "a cup of tea it is then. So long as nobody thinks its favouritism, you getting the job because we're old friends."

"Oh," she sighs. "I didn't realise that's what you were fretting about. I thought you were worried I was being over-friendly. That's all right then. Let's go and get that cup of tea. I'm starving. Aileen from Science said the café do a good spread, and, more importantly, they do vegan food too."

And they do, provoking yet more jingly twirling from my ex-wife, the waitresses exchanging scornful looks as she dances over to a table in the conservatory. The wicker chairs creak as we sit down and look out over beautiful, manicured gardens, swans floating on a grand pond, the sound of a waterfall tinkling drifting in through open windows. The waitresses ply us with tea and tiered cake stands laden with dainty cut sandwiches, elaborate fruit pastries, fat cushiony scones, and jam. I freeze at the sight of so much food, the unease at what exactly I might be eating comes creeping up from my gut and strangles my appetite, but Rebecca is chatty and cheerful, and I don't think she's noticing she's eating far more than me.

"Ah, that's better," she says, her mouth full of sandwich, wiping her fingers on a napkin embroidered with pink daisies and coiling leaves to match the tablecloth. "I was starving." She looks up and around, her eyes following the conservatory's ornate white frame, its glass gleaming in the late afternoon sun. "Rick would love this place. I must bring him here some time."

"How long have you been married?" I ask, my mouth souring. It's not that I want to know, but I think social niceties dictate it is long past time I asked this question. 'Small talk', that's what they call it. I don't want to know, I don't want to hear about it, and yet, there is a perverse side of me that wants to listen, to savour the pain of her revelations. God, I'm such a contrary sod. I don't know why I do this, fluttering around like the proverbial moth to the bloody flame. There is something ingrained deep in my psyche that likes it when I hurt. It's comforting. I haven't felt the need for a long time. Actually, never mind moths, it's a bloody great big vulture circling lower and lower, obsidian eyes fixed on my every move. I want it. Come on Rebecca, hurt me.

"Seven years." Sunlight breaks out across her face and radiates the insular, smug happiness of two people in love. I look down to hide my scowl. Had I the inclination, I could spit bile.

She lifts up her patchwork bag and rifles through a hazardous pit of old receipts, half-used tissues, leaflets and notes.

"Here you are," she hands me a photograph. "That's Rick on the left."

Well, obviously it's Rick on the left, since she's the one on the right. The dark-haired Adonis with his wide, perfect smile does nothing to make me feel better, although I conclude he's obviously a bit of a dick since he looks so pleased with himself, that much must be certain. But I force myself to say pleasant things, digging the nails on my left hand into my thumb and I make such a good job, Rebecca is still beaming as she puts the picture back in her bag. Did I ever make her look so happy, I wonder. Was there ever a time she looked like that whenever she thought of me? The answer lies somewhere deep, dark and cold, and the thought makes me shudder. I don't want to look. I like clinging to my comforting blanket of delusions that we were happy.

"So how come you're not married?"

That's quite a question, don't you think? I listen to my clumsy mouth stammering through a rubbish answer about not meeting the right woman, and watch how I squirm in the glare of her spotlight, inadequacies seething just beneath my surface.

"Yeah, but I am surprised," she says, twiddling with a teaspoon, tracing the pattern on its handle with the tip of her thumb. She gives me a fleeting glance, and looks back down at the spoon. "I thought you'd be married with a little ensemble of budding musicians running around your house."

"I thought you'd have children too," I say, sidestepping the question and deflecting it straight back. She'd been desperate to breed, I'd thanked every god I could name each month when it turned out she still wasn't pregnant.

She shakes her head, and a cloud steals across her sun so dark, I regret, and even feel a little guilt at the strength of my antipathy towards the thought of her carrying a child.

"I had tests done," she stirs her tea, lost for the moment to her own drama. "It turns out I can't have children."

Ah, so that was one thing that wasn't my fault. Much as the thought fires a little triumphant glee rocketing through my veins, I am sorry for her. She would have made the perfect mother hen, shooing her little flock around with a flap of her flowery skirts. I go to put my hand over hers, but she pulls away.

"It's all right, I'm fine," she puts the spoon down. "We've talked about adopting, but you know, I'm just not sure I'd feel the same, you know, if it wasn't my own."

"Does that matter if you want to care for a child?" I've never understood the 'it must be mine' anguish of parental dreams denied. Still, who am I to throw down the challenge? I don't understand the need to produce an ugly, red-faced squalling infant in the first place. And Alex has a fourth on the way? The man is insane.

"Maybe," she muses, and then lifts her head and fixes me with such a pointed look, I can't escape. "Anyway, never mind all that. Back to you, why aren't you married, Ewan?"

"I told you," I sigh, toying with a sandwich. "I've just not met the right person."

"I wish you would," she says in a voice so gentle, it re-ignites the hope I'd like to deny that she's about to profess undying love, and wash away the festering hurt with her tears. What will I say if she does, I wonder. But there's no need for me to worry. She squashes the prospect underfoot like a delicate flower in the path of a field full of grazing cattle. "I sure as hell wasn't that woman, but Alex is right. You need someone to look after you, you of all people."

Alex? What does he have to do with this? My eyes narrow. What has he been saying to her now?

"You need someone to remind you to eat, if nothing else," she says, her eyes running over me as though she were the farmer eyeing up his livestock. "You're very thin, you know. It's not flattering."

"Why, thank you Rebecca. That's very nice of you to say so."

"There's no need to be like that," she huffs down from her self-righteous platform. "I'd want you to tell me if it was the other way round. We know each other well enough to be honest with each other, don't we?"

Honest? I throw a quick glance over the bones of our relationship and ponder whether we were ever honest with each other. The only thing I know for sure is my version, and it's too twisted to tell.

"I don't suppose there's any point in me asking if you've got back in contact with your family?" She eyes me over the rim of her teacup.

"No, there isn't."

I'm surprised she's even wasted her breath in asking. We sit in silence, sipping our tea as the late afternoon sun filters through the trees behind her head, illuminating her unruly hair with a soft halo. Her bangles clink and chime as she puts down her cup, and I wonder if she kept any I bought for her, I don't recognise any of her rings. I used to like to buy her jewellery. She was so easy to please, anything silver and quirky, such a relief after growing up with a woman who would reject any gift unless she'd chosen it herself. "It's not just that I don't like it darling, I don't understand why on earth you thought I would," my mother would pout, and I would stare at the floor knowing I'd let her down, yet again.

"Goodness, it's nearly five. I suppose I'd better be getting home," Rebecca says, checking her watch while the waitresses glowering from the counter, arms folded tight across their chests, stir in the hope their last two customers might actually leave. "I'm going out for dinner tonight, just a couple of chaps Rick works with and their wives. All a bit dull really. What about you?"

I have my usual Friday night lined up, choir practice at the church and a pint or two with the vicar and Alex on the way home, but I don't want to tell her this, it doesn't sound very exciting. So I say I'm not sure, I might pop away for the weekend, or nip up to London because it's great having the freedom to be so spontaneous. She sighs in agreement as though I've just dangled something she once valued just out of reach. I pay our bill, fending off her token protests, and follow her out into the street.

"Well, whatever you do get up to Ewan, I hope you have a good weekend," she says. "See you on Monday."

For a moment I think, and hope, she is going to kiss my cheek, but she smiles, and sets off across the road, her long skirt flowing around her ankles. She walks away. I watch her go, my hand ready to wave, but she doesn't look back.

Chapter 6

I walk home, locked in the comfort of my inner world, my feet plodding on automatic. In here, Rebecca is at my side and not only are we going out together for dinner tonight, but we're reminiscing about the little Indian restaurant we used to frequent in Cambridge, in which the owner Clive, a name he'd adopted having grown tired of people being unable to pronounce his proper Bengali name, had an enormous photograph of himself shaking hands with a famous jockey in pride of place behind the counter. I don't recall a single visit there which didn't culminate in Clive referring to the photograph at least once. We used to play a game to see who could be the one to prompt the story of the time his most famous patron came to dine. The only time, as it happened, but this didn't bother Clive. He had his picture and his story, nothing else mattered.

I'm so absorbed, I haven't noticed I'm almost home, and as my feet turn into Orchard Road, I blink in surprise at the sight of my own front door. As I walk up the small path to the door, rummaging in my pocket for the key, I'm thinking about the day I moved here, nine years ago. It had felt so strange moving here, I had never lived by myself before. At first it was disconcerting, the silence roaring in my ears as I moved around empty rooms with no one with whom to share a remark about what furniture would look nice where. After a while it became monotonous, and I went through a spell of talking to myself, wondering if I should get a cat. But these days I can't imagine sharing my precious space with anyone, the reason I suppose, despite the teasing and underhand suggestions there must be 'something' wrong with me, I still live here alone.

"Coo-ee!"

Key in hand, I spin round. Vi is waving at me from her front door. She's talking to old Mrs. Harris, my next-door neighbour, the two of them standing with their arms folded, passing judgment on everything from what they've seen on television, to what the queen might have worn yesterday.

"Late home eh," I hear her voice in my head. *"What have you been doing, I wonder."*

I lift my hand and wave back. Why is she really standing outside if not to warn me she knows I'm trying to resist? I'm beginning to wonder if I ought to keep notes, record the times I see her.

My door opens wide, scraping across the day's post sprawling on the floor. As usual, there is nothing of any value, just garish leaflets, innocuous letters addressed to 'the occupant', and a letter from the council notifying residents of another planning application which will be turned down through a concerted campaign from those who like the town being mired in the past. 'Protecting our heritage' they call it, more like 'protecting their damned property values', I think, tossing the letter down on the hall table. I drop my briefcase, and shove the door closed with my foot.

I go to pull off my tie and leave my jacket hanging to air on the bottom of the banister, but freeze. There is a whiff of furniture polish in the air. Alarm strums my nerves. It's Friday, of course. That means Vi's been in here cleaning. I swallow, and finger my collar. Cleaning eh? What else has she been doing? I can picture her snooping, opening drawers and checking cupboards. A shiver stalks down my spine. I hope she hasn't been looking in the bin, she might have found the packet of salmon rotting in the heat of glorious September sunshine. The binmen won't call again until next week.

In the kitchen, the wooden clock above the door points out it is nearly six. I make a cup of tea out of habit rather than genuine thirst. Choir practice begins at seven, so I have time to sit down, maybe watch the news for any reports on food safety before I need to swap my school suit for something less formal. At least Vi will have ironed my shirts, I was beginning to run out.

I turn on the television and settle down in my leather armchair to sip my tea. Last night's whisky glass is still where I left it on the coffee table, one of the set of cut crystal tumblers to which I treated myself last Christmas. Vi's getting sloppy, I think, but perhaps she's left it there on purpose, wordless disapproval of my drinking habits. Mind you, I shouldn't have left it there either. I bin my empty Scotch bottles on the way to work rather than put them out in my recycling box for the neighbours to see.

There is nothing of interest to me on the news. Bored, I turn it off after only a few minutes. I'm glad I forced down a few sandwiches over afternoon tea; I'm not hungry now, so this absolves me from another night of agonising over what on earth is safe to eat. I've spent every lunchtime this week trying to educate myself by researching food safety online. The more I read, the worse it becomes. I found one website which says the only way you can be sure you're safe is to grow your own food. But when am I supposed to find time to do that? Yes, so I grow a few tomatoes in the greenhouse every year, but that's as far as my smallholding inclinations extend. And that reminds me, there should be some ready. I lever myself up out of my chair and head outside to investigate.

My feet crunch along the winding gravel path. It isn't a big garden, but I designed it myself. When I moved in, it was paved with cracked, utilitarian grey stone, couch grass, dandelions and other weeds seeding from the copse at the end of Orchard Road sprouting up wherever they could, such a waste. I made the path to lead down to the greenhouse hidden behind a long wooden trellis which supports the curling, thorny stems of a delicate yellow climbing rose. It has been rampant this year, sporting a never-ending procession of perfumed blooms which have delighted the bees. Twisting and twining amongst it grows a Clematis, its Chinese-lantern-style orange flowers on the turn into fluffy, feathery seed-heads. I pause to snap off a dead flower here, a spoilt leaf there, my ears full of the sounds of sparrows and coal tits squabbling over ripe sunflowers swaying in the slight breeze.

The greenhouse door squeaks as I push it open wide enough to let me in. The hot, humid air is spiked with the leafy, pungent smell of my tomato plants. Today's sunshine has gifted me a crop of ripe red fruit to harvest. I start to pick them. They feel warm, their scent wholesome and safe. I've started buying only organic food, but I'm worried about it too. Can you trust a label, and, more significantly, can you trust the authorities not to tamper with so-called 'organic' food to make sure it meets their requirements? I shudder, and examine my tomatoes more closely. An image appears in my mind of Vi in here injecting them with poison, but I try to suppress it. I must eat, I remind myself. I mustn't scare myself, I have to eat.

"Ewan."

I gasp and drop the tomatoes. They roll off across the paved floor.

"Ring me. I want to talk to you."

It's Rebecca talking in my head. I keep very still, my heart thumping loud and fast, my breath coming in and out in shallow little gasps as I wait, wondering if I really heard her, or if it was just my imagination. Before we parted at the café, I insisted we swap telephone numbers in case there was anything she wanted to ask over the weekend. I didn't expect her to ring, and I didn't expect to hear her in my head.

"Rebecca? Is that you?"

"I want to talk to you. Please ring me."

The mobile phone stuffed in my back pocket begins to ring. I yelp, my heart racing faster. My hands are shaking as they pull out the phone. But it's not Rebecca. It's Neil, the vicar.

"Hi, Ewan? Look, in case I forget to ask you later, can you do the organ on Sunday, only Henry Winterton's been rushed to hospital this afternoon, they say he might have had a stroke, so I was thinking maybe you could cover for Della this weekend?"

I shake off my fear with a jubilant punch of the air. Thatchington Parish church is a splendid early medieval building with a tall, vaulting roof which offers the most marvellous space and acoustics to show off the rich, mellow tones of its beautifully restored, eighteenth century organ.

I love that organ. The first time I persuaded Neil to let me play it was one wet Saturday afternoon. He thought I meant to have a quick dabble with its ivory keys and wooden pedals, and stood fidgeting by my side, hoping I wouldn't take long, what with all the things he had to do that afternoon. But I was so bowled over by the sound, by the vibrations I could set shimmering in the air, that by the time he'd dealt with all his paperwork, finished writing his sermon, drunk two cups of tea and even swept the steps leading up to the alter, the only thing that prised me away from playing was his promise I could stand in on the occasions Della Winterton, his regular organist, was unavailable. I like Della and Henry, they're good, honest people, but I can't help my spinning, fizzing delight, my enthusiasm like fireworks exploding in my head. What shall I play before and after the service? Yes, I know, I think I'll go baroque. Yes, yes. That will be nice, the perfect contrast to Della's safe, repetitive repertoire.

"I know it's really short notice, but it's not just Sunday, I've got a wedding tomorrow afternoon as well. Do you think you could manage?"

"Neil! Not a problem," I say, wondering if I could manage to turn cartwheels if I tried. "As long as they haven't chosen anything completely tasteless."

Della says she despairs when they want some ridiculous pop song played, the scant, thin melody incongruous with the organ's majestic tones. The worse thing she says she's ever seen was the bride walking down the aisle to the theme tune to a television soap opera. Given that particular programme is notorious for its overblown story lines of family strife, it seems a foreboding choice to begin a marriage, but there you are. When Rebecca and I got married it was in a tiny registry office. Her family might have been tight-lipped at the lack of theatre; I still think it was commendable.

"No, I think you'll approve. They've got a harpist as well, so that should be interesting. Thank you old chap, I knew I could rely on you. It's my shout when we get to the pub later."

We adjourn to 'The Dolphin' one of Thatchington's liveliest pubs every Friday night after choir practice. It's a rickety old building with an uneven wooden floor and lopsided doors, the dark bar so small, patrons spill out into the pavement, ducking their heads to avoid a series of hanging baskets groaning under the weight of big, brash petunias and trailing geraniums. Neil and I push our way through the bodies, and find a place to stand near the bar.

"Thought I might find you in here, mate."

I turn round to find Alex standing behind me. His large features are sporting an enormous grin, and I shuffle aside as he shoves his way up to the bar, nodding in greeting to the various assembled figures. In front of the bar sits Jeremy Fotheringham, who proclaims himself 'Thatchington's only independent estate agent', a man whose elegant fingers are wedged in so many pies, very little happens in the town without his knowledge, without his being involved in some way. He holds court in the pub every Friday evening in The Dolphin, and whilst much of what he has to say leaves ordinary mortals' eyebrows raised, it is preferable to humour him than to discover too late you have inadvertently marked yourself in his elephantine memory as having disagreed with him at some point over some trifling matter you had thought inconsequential. Jeremy is throned on a bar stool, leg crossed high over the other to show off expensive Italian brogues, and he only has to raise his hand to have the barmaid, a fawn of a girl, skittering to his side.

"Alex, my man," he booms. "What'll you have?"

I turn away to hide my snort. Neil catches my eye and smirks. We are small fry in Jeremy's world and while he might want to keep friendly with the vicar, he usually has very little to say to either Alex or myself, especially now his daughters have left public school and there is no need for him to continually point out how much higher their standards compare to ours.

"You're honoured," I say when Alex rejoins us, beer in hand. "What does he want?"

"A picture. He's been onto Tessa about it. I told her to tell him to get lost, but I think she has him eating out of her hand. That's my wife for you."

"A picture?" Neil echoes, his chubby red face twitching with laughter. "Don't tell me, he wants you to paint his portrait."

"No," I say, amusement warming. "A family portrait of all the Fotheringhams in a classical pose."

"No, no," Neil giggles. "Acting out a famous scene from the Sistine Chapel."

"Mrs Fotheringham as The Mona Lisa," I say. Neil leans with his hand on my shoulder, helpless with laughter, his face scarlet. The thought of Verity Fotheringham, a humourless matron with a helmet of coiffed yellow hair, posing for such a picture makes Alex guffaw too. We're laughing so much, it's only when we hear Jeremy make a loud remark wondering what the peasants find so funny, that our hilarity subsides. Neil wipes his eyes, tells him it's too complicated to explain, and that sets us off laughing again.

"Anyway," Alex says once we've recovered our composure. "Never mind all that. There's something I've been meaning to ask," he looks at me, takes a long, appreciative sip of his beer, and lets fly the question I've been dreading all week. "How do you come to know Becks?"

"Becks?" Asks Neil, as my chest tightens, his pricked-up ears vaulting to the conclusion I am acquainted with a certain famous footballer whose presence at a future church fundraiser might rather boost attendance and takings.

"A new teacher," I say, my breathless voice dashing his plans before he gets any more excited. "Her name's Rebecca. We met at uni," I give my shoulders a nonchalant shrug while I scrabble around in a bucket of alternative topics to toss into the conversation. Weather's nice, maybe. Is Alex doing anything with the kids this weekend? Yes, that's probably the best option. Or ask Neil about the brass band? No, we'll be here all night. I don't want to start him off talking about the concert he's planning to raise money for the repair of the church roof, prey to the elements ever since the lead flashing was spirited from the roof one night last January. He'll never shut up.

"You never went to 'uni'," Alex points out.

God, why does it matter?

"She was at uni, I was at college," I say.

"Rebecca?" Neil says, arching one bristling eyebrow as he sips his beer, and launching me into a cold sweat at the sudden realisation of what I can see is coming next. Oh hell, I forget how well he knows me. Quick, think of something. Change the damned subject. No, it's too late.

"Wasn't your ex-wife called Rebecca?"

Alex's mouth falls open. Nice one, Neil, thank you very much.

"Yes, but it's not her," there is a note of hysteria behind my laughter I'm praying they won't notice. And perhaps the fierce heat raging in my face is only obvious to me too, I hope. "Not that Rebecca. Could you imagine?"

I take a deep swig of my beer and look round as Jeremy Fotheringham's voice rises, yet again, above the general hubbub of the pub as though he is reminding all assembled, just in case anyone should dare forget, how much he likes to be the centre of attention.

I turn back to my friends to find Alex drinking, but watching me over the top of his glass. I look down at the floor, scanning through conversations I've had with Rebecca in front of him this week, looking to see if I've made any comment which might indict me. The air in the pub is hot and pressing in on me from all sides. I think I'll just have this one drink, and then head for home.

Alex waits until Neil announces it's his round, the vicar brushing off my announcement I'm going home with a sound harrumph, and then he tries to pin me down with logic.

"It's true, isn't it? What Neil said about Rebecca, it all makes sense. I thought you two were unbelievably chummy. I've never known anyone make you laugh like she does. Remember the other day when I walked into the office; you were laughing so much you had tears running down your face."

I hadn't been able to stop laughing, that was true. She'd been telling me the story of how she'd got tired of 'grubbing around in muddy fields' as she put it, explaining the final straw for her career in archaeology when she had to work under the supervision of a much detested colleague from Cambridge, one Daniel Gallagher. He'd had a crush on Rebecca when we were students, so he and I had never been friends. The last time I saw him was after their graduation ball. A crowd of us had been trawling the streets of Cambridge in full song at around four in the morning when we encountered Daniel's inebriated figure on a bridge over the Cam. What can I say? It seemed like a very good idea to help him sober up by pitching him over the side and into the water. My last memory is the sight of him standing, his formal dress suit muddy and dishevelled, thigh deep in water squealing 'Davies, you ignorant Scotch bastard,' at the top of his reedy thin voice. Rebecca had just been telling me he still bears a grudge for that night, when Alex had walked in.

"I thought I was being paranoid. I even said to Tessa I felt like a bloody gooseberry."

I put my hand on Alex's shoulder. Now the initial shock of Neil's blundering revelation has worn off, I can lean right back into the lie.

"Believe me," I say. "That's not my ex-wife." I sound great. Hell, even I'd believe what I'm saying if I were listening. "Different Rebecca. Same name, but a totally different person. There's no way I could ever work with my ex. It would be all 'why haven't you done this, why haven't you done that?'" "I'm quite good at mimicking Rebecca in full flow vitriolic outburst, and since Alex will probably never witness her standing there, hands on hips, going 'you need help Ewan, H-E-L-P help," I feel quite safe and justified at giving my rusty performance an airing.

"Blimey," Alex says. "Just as well it's not her at school then. Ta, Neil," he says as the vicar reappears with our drinks.

The conversation meanders off onto safer territory, such as the chances of Spurs winning their match this Saturday, the Dolphin's proposed Halloween beer festival, and Alex's kitchen renovations, which he hopes will be finished in time for his birthday bash in a couple of weeks time. As he and Neil become embroiled in a debate over the best method of tiling kitchen floors, I am only half-listening and enjoying my beer, my eyes following the twisting lengths of hop vine twined round and around the ceiling's gnarled timbers.

The landlord, Nigel, keeps a good cellar, and has recently started up his own micro-brewery in some outbuildings behind the pub. I'm not one of the chosen few who've had the chance to taste any of his offerings yet, but reports have it his beer is very good. He's so pleased with the results that he's decided to hold a beer festival at the beginning of November. 'Give me a chance to make enough for all you regular gents," he told us when we arrived earlier, leaning across the bar, stroking his walrus-like silvery grey moustache which balances on his ruddy face in counterpoint to his sprouting, matching eyebrows made all the more striking by the fact his head is so bald, it has almost a mirror gleam in the lights behind the bar. This is a nice pint, I think, lifting my glass to examine the beer's reddish brown hue, my mouth full of malt with a delicate flowery aftertaste. I freeze. My pleasure turns to revulsion. There is something in the bottom of my glass. I hold it up to the light. It is a big round black beetle with curved, barbed legs.

"Ugh, that's disgusting," I exclaim, silencing conversations babbling around me. Heads turn.

"What is it?" Alex and Neil press in for a look.

"There's a bug in the bottom of my beer," I say, holding up the glass so they can see. "Oh my god, I hope I haven't swallowed one." My stomach churns at the thought.

"Where?" Alex takes the glass out of my hand, and holds it up. "No there isn't."

"Everything all right gents?" Nigel and his moustache lean across the bar. Even Jeremy has gone quiet. Neil cranes his head to examine my glass, but he can't see anything either. And I realise that's because there's nothing to see when Alex passes the glass back into my hand. I stare into the beer, but there's nothing there, no beetle, nothing.

"S'all right Nigel, Ewan's seeing things. Either means he's had too much beer, or not enough. Better make sure it's too much. Can you get us another three pints, mate? Cheers."

"Yeah well, just watch what you're saying, Mr. Davies," Nigel folds his beefy arms across his chest. "Can't have you teachers going round saying there's things in my beer, be bad for business that."

If I was red-faced over Rebecca before, that is nothing to the inferno burning in my face now. Everyone is staring and laughing. I mumble an apology, and eye the door. There was something in my glass, I was sure of it, and now I can't bring myself to finish my drink. The queasiness hasn't left me; I don't want the pint Nigel is pouring. It's been a long day, a never ending week, and this time I really do want to go home. As people lose interest and turn back to their chatter, Alex and Neil drain their glasses and reach for the beer waiting on the bar.

"You know, it's good of you to buy me a drink," I say to Alex, the door a magnet whose pull I don't want to resist. "But I think I've had enough. You don't mind sharing it between you, do you?"

"Ah, come on," Neil says, his eyes widening with disbelief. "Nigel's only pulling your leg. Look, everyone's forgotten about it now. We all make a bit of a tit of ourselves from time to time. In fact I think I manage every Sunday if I'm going to be honest."

That much is true. I have rarely sat through one of Neil's services without him dropping something, or announcing the wrong hymn, although the worst episode by far was last summer when, hung-over as we all were after the town's annual fair, he got the names wrong at a christening. I thought one mother was going to slap him, her fury was so formidable. We haven't let him live it down yet. 'I baptise thee Darcy Isabella.' 'No vicar, this is William. That's Darcy. In the pink dress, Vicar.' It didn't help that both sets of parents heard him mutter to the curate that how could he be expected to remember which one was which since all babies looked the bloody same.

"And anyway mate," Alex adds. "When have you ever left a pint? It's not like you."

No, it isn't like me. But my eyes saw a beetle, a vicious looking brute swimming in my beer, and no matter how earnest sense is in telling me I imagined it, I'm so revolted, I have lost my appetite for beer and good company. I fend off their protests by joining in with the banter about me being a lightweight, and then I make my escape. Hands sunk deep in my coat pockets, I hurry home. My footsteps echo in the quiet, dark streets. I make my way past dimly-lit shops, up Market Hill and past The George Hotel, the sound of cheery chatter and bright lights spilling out from doors and windows, mocking my solitary retreat back to the reassuring comfort of my lair on Orchard Road. And as I walk, I whistle the tune, the theme from my ongoing composition. But no matter how often I whistle it, I can't take it beyond the part I was writing on Monday. I try and try, reaching for it throughout the eternity of another sleepless night, but it lurks beyond my fingers, curled up out of reach.

Chapter 7

To my relief, Saturday's wedding turns out to be a tasteful, understated affair with well-behaved guests, no wailing children, and a harpist, a dark eyed wraith of a girl, whose beautiful, ephemeral playing haunts me for hours after. I make a note of her name, Norah Whitton, and she tells me I can download music from her website for free. She won't commit to coming into school to play a recital for my students, her nervous eyes darting here and there, too timid to hold my gaze for long, but she promises, as I struggle through an out-of-practice show of charm, that she will think about it.

Sunday's service however, leaves me wishing I'd never looked twice at the organ. For a start, Neil is reduced to a trembling wreck by the unexpected appearance of the rotund figure of his archdeacon. He fluffs his lines and gets in such a muddle whilst administering Holy Communion, part of me wonders if I should jump down from my perch in the organ loft and give him a hand. The church is packed, and as I play each hymn, I am dragging the congregation's torpid singing as though I was pulling a broken-down car. It is a lengthy service, dragging out minute by painful minute.

I smother a yawn as Neil continues droning on from the pulpit. It's not that his voice is especially dull, but he lost me about five minutes into his exposition on Paul's conversion on the road to Damascus. I have no idea what he's talking about, and, from my vantage point overlooking the church, neither do most of his flock. My eyes drift across the church, too bored by the familiarity of the intricate stained glass windows, the flickering candles, and the four hundred year old carved stone Madonna to find any of them remarkable. Confident no one can see what I'm doing, I sneak my mobile phone out of my pocket under the guise of checking the time, to see if Rebecca might have sent me a message. She hasn't. I hope she isn't cross. I didn't ring her, and I haven't heard her again since Friday evening.

The organist's bench is lumpy and hard, and I find myself wondering if the restorer stuffed it with some sort of authentic filling, horsehair for example. I shuffle my bones, wishing Neil would hurry up and get to the end, and wondering what Rebecca's doing this morning. One thing is for sure, she won't be sat, bored, in church. We used to spend Sunday morning in bed. One of us, it was usually me, would go and fetch tea, toast and marmalade, and the Sunday papers, and we'd spend blissful hours eating, reading and making love to the sound of church bells calling in the city's faithful. My stomach churns at the thought of her entwined in crisp white sheets with the sculpted vision that is Rick Cartwright, my replacement.

I'm so rapt in the torture of this scene, it isn't until the weight of the entire congregation's stare jolts me back to reality, back into the moment, I realise Neil is literally flapping, waving his robed arms to try and get my attention. Damn. I swivel back into position. His sermon finished, it's time for the collection, and I'm supposed to be playing. Nice work Ewan, you idiot.

I bow my head, repentant, as Neil blesses the collection and leads his people in one last prayer. Forgive me Father for not paying attention, for thinking too much about my Rebecca, oh and for still referring to her as 'my' Rebecca when, obviously, she isn't. And then it's time for one last rousing hymn, 'Onward Christian Soldiers' followed by lunch at the vicarage in payment for my services. I tried to refuse, but Neil's partner James is a fabulous cook, and loves to show off his skills. The prospect of a pleasant afternoon of amusing company and good wine outweighs my fears over what I might be forced to eat in the name of politeness.

Everyone is singing with great enthusiasm, the end in sight. We swing into the last verse, and I pull out the organ stops to let the majestic instrument sound its full, throaty voice all the way up to rattle the rafters at the top of the roof. I don't really need to look at my sheet music, besides, I'm busy admiring my fingers flying up and down the keys, but I do glance up for a moment, just long enough to see an enormous black beetle with jagged-edged legs. Damn. The ghastly thing falls off the page and lands on my hand.

Thinking about it afterwards, as I have, going over and over the details in my mind, I wish I'd had the presence of mind to just play on. It was only a beetle, after all. But I didn't. I screeched and snatched my hands off the keys, my heart pounding with horror.

There was a collective gasp from below as the enthusiastic singing stumbled without my lead, and the entire church gawped up at me.

"Mr. Davies, are you all right?" Neil vocalised everyone's thoughts.

"I, er," I raked my fingers through my hair. This was too much. How could I explain to everyone that a beetle, and I couldn't see where it had gone, had startled me to this extent? "I'm sorry, something made me jump. I'm really sorry." I could see the archdeacon staring, his arms folded across his chest as though he couldn't quite believe what he was witnessing. "Shall I carry on and finish the last verse?"

Neil said no, we should just leave it there. He pronounced the benediction, and I began playing to usher everyone out, not the triumphant march I had planned, but a quiet version of the last hymn, my trembling fingers fumbling over the notes. It sounded awful, and I knew it. The instant I could escape, I closed the doors around the keyboards, and fled.

I didn't get far. Neil was waiting for me at the bottom of the stone steps.

"Ewan, what on earth happened?" His face was grey, the dark shadows growing under his eyes a testimony to the trials he'd endured this morning. The archdeacon, a short, round man with a half-moon of curly black hair peered at me through thick, black-framed glasses, his hands planted on his hips, and muttered something about it being 'a rather unfortunate turn of events.'

"There was this enormous black beetle, it fell on my hand," I shuddered again at the memory.

"Beetles again?" His concern morphed into disbelief. "Excuse us for one moment," he said to the archdeacon, who nodded and walked back into the church. Neil waited until he was out of earshot, then he took my arm, and steered me to one side so no one could blunder in and overhear our conversation. "Are you sure you're all right?"

He asked me over and over again. I keep thinking about it. It seems to me that everyone keeps asking if I'm all right. And, although I've denied it, if I'm going to be honest, I don't feel right. I imagine this is how a snow-globe feels after someone picks it up, shakes it, and sets its innards swirling. Of course, I told Neil I was all right and there was no need for him to over-react after one simple mishap, but he corrected me on that.

"Two mishaps during the service," he said, his eyes studying my face. "And three if we count the episode in the pub. You seem, I don't know quite how to describe it, Ewan, 'edgy', I suppose. Like something is really bothering you."

"Nothing's bothering me," I lied, thinking of Rebecca, of Vi, and my growling stomach.

"It doesn't matter if you don't want to tell me," he said, his voice a gentle balsam dripping calm in to soothe my chaotic mind. "But don't forget I'm always here if you need me, as a friend as well as a vicar. And look, I'm sorry old chap, but I'll have to skip lunch." He nods ever his shoulder in the direction of the church. "Trust me: you don't want to dine with Wilbur."

"Wilbur?" I smothered my smirk, indiscretions forgotten.

"Wilbur. Enough said. See if you find it in your heart to feel sorry for James and me. And look Ewan, make sure you go home and take it easy the rest of today. I know you; you've probably been working too hard. Maybe you need a relaxing afternoon doing nothing eh? Good man."

But you know, hours have passed, and no amount of relaxing, nor the large glasses of whisky I've been swallowing have helped shift the unease that's left me jumpy, nerves jangling at every last creak as the cottage shifts its ancient bones. I keep getting up and creeping to the window, peeping out into the street to see if I can spot Vi watching me, but everything is quiet under the pall of a Sunday evening. Everything is quiet, but nothing feels right. And nothing has felt right from that very moment when I looked up from my piano and realised Rebecca was there in my classroom. I stand by the window, chewing my nails and nursing my glass. What a mess, and I don't understand how I got into it.

Chapter 8

Monday morning, and in the light of Alex's suspicions, I resolve to spend as little time as possible in our office. The fewer opportunities I give him to witness my interactions with my ex-wife, the fewer conclusions he can draw. I go straight to my classroom and, after playing a few scales and arpeggios to warm up my fingers, remember I need to look out some music I've promised one of my students.

I go and unlock the door to my storeroom. Its door creaks open. There are no windows in here, and the single electric light bulb does a poor job of illuminating the dark shelves. For a second I pause in the doorway, my thoughts conjuring images of black, horrible beetles until I shake my shoulders, remind myself to stop being so damned hysterical, and get on with my work. I step into the storeroom and the door grinds shut behind me.

The lack of light doesn't hamper my search for I know the precise location of everything in this room. I have a strict system, which even Nancy has grasped, a testament to the number of times I've had to drag his stupid bulk in here to castigate him for leaving things out of place, thrown down on any old shelf instead of being neatly filed where I expect to find them. Mousey Miss Harris, Rebecca's predecessor, also courted my wrath by dumping things in the first available space. To me it's simple; put everything back where you found it. I can't understand why everyone finds my concept of order so challenging.

Third shelf on the left, second from the bottom, and there is the pile of sheet music for the GCSE syllabus, incidentally, in a box labelled 'GCSE-P', the 'P' standing for piano music. It's so obvious it pains me every time I have to explain it to my dull-witted colleagues. Of course, I don't need to say my pupils are not allowed in here.

Music in hand, I rifle through a collection of old records for a recording I want to play my class this morning, when the door creaks open. My heart skips a beat. It's Rebecca. Her head cranes, her neck snaking this way and that, her wild hair already escaping from the confines of a bun skewered with a pen. I step out from between the shelves and her mouth breaks into a wide smile.

"Morning," she says. "I wondered where you were."

Ah, she doesn't seem to be annoyed with me for not ringing. That's a relief.

"Did you have a good weekend?" She says.

"Yes, thank you," though I'd prefer not to think about it since the slightest mention sets another wave of embarrassment prickling through me. "You?"

"Oh yes," she sighs, wiping her hand across her forehead with a dramatic flourish. "Went out for dinner on Friday, like I said," she glances at me and I smile to show I remember her telling me. "Then Saturday we drove down to the South Downs for a picnic with Rick's sister and her family, they've got five kids, can you imagine?" I grimace. "Then yesterday we went to one set of friends for lunch, and the theatre last night with a different set of friends to watch a friend of my cousin, you remember Bella, don't you?" I nod. "Well, her friend is in one of the drama groups at Cambridge, so we went to watch that. It was quite good really, a play by the writer David Cunningham, don't know if you've heard of him?" I shake my head. "Well it was great. It was set in the nineteen-fifties and was all about this woman who, oh look, I'll tell you about it later. I don't think I've got time for it now, I'd better get ready for class."

She's been talking so quickly, she's almost out of breath. I watch her, my sinking sense of being an uncultured dullard looking in on her glittery, whirlwind life subsiding at the thought of her breathless, astride me, her full breasts swaying as she rocks backwards and forwards, driving me to the very edge of reason. Make of it what you will, I love to be dominated by a woman in bed, to have her take the lead and use me for her own pleasure. I lean against the shelves, my legs weak at the thought.

"By the way," she is saying, innocent of my thoughts. "I've been thinking. How about I get Nathan to help me sort out this mess," she indicates the shelves with a swivel of her head. "Wouldn't it be a great help to have someone tidy it up for you?"

What? My mouth falls open. Colour floods my face and I go to speak, but indignation hampers my words and all I can do is splutter with disbelief. Did I hear her correctly? My storeroom is not 'a mess', it's a vision of order and I don't know how she has the nerve to suggest otherwise. I press my lips together. We are not in bed now, and we do as I say in my department.

"There's no 'mess' as you put it, in here. I know exactly where everything is. The only time it is a mess is when other members of staff," I glare my warning, "fail to put things back in their proper place. So no, I do not want you to muck everything up. There is a system, it's my system and it works perfectly well."

She folds her arms, amusement playing around her mouth, although I can't think why; I'm not laughing.

"Would it kill you just to listen to someone else's suggestion?"

"Would it kill you just to follow my instructions?" I hit back, and because I'm so rattled both at the thought of her messing up my cupboard and that she's been flagrant enough to suggest doing so, today it's me dredging up old arguments by adding "for once."

She arches her eyebrows, and I regret letting those last two words go.

"Whatever you say, Mr. Davies," she says, belittling my precious order with the contemptuous look she throws around the storeroom. "Whatever you say."

She holds the door for me. I snap off the light, and step back out into the corridor as she walks towards her classroom door. As she moves, I think I see something black disappear under her hair at the nape of her neck. I open my mouth to say something, but self-preservation stays my tongue with a firm 'no'. It points out I have humiliated myself enough this weekend. I do not keep seeing beetles. And she has stirred me enough this morning, I don't trust myself to keep calm. As soon as the door closes behind her, I take the storeroom key out of my pocket and lock it. I don't care if she does have to come and find me every time she needs something, the thought of her and Nancy moving everything, rearranging my things, sets my head swirling.

Eschewing lunch in the school canteen yet again, I head upstairs for a peaceful cup of tea, aiming to leave the office long before either Rebecca or Alex appears. Shutting the door, I settle behind my desk, my stomach growling. Out of my briefcase, I take a packet of sandwiches I made this morning, organic bread, organic butter, and sliced tomatoes from my greenhouse. I lay them out on the desk, and examine them, but my appetite wavers. They lie there on top of their paper wrapping looking wholesome and innocent, but what poisons lie waiting for me to ingest with every bite? A line of sweat breaks out on my top lip

I poke at a red tomato slice sticking out between the bread. Ever since the thought occurred to me, I've been worrying about Vi tampering with them, but what about the bag of compost I've grown them in? There was something in Saturday's newspaper about people getting food poisoning, no, wait, it was worse than that, Legionnaire's disease from new, peat-free compost. I don't know what Legionnaire's disease is, but outbreaks of it make the news, so it must be serious. What is this new, 'peat-free' compost anyway? Maybe it too contains chemicals, the government's attempt to infect even those who might think they're safe by growing their own food. Nothing is safe, not even the paper I wrapped around my lunch.

Nausea wafts through me, and the room gives a slight lurch. I grip the desk, staring at my lunch as though it might savage me if I look away. The office seems very hot and it is as though my shirt, my collar is tightening, trying to throttle me. I undo my top button with hot, sweaty fingers. And all the while, the sandwiches go on sitting there, challenging me to take a bite.

I must eat, I tell myself. That's why I'm not feeling well, I'm hungry. On the count of ten, I tell myself, I will eat one mouthful. I take one modest bite. But although I chew and chew, I cannot summon the will to swallow. I wind up spitting it out into the bin.

The door opens and Alex saunters in. Damn. I've spent so much time staring at my lunch, I have lost track of time. Mercifully, he is alone. He shuts the door, throws himself into his chair, which squeaks as though in surprise at being disturbed, and puts both feet up onto the desk.

"What the hell is this?" He catches sight of my lunch and cranes his neck to have a good look. "Sandwiches? I know the food in the canteen is pretty lame, but sandwiches, mate?"

"I fancied a change," I say. "Anyway, I've got a glut of tomatoes this year. Got to use them up somehow."

"Tomato sandwiches?" He frowns. "Look, I hope you don't mind me saying this, but are you sure you're all right?"

"What do you mean? Why does everyone keep asking me that? Of course I'm all right. What, is it so weird for a guy to bring in his own lunch for a change? I knew I had a lot of stuff to sort out this lunchtime," I indicate the pile of paperwork on my desk, "so I thought I'd have lunch up here and get on with it."

"All right," he grins, holding up his arms and getting up out of his chair to turn the kettle on. "I still haven't got over the fact you left a pint on Friday, that's all. If that's not weird, I don't know what is. That and you babbling on about beetles in your beer," he snorts with laughter. "Thought Nigel was going to slap you, I did."

I sigh, trying not to dwell on the memory, and turn back to my lunch. One bite of sandwich, Ewan. Come on, you can manage one bite.

"Would it kill you to take just one bite?" Rebecca says. I startle, and look round, but she's not here. It's only me and Alex.

"What is it?" Alex is watching me and chuckling. "Jumpy, aren't you?"

"I thought I heard Rebecca."

"Nah, she's in the staffroom mate," he says, busying himself spooning coffee into his mug, fishing out a teabag for mine. "She's made the mistake of telling Smarmy Stu she was an archaeologist. There'll be no escape for her the rest of term. You know what he's like with his bloody metal detector. A tenner says he badgers her into joining him one weekend."

"Nice," I mutter, imagining Rebecca with Smarmy Stu, the English teacher, so-called for his approach to dealing with the head is to agree with her every word. My appetite rasps out its last breath as I'm worrying whether or not the beetles I keep seeing have been crawling over the tomatoes in the greenhouse. Thank goodness Alex wasn't there to witness my performance in church yesterday, although I'm sure it won't be long before someone mentions it. I crumple my lunch in its paper, and drop it in the bin beside my desk.

"Talking of wanting to slap people," he says, putting a mug of tea on my desk. "I forgot to tell you. Our glorious leader was looking for you in the canteen. Something about a key?"

I huff, and smack one hand down on my desk, which startles Alex so much that he spills coffee down his corduroy trousers, the dark stain mingling with the multicoloured smears of paint.

"That bloody woman," I groan. "Sorry, didn't mean to make you jump."

"That's all right," he grins. "She has the same effect on me, right from the moment I hear her horsy heels clippety-clopping up behind me."

"No, not that bloody woman, the other one. Rebecca," I explain to his blank look. If Mrs Phillips has been asking Alex the whereabouts of me and the key to my storeroom, I can deduce Rebecca has taken revenge for having her suggestion dismissed by reporting me. I can picture them together, cosy in sisterhood. 'Ewan won't let me do as I please, Mrs Phillips. He won't listen to anything I say.' 'Don't worry Rebecca, I'll sort him out. You have such lovely suggestions. Of course you can do whatever you want.'

"Rebecca? What's she done? She hasn't been here long enough to piss you off already, has she? I thought you two were friends."

"She wants to rearrange my storeroom. In fact, as she put it this morning, in her opinion, my system is 'a mess'. I've locked the door to keep her out, so she's obviously gone whinging to Mrs Phillips."

"Ouch," Alex says, sipping his tea. "What is it with new members of staff feeling as though they've got to do something to prove their worth? I don't blame you there, mate. But she's quite a reasonable person though, isn't she? Maybe you should just let her get on with it."

Let her get on with it? My head jerks up, mouth falling open as I reel from the impact of this unexpected blow. Alex is siding with Rebecca. My body chills with disbelief. I cast a critical eye over my standpoint, but I don't think I'm being ridiculous. It isn't un-reasonable of me to expect a new member of staff to go along with my tried and tested methods, and furthermore, I resent the fact she's gone running to the Head instead of apologising to me. I glare across the office, stung by the thought my usual ally inside these four walls has taken against me, and I notice Alex's broad shoulders shaking. As I watch, he can hold it in no longer. He throws his head back and erupts into gales of loud, convulsive laughter.

"That's a classic," he sobs, once he recovers the ability to speak, and wipes his face on an enormous, paint-covered handkerchief he produces from a trouser pocket. "Your face: I thought you were going to throw something at me. No need to fret, mate," he blows his nose. "No one in the school would dare muck with your cupboard. She'll soon learn."

"Wretched bloody woman," I mutter, and, as if on cue, the door opens and Rebecca steps into the fray.

"Oh there you are," she says to me, her colourful skirt swirling as she shuts the door. "I wondered where you'd got to." One hand on her hip, she greets Alex, who's trying to make it look as though he's not laughing, and flounces over to my desk. "I need the key to the storeroom," she folds her arms tight across her chest. "Mrs. Phillips says you will have to cut me a spare if you're going to persist in keeping the door locked."

"She does, does she? Good of you to mention it to her. And anyway, why wouldn't I keep it locked? I don't want anyone and everyone messing around in there."

"Don't worry," she gives a weary sigh. "I promise not to interfere with your so-called 'system'. I just need some music stands for a group of pupils interested in starting up a lunchtime guitar group."

"Who?"

No one has approached me to say they want to start a guitar group. Not that I'd be any use since it's not an instrument I can play, but why ask

Rebecca? Irritation bubbles through my veins. It's the principal of the matter; as Head of Department, it would be courteous to ask my permission first.

"Some of the year eights," her breezy tone dismisses me as inconsequential. "Might be a good way to get them more interested in lessons." She holds out her hand. "Key, please."

If I'm going to be honest, it is a struggle to keep the non-musical pupils interested. I can't understand their antipathy any more than they can understand my passion. But I'm not happy at the thought someone new can waft in and inspire where I have failed, just like that. As I sit there, I remember how dull and uninteresting I felt listening to her enthusing about her action-packed weekend earlier. When I first arrived at Thatchington, I was the dynamic, inspiring one. The thought she has stolen the role I thought was mine, makes me want to grind my teeth with jealousy. Next time I see Vic I must ask him if he found me this annoying, and apologise. I hand over the key without uttering another word.

Alex waits until the sound of her footsteps walking away gets faint.

"She's just trying to impress. Give it six months, mate. The novelty will have worn off."

Six months? I'm not sure I can endure this for six whole months. And as I sit there staring at the door she's just walked through, something becomes blindingly apparent to me.

"She's after my job," I say, my voice raw with disbelief, reeling in the glare of what's just occurred to me. It's no accident, no mere coincidence she's turned up here. I loosen my collar further, the hot office becoming unbearable. She's here to undermine me, to push me out. It must have something to do with Vi and the fish; I knew my neighbour had guessed I've discovered what she's up to. Rebecca must be involved; she has to be working for the same people.

"Aren't you clever?" Rebecca's voice is snarling in my ears. *"You've worked it out. Think it's going to save you, do you? Ha."*

"Nah," says Alex, oblivious to my turmoil. "That's never gonna happen. She's not you, mate. Trust me, once the novelty of being here has worn off, and once the little bastards have pissed her off enough to make her shout at them, she'll settle down. And at least it looks like you've got someone you can trust with some of the workload. Be nice for you to be able to relax for a bit, knowing it's not all up to you, won't it? Don't know what I'd do without Joan picking up all the stuff I can't be arsed to do. Means I can get on with the important stuff like this picture I'm doing for one of Neil's ecclesiastical cohorts. It's a retirement gift from his congregation, and boy, are they paying nicely for it. I'm thinking of buying a boat with the money."

"A boat?" I say, admiring how calm I sound when all I can hear is Rebecca's poisonous prattling. "Haven't you got another baby on the way?"

"Yeah," he squirms, and I smile, guessing from his reaction this is exactly what Tessa had to say on the matter too. "But me and the nippers need something to do while Tessa's busy with the baby. Seen this great tub," he says, his enthusiasm firing. "Have you got your computer on? I'll show you a picture."

Tempting though it is to indulge his childlike enthusiasm, I have a department to run, and a job to protect. I make my excuses, gulp down my tea, and head for the door. Rebecca might think she can outfox me, but Alex is quite right; she isn't me. I need to take charge, and I need to show 'them', whoever it is she and Vi are working for, that I'm not easily cowed. It took a lot for me to get where I am today, and I won't let go without a fight.

Chapter 9

The doorbell rings. I look up from the piano to the clock on the mantelpiece, but it's only six, too early for Mrs Harris to be round complaining about the music. Despite my attempts to soundproof the tiny room which houses my piano, my neighbour swears she can still hear me playing. The sight of her bent form hobbling up to my front door and the ensuing 'now Mr. Davies, about the noise' darkens even my sunniest mood. I don't, I might add, complain about her wretched dog, an overfed Jack Russell, a sausage on stubby legs, yapping at all hours of the day and night. And my tastes are classical, so it's not as though I'm playing outlandish, experimental music. You'd think she'd appreciate it.

I mean, I could have been a concert pianist, had my interests not lain elsewhere.

I decide to ignore the bell and set my fingers sauntering down the swinging lines of melody once more. This evening I'm in the mood for a little soulful jazz, and I'm playing Nina Simone's 'My Baby Just Cares', throwing my voice in good measure. And as my fingers romp up and down the keys, I'm imagining Rebecca sitting next to me, playing along as I taught her, echoing the melody with the tinkling, upper keys of the piano. She rests her head against my shoulder, and I play on. Music, love: in this moment my life is complete. This is my Rebecca, I might add, not the one at school who makes disparaging remarks about my methods and questions my authority. No, this is the other one, the one I fell in love with. This is the Rebecca who makes everything all right.

Above the music sounds discord, something that doesn't fit. I listen as I play, as Rebecca plays, and recognition sinks in, a heavy stone cast in and sinking down, stirring the waters of my contentment. It's the doorbell again. My caller is persistent.

"All right, I'm coming," I get up from the stool in a pique, sulking at being compelled by ingrained notions of socially acceptable behaviour to leave the warm, cushioned comfort of one of my favourite fantasies. My feet drag as I head for the door, and my fists clench, ready to savage my caller if their need to disturb me is anything other than life-threateningly urgent. I throw open the door. Expecting to see old Mrs. Harris, the shocking vision of beads and flesh jolts me on guard. Damn. It's Vi.

"Hello love."

I gawp, my mouth opening and closing. It must be time for her to check on me. Earlier, when I'd had time to think things through, it had been my plan to be ready to confront her the next time she came to the door, but I've been so busy with Nina and Rebecca, my wits are lounging, glass of wine in hand, enjoying my performance. Get up, I snap at them. I need you now. But they huff, roll their eyes and complain they're much too comfortable to be bothered. I take a deep breath. I'm on my own with this one.

Vi is as voluptuous as ever in her vest and beads. Tonight you can see the faded, grubby trim and straps of a coral lace bra that must last have fitted her some decades ago, and her tanned, wrinkly hide rolls over the top and sides. It looks so uncomfortable, I am too distracted by visualising myself doing her poor breasts the service of releasing them from their confinement to see the package she's holding out to me until she shakes it, as though trying to snare a baby's attention.

"Oh, sorry Vi, here, let me," I take the package from her hands. It's a parcel of books I've ordered from the internet about food additives and safety. Parcelled up like this, she has no idea I'm onto her. At least, I hope not. I don't think she's opened the package, it looks intact.

"Got you a nice piece of fish too, I have," she says, holding up her arm from which dangles a plain white carrier bag. "Some for you, and some for Mr. and Mrs. Gregory next door."

Mark and Phillipa Gregory whose driveway borders mine, are both lawyers working in London. I wonder, with their skills, if they've realised what Vi's up to. Mark, for one, is a defence barrister, so he must be used to identifying underhand schemes. Perhaps I should try to have a chat with him. No, wait a minute, maybe I should be thinking about organising a resident's meeting so I can make sure everyone's aware of what's going on. But I break out in a cold sweat at the thought of what she might do if she discovers I know what's going on. Perhaps for now it's better if I keep it to myself, and monitor her activities, just as she is watching mine. I've bought a diary to record notes, instances of her strange behaviour. Yes, now I think about it, if I'm going to mention it to Mark, he will appreciate hard evidence over mere conjecture. I will have to prove my case.

"You know Vi, I've been thinking. I don't want you to get me any more fish."

"Why?" She looks crestfallen, hurt that I'm trying to defy her clever plan. "Are you feeling all right?"

"I'm fine, thank you," though tired of everyone asking. "I just don't want any more fish."

"But it's good fish from the fish-man. It's fresh. He goes and gets it from the market in Covent Garden, he does, every morning. I thought you liked having your bit of salmon. I can ask him for something else for you, the fish-man, I mean. You've never said you didn't like it before."

"I just don't think I want any more," I say, clinging to the door as though it has the power to shield me from her antipathy.

"Well, I don't know what I'm going to say to the fish-man, I don't," Vi says, her eyebrows raised to heaven. "He's going to say 'why' and I'm going to have to say 'well he didn't really say, like'. I tell you what; it's a shame to take business away from a man who's trying to earn an honest penny. It's a crying shame that."

"I just don't want any more."

"Oh well, if you're sure," Vi shakes her head as though I've just made the most stupid decision she's ever imagined possible. "I'll just have to tell him, I will. I don't know what he's going to say though. Oh, and that reminds me," she says, folding her flabby arms across her tortured bosom. "That was a bit of a queer do in church yesterday, wasn't it?"

As my face flames hot and scarlet, I mutter that I'm trying to forget about what happened.

"Gave us all a scare, you did. Not like you, that. He usually plays so nicely, I said to our Lucy, I did. Well, I'll tell the fish-man. He's not going to be happy, though; not happy at all. Are you sure you're all right? I'll be off then."

She turns, and waddles back down my path, still shaking her head and muttering. I close my door, cringing at the mention of my faux-pas in church and how one small, tiny incident can leave a man marked for life. I can imagine the tittle-tattle, the sniggering. Mr Davies? The school teacher? Oh, didn't you hear, he got all hysterical in church over a beetle, fancy, made a right mess of playing the organ, he did. It's just not the same when Della plays, good old, reliable Della. My inner self slumps down into the filthy cold depths of a puddle of shame. Neil will never ask me to play again.

I peek through the spy-hole fitted to my front door, making sure she really is walking away, and congratulate myself. It wasn't easy, but it was a victory of sorts, albeit an inconclusive one, and I'm happy I think I've proved one thing to myself. There can only be one reason why she made such a fuss over something as innocuous as me not wanting to buy fish, and that is because she wants to make sure I go on eating it, eating up my drugs. Because if everyone stopped taking them, I guess we'd all wake up. There would be a revolution, an uprising of ordinary people, the common man against the age-old institutions, the 'old-boy networks' and the stratums of hypocrisy that keep us held down in our so-called rightful places. The authorities don't want that. I open the diary, and make my first entry.

1856hrs. Told Vi no more fish. She wasn't very happy, tried to persuade me to keep buying, claimed it was because she doesn't want to upset the fish-man.

But through my bravado, a thought comes flitting into my brain. My blood chills. I am in danger for my non-compliance. A vision, a memory of being held, of being dragged, pleading, crying for mercy stirs in my brain, but I gulp it away. No, that didn't happen to me. Maybe it was something I read, something that happened to someone else. Nina Simone forgotten, it's to the kitchen I head. I need a drink, some whisky to anesthetise the fear curled up and quivering in a corner of my mind. It's only after I pour the third large glass, I remember I was going to tell Vi I don't want her cleaning for me any more either.

Eventually I fall asleep on the settee and wake up in the pale, grey morning with a stiff back and painful crick in my neck a hot shower does nothing to soothe. Worse still, my head is pounding with a dull ache situated right between my temples as though my skull is caught in a vice, as I myself am caught by my own vices, the bones tightening, pressing against the pinkish, cushion of brain inside. The slightest movement sets it throbbing anew. I spend lunchtime sitting at my desk in the office, berating my stupidity for not going to bed earlier while toying with the latest packet of sandwiches from home. The door opens and Rebecca swishes in. I don't look up, I daren't lift my head.

"Ewan, you look awful," she says, pulling out her own chair and sitting down in front of her computer in a flap of flowing flowery fabric. It was Alex's brainwave she should share our office. I had no rational reason for refusing.

"Thanks."

"Are you all right?"

I tell her from behind gritted teeth, that yes, of course I'm all right, but I'm quaking at the thought she'll realise I'm hung-over. She knows me well enough to guess the source of my malady. So much for running such a tight ship she won't get the chance to slide her feet under my desk, today I feel as though I've handed over the whole chessboard and asked her to make my moves. Mind you, her assumption that she knows me so well she can predict my every move is a conceit, and I long for a way to shake her out of her judge's chair and pitch her headlong into seething doubt. I've changed, but she doesn't see it. I am not the man she loved and left, if indeed 'loved' was the word. I am different, even if I do still drink too much when I'm feeling besieged. Well, how else am I supposed to sleep? Sober, I haven't slept for weeks. How can I switch off knowing what I know? And if it isn't Vi or Fiona prattling on in my head, it's Rebecca. It's enough to turn anyone to drink. But, I think, glaring at my lunch, none of this would seem so bad if I didn't need to eat.

"Sandwiches?" Rebecca says, curiosity craning her neck to peer across our desks to see what I'm doing as I sit, steeling myself to take a bite. "You've never been a packed lunch sort of a guy. What's the matter with the food in the canteen? Carmen and the girls do a wonderful job, great choices and some really healthy stuff."

I wonder out loud just who the hell is 'Carmen', but, of course, my ex-wife has made friends with everyone, and thinks it's disgraceful I'm not on first name terms with the dinner ladies. But I shouldn't be surprised to find her cultivating allies in the unlikeliest of places. 'Oh Rebecca, she's so marvellous. She's lovely, isn't she?' No one will suspect this is all part of her ploy to shake hard enough to dislodge me from my post. I massage my temples with my fingers. None of this conjecture is helping my aching head. Damned whisky. Damned meddling women.

"I can't believe you didn't know that," she sits typing at her keyboard, the tippety-tap of the keys a snare drum rattling in my ears heralding her occupation of the moral high ground. "Perhaps if you were nicer to them they'd make you something special for lunch. They're very good like that, you know. No problem at all getting a vegan meal, they even asked what I like to eat. Such a nice change from being made to feel like a prima-donna in field kitchens."

"Ah, so what you're actually saying is that you don't eat the muck they dish up either, you have them make 'a special meal' just for you."

I mustn't laugh; it'll set off fresh spasms throbbing in my head.

"That's very trusting of you. How do you know they're not going to slip a spoonful of beef jelly into your lunch? Better hope 'Carmen' is as friendly as you'd like to think. You can't trust anyone, you know. You wouldn't believe the stuff they put in food these days: additives, pesticides, fertiliser, growth hormones. It's terrifying," I'm talking so fast it's as though I can't stop the words falling out of my mouth. "I read all this stuff in the newspaper about them stuffing poisons into farmed fish to make their flesh a nice colour. It was horrific, and my neighbour buys it for her grandson. It shouldn't be allowed."

I look up, my pounding pulse as wild as my loss of control. What on earth am I doing? I mustn't say all this stuff in front of Rebecca, I'm sure I can't trust her. But she is nodding, all wide-eyed and hanging on my every word, her fingers poised above the keyboard. I gulp, wondering if she's taking notes, evidence against me.

"Oh, I've been worrying about the same things for years," she says, pausing to push wisps of hair out of her eyes. "It's one of the reasons I decided to go vegan. Meat, urgh," she shudders. "I only have to think about the things they feed animals to fatten them up and I can be physically sick. Did you know, for example, what they do to chickens? And it's all in the name of profit. Disgusting," she says, shaking her head. "Dreadful karma. We're all going to suffer, you know."

"What do they do?" I put my palms flat against the soothing solidity of the surface of my desk as queasiness sends my head swirling. The door opens, and Alex strides in. He tosses a pile of folders down on his desk, and saunters over to see if there's any water in the kettle.

"They feed them processed pellets made from actual chicken," she says, her eyes huge, her lashes trembling.

"Not 'actual chicken'?" Alex cuts in with a scoff, filling the kettle with water from a jug. "What is that, as opposed to 'virtual chicken'? What are you talking about? Sounds like the sort of moronic conversation my kids would have. I get it all the time. 'Dad, who do you think would win in a fight, the virtual or the actual chicken? Answer: I don't care. Are you all right mate? You look rougher than a badger's, ah, never mind," he says, blushing and glancing at Rebecca, the grown-up in the office.

"Whisky-itus, I expect," she sneers.

I sit up, stung. This gets worse.

"Don't worry Alex, so far it's never proved fatal," she arches her eyebrows, a smirk playing around the corners of her mouth, and cuts off my retort by answering Alex's other question. "We're talking about food safety and cruelty to animals in the food-chain," Rebecca says, reaching into her bun for a pen.

"Nice conversation for lunchtime. Don't tell me you're thinking of joining the sandwich brigade too," he says, indicating me with a nod of his head, and throws his arms up into the air in mock supplication. "I'm surrounded by nutters."

"I still don't understand what you find so weird about me bringing in my own lunch," I say. "And no, Rebecca, I am not hungover, I just have a headache. Anyway," I point out to Alex. "It turns out she has the dinner ladies make her a special, personal meal so she doesn't have to eat the crap they serve up to the rest of us."

"That's because I'm a vegan," she glares across the room.

"Who's a vegan?" Alex groans. Rebecca flashes him her brightest smile, and he pretends to faint across the desk. "Oh well, lucky you've told me. I'll have to have a word with Tessa, make sure she's got food for you puritanical types laid on for the buffet on Saturday. Mind you, I'm guessing we won't have to worry about you, mate. Expect you'll be bringing your own sarnies."

"Saturday?" Rebecca asks.

"Saturday. You know; my birthday party? Don't you dare tell me you've forgotten all about it. Is Rick coming?"

"Yes he is."

Oh great. So he's invited the Cartwrights too. Now I'll have to think up a decent excuse to get out of going. There's no way I'm spending Saturday evening watching Rebecca flitting around in 'happily-ever-after' world. I take a bite of my unwanted sandwich, anything to detract from the bitter taste in my mouth

Alex plonks a mug of tea down on my desk, and I wind my cold fingers around its warmth in search of some comfort from the depths of the cold, toxic sea which long extinguished my passion for Rebecca. To think my first thoughts when she reappeared was to entertain a woolly, fluffy notion that she'd spent all this time waiting for me; thank god I managed to keep that to myself. I say 'thank god', whatever 'god' means. Yes, so you'll find me in church every Sunday indulging my passion for choral music, but 'God'? Whatever 'God' is, he's never been there, never stepped in to save me when I needed saving, and 'god' knows, there have been many times.

"You're not bloody-well listening to me, mate, are you?"

Alex's voice cuts into my musing, and I look up, bewildered in the shock of being dragged back into the here and now, to find both he and Rebecca watching me, their faces animated with mirth. As I look from one face to the other, they laugh together, and again I am conscious of being on the outside looking in. And now, never mind 'god', I'm not sure who 'I' am. Am I the body sitting at his desk, the subject of a joke he doesn't understand, or am I the observer, watching the scene unfold as the actors strut and utter lines written for them by some universal hand, an elaborate cosmic script? I shake my head. I must stop thinking. My head is already sore, and I must remember to note this in my diary.

R laughing at me, accusing me of being hung-over in front of Alex. She's after my job.

"Sorry, no. What did you say?"

"I said I spoke to Neil last night. Beetles, mate."

You see? This proves there is no such thing as 'god'. If there were, he wouldn't have let me humiliate myself in public, or he'd magically remove all memory of the incident from peoples' minds. Instead, Alex is doubled up whooping at the thought of me frightening churchgoers by being in hysterics over a beetle, and Rebecca's making stupid remarks about how I must have been playing 'All Creatures Great and Small'. I bury my head in my hands as my companions go on laughing, go on having a bloody good laugh at my expense, and wish I was anywhere but here.

Chapter 10

Unable to face any more aftershocks in the aftermath of my faux-pas in church, I don't care how much Neil relies on me to organise it, I'm not going to choir practice on Friday. I pick a time when I know he and James won't be in, the weekly service they hold up at the hospital on Thursday night, and leave a message excusing myself on their answering machine. After last week's debacle in the pub, I'm not going to 'The Dolphin' either. Instead I turn off the ringer on my telephone, open a new bottle of whisky, and try to settle down with a book, although this doesn't last long before I relent to temptation, turn on the computer and lose myself in another evening of searching online for more clues about the food conspiracy.

I spend a lot of time on Saturday pondering various excuses for missing Alex's birthday bash, but nothing believable comes to mind. Pottering around my garden, I wind up cutting a bunch of pinkish-orange dahlias for Tessa, and promise myself two things that will keep me safe from any embarrassment in front of Rebecca and her husband during the evening. Firstly, I will not drink too much, and secondly, I will leave after an hour or so. It will be a pleasant evening with friends, I tell my reflection as I shave before having a quick shower. I will not disgrace myself. Oh, and that's another thing, I use a stern voice to make sure my reflection is listening as I button up my shirt. I will not be seeing any beetles.

Alex and Tessa live near me, but not in a small cosy street of quaint cottages. Theirs is a splendid Georgian townhouse set back in gardens up a private driveway. Alex said it belonged to Tessa's great aunt, a spinster who'd lived there until she died at the ripe old age of one hundred and one. The aunt had insisted upon Tessa and Alex moving into the house as soon as they discovered they were expecting their first baby. 'It's a family house', she'd insisted, time and time again. 'It needs to be filled with a real family'. And despite how much she adored Alex, who liked to sketch her dozing in her chair, she would say not only to Tessa, but to anyone who came to visit, 'well it's not like he's ever going to be able to afford to buy a decent house, now is it, the poor boy. Gifted, yes, but utterly, utterly useless."

I chuckle at the memory of Alex telling me this story, tipping back his mane and laughing, unafraid of the aunt's prognosis. She could have been talking about either of us. Alex and I might both like to think teaching is just a stopgap before I publish my seminal composition, and he sells enough paintings to sustain his family, but we've both been working in education now for over fifteen years. I've been at Thatchington High for nine, and Alex, twelve. Given the evidence, the aunt may have had a point.

I turn the corner and into their drive, my feet crunching on the gravel, as I think I am relieved I have never had any wealthy, elderly aunts to impress. The drive is flanked by a line of tall plane trees with little white lights twinkling from among their roots, solar powered lights dotted here and there, and giving the garden a fairyland feel. As I near the door, a large security light blinks on, blinding me with the sudden switch to brightness. I just miss stumbling over a gaggle of children's bicycles left strewn where their owners have abandoned them, and make my way up to the imposing front door. The nearer I get to the house, the more I can see of the lights and colours of a party in full swing, music playing, bodies swaying, and a hubbub of bubbling conversations seeping from the windows.

I jog up the steps to the front door, trying to ignore the twisting unease contorting in my gut. It's Alex's birthday, I remind myself again, and I can manage his party. I will be all right. I'm not going to drink much. I'm not going to stay long. And I'm not going to make a fool of myself. There's no need for me to worry about the food; I don't need to eat anything, and then I can go home. I can do this.

The door springs opens as I go to reach for the lion's head door knocker, and Alex stands in the doorway. He throws up his arms, the wineglass in one hand sloshing red wine down his sleeves.

"Ewan, mate! At long last! Didn't think you were coming. That for me?" He says as I hold out the bottle I have tucked under one arm. "What's this? Twenty-one year old Bowmore? Well, hello baby. Christ," he says, dropping his voice as I wriggle my arms out of my coat. "Tessa's invited a right bunch here. I think me and you ought to take this out in the garden and leave the tossers to their wine."

"You've certainly got a houseful," I say, looking past him to where people are chatting in the hall, on the stairs, and drifting from room to room. "Where are the kids?"

"Upstairs with the footie," he says, taking my coat. "Which is exactly where I'm heading in a minute, but don't tell Tessa. Rick's up there too, Rebecca's Rick," he explains to my blank face.

"Don't tell Tessa what?" Tessa Garvie appears in the hallway, her pregnant belly swathed in purple chiffon. Her short blonde hair is slicked into place, and set off with a pair of dangly, glittery earrings. She doesn't need a crown to mark her out as queen of her domain. "Alex, I hope you're not sneaking off to watch the football upstairs with the boys; that would be intolerably rude. Ewan, darling," she steps forward and pressed her warm lips against my cold cheek. "I'm so glad you're here. It's lovely to see you."

"These are for you," I say, holding out the bunch of dahlias.

"They're beautiful," she gasps, taking them from my hands, and turning them round and round to admire every angle. "Look at the colour. I think I'm going to have to pester you for some tubers. Do you dig them up in the autumn?"

"Oh here we go, gardening talk," Alex rolls his eyes. "It never takes you two long to get started, does it?"

"That's because Ewan and I are civilised sorts," she says, slipping her arm through mine. "Not the type of person who'd neglect his own guests in the name of watching football. Come on Ewan, let's go through to the kitchen and I'll get you a drink."

She tells Alex to put my coat with the others, and he goes bounding off to do as she says. Shaking her head at his exuberance, she winds her arm tighter around mine, and leads me through to their handsome kitchen with its granite tops and seasoned Dutch Oak cupboards gleaming in the light from a bespoke chandelier, a commission from an artist friend of theirs whose work the Garvies both admire. It hangs from the ornate Victorian ceiling high above the gathered heads. Most people have congregated in here. The downstairs rooms are stately, beautifully decorated with Tessa's eye for design, but the kitchen is the newest, and the most impressive. Yet everything, from the worktops to the chandelier, has either been salvaged or given to her for free. She has a knack not only for aesthetics, but for persuading people to do things for her. She leads me into the kitchen, but as I step in, my eyes fall on a familiar figure, and my nerves jolt.

Rebecca's eyes meet mine, and she raises her glass in salute. I give her a nod to be polite, but now I am conspicuous, my face flushing in the spotlight. Tessa notices, and asks me if I'm all right.

"What? Oh yes, sorry Tessa. It's just rather warm in here, but I think it's because it was so cold outside."

"Are you sure?"

She hands me a glass of red wine, the glass so large, it looks as though it holds at least half a bottle. I must not drink too much, I repeat to myself. I must not drink too much and I must not see things. I must not make a fool of myself in front of Rebecca.

"You know, I hope you won't mind me saying this, Ewan, but are you all right?"

Why does everyone have to keep asking me if I'm all right?

"It's just I think you look as though you've lost a lot of weight recently," Tessa says. She reaches up and strokes her fingers across my cheek, her fingers soft and cool like feathers across my skin and I catch my breath at the ache, the pain that opens up inside at the thought I have no one to care, no one of my own to touch my face with such gentle concern. "It's not as though you were exactly overweight in the first place."

"I can't say I've noticed. Have to say though Tessa, the kitchen looks fabulous. Are you pleased with it?"

I sip my wine as she enthuses over her latest creation, her eyes sparkling with pleasure at the opportunity to talk about it. Do I like the chandelier? It's made entirely from recycled beer cans and glass bottles, although nobody can tell. That's the genius of their artist friend, she tells me. He can create something beautiful out of nothing but rubbish. She'll introduce me to him, she says. He's in the dining room.

"Ah, but first there is someone I want you to meet," she says, taking my hand. "Come on now, and don't be shy."

"Tessa, no," I protest, my feet trying to force roots down through the solid tiled floor, but with her three boys, and Alex I suppose, she is accustomed to dealing with children who don't want to do what she thinks is good for them. It is one of the most tedious pitfalls of being single and surrounded by married types. They don't like having one in their midst who bucks the trend, challenges the order of things, and, like a solitary daffodil growing up amidst a bed of tulips, the one must be dealt with. It can only be considered pleasing to the eye if it is surrounded by other daffodils, so any opportunity to pair up single friends must not be dismissed. Tessa is determined to see me married off. 'What you need is a good woman to look after you,' she tells me every time it can be dropped into a conversation.

"And Trudy might just be that woman," she says, her aqua eyes twinkling with mischief as she leads me out of the kitchen. I feel Rebecca's gaze heavy on my back.

There is a plump woman with curly, conker brown hair sitting on the stairs with a gaggle of Tessa's friends, fiddling with the stem of her wineglass, her wide eyes darting here and there, her laughter a little too earnest, and I get the impression she is a kindred spirit, lurking on the fringes of the conversation, counting down the minutes until she too can make her excuses and slip away home. Her dark eyes widen with a smile as Tessa shoos the other friends away, and steers me to the step beside her. A whiff of something familiar about her stirs in my brain, but I can't think why. We are introduced, and then Tessa invents a reason to leave us, waving crossed fingers at me as she retreats. I sip my wine and sigh.

"Let me guess," Trudy matches my sigh, and fiddles with her glass with long nails painted the same dark wine as her dress. "You're here on your own as well, so as the only two single people at the party, we have," she uses her fingers to make quotation marks, "so much in common."

She has a beautiful, melodic voice, slightly deeper than I might have expected, and the earthy lilt of her local accent suits her. I wonder how well she can sing, imagining her as a busty milkmaid belting out folk ballads as I try to look anywhere but down between the ripe curves swelling under the neckline of her plain, fitted dress, her tanned flesh suggesting a recent holiday. No, I tell myself, I mustn't start thinking about the scent of sun-warmed skin. I promised I wouldn't make a fool of myself tonight.

"I need a good woman to look after me, apparently," I guffaw into my wine.

"And I need a good man to care for me after my divorce," she says. "Apparently."

"Well then, it seems we're perfectly compatible. Shall we set a date for the wedding now, or would it be more prudent to wait, do you think?"

She gives into snorty giggles, but stifles them with her hand, glancing at me as though wary her unfettered laugh will be too much, but when she sees me laughing, she relaxes into a full burst of laughter. I watch her; I watch the way her shoulders shake and how merriment animates her, setting her dark, shiny curls bobbing, and driving away the shadows lurking in her eyes. She grins, flashing slightly crooked, white teeth. The discomfort at being forced to socialise with her fades away as though it never existed and I begin to think that for once, Tessa might have played a winning hand in her matchmaking.

Trudy is explaining how she knows the Garvies, when there is a commotion of footsteps and voices above us on the stairs, and Alex appears followed by a tall man with neatly clipped dark brown hair who has to duck to avoid the light fittings on the stairs. Trudy and I move apart to let them past, Alex's big feet struggling to fit between our bodies.

"Hello Trudy," he says, pausing to kiss her cheek. "How are you? You got a sitter then. Kids okay?"

"Yes, yes they're fine, thank you, staying with their dad tonight."

"That's good, 'bout time you had a chance to enjoy yourself. Mind you, I see Tessa's lumbered you with Ewan, and that's enough to spoil anyone's evening, isn't it? Don't worry; Uncle Alex will save you." He puts an arm around her shoulder and winks at me. Trudy blushes, resuming the look of someone planning their escape, her darting eyes weighing up the options. The man standing on the stairs lets out a deep laugh. Alex releases Trudy and turns to me with a wide grin.

"By the way, mate," he says, draping his arm around my shoulders this time. "This is Rick Cartwright. Rick, this is the one-and-only, Thatchington High's musical maestro, young Mr. Ewan Davies. This is who your Rebecca has the misfortune of working with, the poor girl."

Rick Cartwright gives me a broad smile as he shakes my sweating hand with a firm, cool-handed grasp. He tells me it's nice to meet me in a large, deep voice that echoes out of his broad, muscular frame, but I only half-hear him, I'm too busy fretting over whether or not he knows exactly who I am. His clothes look expensive and radiate that air of 'oh, I just threw this together' meaning 'actually I spent hours getting it just-so', quite the opposite to Rebecca's hippy, fair trade garments, but in case I may have had any trouble comprehending why my ex-wife prefers this charming, swaggering man to my own humble self, I notice Trudy is sighing, luxurious eyelashes fluttering, her giggles coquettish. Or at least, she was, up until the moment Alex introduced me to Rick. Now it's me holding her attention, her eyes wide and shining.

"You're Mr. Davies, the music teacher," she exclaims as Rick and Alex head for the kitchen, nodding as though she's solved some great mystery. "Wow." She goes to shake my hand. I chuckle, a little bemused. My title doesn't normally inspire much wonder. "You must be a very good teacher."

Well, I certainly like to think so, but when so much of what I do is measured only in terms of my students' exam performances, and given that music is not held in such high regard as other subjects, my efforts tend to go unreported, remarkable only to me. I can't resist but ask why she draws this conclusion.

"You teach my son Toby. Toby Smith. He's in year seven," she explains as my memory for the children in my classes splashes about instead of diving straight in to connect name and face. Wait a minute: ah yes, young Toby. A quiet, shy boy, he appears to have quite a talent for the violin. I spot the likeness between mother and son now; the same dark eyes, the same air of composure. Damn.

"He talks about you all the time. It's all 'Mr. Davies says this, and Mr. Davies says that.' You've made quite an impression on him. It's about time someone captured his enthusiasm," she sighs.

A strange thought to imagine my words being taken home and repeated to parents as though they were some sort of gospel, 'The word according to Ewan Davies'. Perhaps I'd better be a little more mindful about what I say in class if I'm creating that sort of an impression. Trudy is still smiling up at me, but regret is raining cold on the warming pleasure I'd been finding in her company. A wall has sprung up between us and fantasy turns on its heel and walks off, back into the darkness. I can't be involved with one of my pupils' parents. It isn't professional.

"He's a very talented boy. Do you play an instrument?"

"No, he gets that from his father, I'm afraid. Nothing to do with me." She lifts her glass to her lips, still giving me that wide-eyed smile of hers, but it can't reach through my defences. She suggests we get another drink, and I agree. I'm not sure I want to stay sober now.

I hold out my hand to help her up. Her warm fingers curl around mine, and as she gets up, she beams, her eyes lingering on mine until she looks away, a hint of colour blushing across her freckled cheeks. She is at least a head and shoulders shorter than me, even in her heels. As she walks, her ample hips sway with such grace, I am entranced. We reach the kitchen, and, because I'm such a gentleman, I put my fingers against her arm, to guide her past Rebecca. And because I'm anything other than a gentleman, I can't describe the depths of the thrill I get when Rebecca turns to see who is passing by, and sees me with Trudy. An electric shock ripples through me when I see her looking, made all the sweeter as I make a huge point of ignoring her. Trudy might not pass muster as a trophy of Rick Cartwright's calibre, but she is a prize nonetheless, and for once, I can hold my head up around my ex-wife; I am not on my own.

"Ewan."

Rebecca catches hold of my arm as I pass. You see? She can't resist. I bet she hates seeing me with another woman.

"I'd like you to meet my husband, Rick. Rick, this is Ewan, Ewan, Rick."

"You're too late dear, we've just met," Rick says, his whole, perfect face smiling with that good-natured, lazy smile I'd always thought was airbrushed onto sultry male models by magazine editors. "Good to meet you though Ewan, I've heard a lot about you. It's a brave man who works with my wife. Haha."

What the fuck has she told him?

"I asked for a pay-rise, you know, danger money," I cock my head towards Rebecca who arches both eyebrows and gives a mocking 'harrumph'. "But the Head's a woman too, so she didn't understand." This prompts much guffawing from Alex and Rick, and I bask in their laughter, savouring the attention until Trudy catches my eye. She holds my gaze, and rolls her eyes. I introduce her to Rebecca, and then before anyone asks a question that will show we've only just met, I usher her over to the table groaning under many bottles of wine.

"Are you all right?" Trudy asks.

"Why does everyone keep asking me if I'm all right?"

"Your hands are shaking."

I look down. She's right. I'm trying to pour wine into our glasses, but my hands are shaking so much, I nearly knock a chunk out of one of the glasses with the neck of the bottle, and everyone looks round at the bang of glass on glass. Trudy takes the bottle out of my hands, and pours for me.

"Is it too much, when we've only just met, for me to ask what is it about your tall, arty-looking colleague that makes you so flustered?"

She looks me full in the eye, and raises one brow in challenge. I gulp at the clinical precision of her assessment. Her directness warns me she will see through the most tapestried of my lies. But it is as though there is no one else in this room but she and I, and I feel safe, cocooned in her company. I open my mouth to speak, and, to my amazement, it's the truth which comes blurting out. This is dangerous territory, I know, but the warmth glistening in the depths of her dark eyes promises me I can trust her. Then again, maybe it's the wine. I promised myself I'd be careful. Trudy is gorgeous, but perhaps it's time I was heading home.

"So let me get this quite straight," she says, her forehead knit together in a frown. "Not only are you and your ex-wife both at a party, but you're working together too? Wow. How does that work exactly? No way could I be in the same room as my ex, Richard. You either still adore one another, or one of you is compromising way too much. And I don't think I'm going to get a prize for guessing which it is," she sips her wine, studying me over the top of her glass.

"No one knows," I say, aghast that this woman, a virtual stranger, could have picked apart my façade with such ease. Taking her arm, I turn her to one side so no one can overhear what I'm saying. "No one knows, and no one must know. Trudy, you have to promise me you won't breathe a word to Tessa or Alex."

"Ewan, you're nuts," she says, shaking her head at me. "Of course I won't say anything, but you must know whatever you've got yourself into, it isn't good for you. No wonder you're shaking. I hope you know what you're doing."

Unease blooms feathery fronds like ice crystallising across my shoulders and down my spine as she casts doubt into the melting pot of my psyche. I take a step back, and examine my motives. What am I doing around Rebecca now the chaffing reality of her company has chased away the last of my reconciliation fantasies? No, it's quite simple; there's no confusion. I'm helping out an old friend, that's all, just as she once did the same for me.

Trudy watches me wince as Rick's braying laughter leads the mirth erupting from his group, as Alex laughs along, as Tessa puts her arm through Rebecca's, the two women sharing a moment. She reaches out and puts her warm hand on my arm, wonders if I'm hungry, and suggests we go and find the buffet. My resolve to avoid eating melts in the heat of her compassion, and I follow her out of the kitchen. No one notices us leave.

She takes my arm as we cross the hallway to the dining room, but I'm eyeing the front door, and the darkness beckoning beyond. Just as no one noticed us leave the kitchen, we could just slip away, unobserved. I could take Trudy back to my house, and we could relax on the settee, music playing quietly in the background talk properly, not snatched moments here and there while a rabble of merrymakers, a circle of barred friendships, strut and crow their allegiances. But in the doorway to the dining room, Trudy lets out a gasp at the extravagant buffet. Tessa is a marvellous cook, and as I look at the table laden with salads, pasta, quiches and savouries, I'm thinking of dinner parties I have enjoyed here, back in the days when I didn't have to worry about sharing a table with my past, and had no fears about things being done to our food.

Trudy squeezes my arm, and I startle at her touch. She frowns.

"Are you sure you're all right? Why don't you go and sit down, and I'll go and get us some food. It looks fabulous. What do you want? I think I'm going to have a bit of everything."

"I'm not sure I'm hungry," I say, balking at the thought of having to put on a show of normal eating. The wine is working on my head, fuddling my senses and threatening to put me off-guard. I mustn't drink too much. I must not. "I'm feeling rather hot. Why don't you go ahead? I'm going to get a glass of water."

I head back to the kitchen, taking great care not to make it look as though I'm swaying on my feet. No one notices as I scuttle in. The shiny glittery people are all busy talking and laughing at one, trying to outdo each other in a contest for social kudos. I make my way over to the sink, one of those trendy white ceramic troughs, and fill my glass with good, clean cold water.

"Well?"

I look round as Tessa sidles up beside me, her pale eyes and glittery earrings twinkling in the light. Her elfin face is grinning, and she looks poised to don a cloak of self-congratulation. She slips her arm back through mine.

"You seem to be getting on with Trudy. What do you think?"

"She's lovely." I indulge Tessa with a smile. She squeals, and grabs my arm in delight.

"I just knew you two would get on. Shall I start saving up for a nice hat?"

"Hardly," I say, patting her hand as I deflate her excitement. "I teach her son at school."

"So?"

"Well I can't start seeing her. It would be unprofessional."

"Oh." Tessa frowns, folds her arms and purses her lips, leaning back against the sink as though she's pondering the best way to unravel this unforeseen complication. She glances up as Alex appears beside us with another empty wine bottle to add to the pile gathering on the draining board. "Unprofessional eh?"

"What's unprofessional my love?" Alex asks, sliding his arm around her thickened waist. Their cosy togetherness deepens my misery.

"Ewan likes Trudy, but he's afraid it might be 'unprofessional' for him to take things any further," Tessa explains. I squirm, darting glances for fear other ears are listening in, but the party swirls on around us, oblivious to we three standing at the sink. My fears sound ridiculous coming out of Tessa's mouth and I am ashamed to hear them being spoken aloud. Alex gawps and scoffs.

"Her son's in one of my classes," I explain.

"So?" Alex shrugs, screwing up his face as though I'm either saying something too stupid or too complicated for him to understand. "I don't get you."

"We're not allowed to date parents," I hiss. "Fiona would go nuts."

"Oh, and you always do what she says and go along with all her stupid rules, don't you mate? Honestly Ewan, no one's forcing you to marry Trudy. If you like her, and she certainly looks as though she likes you, poor girl, why can't you just let your hair down and have some fun for once? How the hell is anyone, let alone Fifi P going to know if you see Trudy a few times? Go on mate. You know, you can be really dense sometimes. Get in there and stop faffing around."

"That's a bit harsh," Tessa chides, stepping away from him and taking my arm once more as he laughs and says he's being harsh, yes, but fair. "Ewan, why don't you just try to enjoy yourself," she smiles, squeezing my arm once more. "Here," she reaches behind me and produces another bottle. "Have some more wine. Relax and see what happens."

As the wine sloshes into my glass, something catches my eye. There, on Tessa's shoulder. I catch my breath. There was something black, and now it's disappeared into the folds of purple material arranged across her shoulder. I hold my breath. There it is again. It's a beetle. I'm not imagining it this time. There really is a beetle.

"Tessa," I say, keeping my eyes on the insect. It's the same as the others, a black, bulbous thing with shiny wing cases and serrated legs. I wonder if it's poisonous. Maybe it's some sort of foreign beetle tempted here by climate change, our summers so much hotter than they used to be. Or maybe it got here in supermarket fruit, you hear about deadly spiders, why not beetles? Either way, I must get it off Tessa's shoulder. "Don't move."

"What is it?" She blanches at the seriousness on my face, and holds still. Alex leans in, trying to spot what I've seen. She follows my eyes, twisting her neck to look for herself.

"There's something on your shoulder." I put my hand out, but I'm afraid of being bitten, and I don't really want to touch. "It's in the fabric."

"What is it?" Tessa's voice is quivering, panic shattering her usual composure. "Is it a spider? Ugh," she shudders. "Get it off, Ewan, please."

"I can't see anything," Alex says, glancing at me as he tries to calm his wife. "Look Tess, let's nip in the pantry," he indicates the door. "Take your top off, and I'll shake it out, whatever it is."

"I think it was a beetle," I say with some reluctance.

"Not one of your imaginary ones, I hope," Alex is stern as he ushers Tessa through the door. "Come on love."

They emerge a few minutes later, Tessa still pale and shaken. She steps past me without a word, but tells Alex she'll be back in a minute, once she's had a chance to get changed. He tries to catch her arm, misses, and calls after her to lie down for a bit, but her momentum has her hurrying across the kitchen in a flap of fabric, repelling enquiries from concerned onlookers.

"You and your bloody beetles," Alex appears at my side and folds his arms. "It's getting a bit beyond a joke now mate."

That's it. I'm going home. It's happened again, despite my best efforts. I did see a beetle, I know I did, but yet again I've been left looking like a fool. Excusing myself, I leave Alex to his other guests, and slip out of the kitchen. I don't announce to him that I'm leaving, I'm just going to let myself out and go back to the safety of my quiet house where there is no one to see if I do something silly, no one to ask if I'm sure I'm all right, and no one to look at me with Alex's disgust if I think I see a beetle.

I'm crossing the hall to the front door when children's voices hail me and their owners come bounding up to me, red-cheeked and wild with excitement.

"Uncle Ewan! Uncle Ewan! Are you going to play the piano Uncle Ewan?"

Putting my finger to my lips, I crouch down as Alex's three boys, Jamie, Will, and the youngest, Henry, clutching a grubby white teddy I bought for him when he was a baby, crowd round me, begging me to entertain them as I inevitably do every time I come to visit. Henry tries to climb on my knee. He's only three, but already he shows potential. Tessa wants me to give him piano lessons and I'm more than willing.

"Aren't you all supposed to be in bed?" I say, not wishing to be the source of more vexation to their parents.

"Mum said we could come down," Jamie says with all the authority he can muster as the eldest. "Will you play for us, Uncle Ewan, please?" Will echoes 'please' with his hands clasped as though in prayer, his mischievous face beatific, anything to win my compliance.

I let them persuade me. They take my hand and drag me through to the small sitting room where the piano lives. Henry sits beside me on the stool as the other two sing, dance, and shout out requests for me play, and it isn't long before the rest of the party drifts through to investigate. I'm happy. Sat at a piano, I am king in my domain, my ever-increasing capacity for making an arse of myself nowhere to be seen.

The children grow tired as others ask for songs they don't know, and disappear off to bed. I'm waltzing through some of my favourites, singing along to Sinatra, Ella Fitzgerald and, of course, my beloved Nina. Someone smiles at me from the doorway, and I stumble over my lyrics, losing my place as my fingers fumble for the right notes. It is Trudy, her eyes dancing with delight. To my astonishment, she picks up where I've faltered, her voice husky as though she gargles with my favourite whisky, Lagavulin, smooth and smoky, warming me to my core. She sits down beside me where Henry sat, leans against me, and sings along as I play and play. Her voice is more beautiful than I imagined, and her body sways along to the music. The room is full of revellers, but to me there is no one here but she and I.

The evening wears on. Someone, I think it's Tessa, brings me more wine and keeps topping it up, but I barely notice how much I'm drinking, I'm so engrossed. I ask Trudy if she knows the words to Gershwin's 'Summertime' because I think it will suit her voice, but she doesn't, so I sing it for her. She rests her head against my shoulder as I sing, and smiles up at me. I lose my place. I forget to sing, forget to play, and instead, my fingers slide along the soft warm line of her jaw as she tilts her head, as my eyes close, and I claim my first taste of her pouting, inviting mouth. I thread my fingers through her hair. Time stands still, even if the room is spinning around me. All I can hear is my own heart beating and my breath in my lungs deepening.

She whispers 'yes', when I beg her to come home with me. Outside the cold hits me like an icy hammer. I thought it might have sobered me up, but it seems to amplify my drunkenness, and we are halfway down the street, me lurching, and squawking with laughter at every wobbly step, before I realise I'm leading us in the wrong direction. When we do arrive back at my house, she has to take the key from me, so useless are my fingers. I'm beginning to wonder if it was wise to bring her back here. I feel ready to crash down into the oblivion of sleep, never mind anything else. Even the front lawn looks soft and tempting. But she presses herself against my aching body, and kisses me, and I tell myself surely I can resist the spinning to make love to the real live woman here in my arms.

What I should have done, was to refuse the many glasses of wine, and taken her home, undressed her bit by bit as though I was unwrapping a bar of rare and expensive chocolate, slowly, savouring every moment from the scent of her skin, to the warmth of her body, loving her over and over again as the velvety night thinned into a silvery dawn. That would have been the gallant, considerate thing to do. But I am too drunk to be either of these things. Instead, we kiss in the hall, and fumble down onto the sofa, and then she has the bright idea of going to make coffee to help sober me up. The next thing I know is when I wake up to the crushing headache and nausea of a red wine hangover, my body hot and cold and stiff-limbed, and guess what? Yes, she's gone.

Chapter 11

My hangover is so ferocious, I spend Sunday huddled under a sweaty green fog of self-chastisement, furious with myself for being so easily led into making myself feel ill. All I had to do was say 'no' to another glass of wine, not swallow it down. The thought of red wine sets me on another bout of retching, and moving around doesn't help the pounding in my head which feels as though my brain decides its had enough and wants out. I am cross with myself too for all the things I was going to do today, each of which must now languish on the list of things I must do when I feel better. All I can do is huddle in bed, force down fizzy hangover remedies, and feel sorry for myself. And perhaps, if I don't think about it, I never really brought a woman called Trudy back here at all. Ah, the exquisite pain that is shame.

My head is still reeling when I wake up on Monday morning. It's okay so long as I'm lying down, but upright, I'm nauseous, my senses disorientated, so I force myself to abandon my 'no breakfast' policy in favour of a couple of scrambled organic eggs, a slice of organic toast, and a pot of tea. I sit at the kitchen table fighting my reluctance with every mouthful, but once I've finished, I conclude it was worth the effort.

0750hrs: Vi waving at the window as I leave for work.

In my office I help myself to another cup of tea, and rifle through Rebecca's drawers for the packet of paracetamol tablets I know she keeps in here. I swallow a couple, hoping these will nip the lurking niggle in the back of my skull, and scoot back over to my desk as I hear footsteps approaching.

"Morning!" Rebecca comes bustling in, dressed in a brown smock adorned with enormous splodgy crimson flowers, and drops her bags down on her desk. "How are you?"

I don't know why it always sounds like a loaded question coming out of her mouth, but 'how are you' from Rebecca could incite fear in the calmest mind.

"I'm feeling much better than I did yesterday, thank you."

"It was some party, wasn't it?"

"I'm not sure I can remember that much about it," I say. It's all a bit hazy in my mind. I know I drank a lot, and I remember how much I wanted to take Trudy home, but that's about it. And I've been very successful up until now avoiding thinking about why she wasn't there when I woke up. Disappointing women is a recurrent theme for me. No, mustn't think about it. Must think of something else.

"How long have you known your girlfriend? What was her name, Tanya?"

"Trudy," I say, blushing. "She's not really a girlfriend as such." I'm not sure I'm ever likely to see her again. The fact that she left my house without leaving a telephone number doesn't bode well for a future relationship.

"You seemed pretty friendly," Rebecca mutters, but I choose to ignore her. The humiliation is too raw, and I can't be smug in front of Rebecca while I feel like nothing other than a fake.

Alex seeks me out over morning break. I'm climbing the stairs having just ticked off a couple of year eleven pupils for pretending the rules forbidding children from being upstairs at break-time doesn't apply to them, when I hear him shout, and catch sight of his dishevelled locks bouncing above the milling heads of pupils pottering around on the ground floor. He bounds up the stairs, and presses in close.

"Great party mate, or what?" He grins. "Was I sick yesterday though. Threw up on the sidelines at the nippers' footie match. None of the uppity-mummies in their flowery wellies are ever going to speak to me again."

"I'm sure you'll be able to charm them all back onside," I laugh and shake my head. "I don't know how you managed to get to their football match. I spent the day in bed."

"Yeah, but isn't that because you were with Trudy?" He gives me a hard nudge. "Eh? You old dog. All that crap about being 'unprofessional'. Right in there, mate. You were right in there you were."

"No," I sigh, pulling open the fire doors at the top of the stairs. "It didn't go well. I was so drunk I passed out. She didn't even leave me her number."

This news tickles Alex, and he laughs so hard, he has to lean against the wall for support. A couple of our colleagues hurry past, staring at him as though there is something very wrong, but he can do nothing for the tears of mirth rolling down his cheeks.

"I tell you what," he wheezes between fits of laughter. "Who'd be you, eh? Years in 'no-woman land' and then the first chance you get, you're so pissed you pass out. God, but that is funny." He wipes at his tears with the back of his hands, and puts his arms around my shoulders. "I tell you what, Ewan, mate, what say I give Tessa a call and get Trudy's number for you? Eh?"

"Thanks, but I doubt she'll want to speak to me."

"Ah, I wouldn't be so sure," Alex says, serious now. "She's all right is Trudy. Husband ran off with her best friend last year. They've got two kids and she's had to fight him for every last penny to feed those boys. She needs someone safe and boring like you, no offence mate, someone who's not going to dick her about, if you see what I mean. Leave it with me, I'll talk to Tessa. Got to give her a ring anyway. Why don't you put the kettle on, and I'll phone home."

I try not to listen as he talks to his wife, but he keeps catching my eye and winking the whole way through their conversation, rolling his eyes and making wry asides to me. As soon as I've made us a cup of tea, I turn the computer on and sit down at my desk. I sat up into the early hours this morning trawling through the internet for information about 'the great food conspiracy', as I'm calling it in my head. Using the internet at home nearly paralyses me with nerves, I'm so afraid the authorities might be monitoring my searching, but I daren't do too much at work. The school's mainframe is probably even less secure.

There is a great deal of hilarity between husband and wife over the subject of my disastrous night with Trudy. My face flares with colour, and I'm relieved Rebecca isn't in the room to overhear. This is the up-side to her popularity. She's sat in the staffroom tittering and gossiping at break-times, so for the time being, Alex and I have our office to ourselves.

"Right, here you are," Alex says, picking up a piece of paper from his desk. He steps over to my desk and plonks it down. "Apparently you've made quite an impression, drunk or not. Mind you, whether that's because Trudy was tiddly herself is another story. Tessa says she's already asked her for your number. Go on, get in there," he slaps me across the shoulders and gives a huge belly laugh. "Hey you've got your computer on; I'll show you a picture of my boat." He leans across my desk for my keyboard. "What's this crap you're looking up? Conspiracy theories over food safety?"

"It's true," I stammer, my face firing hot with colour. "People don't realise. There's a huge cover-up going on, you know. I wanted to tell you about it before, so you'd be able to protect your kids, but I wasn't sure you'd believe me until I found proof. And look at this, it's all true."

I flip through the pages I've been reading online, pointing out the bits and pieces I think are important. Pesticides, growth hormones, chemicals for preserving: it's all here. No wonder I can't sleep at night, no one would sleep if they knew about it. It's terrifying, and yet it's all perfectly legal.

"What's terrifying is that you're taking this crap so seriously," Alex says, frowning. "This is a load of bollocks you've dug up here. Come on mate, you might not be the sharpest tool in the box, but you're not that gullible."

"It's true," I protest, stuttering with indignation. "It's all true. You're playing into their hands by refusing to accept there's a problem."

"There's a problem all right mate, and it's in your head. This is why you've stopped having lunch in the canteen, isn't it? Aw, come on. You don't seriously believe in all this stuff, do you?"

He doesn't believe me. I wring my hands together under the desk. He hasn't understood. I can't have explained it properly. This was my one chance to explain what's going on, and I've blown it. I should be doing what I can to protect people, innocent people like Alex, but what is the point of me knowing what's going on if I can't help anyone. A line of sweat breaks out along my top lip. As I go to wipe it away, I notice my hand is shaking.

"The internet is full of shit like this. You know that as well as I do."

"Yeah," I make myself laugh. This has gone so wrong, I'll have to go away and think about how I can get the message over to people without them thinking I'm insane. "Just something I read about, that's all."

"You can read something about anything if you look hard enough. Look, I bet if you type in the words 'Alex Garvie is Elvis' you'll find something to prove I'm his incarnation. Anyway, look, here's the new boat." He types away, and brings up a snapshot of a dilapidated, peeling wooden boat with mouldy sails. I start to laugh.

"Is it meant to have a hole in the side?"

"Where?" He leans in close to the screen, tilting his head from one side to the other. I'm laughing, tickled by the thought he's actually paid for something which doesn't look fit to float, never mind sail. The door opens and Rebecca walks in. She looks over, and grins at my laughter.

"Rebecca, come and look at what Alex has bought. Word of warning though, the salesman saw him coming." I'm laughing so hard, the tears are rolling down my cheeks. "I bet Tessa's relieved she's pregnant."

"Let me see," Rebecca bends over my shoulder. I catch a waft of her warm, citrussy perfume, but it's just a smell. It does nothing other than point out that Trudy has chased away the last lingering threads of my attachment to my ex-wife. "You bought that Alex? You actually paid for it? Oh dear. Tell me you didn't pay very much."

I take my glasses off to wipe my eyes, and put them down on the desk. But no sooner have I gained some sort of composure, than I take another look at the wreck on my computer screen, and start laughing anew. Alex is good with his hands and likely to make a good job of restoring it, but for the moment, the joke is firmly at his expense, eclipsing my earlier perceived stupidity. I'm happy to laugh.

Fishing a handkerchief out of my pocket, I polish my glasses, and put them back on my nose. I forget how blind I am without them. The room comes back into focus, and I catch a glimpse of movement beyond my desk. There. Something just moved on the wall behind Alex's desk. It's another bloody beetle. Damn it. I haven't seen one since Saturday.

"Look, what's that on the wall?" I get up from behind my desk, seizing a roll of papers as I rise. If I could just kill one, it would prove, no less to myself, that I am not making the whole thing up. Alex and Rebecca look up from the computer screen as I pounce. I whack the wall with a resounding smack which makes Rebecca screech.

"Ewan! What is it? Is it a spider?"

I pull Alex's chair out of the way, looking for my victim. There's no sign, but I know I got it. I bend down, searching for the corpse. My knees creak in complaint. I look and look, but I can't see anything.

"Damn. Must have missed," I say, straightening up. Rebecca is peering, her head weaving this way and that, ready to flee squealing at the first hint of a creepy-crawly, but Alex has his hands on his hips, the sort of look on his face I'd imagine he uses to chastise his boys. "Can't find it," I add, avoiding his eye.

"Hmm, well perhaps that's because it wasn't actually there," he harrumphs. Rebecca looks at him, ready, for once, to defend me, but he ignores her. "You and your bloody beetles. It's just a figment of your imagination, mate." He walks past, picks up his jacket, and continues out of the office without another word.

"What's he talking about?"

"I don't know," I tell Rebecca. "I just don't know."

Chapter 12

I wait until the evening before I phone Trudy, and I spend a lot of time rehearsing my apology. It takes me a few attempts, a few episodes of dialling the number and hanging up before the call connects, and a lot of pacing up and down my hallway, my footsteps echoing through the quiet house before I summon enough courage to calm my shaking fingers, dial the number, hear it ring, and wait for her to answer. It rings and rings, each one more agonising than the last as it's either a ring closer to her answering, or a ring closer to me deciding she's not in, and having to repeat the whole damned ordeal later.

"Hello?"

"Trudy? Hi, it's Ewan. We met the other, oh yes, of course you remember."

Even the sound of her voice excites me, her rich, lilting tones laced with huskiness makes the hairs quiver on the back of my neck, and I acknowledge just how much I do want to see her again. I recite my apology, she tells me not to be so silly, we'd both had a lot to drink and she'd only left because she wasn't sure about putting herself to bed in my room while I was comatose on the couch. As I listen, I am aching to feel her soft warm body pressed against mine.

But there is nothing I can do until the weekend, Saturday night to be precise, as that is the only night she has to herself, the children spend the two days of the weekend with their father. She invites me round for dinner, and just a moderate amount of wine, 'so we can pick up where we left off' as she puts it. Damn. I can't wait until Saturday. I have to see her, and having to wait another four whole days feels too long. And I'm not comfortable with the 'dinner' part either.

Half past seven on Saturday evening, a bottle of red wine tucked under my arm and a bunch of pink roses in my hands, you've no idea how I annoyed the florist agonising over what colour I should buy, I stand outside Trudy's house and ring the bell. It's on one of the housing estates on the other side of Thatchington, rows of identical houses all overlooking one another, the feeling of being watched by many neighbourly eyes pressing down on you as soon as you turn into the road, a stranger walking into the neighbourhood. I glance over my shoulder as

I wait for Trudy to answer, and hope none of my more insolent pupils are watching, gathering ammunition for their backchat. Footsteps approach, coming closer down the hallway and Trudy's muffled voice calls out in greeting. The door flies open, and there she is, her warm eyes and wide smile inviting me in.

She holds the door open, and I trot up the steps into a colourful, brightly lit hallway painted not only with terracotta, but swirling gold and silver motifs. I look round, amazed. It looks like something out of a magazine, bold and adventurous, not dull and predictable like my nice, safe white. She sees my expression, and laughs.

"Do you like it?"

"I love it. Is this what you do for a living?" Maybe this is what I need, a bit of colour to brighten up my staid and predictable existence.

"This? Nah, it's just a hobby. I work up at the hospital. I'm a paediatric nurse."

"A nurse? I wouldn't have guessed. And look, about the other night, I'm really sorry."

She puts her finger on my lips, tells me to shush, and steps in close. I would put my arms round her, only I'm still clutching the wine and flowers. She grins, takes them from me, and puts them aside on the hall table. My hands slide around her waist, and I draw her into my arms. She smells delicious, of vanilla and freshly cut apples. I can't resist, and press my nose against the soft warm skin just beneath her ear to breathe in her scent. She shivers and sighs, her fingers travelling over my shoulders, smoothing the tension from my neck. Our lips meet, and brush together, a shy, inquisitive taste.

"Are you hungry?" She whispers, her eyes full of stars. "Dinner's almost ready."

"Sod dinner," I mumble into her mouth and tighten my arms around her, but she twists out of my grasp with a wicked laugh.

"Ah-ah," she wags her finger, fending off my attempts to pull her back into my arms. "I'm starving. Let's eat first. And anyway," she winks. "Anticipation makes everything worthwhile. Come on."

She leads the way through to the kitchen where she's set the table, candles glowing in jars. I offer to open the wine, and she sets about dishing up, but my attention is monopolised by a huge canvas print on the wall. She is smiling down at me, her two boys in her arms. I try not to look, but I can feel Toby's dark eyes watching me from the photograph, telling me I shouldn't be here. But dinner smells good, and my mouth is watering. 'Your mother has cooked for me,' I silently tell the picture. 'The very least I can do is eat the meal she's made.' I will eat, and as I eat, I will explain to Trudy why I can't see her, no matter how sensuous her voice, her mouth. And then I will go home and everything will be all right. Toby says he's happy with that.

"Mmm, this is delicious. Here Ewan, try some," Trudy says, feeding me slivers of roast beef as she carves the joint, licking the gravy dripping from her fingers with her long pink tongue, watching me, teasing me. "You don't look like the sort of person who spends a lot of time cooking. Me, I didn't get these curves from eating salad."

She's quite right. One of the things in life that bores me the most is how we constantly need to eat. No sooner have you finished one meal than the human body is gearing up for its next. Think about it: we might not need to go charging out with spears any more, but how much time is taken up with shopping, preparing and cooking food? My fears we're being drugged aside, I'm waiting for someone to invent a pill, a tiny capsule to take the place of eating. Now that would be something useful I'd love to see. It astonishes me it hasn't already been done.

That's not to say I don't appreciate a nice meal; I do, just so long as I don't have to make it myself. And Trudy has prepared something fabulous. Crisp roast potatoes, fat baby carrots, brussel sprouts glistening with butter, broccoli spears she dips in gravy and nibbles, her eyes locked on mine. There are big blousy Yorkshire puddings straining to burst free of their tins and what feels like half a cow. 'Eat up,' she says, and I might have managed to make more of an impression on a plate piled with more food than I've eaten for week had she not then winked and added, 'you're going to need your strength.' It just isn't food I want, it's her. My resolve to go home weakens with every mouthful.

"That's better, isn't it?" She says, pushing aside her empty plate at last and pouring another slug of wine. "I don't think I could manage another bite. I do have some strawberries for dessert; maybe we should have them later." There's something about the way she says 'later' that sends a delicious shiver tingling down my spine. I help her carry the plates over to the sink, but when I ask her if she'd like me to wash or dry, she pushes me back against the cupboards, presses herself against me and tells me how dinner has only wet her appetite for what she really wants. I groan as I watch her lick her lips, every cell in my body quivering with anticipation. Sorry Toby. I shouldn't do this, I really shouldn't, but I don't have the will to stop my hands from sliding around her body.

The candles have almost burnt down in their jars by the time she decides we've worked up a thirst. She pulls a fluffy pink dressing gown around herself, and goes pottering off downstairs to make some coffee, tea for me. I lie back in her bed, gazing up at the ceiling, almost purring with contentment. I stretch out my arms and legs, and curl myself back up in the duvet. To think I nearly denied myself this? I see my fears as dim spectres, the disapproving figure of Mrs Phillips among them standing around the bed, shaking their heads, but they are powerless to touch me. They vanish as Trudy reappears, bearing with cups, glasses with some sort of cream liqueur, and a trifle bowl filled with strawberries.

I prop myself up as I reach for the cup she hands me, and I see her eyes take a closer look at the scars on my arms. Unease goosepimples my skin. She's a nurse, I remember. I don't want her looking. Once upon a time I took great pains to bandage my arms to fend off a lover's curious eye, I'm so out of practice, I forgot.

"Glass door," I say, rearranging the duvet to foil her gaze. "I fell and put both arms through a glass door at my Granny's house when I was little." This is my favourite excuse. I don't even have to think about it, it glides off my tongue like hot liquid glass pouring into a mould. But cooling glass can shatter, and right now I watch as my lie shatters, as Trudy's lips purse, reigniting a little tongue of fear within the smouldering kiln at the core of my inner self. She doesn't believe me. This can't be undone by merely sweeping up the pieces and throwing them back into fire. Trudy has spotted something gleaming among the fragments. All I can do is watch as she pounces. I am impotent to stop her.

"That's where I've seen you before," she throws her hands up in a 'eureka' moment. "I knew I'd seen you somewhere. I said to Tessa, 'I definitely know him from somewhere' and that's it. You're one of Rod's patients, aren't you? Roderick Henderson," she explains, mistaking my silence for confusion. "Of course! I remember now."

"No." No-no no-no no.

"Yes, don't you remember? You met me the first time you went to that support group he used to run. I was on reception that night. I knew I knew you from somewhere. It's such a small world! That was awful though, that girl who died. Poor Roderick, he took it badly. It really knocked his confidence. Do you still see him?"

"I don't know what you're talking about."

I've put my drink down and I'm gripping the edge of the duvet, my breath coming and going in shallow bursts as I try to keep still, trying to control the trembling now threatening to shake my whole body. The only thing I know is that I've got to get out of here. I look round. Where are my clothes, damn it? Wait a minute, I took them off downstairs. Damn.

"Ewan, what's the matter?" She asks me this a few times before I realise she is waiting for an answer.

"I have to go home," I look round for something to cover my nudity while I head off to get dressed.

"Why?"

"I just have to."

I am wondering how I can be so stupid so as to have fallen into this. She knows about me. Perhaps this means everyone knows about me: Alex, Tessa, people at school. Perhaps everyone knows and the joke is that I don't realise. Or perhaps this is something to do with the plot I've uncovered. The authorities have sent Trudy, someone they knew I wouldn't be able to resist, as a warning. She knows about me. They know about me. So if I make a fuss or try to tell people about everything I've discovered, they will expose me as a freak and ruin my life. The thought of my friends, my colleagues, my students knowing what I used to do makes me want to shrivel like a grape drying up into a raisin. I have to get home. It's not safe here. I have to get home, and the only place I know to be safe is for me to be completely and utterly on my own, alone.

"Because I've remembered where I've met you before, is that it? I won't mention it again if you'd rather I didn't. I didn't mean to be insensitive; I just think it's amazing we should bump into each other again. What a coincidence."

"I don't know what you're talking about. I fell through a glass door and we haven't met before."

"Okay, okay," she holds up her hands. "Forget I said anything, will you please?"

She's got to be kidding if she thinks I can pretend none of this has just happened. It isn't 'a coincidence'. I've been set up. Her brow furrows in thought as she watches me slide out of bed, my spread hands my only means of modesty. Frankly, I'd prefer to hide my arms behind my back away from her all-seeing eyes, but that would mean exposing myself and right now I'm not sure which would make me feel worse. Marcia was clever. She used to cut her thighs to make sure she never roused her mother's suspicions. I never had that foresight, and I often think of the trouble that could have been avoided if I had. Mind you, if my scars were tucked away under the duvet, out of sight, I'd be enjoying Trudy back in my arms, ignorant to the truth of what's really going on. I have to get out of here. I am no longer safe.

She stands in the doorway, blocking my way out, one hip jutting, ripe with invitation. I will have to push past her ample, naked flesh to get out. She fixes me with a wicked smile.

"Come back to bed Ewan, let's enjoy these strawberries."

Her eyes hold mine as she brings a ripe, red berry to her warm, luscious mouth and nibbles it. She sucks noisily, dribbles of strawberry juice dropping down onto her left breast. I watch, slack-jawed, my tongue begging to be unleashed, to follow the droplet's trajectory down and down onto her hard, erect nipple, but it isn't until her hand reaches to caress my inner thigh that my brittle fear and desire to flee melts down into molten need.

The door to the past slams shut, and that's just the way I like it.

Chapter 13

It's still dark when I wake up, disturbed by the sound of the wind smattering squally rain against the window. My eyes adjust, and by the time I conclude the dark room is unfamiliar, I remember where I am, and realise I can feel Trudy's soft warm body pressed up against mine. Her bed is so comfortable, and I can't remember the last time I slept so well. I yawn and stretch, grinning at the slight ache from the vigour of exertions I had almost forgotten possible, and wonder the time. I prop myself up on my elbow, and see from the clock it is already half-past six. If I was at home, I would be up and pottering around already. Restlessness fidgets in my limbs. I have never been able to loll in bed. Trudy gives a little sigh, and shifts in her sleep.

I hold my breath, hoping she is waking, but her breathing settles back into the rhythmic rise and fall of sleep. A pity: the bed smells of her perfume, of the scent of her skin, and the thought of her warm flesh makes me hungry to make love to her again. Perhaps I should wake her, I think, rolling onto my side and snuggling up to her skin. I slide my hand under her arm and let my fingers close around her full, ripe breast. She stirs, but she doesn't wake up.

I roll onto my back, but it is no good, I cannot lie still. It isn't that I want to get up, but I think I ought to let Trudy sleep on. She's told me she works long shifts at the hospital, and it can't be easy caring for her children. Maybe I should make her some breakfast. Besides, I've never fared well in the thorny company of a woman woken too early. I tiptoe out of bed, and downstairs. It's chilly, so I slip on my clothes, make myself a cup of tea, and fill the sink with hot soapy water to start clearing up the plates from last night's feast. As I plunge my hands into the water, I catch sight of my puckered forearms and decide now is the best time to confront my thoughts and examine last night's wreckage, the fallout from my worlds colliding.

It's beginning to grow light. I watch the rain streaking down the grey windows, the world drenched in a soggy gloomy light which makes the marks on my arms look silvery, like ghosts of the turmoil each one was meant to release. Once upon a time I could recite every occasion, a litany of pain, but now they are too numerous, and my memory too short. In truth, they are nothing more to me than souvenirs, faded postcards from times in my life I'd sooner forget, but I do remember the first. I turn my arm over to peer at it, the faintest line lurking beneath bolder, more savage cuts. It had been a revelation to find such calm. I could do with a little of it now, and go rummaging through Trudy's drawers for a suitable blade, but I won't. I stopped it after Marcia died. Her death helped me to become 'normal', because 'normal' people don't have urges to cut their flesh, and being 'normal' is the key that keeps the box, one even Pandora would have resisted, locked, and I need it to stay that way.

I run some fresh water, and as I wait for the bowl to fill, I turn my arms over and over, examining their lumpy, gnarled flesh, trying to imagine what it must be like to see them for the first time, to see them as they must have appeared to Trudy last night. It's been so long since I had to think about them. Besides, pretending they don't exist helps me pretend I never needed to inflict them. I like pretending a lot of things never happened. And that's when I remember something that did, and my gut liquefies with cold dread. 'You're one of Roderick's patients, aren't you?' That's what she said.

I'm shivering, even with my hands in hot water. You know, sometimes we think we can lock a memory away somewhere deep and dark, incarcerate it in some dusty hole and forget it, but this is an illusion. Memories have a nasty habit of escaping and creeping back into sight when you least expect it. I remember meeting Trudy now she has reminded me. I can see her face, her plump pink cheeks and dark eyes smiling up at me from the desk at the entrance to The Alexandria Suite in Thatchington's general hospital.

I hadn't wanted to go. God knows how much I didn't want to go, how much I prayed I might develop some illness that would prevent my attendance, that my car would break down en route, that the telephone would ring and I'd hear that pushy, pony-tailed Glaswegian, to whom I'd been referred by my doctor, telling me the meeting had been cancelled. But none of these things happened, and it was either do this or lose Rebecca forever. So at half-past-seven that Thursday night, there I was trying to find my way to the Alexandria Suite, to attend Roderick-bloody-Henderson's self-harm support group.

Seven-thirty, the Princess Alexandria suite, Thursdays. I kept repeating these words over and over again, a mantra, although an unsuccessful one, to smooth my quivering nerves as I scurried along the buffed linoleum floor of Thatchington's General Hospital. Seven-thirty, the Princess Alexandria Suite, Thursdays. I'd only ever visited the casualty department on the couple of occasions I'd been a little over-zealous with my knife, and had no idea where to go, glancing up at signs suspended above heads. X-ray department, fracture clinic, paediatrics, antenatal admissions, casualty, genitor-urinary medicine, psychiatric ward, chapel, toilets, lifts, shop, and cafeteria: the hospital had it all. Late, I hurried along, my heels clicking against the floor, eyes darted this way and that, trying to spot the sign for the Princess Alexandria Suite, while avoiding contact with any other person travelling up or down the endless corridor, the hospital's artery, throbbing with people.

I felt as though I must have a neon sign flashing 'lunatic' in enormous lurid letters above my head, because it seemed to me everyone looked twice. I kept my eyes to the floor, but everyone I passed seemed to stare, their eyes burning into me, trying to discern the reason I was here. I could hear all their thoughts that night,

"Look at him, he looks funny."
"He looks weird."
"He doesn't look right."
"Where do you think he's going?"
"Do you think he's one of them? You know, the nutters from the Princess Alexandria Suite?"
"Yes, he's not right in the head. You can tell, just by looking at him. I've heard he cuts himself. He gets a sharp knife and slices through his arm when it all gets too much, when he can't cope, and he likes to watch the blood run out. He's not right, you know: not right at all. I've always said there was something wrong with him. He's not right in the head. He's sick. He's a weirdo. God, could you imagine being like him? Just imagine! Nah, I can't. People like that, they're just not normal."
"I heard he's a teacher."
"Oh my god, that is outrageous."

I stood at the double doors and stared at the plaque which announced this was indeed the Princess Alexandria Suite. Why Princess Alexandria, I wondered. Had she possessed lunatic tendencies too? I dithered, pride urging me to run while obligation plonked her hands on her hips and said if I didn't get on with it, this time she was leaving. L-E-A-V-I-N-G: leaving, Ewan, and just see if I don't mean it this time.

"Good evening, can I help you?" Trudy gave me a welcoming smile. Of course, I didn't know then it was Trudy, but I remember wondering if there was a training course for nurses to deal with people like me, where they learnt to smile a smile designed to be non-threatening, friendly, but anonymous, with the aim of putting your average mentally-unbalanced patient at ease. And I'd felt a gush of relief at the certainty we'd never met before. She didn't know who I was then, thank goodness. Funny how that's come back to haunt me.

"I'm Ewan Davies. I have an appointment. Um, well, not an appointment exactly." I leaned in closer, and lowered my voice. "Roderick Henderson said I should be here at seven-thirty." And I added just enough intonation to turn this into a question, to add just enough doubt into the mix to point out I didn't really need to be here, it was just a mistake, that's all.

"That's right," she said, smiling that smile. "Go through the doors behind you, and to your right. You can't miss it. You'll see the others. Roderick's not here yet, but he'll be along in a minute. Help yourself to coffee. Or there's tea, if you prefer."

Prefer? Preference had nothing to do with it. I'd have 'preferred' not to be there at all, but I thanked her, and followed her directions, my steps hesitant, but my feet obedient. And I felt a wave of disgust at the thought of encountering 'others'. I knew there would be other people here, but I hadn't given it much thought. It made me feel jittery, nervous about what freaks I was about to encounter. Obviously none of them would be ordinary, unassuming people like myself, perfectly, completely normal in every respect save for that one tiny aspect, and to me it was tiny, that sometimes a little cut was needed for life to continue as normally and un-remarkably as always. As I reached the door, I had to fight the urge to run away. It will be all right, I told myself. It will be obvious to everyone, and to Roderick too, there was no need for me to be there. No need at all.

I found myself in a low-ceilinged, magnolia room. There were chairs, brown, plastic chairs arranged in a circle, and a number of people sitting, none next to one-another, rather they had left a seat empty between themselves as though each had some hideous, incurable disease none of the others wished to catch. They all looked up and forced smiles, rather like the nurse. No one spoke.

I stood in the doorway. It still wasn't too late to run. I had nothing in common with this gaggle of misfits, and I began to wonder if this was actually an elaborate joke. Mercifully though, I noted too, through the fog of self consciousness, there was no one there I knew; no former pupils to titter up their sleeves at Mr. Davies and his psychological difficulties. My eyes found the collection of cups and saucers. Oh well, I thought. I'm here now. I might as well have a cup of tea.

My hand shook as I poured a cup of tea. It was the silence which was the most disconcerting. No one was saying a word to anyone. I had imagined a ghastly 'high-fives' affair with everyone brimming with tales of how they'd been saved, but there was nothing. I took great care to stir my tea without rattling the cup, not wanting to be the one who destroyed the atmosphere, the ambiance created by people, each of whom wished to be a million miles away from here.

The room stirred when Roderick arrived. He strode in like the winds which precede thunder, vaguely refreshing, but ominous with the threat of the gathering storm, and shut the door. I had been on the cusp of summoning enough courage to put down my cup and leave, and Roderick's arrival thwarted my escape. The closed door seemed to make the room oppressively hot. There were no windows. My top lip broke out in a sweat. I was trapped.

"Ewan," Roderick saw me, and nodded, and I scowled at the gleam of self-congratulation that sparked across his face. My face was burning, and wet with sweat. I put down my teacup, and took out a hanky. Coming here was a mistake, I thought as I wiped my face. It was a waste of time. I should speak up and tell Roderick exactly what I thought of him, and leave, but I couldn't. I stood shuffling, my mouth clamped shut. But it flexed into a small, wry smile. How could forcing me into this abhorrent situation be the key to unravelling my mind? I could think of nothing I'd rather do than go home, shut the world outside, and use a knife to instil that heady, dreamy calm I felt when I dragged a blade across my skin to watch the beautiful ruby blood well up and out. I'd been doing it for years, and it had never failed me yet.

"If everyone's got a drink who wants one, then take a seat and we'll get started," Roderick had said, reeling me into his circle. I'd sat down on the last remaining chair, taking care not to catch anyone's eye, and fixed my gaze upon a spot in the centre of the circle, and staring at it as the world would dissolve if I stopped looking.

I was sitting next to a stroppy-looking girl with tumbling dark hair, who could be no older than sixteen or seventeen. She was wearing a yellow jumpsuit patterned with teeny pink roses, and sniffed constantly. I had to bite my teacher's tongue to tell her to stop, desperate to point out how rude and how unbecoming I found this habit of hers. She sniffed again. I shuffled in my chair, and pinched the palm of my hand to try and distract my attention.

Roderick cleared his throat with a loud cough, and perched on the edge of his seat.

"Okay everyone, I'd like to welcome you all, and thank you for coming. It takes courage to come here," he said, looking at me as I continued to stare at the floor, burning under the spotlight of his attention. The room was intolerably hot. I wondered if I should take off my jacket, and loosened my tie and collar with my fingers.

"Sniff," went the girl in the yellow jumpsuit, twisting her rings around her fingers.

"Now I know many of you have been coming here for some time."

For some time? Some time? I thought once or twice would be all. So it obviously doesn't work, if you have to keep on coming back. Why am I here?

"Sniff."

"But we have a new face here tonight," I squirmed as the spotlight turned back to me. "So I think we'll take a minute to go around the circle and introduce ourselves."

Oh, that's just great. Like I really want to stand up and introduce myself. Oh no, I hope I don't have to stand up. Surely he doesn't expect me to stand up. Why am I here? I bet he's enjoying this, the sanctimonious bastard.

"Sniff."

"You can say as much, or as little as you like," Roderick sat back in his chair with an air of great expectation. And don't worry," he addressed this remark to me once more. "We are all here to support each other.

What we say in this room stays in this room. There are no records. There is no discussing what we've talked about with people outside of our group. And my role here is as a facilitator. I'm not here to judge, or diagnose. None of us are. We are here to offer what support and help we can to each other."

Oh, I don't need this. I don't need anyone's help or support. A 'facilitator'? Sounds like he'd get on well with Fiona.

"Sniff."

Oh for god's sake, will you stop sniffing and use a bloody handkerchief?

For a moment, I sweated at the thought I'd spoken out aloud. I held my breath, braced for a backlash of protest against a lack of manners, but there was nothing. Roderick was answering a question someone had asked. I tuned back into the conversation, rattled by my discomfort, and shifted in my chair. The girl with the sniff glanced at me.

"Sorry," I whispered. "It's just so hot in here."

She agreed, but our brief exchange drew unwanted attention.

"What is it?" Roderick asked.

Twelve pairs of eyes followed his gaze and stared at me. My face erupted with colour in their attention, and my tongue stammered, dry and uncooperative. I tried to take a deep breath to calm myself, to speak clearly, but it didn't work. Sensing my distress, the girl spoke up.

"It's really hot in here tonight, Rod. Does anyone mind if I open the door." She got up before anyone answered, and swept over to the door. I took the opportunity to shrug off my suit jacket, and draped it over the back of the chair, giving the girl a grateful smile as she sat back down in a rush of flowery material and matching perfume.

"Thanks Marcia," Roderick said. "Okay, if we're all ready, I'll go first. I'm Roderick, and I'm a psychiatric nurse here at Thatchington General."

Yes, we all know who you are. God, this is pointless. Just think of all the things I really needed to do tonight. Those essays I need to mark. I don't know when I'm going to find time this week.

"I specialise in helping patients who self-harm because I have a history of cutting, myself." He looked straight at me, and folded his arms, a triumphant gleam on his face. "I know how it feels."

There was a pause, and a flurry of awkward smiles. Most had heard this before, so they were busy inwardly rehearsing what they themselves would say when it was their turn to speak, but I sat and gawped at Roderick. I had thought of the man as officialdom, sanity personified, and it had never occurred to me to question what might qualify him to unpick the minds of the certifiably unstable.

They went round the circle, taking turns to bare their souls, and yes, they did applaud and back-slap one another with evangelical zeal, Roderick presiding with a pastor's quiet pride at having guided his hitherto misguided flock this far. When it was my turn to speak, I just gave my name and said I didn't want to talk, but they applauded me nonetheless as though I'd said something particularly insightful. It took months of coming to the Alexandria Suite before I was brave enough to be willing to blurt out something of a tearful confession to their forgiving ears; not much of a confession I might add, since I have suffered the consequences of being too willing to discuss the facets, the twinkling yet cracked layers which mould together to comprise the man I am. There are many things better left unsaid. 'Trust us', I was once told, and I did, talking away, telling everything, thinking I was making everything better by doing as I was told, too naive, too stupid to know I was condemning myself deeper, further with every word. But I was only seventeen, damn it. I was only a child.

The group helped me through the fog and the mess Rebecca left reeling in the wake of her departure. First we'd sit round in the Alexandria suite revealing all, and then we'd adjourn to the Windmill, the pub opposite the hospital where the real work was done. There, unfettered from the claustrophobic pressure of confessing in front of Roderick, friendships were made, alliances created. Sometimes he joined us, and most of the time he didn't. We'd get together, moan about his stupid suggestions, and swap ideas ourselves. He encouraged us to be 'buddies', swapping telephone numbers so if one of us felt tempted to harm ourselves, we could ring our 'buddy' and talk things through.

Marcia was my buddy. She helped me, but I told her to go away when she needed me. None of Roderick's crappy happy-clappy guff could save her, and it's the one thing in my life I wish I could undo the most. I haven't seen any of them since her funeral, and I certainly haven't needed Roderick. Marcia's death, her life bleeding away in a hot bath, has kept a knife out of my fingers, out of my arm. I'm sure Trudy can tell none of my scars are fresh, but it doesn't really matter. I can't see her again after this.

I dry the plates, and leave them in a neat stack on the side. The mug of tea I made has gone cold. I will make another at home, I have to go. This time, it is me who will leave, slipping out of the door and away while she slumbers, as I slumbered, unconscious in the soft warmth of sleep. Toby is still staring at me from the picture, but this time it is Mrs Phillips' voice I hear, not his.

"Mr. Davies, you know very well I do not expect my staff to fraternise with parents."

Does this mean she knows? I've got to get out of here.

But as I listen at the bottom of the stairs for any sound which might suggest Trudy is awake, something unfamiliar comes sidling up to me, creeping through the thick, early morning peace of her house on soft, velvety feet that move with such stealth, I never heard their approach. Fingers slide around me, gliding through my hair, sweeping across my skin on and on deep into my heart, wrapping around it a muffling, fluffing heavy cloak. My assailant is so unfamiliar that it takes me a few minutes to identify it as regret. I don't want to leave.

I shiver in the morning's grey gloom, torn. The hermit, in his mind, is already halfway home, scuttling for the safety of his shell. But there is another man in here this morning, and he craves the warmth of Trudy's bed, the solace in the comfort of her arms. And this man frightens me: I don't know what he will do. If Trudy wakes, she will precipitate a confrontation in which I am uncertain which fractured part of me will stand or fall.

My coward's heart wins. I grit my teeth as I pull the door shut behind me, letting the catch fall back into place without a sound, and I walk away, slipping through the empty Sunday streets, half-hoping to hear my name in her mouth, her heels clicking on the pavement as she runs towards me, running to catch me up, to persuade me back into her arms with her full, pouty lips, her fabulous body and the comfort of her caring company. And as I walk, it's not peace I find, nor the sense of having done the right, the 'safe' thing, but more regret sighing sighs into the deepest corners of my soul, drawing its cold blanket tighter around me until I too feel as grey, cold and sullen as the morning. I am a prisoner inside the walls I have constructed around myself, and there will be no escape for me today.

Chapter 14

Trudy tries to ring me a few times over the next week, but I don't answer, and I don't return her calls. And gradually, as the time goes by, I am able to answer a ringing telephone without breaking out into a sweat that it will be her calling up to admonish me for not being brave enough to talk to her, and my life goes on as normal.

I say 'normal', but that's only because I'm working so hard to make sure everything I do seems unremarkable and as 'normal' as is possible, the authorities don't realise what I'm up to. Since I've started monitoring Vi, more and more strange things are coming to my attention, and I've finally realised I'm not alone. It turns out half the street knows what she's doing. While I was pulling up one or two weeds that had sprung up undetected amid a bed of lavender, I overheard old Mrs Harris telling Vi she was tired of buying from the fish man, only she was cleverer than me, and said it was because she didn't think his produce was fresh. Vi harrumphed her way through protests, but my elderly neighbour was steadfast in her decision. I could learn a lot from her, I realised, and I waited until Vi had gone before I tiptoed around the front where Mrs Harris was pulling up dandelions from her path. It took a couple of attempts before her hearing aid picked up what I was trying to say.

"I said, I know about the fish too," I darted a quick glance to check we weren't being observed, but Vi had disappeared off indoors, and I couldn't see her at the window.

"I'm sorry dear, I don't know what you're talking about," Mrs Harris said, her opaque blue eyes peering at me through her thick-rimmed glasses. "Lovely weather we're having though." She turned to go, her shuffling body rigid with pain. And I understood. She must be more practiced than me. We mustn't talk about what's going on out in the street, it's far too dangerous. I wanted to tell her it had dawned on me, tell her I've got the message, but she was halfway up her path. So now when I'm peeking out of the window, checking up on Vi, I look over to Mrs Harris's window. If anything is amiss, I know she'll find a way of letting me know.

Other neighbours seem to understand what's happening too. I notice things everywhere now I'm remembering to pay attention, remembering to look. Mark and Phillipa have a clever way of communicating with the rest of the street. It's all about the position of their coloured bins. Previously, it's been a source of chagrin to me they leave their bins at the bottom of their drive, but that was before I woke up to the plots surrounding us. Now I realise that if the blue bin is on the right hand side, everything is safe. If it's the brown bin, then we all have to be extra careful. Jane, who lives next door to Vi, does something similar parking her car. Over to the right, everything is all right. To the left, and she's warning us. It staggers me I had no idea what was going on before. I make a special point of recording it all down in my diary each day.

This morning as I'm writing everything down, I wonder if there's something I should do to let everyone know I'm part of what's going on, to let them know I understand. For instance, I've got to work late this evening, an informal parent's night so the parents of year seven pupils can come in and discuss how their little darlings are coping in high school. I don't want any of my neighbours to worry if something has happened to me. As I tap my pen against my cheek, trying to think, there is a muffled sound in the wall beside me. I step away, my heart thumping in alarm.

These damned beetles. I've bought tubs of insect repellent and trailed powder throughout the house, but nothing seems to work. Even if I don't see any, I can hear them scratching and scuffling. I think they're living in the walls. There's even an infestation in my classroom. It's not so noticeable when I'm teaching, but when I'm working quietly on my own, it isn't long before I can hear their horrible scurrying, little barbed legs scrabbling as they come closer and closer. I've even found them crawling inside the piano. Horrible things: I keep seeing them more and more, and I don't like it.

They're everywhere. Even the tailor's shop on the high street is overrun. I called in the other day with some trousers. Mr. Findlay appeared from the back room, his wizened face beaming when he saw it was me. I'm a good customer, I suppose, although he is always busy. He retired here after working in London, but in spite of his wife's well-planned intentions, he couldn't keep his fingers free of a needle and thread. It'll be lovely in the country, she says she told all of her cronies, conjuring a gentle retirement of trips to the garden centre, and pottering around with friends. But they hadn't been in Thatchington a week, before he'd signed an agreement to rent a small shop. He tried to wheedle a thaw in her cold, wordless wrath by suggesting it would keep him out of mischief, but she merely pursed her tight lips tighter still, and refused to talk for a week. Silly old fool, she always says to me. He'll sew himself into the ground.

"What can we do for you, Mr. Davies?" He asked me, his asthmatic wheeze worse than ever.

"Can you take these in for me?" I don't know; all my clothes seem too big these days.

He told me to hold my arms out, and wound his tape measure around my waist, around my hips. I watched as his wiry white eyebrows moved towards one another, as he checked his measurement, and turned to the little box on the counter in which he kept his regular customers' details. His bony fingers leafed through the cards.

"My goodness, Mr. Davies," he said, looking at my card. "I'm not surprised your clothes don't fit. You've lost a lot of weight. Have you been ill, or is this an ongoing condition?" He peered at me over the top of the half-moon spectacles he wore with a chain around his neck. "You don't look well, if it's not impertinent of me to say so, of course."

"I'm fine," I said. His eyebrows gave the tiniest arch, and I realised I'd spoken far sharper than I'd intended, so I added "thank you" to soften my words. He nodded, and reached for his pins.

I'm not sure what he was talking about as his practiced fingers worked the fabric of my trousers, because I'd spotted movement out of the corner of my eye. There, on the dressmakers' dummy, an antique construction he kept in the window to advertise his trade, I was sure I'd seen something. And as I watched, hardly daring to blink for fear I missed it, a large, round beetle ran up over the shoulder, and disappeared down the front.

"Are you sure you're all right, Mr. Davies?" He looked up at me, his mouth full of pins.

"Yes, yes I'm fine," I said, looking round at the sound of a soft, but unmistakable noise on the shelf of cotton reels by my head. Another beetle scurried out of sight.

"You're very jumpy."

There was another one on the counter. I gasped, and took a step backwards. My arm shook as I tried to point it out to the tailor, but he couldn't see it. He was staring at me as though I'd gone quite mad. But all I could think was how could he go on kneeling there on the floor with the damned things crawling over his legs? Perhaps it's his age, I thought. Perhaps that's why he can't see them. I took another step backwards, went sprawling over a pile of fabric by the door, lost my balance and landed in a heap on the floor, beetles scuttling towards me.

"Good heavens. Are you all right, Mr. Davies? I'm terribly sorry. That material's only just been delivered and I haven't had a chance to put it away. Madeline!"

His wife came bustling through, and she too fussed over me, as I scrabbled to my feet, the beetles coming closer and closer. She couldn't see them either. I refused her offers to make me a cup of tea. All I wanted was to get out of the shop and away. Even as they both dusted me down asking over and over again was I all right, I could still hear the scurrying, scratching sounds going on all around me. And the tailor's voice followed me off down the high street, calling after me as I retreated.

"I say, Mr. Davies, are you sure you're all right?"

But if there are any beetles in here tonight, it's too noisy for me to hear them. The school's gymnasium is a hubbub of conversations bubbling, chairs being scraped across the floor as pupils with their parents arrive and depart, as we struggle to fill, or limit our five minutes of time, depending upon our opinion of each child. They gravitate towards Rebecca, I notice, giving her shy smiles in response to her gushing enthusiasm. I am happy to sit back and let her perform her nauseating routine, watching how fathers become besotted, while the mothers assume her sex means she's on their side. But I don't permit her a word in edgeways when we're talking about one of my favourite pupils. The gifted children are my domain, and I will not indulge her intervention.

"Not many left now," she says, ticking off the latest name on our sheet, getting her pen to the page before I have the chance to reach for mine. I glare at the back of her head, and sip the coffee Nathan has just produced. It's not that I trust him to bring me a drink, but it's warm in here with so many bodies, my voice has already dried to a cracking, unrecognisable husk. As I dab at my sweating forehead, taking from the top pocket of my suit the violet handkerchief which matches my tie, Rebecca lets fly the remark it's a shame I can't roll up the sleeves of my burgundy shirt. We have spent the evening locked in a point-scoring battle, gouging at each other with the serrated edges of love soured into mutual dislike, but with no clear winner and it's growing tedious now. I roll my eyes, and glance at my watch. A half past seven. Only another hour, and then we can go home.

"Who's next?"

"Toby Smith," she says, and I swear my heart stops beating for a second as I splutter into my mug, sending coffee splattering down my navy waistcoat.

"What?" I snatch the list out of her hand. When I'd summoned the courage to ask Trudy's eldest son if he wanted to make an appointment for her to see me tonight, he said she didn't, and I settled down into cool, quiet relief. But sure enough, here on the list, pencilled in Rebecca's near illegible hand is a scrawl which could, in a certain light, pass for his name.

"Oh, did I forget to tell you? He asked me earlier if he could make an appointment to see you." She sneaks me a sideways glance. "Oh look, here he comes." I look up and see his dark head appear around the door to the gymnasium. "Wait a minute, isn't that your girlfriend?"

Trudy is walking towards us, her reluctance a dark ominous presence bearing down on me.

"Gosh, I didn't think we'd be allowed to date parents," Rebecca is jabbering. "It seems rather unprofessional. Why Ewan, you've turned the same colour as your shirt. How unfortunate, it's really not flattering." And without pausing to draw breath, she flicks on her most dazzling smile and gushes "Toby, how lovely to see you. And you too, er, Mrs. Smith. Thank you for coming. It's nice to see you again, isn't it Mr. Davies?" She gives me a sharp nudge with the hard point of her bony elbow when I fail to answer.

Rebecca can nudge as hard as she likes, there are no words coming from my lips. I'm too busy reeling in the shock of coming face to face with Trudy after the night we spent together and having not spoken to her since. She shakes Rebecca's hand, and makes a point of not reaching for mine, sits down and fixes me with such a glare, I can barely look at her.

I look to Rebecca to speak, but she sits back and folds her arms, amusement playing around the edges of her mouth.

"Toby, uh, Mrs. Hennigan, your violin tutor, and I would like you to know just how impressed we both are with your progress. He's very talented," I say to Trudy, finding the strength to meet her eye for a second, before looking away, scorched by her stare.

"So you've said."

Beside me, Rebecca makes a faint sound that sounds like a suppressed snigger. I make the mistake of giving her another glance, pleading for support, but she merely arches her eyebrows, savouring my discomfort. My voice stammers, and I make a mess of trying to explain why we think Toby should be put forward for music exams. Trudy sits, her arms folded, her lips pursed shut, and addresses every remark to Rebecca. I wish both Rebecca and Toby could be transported somewhere else so I could talk to her. Trudy, I want to say. I'm sorry. I ran away because I was afraid, afraid you'd wind up looking at me just like you're looking at me now. The five minutes drag like five decades. By the time she gets up out of her chair, I am exhausted.

"Well, that was intense, wasn't it?" Rebecca sneers as I watch Trudy walking away. "Any more ex-girlfriends amongst the parents? I could have sold tickets to that performance."

"You think you're so damned funny, don't you?"

I grit my teeth as Trudy reaches the door. Don't walk away, I let out a silent plea, but she pulls the door open, and steps outside. No. Before I have time to think about what I'm doing, I'm levering my body up out of my seat in pursuit.

"Ewan, where are you going?" Rebecca calls after me.

"Cover for me for a moment," I say, and then I'm running, pushing past milling bodies, through the door and out into the corridor. I look up and down, and there goes her swaying hips, her heels tapping on the polished floor as she reaches the door at the end of the block. "Trudy! Mrs. Smith, wait!"

She pauses in the doorway, and turns round. I run towards her, my feet clattering, my lungs protesting at being forced to hurry, and stop short, turned to stone by her glare.

"Can I help you Mr. Davies? Is something the matter?" Beside her Toby's eyes grow wider. I try to smile at him, try to summon some sort of semblance of rational behaviour rather than scare him, but I must speak to her. I can't let her leave without trying to smooth things over. His sobering look is one of pity. I'll bet he was wondering just what the hell was wrong with me while we were talking too.

"I need a word," I say, trying to catch my breath. "Just a quick word. Please," I say, putting my hand on the door she'd trying to open. "Please hear me out."

She gives Toby a long, lingering look as though he holds the key to whether or not she should give me the time of day. Unspoken words pass between mother and son before she rummages in her bag, hands him a pound, and tells him to get a drink, she'll meet him in the canteen. He takes her money, throws me another pitying glance, and steps through the door. As it closes, she turns to me and folds her arms.

"Go on then," she cocks one eyebrow. "This ought to be good."

"Look, er, Trudy, I didn't mean this to happen." If I'd had time to think about this properly, I might have rehearsed a grand speech, but scrabbling with the disadvantage of surprise, coherent speech isn't coming easily to my lips.

"You didn't mean what to happen? Now, let's see, what would that be; me having to see Toby's 'Mr. Davies' on parent's night, also-known-as the low-life cretin who, once he'd got what he wanted, was never to be seen or heard from again, or was there something else?"

"No, you don't understand. It wasn't like that," I protest, wishing I knew how to begin untangling the knots of explanation.

"Wasn't it?" She unfolds her arms and plonks them down on her hips. "You know, at the very least, I might have expected this to be the part where you apologise for running out on me like that. After all, and correct me if I'm wrong, we had spent a pleasant evening, had we not? If you didn't want to see me again, the very least you could have done was rung and left a message. But you didn't, did you? No thanks, no apology, no word of explanation, and then, if that's not all bad enough, because you're Toby's music teacher, I have to sit there watching you squirm while that wild-haired witch laughs up her sleeve. You're a class act, the pair of you, do you know that?"

"Trudy, I'm sorry," I say, leaning against the wall for support. Funny, I haven't run that far, but I'm finding I tire easily these days. Last night I sat down with the newspaper to search through it for messages about the food conspiracy, and woke up just after midnight. All I've done is run out of the gymnasium after Trudy, but it feels as though I've run a marathon. My legs and shoulders are aching, and I'm wheezing as though I need to cut down on the cigarettes. "I can explain, but it's difficult."

"How so?" Trudy folds her arms tighter. "The way I see it, you've got nothing to lose. And you've got precisely two minutes of my time before I go to find my son, so you'd better start talking if you're sure explaining is what you want to do."

I look at her, trying to calm my noisy breaths and trying to work out where to start, but I'm more accustomed to keeping things to myself, and I don't know where to begin. She makes a show of looking as her watch, an oversized dial with Roman numerals, and tells me I have only one minute left.

"Right, time's up," she turns on her heel and makes for the door.

"No, wait, please," I put myself between her and the door, and let slip the hound from its leash. "I couldn't stay, not after what you remembered." When I see her blank eyes fail to register understanding, I hold up my forearms. "You know, about seeing me at the hospital, my scars and that. It's embarrassing."

I bite my lip and look down at the floor, looking at the way the strip-lights reflect against the polished linoleum, unable to hold her eyes. It never got any easier at Roderick's support group either, holding up my head and confessing that I cut myself out aloud. The people in whom I've tried to confide, my parents, Rebecca, they recoiled in disgust, their revulsion too insurmountable to toss me even so much as a scrap of understanding. Describing my fear of Trudy's thoughts, of the conclusions she would form concerning my deviant nature as 'embarrassing' doesn't even begin to define the shrivelling, paralysing terror it strikes deep into my core.

"I was afraid of what you really think of me."

"That's what all this has been about? You couldn't bring yourself to talk to me because you were embarrassed? Why? I thought we were friends."

"Oh come off it Trudy," I huff. "How many people do you know with scars like mine? You must be able to see that it would be embarrassing to say the least, when the woman in your bed remembers she's seen you from a support group for pathetic, wounded freaks." I spit the last few words from behind gritted teeth, from the depths of the gutter housing my self-esteem, flinging them up into the shiny road to land beside her feet, beside the paths of ordinary people, so they may all gawp and count themselves fortunate indeed.

"Is that what you really think of yourself?"

"Yes it is," I say, and this time it's me who turns to leave, turning back to the charade of sitting alongside Rebecca and putting on my bravest face for appearances' sake.

"Ewan, wait." I hear the click of her heels as she runs up behind me. She grabs hold of my arm, and turns me round to face her. Her eyes study my face.

"There is nothing to be embarrassed about," she says. "Not in front of me. If you'd stopped long enough to talk things through, I could have told you that, and we could have gone on seeing each other instead of these long, miserable weeks I've spent trying to guess what was going on with you. Doesn't that sound more sensible?"

"You'd really want to go on seeing me? In spite of everything you know?" I shake my head. "I don't think so. My father could never look me in the eye again after he found out, and my wife left. I hurt the only person who ever did understand so badly, she took her own life. So there you are Trudy," my voice cracks. "There's nothing left to say." I turn to resume my path back into the hall, but she won't let go of my arm.

"So that's it," her huge eyes are glistening with tears, but her mouth twitches as though she could laugh just as easily as cry. "We can't see one another because you're too busy feeling sorry for yourself. You're such a fool, Ewan Davies."

She reaches up on tiptoe, puts one hand on my shoulder and grabs the back of my head with the other, dragging me down to meet her lips. Stung at being called a fool, I might have pulled away, only she presses her soft, ripe body against mine, and deepens her kiss. I slide my hands around her waist, thinking that in denying myself her ministrations, she may have had a point calling me a fool, and I hold her close as her probing tongue explores my mouth, kissing away my defences and fears. There is a sort of strangled screech that sounds from somewhere down the corridor. I don't know what it is, and I'm too engrossed to care.

She breaks apart, and cups my face between her hands, her eyes smiling into mine.

"Tomorrow," she says, her husky tones setting the hairs quivering on the back of my neck. "I'll see you tomorrow evening. The boys play football for a couple of hours, I'll call round then. I'd better go and find Toby."

She presses one last quick kiss against my lips, and then she's off, sashaying down the corridor as I lean against the wall in a haze of pleasure, interrupted as Mrs. Phillips clatters, red-faced, to my side. There is a field of anger quivering in the air around her.

"Mr. Davies," she screeches, and I realise it was she whom I heard while I was kissing Trudy. "Might I point out this is a school, not the sort of hotel where one rents rooms by the hour. Have you no shame?"

So much shame I could share it around and still have too much, but I decide not to say this to Mrs. Phillips, she wouldn't understand. She is so angry, she tells me, she'll deal with me tomorrow once she's had a chance to calm down, but for now I am ordered to return to my post beside Rebecca and to "try to remember 'parent's night' is supposed to be about the children, not giving me the opportunity to dally with their mothers." I go to protest this is a rather harsh assessment of what has just happened, but if she had safety dials, they'd all be pointing to red, and I fear any further input from me might well lead to a full meltdown. I sidle back into the hall, duly chastised, but beaming from ear to ear.

"Finally," Rebecca quips as I resume my seat at her side. "Where the hell have you been? Fiona was rather upset when I had to say that I didn't know where you were."

"Ah well," I say, smirking as I smooth my shirt sleeves, my feathers, back into place. "She's even more upset now. You'll just have to face it, Rebecca, you might be a good teacher, but you'll never have my skills when it comes to winding up our glorious leader. Now," I take the list out of her hands. "Who's next?"

Chapter 15

My diary entry for the following morning goes like this:

Vi: lights out 2235/ curtains open 0715/ glimpses at window 2
Mr/Mrs Gregory: blue bin in normal position/ left for work on time.
Jane: car in normal position on drive
Mrs Harris: curtains open 0730/ sitting at window 0745

Because it takes Mrs Harris so long to let me know everything is okay by assuming her habitual seat by the window, I am running rather later than normal as I hurry out of the house just before eight, my briefcase tucked under my arm. As I leave, I wonder if my tardiness will trouble my neighbours. I'm going to drive to work today too, and I hope no one thinks this is my signal something is amiss. My feet crunch across the gravel to my car, and I look up and down the street to see if anyone is watching, but everywhere is quiet. There is no one around. I clamber into the car, and drive the short distance to work.

Mrs Phillips is waiting when I shuffle into the school's office to check for post before heading through to my classroom. Any hopes I might have entertained that she might decide she'd made enough of a fuss last night over the small matter of my kiss with Trudy are vaporised by the way her eyes laser across the office the moment I walk in. As she orders me into her office, the secretaries sit up, rabbit noses twitching, emboldened by the knowledge they are not the ones meriting a dressing-down today. The Head holds open her office door, but as I follow her in, she turns and stares at me, a frown creasing her forehead.

"Is there any particular reason why you are unshaven this morning?"

Puzzled, my fingers reach up to check, and, sure enough, instead of meeting soft, smooth skin, they graze against the fine stubble fuzzing my chin. Damn. You know, when something is such an ingrained habit, you wouldn't think it possible to forget, but I have. And not only I have forgotten to shave, but I've handed Mrs Phillips another reason for complaint.

"I'm growing a beard," I tell her, hoping this will neutralise her antipathy.

"Not in my time you aren't," she says, putting her bony hands on her hips. "You can sprout as scruffy a beard as you like during the holidays, but I won't tolerate it here. You know the rules. Now, you either go home and get yourself ready for work properly, or you take yourself down to the chemist this instant, and buy a razor. Either way, sort yourself out Ewan. And I haven't finished with you either. Once you've made the effort to make yourself look presentable, I want you back here in my office so we can discuss last night's antics. Nathan can take your first class"

"There's no need for that," I protest, paling at the thought of Nathan let loose with my year eleven GCSE pupils. "Can't we talk about it later? Nathan doesn't have the wherewithal to deal with my students. Standards don't achieve themselves, you know."

"Nathan is perfectly capable, and the man whom I caught canoodling with a parent last night has no grounds to preach to anyone about standards. Now Mr. Davies, go and tidy yourself up, and then we will talk. Now," she says, holding the door open. I huff and roll my eyes, but she is quite right; I know the rules.

I walk back to my car, pondering my options. There is a part of me which thinks I ought to go home and not bother coming back. After all, I have more important things to do such as monitoring everything to keep my neighbours safe. But I will be a good employee and face the music, so to speak. If I go home now though, there will be questions asked. My sudden reappearance might alert Vi to the fact I know what's going on, and I can't risk that. I decide to follow instructions, buy some shaving cream, and adjourn to the washroom at work.

Clean shaven, I steal through to my office for a quick cup of tea before summoning the courage to face Mrs Phillips again. I expected it to be empty, so I'm surprised to find Alex in there, dunking chocolate digestive biscuits into a mug of tea.

"What are you doing here?" I open the drawer in my desk, and drop the shaving things inside.

"Too many beers watching a film last night," he says between mouthfuls of biscuit. "Went back to sleep after the alarm went off, so this is breakfast. Anyway, might well ask you the same question. Don't you have a class first thing?"

"Oh, I'm in trouble. Not only is our glorious leader waiting to read the riot act downstairs, but she's forced me to have Nancy take my class. Still, won't hurt her to wait any longer, will it? Any water left in the kettle?"

"What have you done this time?"

"Oh it's good," I take a deep breath, and gaze out of the window. Actually, I can be as flippant as I like, but I know I'm in trouble. Given just how often I seem to wind up in the bad books these days, there is a growing knot of unease tightening in my belly at the thought Mrs Phillips might deem this latest escapade a sackable offence. Damn. It's times like these when a hip flask in the office would be appropriate; I need something stronger than a cup of tea before I face her. I pour boiling water into my mug and watch the teabag float infuse.

"She caught you snogging Trudy? Oh mate," he is helpless with laughter. "That's a good one. Here, have a choccy biccy. Can't beat them."

111

"Technically, Trudy was kissing me," I arch my eyebrow and shake my head at the offer of a biscuit. "But I don't think that's going to be much use as an excuse. She said 'may I remind you, Mr. Davies, the point of parent's evening isn't to provide you with the opportunity to dally with the children's mothers." Alex laughs even harder, spluttering crumbs across his desk and wiping them with his sleeve.

"No, but it's a good idea," he says, leaning back in his chair, his hands clasped behind his head. "Could you imagine that, eh? Oh well, at least you've patched things up with Trudy."

"Be a bit of an expensive patch-up if I get fired."

"You won't."

But facing Fiona across her desk, the cocky me who mimics her and laughs at her every word has his swagger impaled on the sharpened end of her deadly glare, and not being sacked seems in no way certain. She has her arms folded tight across her chest, her shoulders rigid with tension, her thin lips pursed. Her unblinking stare is white hot with reproach, and I'm having trouble holding it. I want to look down and slink away, tail between my legs, head lowered, creeping away to hide out her displeasure in my den. Nothing, she tells me, can begin to capture the utter disappointment she finds in my 'regrettable behaviour'. And, she says, putting one hand down on the desk and leaning forward, her blonde hair swinging without even so much as one hair stepping out of place, what do I think I would say to her, were our roles reversed?

The thought of watching her kissing anyone is so disturbing, it's on a par with realising, around puberty as I recall, the only reason you exist at all is because your parents must have had sex at least once. I manage to stop my lip curling in disgust, but the shudder goes juddering down my spine.

"Why am I even having this conversation with you?" She says, putting her other hand on her hip. "You, of all people, Ewan? "It's always been 'standards this, standards that' with you. But I don't know what's gotten into you of late. Ever since school returned after the summer, you've caused me nothing but trouble. I ask you to do something; you forget. I go to speak to you; you're so jumpy you virtually go through the roof every time. Your behaviour is erratic, to say the least, you look awful, and now this. First I catch you," she pauses and shudders, seemingly as repulsed by the idea of me kissing as I was at the thought of her. "Cavorting' with one of our parents, not only on school property, I might add, but while you were supposed to be working. And then you turn up looking down-at-heel this morning. Is this some sort of mid-life crisis, or is there something wrong with you, something I should know about?"

"No," I say, crossing one leg over the other, and folding my own arms tight.

"Are you in a relationship with Mrs Smith?"

"That's none of your business," I say, not to be deliberately truculent, but rather because I'm unsure whether I can count the few amorous encounters I've enjoyed with Trudy amount to any description of a proper, bona fide 'relationship'.

"You know my rules Mr. Davies. I do not approve of any member of staff consorting with a parent of a child in this school. Any member of staff: that includes you. I just don't understand you, Ewan," she sighs, switching into a softer mode. It's so unlike you. Are you sure there isn't anything you want to tell me? Are you sure you're all right?"

"I'm fine, thank you." I'd be better still if everyone would stop asking me if I'm all right. "I apologise for what happened, and you have my assurance it won't happen again."

"I sincerely hope not," she says, giving another shudder. "I have no choice but to issue you with a written warning for your antics. Now do you think you could try and toe the line for the rest of term? I don't want to have to speak to you like this again. You may go."

I storm out of her office, slamming the door with as much force as I can muster. She yells after me, but I don't stop. I need to be somewhere she can't find me. My legs automatically stride towards the music department, and without stopping to think, I barge into the cupboard, lock the door behind me, and sweep everything, books, papers and instruments onto the floor with a crash. I survey the mess, my chest heaving as my rage cools to a simmer. How dare she speak to me as though I were one of the children? It begins to boil anew. I don't just want to throw things; I want to punch someone too. My anger is a demon sprung to life, too powerful to ignore. If I was at home, even Marcia's ghost couldn't stop me today.

I sink down onto the floor amid the debris of paper and chime bars, reason tiptoeing back in, its head bowed. Well at least I didn't get sacked, although if she knew what I've just done, that would change. I run my fingers through my hair with a sigh, wishing I hadn't indulged my anger. It's going to take ages to get this mess cleared up, and I want it done before anyone sees.

Not long after I get home, Trudy rings to say she will be round just after seven. I briefly consider what Mrs Phillips had to say on the matter, but in the delicious thrill of anticipation of seeing Trudy, any inclination I might have entertained to be a good little soldier vanishes. Excitement chases the tiredness from my bones. I shower and shave, make sure the bed looks presentable, and spend an age trying to decide which shirt would look right with which pair of jeans, ridiculous when you think my sole aim this evening is to remove both my clothes, and hers. But while my mother might have regretted I wasn't a daughter to share her love of clothes, she exerted far more of an influence than she realised. In the end, I choose a soft grey, cashmere sweater for the way it feels against my skin. Every nerve ending's sensitivity is heightened, awaiting Trudy's touch. By the time I hear a car pull up outside, I have paced for miles, the minutes passing as hours.

"Ewan," she says as I open the door, a pinkish blush settling across her smiling cheeks. I hold the door open for her, but much as I'm excited to see Trudy, I can't resist a quick glance up and down the street to check everything is all right. Yes, everything is in its place. Thank goodness. I don't want to be worrying about that now.

"What, are you worried what your neighbours might think?" She says, slipping off her red mac as I shut the door. "Maybe I should have arrived in my underwear, given them something to talk about."

She is wearing a purple sweater, the v-neck showing just enough of the dip between her breasts to make me forget about anything other than the need to see more. I wrap my arms around her, slide my fingers through her hair, and tilt her face to mine. My lips brush hers, trying to be composed, but I want her so much, there is nothing other than to surrender to the ravenous hunger her gentle touch ignites in my veins. I crush her against my body and kiss deeper and deeper into her mouth. She pushes against me, and peels off her sweater. My fingers fumble with the catch of her bra until it falls away, and I cup both warm breasts in my trembling hands, teasing her dark nipples with my thumbs while she grinds her hips against mine.

"I want you Ewan. I want you now," she growls, pulling at the waistband of my jeans. We crash against the hall table sending the telephone crashing to the floor. I want her too; I want her in my bed, so I take her hand and lead her upstairs, my groin throbbing with every step. She is pulling at my trousers, I am pulling at hers, and we tumble down onto the bed in a tangle of half-clad limbs, pulling and stretching until at last we are free from all restraint. Her legs wrap around me, inviting me in. She threads her fingers through my hair and cries my name as I join us, rocking backwards and forwards until relief surges through us.

Spent, I stretch out beside her, my head sinking into the pillows. I'm so heavy and so numb with fatigue it's an effort to keep my eyelids open. The mattress squeaks as she shifts position. I peek through my heavy lids to see her studying me, her head propped up on one elbow. If I opened my eyes properly, I'd be gazing at the enticing round curves of her breasts, but I can't be bothered. I'm warm, I'm content, and I just want to sleep.

"Ewan," she says, tracing the lie of my jaw with a fingertip. "You're not going to fall asleep, are you? I don't have to go just yet. We have time for more."

"More?" I yawn and stretch. "I'm tired. I seem to be tired all the time these days."

"Why? You are eating, aren't you? Only I'm sure you've lost weight in the last couple of weeks since I saw you."

"Of course I eat," my eyes open and I roll away from her. I lie on my back and stare up at the ceiling. "That's a strange post-coital question, isn't it?"

"Well, to anyone else, maybe. But I know you said you hate cooking. You've definitely lost weight and you're tired. I just wonder if you're eating enough."

Is this is what I get for having sex with a nurse, an on-going scrutiny of my health? You know, it was good to see her yesterday, and I've spent the day soaring thermals of anticipation in prelude to having her here tonight, but I mustn't forget this relationship is ill-advised. She already knows far too much about me. My throat tightens as I fret over what else might be glaring, conspicuous, in the spotlight of her professional eyes. It tightens, rather as it does whenever I go to eat anything at the moment, constricting in protest that no matter how much I know I should eat, we, my body and I, have no way of knowing what is safe. I don't even know if the bottled water I drink is free from contaminants. Fear says it isn't.

"Trudy, I'm fine," I say, turning my head to look at her, but managing only a fleeting glance before I have to look elsewhere, trying to conceal the lie.

"Phew," she says, pretending to wipe her brow. "That's okay then. Because I've got vouchers to have dinner at The Dolphin, and I wondered if you'd like to come with me on Saturday night?"

"Oh no, I can't," I say, admiring the depth of regret I manage to convey in my tone. "I'm not around on Saturday. I'm going to a concert."

This much is true. I will be back in the evening however, but Trudy doesn't need to know that. It's a recital at the Royal Albert Hall. The cellist Martin Rutherford is playing. At first I wasn't sure if I dared to go, to do something so locked in my past, but the more I thought about it, the less I could resist the urge to lose myself in the rich decedent sound of a cello being played by accomplished hands. Sometimes at school one of my pupils will achieve a degree of capability which lets me drift into a universe flowing with music, but it's a dangerous place for me to go. Too many bitter memories.

"Can I come?"

"No."

Her eyebrows arch, and I realise my 'no' was rather more vehement than intended. I try to sand away the sharpness by explaining I had difficulty obtaining my own ticket, but truth be told, I would rather not go than attend with anyone else. The awareness of being in the company of someone familiar will spoil my enjoyment. Anonymity is the muffling, neutral blanket I prefer around my shoulders when I want to indulge my secret passion. And it has to be kept secret. If it should step blinking into the daylight, everyone will see the trail of shame it drags along in its wake. So many things I prefer to remain hidden.

"Sunday lunch then?"

I close my eyes, and sigh. What is it with this woman and food? If she isn't eating, she's thinking about eating. Maybe this is the proof she can't be trusted. Perhaps there's more to her job than to warn me to keep quiet, she's to try and make me eat, to make me comply. My eyes fly open. She's like Rebecca and Vi, a secret agent out to get me and to monitor what I'm doing. 'Your mission agent Smith,' I imagine a voice saying, 'is to get him to eat.' So that's why it's all 'you look thin, let's go out for dinner'. Damn. And because my traitorous body can't resist the lure of her salacious charms, I've played right into their hands. That's probably why Toby made the appointment for last night after he'd told me he didn't want to see me. It's all part of the plot.

We both startle as Trudy's phone starts bleeping from the pocket of her trousers lying strewn on the floor. She rolls onto her side to turn it off, and I try not to think about just how much her ample buttocks remind me of a gorgeous, ripe peach. It's a terrible cliché, but so apt, and I cannot resist but slide my hands around their soft, warm contours.

"Sorry Ewan," she says. "I haven't got time now. I'm going to have to go."

"Are you sure?" She gasps as I nuzzle her shoulder and shuffle up to press against her soft flesh. Maybe she can't be trusted, but she is so delicious, why should I resist? I'm wise to their plans now. So long as I keep my wits about me, there's no reason why I can't enjoy being with her. She groans as I work my way between her legs, harder as I push up into her damp, warm depths. My name is in her mouth as I find the strength, the rhythm to thrust us both over the edge and into the oblivion of sweet release.

"Oh hell, I'm going to be late," Trudy says, breathless and kissing me as she pulls on her shoes and tries to fastens her coat with my hands still roving around her body. She is flustered, wide-eyed and dishevelled after our love-making. "I've got to go Ewan. The kids will be upset if I'm not there on time."

I laugh, not at the thought of her children being upset, but because I love the thought of her driving away, going back to duty with an inner glow of satisfaction radiating at her core. Cupping her face in my hands, I kiss her to the door.

"When can I see you? I need to see you," she says, loitering in the doorway, her lips swollen from our kisses. I lean against the doorframe, wishing she didn't have to go, wanting to feel that mouth working its magic on my body once more. "Tomorrow?"

"You're free tomorrow?" My spirits soar as she nods.

"They're going to their Dad's for tea. I usually work late, but I think I ought to be able to get away early for once. I'll ring you." Grinning, she turns, runs down the path, and clambers into her car. Vi's curtains twitch as she drives off waving. I wait until the blue car turns the corner, then I shut my door, and make a note in my diary.

2030: Trudy leaves, Vi watching.

Vi, Trudy and Rebecca: I am surrounded. It's more important than ever that I keep a clear head. I decide against a whisky, and drag my own satisfied limbs with their inner glow back to bed. Sleep eludes me, but the memory of Trudy's gorgeous body in my bed, her legs wound around my hips, keeps me occupied throughout another long, dark night.

Chapter 16

Trudy rings to suggest we meet after school at the café in the town's tiny art gallery. I leave Rebecca flapping in our office, having forgotten she had earmarked this afternoon for the first of the weekly staff meetings she thinks we ought to have. I can't see the point, but she insists I'm not telling her enough about how I run the department. As I pull on my coat, she folds her arms across her chest and presses her tight lips together as though she needed any help to look disapproving. I can't understand the fuss. I mean, it's not as though I leave early on a regular basis to meet women for afternoon tea. She's jealous; yes, that's it.

"You're just making it worse for yourself, you know."

I pause, my hand on the office door and turn round.

"What did you just say?"

"I didn't say anything," Rebecca snaps, folding her arms tighter across her chest.

"Yes you did. You said," I break off and grip the door, reality wavering around me.

"I didn't say anything. Oh, you're not going to tell me you're still hearing things after all these years, are you?" She slumps down in her chair, her eyes glittering with the malice, the contempt that can only grow in a Petri dish of over-familiarity. "I thought you'd have got over that particular fantasy of yours by now. But just for the record, no, you don't know what I'm thinking. You never have. Not unless you're thinking it's high time you stopped trying to control everything and started to delegate. You know: del-e-gate?"

I walk out, giving the door a slam as vicious as her tongue. She's always been jealous of my abilities.

The prospect of Trudy's company smoothes my ruffled plumes back into place, and I set off for the art gallery, whistling as I walk. It's a bright autumn day, russet leaves beautiful against a cloudless blue sky. Autumn was one of my favourite seasons in Aberdeen. The silvery buildings gleam in the sunlight, the huge horse chestnut in our back garden, its leaves turned scarlet and yellow with the cooling air. Nostalgia sweeps through my veins. Trudy would like Aberdeen, I know she would.

"A weekend away would be nice," she says. "But that's a bit of a long way to go just for one night. I suppose I could ask Richard if he could have the boys for an extra night."

"No, I didn't mean 'go' to Aberdeen," I see my error, and backtrack at high speed. "I just meant you'd like it. Stupid thing to say, really."

Yes Ewan, especially as there's no way you could possibly do that. What the hell am I doing even mentioning it to her? I think it's beginning to get to me, the strain of living with everything I know, keeping up appearances while inside I'm quaking with the fear that at any minute, I might be arrested for knowing too much. Arrested, and locked up to stop me from speaking out. I wish Mrs. Harris had been more willing to talk. I don't know what I'm supposed to do.

I hear scuffling. I look round, but there's nothing. A woman with long blonde hair sitting at the table behind glances up as though querying what I'm looking at. I turn back round. Perhaps she's watching me. I mustn't draw attention to myself.

"Are you all right?"

"Yes, of course," I grin, trying to remember I must act as thought nothing is amiss. 'Normal', that's it. I must act 'normal'. "Just thought I saw someone I knew."

Trudy frowns as she pours another cup of tea, but she doesn't challenge me any further. She takes a bite of her chocolate éclair, and I try not to watch as she licks cream from the corners of her mouth. Instead, I sit back and look at the pictures hung against the café's white walls. They are huge colourful works, but I've no idea what any of them are meant to be. It's the sort of thing Alex is fond of painting. As my eyes drift around the room, I hear more scratching.

"Ewan, what is it?"

"It's nothing, Trudy, honestly." I lean closer across the table. "You know, Toby's very talented with that violin. Is there anyone in the family who plays? He's definitely got your ear for music."

Standard tactic for deflecting a mother's unwelcome attention, get her talking about her children. Trudy's eyes glaze over as she sighs over her eldest boy's unexpected gift. I smile and nod in all the right places, but my attention is elsewhere. There's an older couple sitting eating scones, their bored eyes drifting across the café, nothing to say to one another. I can't be sure, but I think they're watching me. I loosen my collar, and force a smile, trying to focus on Trudy while monitoring them.

"You seem very distracted."

"Hmm," I smile, "go on."

"There's a large blue cow with green horns."

"Yes, that's right," I say, watching the woman with the scone watching me. To my surprise, Trudy scoops up her bag and manoeuvres herself up out of her seat. "What are you doing?"

"You aren't listening to a word I'm saying," she says, her eyes glistening with hurt. "So I might as well head home. It's almost time I was going anyway. Thanks for the tea, Ewan," she turns on her heel and stomps towards the door. My face reddens.

Damn. Why does it always end up like this? I don't seem to be able to spend time with anyone these days without them taking offence over something I've said or done. Grabbing my briefcase, I hurry after her. The couple watch me with dispassionate eyes.

"Trudy, wait," I catch up with her in the foyer.

"No, Ewan, because it's always like this. If I'm rolling around in bed with you, everything's fine. But try to talk to you, or spend time with you, well it's like you'd rather be anywhere other than here with me. And if that's how it is, well, that's fine. Why don't you just say-so?" She folds her arms and starts tapping her foot.

"It's not like that," I say, my face getting hotter and redder. What shall I tell her? I don't think I can trust her, but I've got to explain. "It was that old couple sitting across from us," I say, unsure whether this is brave or stupid of me. "They were watching us. Watching me." Come to think of it, I think the blonde-haired woman was too. I am surrounded. Nowhere is safe.

"They were watching you? Why?" She is shaking her head in disbelief as though I've said something particularly outrageous no sane person would entertain.

"They just were, I could tell. You can't trust anyone these days." And then it dawns on me, a truth so extreme, it's blinding in its intensity. "I don't think it's safe for you to see me," I say, leaning in close so I don't have to raise my voice and draw yet more attention. "I don't want you to get hurt." I haven't thought about this before. If Trudy isn't actually a part of the plot, then she could be in serious danger. None of my friends are safe. Any one of them could be rounded up, tortured maybe, as a means of getting at me. Fear strums the nerves in my stomach. Why did I have to find those articles in the newspaper? I wish I'd never read them. I wish I knew none of what I know. Ignorance, as they say, was indeed bliss.

"Ewan, what are you talking about?" Her eyes are narrow with suspicion, but this is the kindest way. I never thought for a moment the enormity of what I've got myself into. No one is safe, least of all me. It's better if Trudy can just forget about me, pretend we never met.

As I walk away, I look back to wave. She is still shaking her head.

Chapter 17

I keep seeing people staring at me no matter where I turn. I hurry to school the next morning, my collar turned up against a squally wind, but it makes no difference. Even motorists sat in their cars turn and look at me as I hurry by. I wonder what it is that's making me so conspicuous. I have become a marked man.

Darting glances over my shoulder, I hurry into the school office to collect my post from the Music Department's pigeon hole. There is nothing there. I check again. The music shop promised they would send the violin strings we need by courier if necessary, but there is nothing here. I look round, examining neighbouring pigeon holes, tutting at the thought the school's team of useless secretaries have obviously put it somewhere stupid, but I can't see anything which resembles the package I am expecting. I'm so busy rummaging, I don't hear the head's approach, her heels muffled by the carpet.

"Are you all right Mr. Davies?"

I jump back from the pigeon holes, strangling my scream with the heavy hands of what I think might constitute 'normal' behaviour, although I'm finding this is getting harder to define. The office's secretaries look up with one judging head. I must be more careful. Any one of them could be a spy, be watching me and reporting my actions. I'm not even sure about the head, who is frowning, her arms folded across her chest. Wait a minute, she asked me something. What did she ask? Oh yes, that. Am I all right?

"Yes of course Mrs Phillips," I say, wiping my sweating face with the back of my hand. "You startled me."

"Are you looking for something?"

"I'm expecting a package," I say, mirroring her pose and folding my own arms. "Reeds and strings for some of my students. They said it would be here this morning, but it isn't. And now I'm going to have to go and telephone them again," I huff, letting my anger flow. "It's all deeply inconvenient."

"The package has arrived," says Monica, the head receptionist. Her rolled curls wobble, her hairstyle somewhat strangely reminiscent of pictures I've seen of the Medusa, as she calls out across the office. I glare, ready to savage her for failing to put it in my pigeon hole which I'm sure is a deliberate act of antagonism on her part, when she gives a smug smile and says "Mrs. Cartwright has already collected it. Haven't you spoken to her this morning?"

"She didn't mention it," I say, my cheeks igniting, but my tongue stayed, conscious of the head's presence.

"Hmm," Mrs. Phillips says, folding her arms tighter. "It does seem as though there is something of a communication problem beginning to crop up in the Music Department, wouldn't you agree, Mr. Davies? If it isn't you in here rummaging around for a package, it's messages not being passed on. As Head of the Department I expect you to take the lead in ensuring the lines of communication flow freely, not making a point of keeping things to yourself and cancelling meetings. You aren't a one-man band."

"I have no idea what you're talking about."

"I thought you might say that," she says. "Anyway, since you are here, don't forget this lunchtime we are showing a delegation from the chamber of commerce around the school and I want you involved since the Music Department is one area they've indicated they are interested in funding. Their money would mean those new instruments I know you want, so my office, at one. Don't forget."

Bloody women: I am surrounded by a sisterhood of conspirators, I think as I walk back through to my classroom, ready to throttle Rebecca for not only making me look a fool, but for running with her complaints to the head. 'Ewan doesn't tell me stuff', I imagine her bleating. 'He doesn't give me enough to do. He won't delegate, no matter how many times I ask him'. Bloody woman: can she make it any more obvious she's after my job? You'd think she'd be grateful I hadn't blocked her own position here by drawing the head's attention to our previous relationship instead of trying to poach mine. And to think my first thoughts were that fate had brought us back together? I shake my head. Fate was having a bloody good laugh at my expense the day Rebecca got the call from her agency to come to Thatchington High.

"Mr. Davies? Mr. Davies, sir?"

Pairs of feet are pounding down the corridor towards me, the sound ringing off the walls. I pause with my hand on my classroom door and turn, ready to berate the owners for daring to run on my watch, but when I see the nervous smiles of a clutch of my GCSE pupils, my irritation melts.

"Mr. Davies, Mrs. Hennigan wants to know if you'll listen to our exam pieces this lunchtime."

Mrs. Hennigan is our visiting strings tutor. I haven't had a chance to speak to her for a few weeks to discuss the children's progress, so this is a marvellous opportunity made all the more straightforward by the fact it is her suggestion and not my demand. I think for a second. Wasn't there something else I was supposed to be doing at lunchtime? I scan through my memory, but I can't think of anything more important.

The four girls and one boy assemble straight after lunch and busy themselves with their instruments, tuning strings and tightening bows. I sit at my desk, Mrs. Hennigan in her brown velvet suit perched on the piano stool, ready to play in accompaniment. She is tiny, like a little wren, and bobs her head this way and that, darting glances at me, at her students, at the door, on a constant lookout for danger. Her huge brown eyes bulge out from under enormous quivering lashes, and I think if I speak when she least expects it she will fly away across the room.

My pupils are competent, if not gifted. Two play violins, and another the viola. The tall, clumsy boy grapples with a double bass, but he plays well, and as I listen, I make a note to suggest to Mrs Hennigan the five perform as a quintet for the school's Christmas concert. I imagine the wren flapping and fluttering over this, but really, it shouldn't be difficult to arrange. The last girl, one of my more promising students, picks up her cello, and begins to play.

I sit up. This melody is familiar. It is a beautiful air, and the cello sighs and mourns its way through the piece, bemoaning the fleeting futility of doomed love. Once upon a time it was one of my favourite pieces of music, but I have not heard it arranged for the cello since before I left Aberdeen. I lean across the desk, wanting to lose myself in my student's performance.

But Clare Patrick scrapes her bow backwards and forwards, the passion in the music squashed flat as though it meant nothing. I glance at Mrs. Hennigan, but she is concentrating on her own playing, her head dipped, her lips pursed. My mouth sours. Perhaps I'm going to need a different strings tutor, one that understands more than the mere mechanics of performance. I slump, supporting my head with one hand, and glance at the clock.

Claire plays the end notes with a flourish, wisps of her fine hair falling free of its clasp, but when she looks up, she's biting her lip, afraid of my verdict. Her friends, and Mrs. Hennigan, break into a round of polite applause, and her red cheeks blush darker. Their encouragement emboldens her, and I watch as she summons just enough courage to glance at me only for a second, seeking my approval, and lingering just long enough to see there is none. She drops her gaze to the floor. I sit and stare, my limbs set like fired clay, as I ponder my analysis. The seconds pass as hours. How to explain my thoughts?

"Miss Patrick." She startles as I speak. "What do you feel when you're playing? No," I shake my head. "Tell me: the piece of music you were playing, Fouré's 'Sicilienne', what is it all about?"

Her face burns with colour. She opens her mouth, but nothing comes out except the self-conscious stammers of a teenaged girl, her words tripping and tumbling as she panics in the harsh glare of my judgment. I sigh, and reach under my glasses to rub the bridge of my nose. We will get nowhere at this rate.

"This particular sicilienne was a composition Fouré worked into his orchestration of incidental music for a play entitled 'Pelléas and Mélisande' by the Belgian playwright Maurice Maeterlinck. As a GCSE student, I would expect you to know this." This remark is aimed at timid Miss Hennigan as much as it is at Claire, the latter's head so bowed I can't see her face. What is the point in merely teaching the children to play notes in order without an appreciation of the context of the music? I will need to have words with the strings teacher afterwards. Standards do not achieve themselves.

"The story goes that Pelléas and Mélisande fall in love, only she is already married. The piece of music you've just played tries to capture the beauty and passion of the forbidden love they share, which ultimately leads to Pelléas's death at the hands of Mélisande's husband's revenging family. But you play as though Pelléas and Mélisande were just two people passing each other by in the street."

Claire's friends smother their titters when I glare. I sit up, and clasp my hands together on the desk.

"What do you think about when you play?"

"Not making a mistake, Sir," she stammers, blushing even harder, her eyes filling with prickling tears, embarrassed at being the focus of so much attention.

"Not making a mistake." I groan, and rub my aching temples. "You are not going to make a mistake, Miss Patrick. You are quite possibly the most technically able cellist I have ever heard, wouldn't you agree Mrs. Hennigan?" The wren nods with such enthusiasm, I can't tell if she agrees with me, or is too afraid to disagree. "But," I let out a long sigh. "You are also the most clinical. There is no feeling in your music. You scrape away from one end of the piece to the other as though the only point in making music is to reach the finishing line. What do you think poor old Gilbert Fauré would have preferred in his air for doomed love, a perfect execution, or passion with the odd mistake? Try again."

The girl readies her bow, blinking back hot tears which must be making the black lines and notes on her sheet music dance and swim before her eyes. I can see she is trembling. She tries, but I have killed her confidence. Nice one, Ewan. I need to pull something out of the bag, something to inspire her, and I can think of only one thing. But do I have the nerve?

"All right, that will do." Mind made up, my chair scrapes and everyone stares as I get up and walk over to Claire. She peers up at me from under her fringe, trying to guess what I am doing and recoils as I stretch out my hand. "Give me the bow."

She gawps, but obeys. I motion her to give me the cello. She releases it, but goes on sitting on the stool, flustered.

"Go and sit down."

I settle myself, and position the cello between my knees. There isn't a sound in the room, just the charge of anticipation. I run my hands over the instrument's wooden belly, admiring its smooth, beeswax finish. It is a fine instrument, though not as good as the one my parents bought me. Now I have hold of it, I feel the years slip away, and I know I can do this. I adjust the bow, and nod to Miss Hennigan. As the piano tinkles through its introduction, I take a deep breath, and begin to play.

Any fears that I might have forgotten everything, and make an idiot of myself vanish as, with the first draw of the bow, the cello sings out with such a rich, delicious tone, the classroom and my small audience disappear. I am my teenaged self again, my eyes close as my fingers fly up and down the neck, the strings nip my soft, unpracticed fingers but it feels as though I have been doing this, performing this piece of music every day of my life. I am Pelléas, I am Mélisande, and I am the certainty that nothing this good could ever last, snatched moments of brilliance whose gaudy, glittering colours could never hope to withstand the darkness that comes crashing in and rolling on, swirling down into a black oblivion of despair, haunting me when I least expect it, swamping anything good or wholesome in my life with the numbing certainty that nothing can ever be truly right.

Clapping breaks the spell. I surface from doomed love, from darkness, and find myself back in my classroom surrounded by open mouthed, enthusiastic applause. I blink, dazzled, having forgotten there was anyone here but me, but the clapping assures me I have managed to make my point. I permit myself a small smile, but it vanishes when I realise I have not only been playing to my pupils, but to a gaggle of suited figures, including Mrs. Phillips and Rebecca, the latter's mouth gawping in astonishment. There is a curious light in her eyes, and I think, for once, I have managed to impress her. I puff with pride. My memory stretches and stirs at the sight of the Head, but settles back to sleep. It has just worked hard, and thinks it deserves its rest.

"Mr. Davies," Mrs Phillip's spiky heels tap-tap across the floor. "What a treat for our pupils to listen to such a beautiful performance. Don't you agree children," she turns her high-wattage enthusiasm on them. "Aren't we lucky we have such a talent in our Music Department?" And to me she adds, "I had no idea you could play like that."

Rebecca sidles to my side as Mrs. Phillips returns to the suits, resplendent in her conviction she oversees a remarkable school.

"How long have you been learning to play the cello?" My ex-wife asks, and I smirk, savouring every crumb of pleasure at the thought she doesn't know me as well as she'd like to think.

"I had my first lesson when I was five," I shrug. She narrows her eyes, and drops her voice so only I can hear as Mrs Phillips goes on singing my praises to the little flock hanging on every word.

"You've been learning since you were five? How come I never knew you could play like that?"

"You never asked, I suppose."

"Only you could keep something like this to yourself," she hisses. "In some corner of your twisted brain, you probably think it's funny. Or clever," she adds as her bile heats up to a simmer. "Don't you ever get tired of your stupid games?"

What is she talking about? This isn't 'a game'. There is nothing funny or clever about the long-buried ache. No, wait a minute, I'm sorry. 'Ache' doesn't teeter anywhere close enough to capture the longing, the utter need I've spent all this time repressing, the feel of the cello pressing against my knees releasing the monster from the prison where I thought I had it chained. All I want to do right now, is play and play on, consigning the rest of the day to a slagheap of inconsequence, obligation sacrificed on a visceral altar to desire. My little lesson has awakened something I thought I could go on pretending to ignore, go on denying its very existence, my vehemence strong enough to erase from my mind the truth behind my own lie.

What was I thinking? I haven't taught anything to anyone here today, but to me myself. The creature has lain, cloaked from sight like a pupae smothered in shimmering, gossamer layers, so light they lay at my core undetected. All I can do now is watch, enthralled, as mistress truth, my muse, rises up, unfurling her magnificent latticed wings. She takes to the air, encircling me, pressing me down with the knowledge I will never be free of the chains which shackle me to her, no matter how adept I have become at pretending they don't exist. And yet all I feel is soothing, calming content. There is liberation for me at last, the crushing weight of all these years of deceit and denial falling from my shoulders as though they have never existed. I ignore Rebecca and run my hands over the varnished body of Claire Patrick's cello. Will she lend it to me, I wonder, or must I suffer another long night until I can find one, and one worthy of my talent, so I may surrender at last in full to the demands of my mistress, and atone at her feet for all the years I thought I could do without.

"No, actually," Rebecca is saying, dragging me back into the present moment and the reality of her bubbling anger. "It's good to be reminded, as if I ever needed reminding, our previous relationship was never based on any semblance of honesty or the truth. I mean, let's be frank; I'm not sure you have any idea what either word means."

Ah, the truth. What is it about women and 'the truth'? 'Tell me the truth,' my mother would say when she got home from work. 'How many hours of practice have you done today? And I mean proper practice, not sitting staring out of the window, or whatever it is you do when you think I'm not watching. All this money I'm spending on your music lessons, the very least you can do is put in a bit of effort.' The truth is that I might need to play, but that doesn't mean I always want to. She never understood the distinction.

There is a very good reason why Rebecca doesn't know I was a talented cellist, but I'll be damned if I'm going to share it with her. But before I get in with a retort, Mrs Phillips calls time on proceedings. The suited posse want to see Alex's Art Department. My memory wakes with a start. Damn, that was it. I was supposed to be involved in showing round the delegation from the chamber of commerce.

"Do you need me Mrs Phillips?" I ask, laying the cello against a desk.

"It's all right Mr. Davies," she beams. "I would never have asked had I realised you were so busy. Mrs. Cartwright very kindly agreed to step in, so she can fill you in on everything later, can't you Rebecca?"

Rebecca smiles a yes to the Head, and a gloat to me. She draws herself up tall, and glides out of my classroom in conversation with a portly man sporting a half-moon of hair whom I recognise as one of Jeremy Fotheringham's associates, leaving me alone with my students and Mrs Hennigan, none of whom are sure what to say to me after my performance. They pack up their instruments and scuttle out, one by one, leaving me alone with my thoughts, with my despair at the thought I've unwittingly aided Rebecca in her efforts to undermine me, and alone with a darkness every bit as deep as Maeterlinck conjured for Pelléas and Mélisande.

Needless to say she doesn't come looking for me to tell me what the chamber of commerce had to say. I knock on her classroom door, but the room is empty, everything tidy and ready for tomorrow. Irritation intensifies into a bitter brew. She's doing this on purpose, keeping things from me. I stamp upstairs to the office, but she isn't there either. There's just time for me to have another quick sweep of the internet to see if any new information has been posted about food additives before I go home. I sit down at my desk, and begin tapping at the keyboard.

My searches find nothing. The clock tells me its half-past four, and I think maybe I should go home. Trudy has already sent me a text suggesting she pop round tonight while her boys are playing football. I thought I made it clear yesterday that we shouldn't see each other, so I am uneasy, wondering if she's checking up on me. I pull out my telephone and read her message again, trying to work out if there is some sort of subtext between the words 'hi, wonder if we can chat while boys r playing f'ball,' but I can't work it out. The door opens. Alex saunters in, swinging the canvas satchel he uses in place of a briefcase, followed by Rebecca. He grins at me, and tosses his bag down. She ignores me, and begins rifling through papers on her desk.

"Hey," he says, his huge grin splitting his face in two. "Just the person I wanted to see!"

"Really? Dare I ask why?"

"Yeah, what's all this bollocks about you being some sort of star performer? The whole school's buzzing with it. Our glorious leader is raving about how you're a genius. You've got to admit mate, going from the scourge of her reign to her pin-up boy is a bit of a turnaround and a half for you, isn't it?"

"Oh that," I sigh, turning back to my computer screen. "Lot of fuss about nothing. I was hoping she might have forgotten."

I mean, I played well considering I haven't played in years, but it wasn't exactly an accomplished performance. My mother would have been horrified. I can picture her face, tight-lipped and hardening stonier, shaking her head in disgust. 'You've let yourself down again, Ewan. All you had to do was play the piece properly, but you couldn't be bothered, could you?' I grip the edge of my desk. It is nice and solid, real, just like it was real that some days I could play better than others, but this wasn't a mere case of simple fact in my mother's eyes. No, it was proof that I was just lazy or stupid. I tried, I really tried, but I never did know what made the not-so-good days not-so-good. If I'd known how to do that, I think, gazing with unseeing eyes at my desk, at the computer screen, I wouldn't be in this mess now.

"I don't remember you ever saying you played the cello before, mate," Alex is scratching his head. "Tessa would have had you play at the nippers' christenings if she'd known that, she likes that sort of thing."

"Yes, well it's funny he's never mentioned it before," Rebecca says to Alex, folding her arms across her chest and swivelling her chair round to glare at me. "I didn't know he could play either, and I've known him for years. Never mentioned it once," her eyes are like sharpened knives ready to strike me down. "You know, even by your warped standards, that's a little bizarre. So come on then, Ewan, do tell. What's all the great secrecy in aid of? I mean, so you play the cello: wow. Since when was there some sort of official secrets act attached to that?"

"It's none of your damned business."

"I'm just asking."

"Well don't. It's got absolutely nothing to do with you. With any of you."

They exchange glances, eyebrows arched.

"There's no need for that," Alex mutters. "We're only asking what everyone else is asking, and it seems to me to be a perfectly legitimate question. But, you know, if you want to be an arse about it, that's fine."

I soften. Perhaps an explanation is appropriate. My remarks were primarily aimed at Rebecca. I've no quarrel with Alex and I don't want to fall out with him, but it's as though I'm cut off from everyone at the moment, and the harder I try to establish normal contact, the worse it becomes.

"I just don't want to talk about it."

"No, no," Alex holds up his hand. "Not interested."

"All right, there's no need to be like that."

"Look, you want to keep stuff to yourself, that's fine. I don't really give a shit," he says, stalking round his desk to the kettle. He looks straight at Rebecca and asks her if she wants a cup of tea. "You?" His voice is cold, and he barely throws me a glance.

I shake my head, smarting. This wasn't how I meant things to go. If Rebecca wasn't here gloating, I might have given him a proper answer. I might have explained, just as I tried to explain to Trudy yesterday. But my ex-wife is poised, ready to pounce at the slightest show of weakness. I can feel her hyena's eyes watching my every move. And now she's getting at my friends, turning them against me. Perhaps she's trying to recruit Alex as another set of eyes to watch me, informing back on my every move. I sit, staring at the computer screen, the atmosphere between the three of us oppressive. It's me who has to move first. I cannot bear their cosy, conspiratorial companionship creeping around me, taunting me, their togetherness amplifying my isolation. The office is getting hotter and hotter. I get up, take my jacket, and lurch out of the door.

I go back down to my classroom. Claire has left her cello. I should ask before I borrow it, but I don't care. I carry it home, and play until my fingers are bleeding, and I can do no more.

Chapter 18

I'm in the kitchen trying to work out what to do with the pulpy, bloody mess that is the tips of my fingers when the doorbell rings. It's Trudy. She has her hands sunk deep in her pockets, and no smile on her face. When she asks if she can come in, it takes me a moment or two before I realise what she means.

"Yes, of course," I hold the door open, thinking how everything has changed since the last time she was here and all I wanted was to peel her clothes off. "Why don't you come through here," I say, indicating the kitchen. "I've just got to find a plaster, and then I'll put the kettle on."

"Why? What have you done?"

I take a step backwards at the tone of her voice. It's laden with both with reproach and the 'no-nonsense' approach of every nurse I've encountered on the few times I've had to take myself to casualty. I put my hand behind my back and tell her it's nothing. She grapples my arm into view, and exclaims at the sight of my bleeding fingers.

"What have you done?"

What have I done? I don't know how to begin to explain. I am so exhausted from the pleasure, the release of playing after all this time, I need to sit down. She guides me into one of my own kitchen chairs, I direct her to the stash of bandages and plasters in the drawer.

"How did you manage to go on playing? I mean, it must have hurt long before you got yourself in this mess."

I laugh, and when she asks just what the hell is funny about this, I point out she's just summed up my life.

"Have you been drinking?"

She picks up the half-empty whisky bottle sitting on the side, waiting along with a new, unopened one, and turns back to me, looking at me as I think she'd look at an injured rabbit she'd hit with her car, dithering over whether to look after it and nurse it back together, or stamp on its head and put an end to its misery.

"Hardly." Not yet anyway. "I'm not used to playing any more." I examine my fingers. "It's been a long time."

"Yes, but to go on playing after your fingers blistered. Ewan, you should have stopped."

"They'll heal. It's not the first time I've damaged them like this."

"You cut your fingers as well?"

"No, no," I hadn't realised she'd draw that conclusion, although I suppose you might say it was the most obvious if you didn't know me. If you couldn't mind-read, I mean. I sigh. It's not in my nature to confess, but I'm prickling with unease over falling out with Alex. My hand has hovered over the telephone countless times before Trudy arrived, but I just couldn't bring myself to make the call. Maybe a little soul-baring will make Trudy think she understands me, and undo the damage done elsewhere.

"It was intentional, but it wasn't part of, you know," I glance into her eyes. "The other thing. There have been times when I've hated my hands so much I could have chopped them off."

"Seriously?" She sits down, threads her fingers through mine, and turns our joined hands over and over as she looks for the scar which will testify my story is true.

"Seriously." I chuckle at her wide eyed horror. She has no idea just how much I mean it, and I was only nine at the time.

School holidays were always difficult for my mother; she didn't know what to do with me. She had to work, of course, not because she couldn't have left the boutique in someone else's hands, she didn't trust anyone with her real baby, 'no one has my eye for detail' the true meaning in her life. Of course, if I had been Stacey, the name she told me she'd chosen expecting me to have been born a girl, it would have been easy. I might have enjoyed being in the shop watching women come and go, rifling through the racks of pretty colours, the myriad of textures and patterns and prints. And I know she would have dressed me up just so, painted my face and styled my hair into a diminutive and prettier version of herself, all wide-eyed innocence dressed up like a tiny tart to wow her customers, but right from the start I had let her down. I was a boy, and boys did not belong in my mother's glossy world.

I remember hearing voices. It was a few days before the long summer holidays, and my mother was in turmoil. Her usual range of childminders to whom I'd be shuttled, bleary eyed in the pale light of morning while luckier school children slumbered beyond their usual wakening time, were unavailable. Mrs Fitzpatrick, the favoured childminder with her own fierce clan of five noisy, boisterous children, had fallen downstairs, and couldn't have me round. Everyone else was booked up. I hadn't long been sent to bed when I heard my parents arguing, their raised voices echoing up the stairs. I crept out of my bedroom and onto the landing to listen, taking care to avoid the squeaky floorboard that lurked just outside my room.

"You'll have to take him,' she was saying. 'I'm busy and he just gets in my way. Oh, damn Mrs Fitzpatrick and her wretched accident. I don't see why she still can't have him. She doesn't have to do anything, he can look after himself."

"Then why don't you just leave him here?"

"Don't be silly Graham. You know what he's like. He'll probably go and mess around in the sitting room. Besides, he's only nine. I'm not sure it's legal. This is so inconvenient, why can't you have him?"

'For god's sake Margot, what am I supposed to do with him? He can't come to work with me. What do you think, there's a bloody playroom in my office?'

They argued, passing me back and forward, each lambasting the other for not wanting the inconvenience of being lumbered with me. I was familiar with these quarrels, they often flared over what to do with me at weekends when both of my parents wanted to be with their separate bands of friends, and I was 'such a nuisance'. They'd no idea how hard I tried, but it was only ever 'why can't you do this, why can't you do that, and why can't you just do as you're told?' I crept back to my room and back under my duvet, hugging my scrawny knees to my chest. If they'd caught me listening, that would have been wrong too.

The next morning when I came downstairs for breakfast, my mother was singing along to the radio in the kitchen, her slim hips shimmying as she danced around the kitchen table. I stood in the doorway and watched in awe. She had a marvellous voice. In church I sometimes pretended to sing, for the sake of appearances, while listening to her trilling, her voice soaring like an angel's, high above the drone of the other mere mortals. And I loved to see her like this, her sparkly happiness spreading twinkling fairy dust shimmering through the air.

"Darling," she danced over to me, caught my hands, and twirled me around the room. I laughed; her happiness was so infectious it filled me with its energy. She bent down and put her face next to mine. "Guess what?" I couldn't guess, so I went on smiling a floppy, daft smile. "You're going to Grandma Felicity's for the whole summer."

The whole summer? I did a little dance of my own. Grandma Felicity was my favourite out of my two grannies, and she lived in a castle on Skye. It wasn't like a castle you see in books, but a rambling old mansion, various wings added from time to time through history depending upon the fortunes of my mother's family as they navigated the treacherous tides of Scottish politics. The oldest part's roof was edged with crow's steps, the nearest thing it had to battlements, and I loved being there. Grandma Felicity had a story for every occasion, rooms full of stuffed animals, crumbling costumes, ancient weapons and an amazing library in which I loved to curl up in the tatty green leather seat she said was my grandfather's favourite, beside the huge stone fireplace and read for hours on end. I could not have dreamed up a more perfect summer, had I tried. Good old Mrs. Fitzpatrick: I could not believe my luck.

My grandmother had a routine. In the morning, we'd go out in her creaking old Landrover, maybe to the village, or over to Portree, and we'd come back past the beach to look for seals bobbing in the water, or, she said, if I was lucky, a glimpse of a basking shark or whale passing. Then, after lunch, she would take a nap whilst I read or played by myself. And later, she would sit and listen while I practiced my cello. There was a competition, a recital, in September and my mother had decided I would win this year 'after all the money I've spent on your musical education'. Furthermore, one of the judges had connections to the conservatoire in Paris. My mother already had her eye on a place there for me, and I didn't dare to think of the consequences if I let her down.

It was a beautiful day, the swallows swooping, chattering around the castle and up into the cloudless blue sky, and I decided to read outside. I pattered down the castle's stone steps, crunched across the gravel drive and went off across the mossy, springy lawn with my book until I reached the cool sanctuary of the ancient bench that sheltered under an enormous redwood, a specimen one of our ancestors had brought back from America. The book was from the castle's library, a ripping yarn of knights and daring deeds, and I was soon engrossed, oblivious to the afternoon passing, until a sudden sound, a twig snapping, jolted me back into reality.

I kept very still, only daring to take tiny breaths through my mouth, my heart thumping. Mrs McLeod, the housekeeper, had been telling my grandmother at breakfast about 'the beast', some creature slaughtering sheep on a neighbouring estate. Grandma Felicity had taken one glance at my gawping face, and shooed away the story with a snort of disbelief, but now I wasn't sure she should have been so dismissive. A second twig snapped, and I startled to my feet.

"Who's there?"

"Put your hands up soldier, you're surrounded."

This was reminiscent of being back at Mrs Fitzpatrick's in Aberdeen, where, as the weediest kid, I was usually pressed into being the prisoner, no matter the game. Since experience had taught me to do as I was told, I duly raised my hands. The branches of the rhododendrons nearest my seat parted, and a grubby girl swamped in combat gear, the legs and sleeves rolled up to fit, her brown hair bristling with leaves and twigs ruffling out of a ponytail as she held a gun shaped stick trained at my head, a look of murderous intent grim on her tanned face. I stared, my mouth wide open.

"Give your name and rank, soldier."

"I'm not a soldier," I protested, keeping my arms up. "I'm just reading."

"Well are you with us, or against us? I must warn you though, if you're not with us, I will have to kill you. Step away from the bench, and kneel down. No, not like that," she put the stick down, took hold of my arm, and dragged me back onto my feet. "You're supposed to say 'you'll never take me alive', do this," she demonstrated a couple a karate-style kicks, "and escape through there." She pointed back into the bushes. "Do it again."

She repeated her threats, I stammered my line, and made a half-hearted move for the bushes. But she let out such a savage, whooping war cry, it fired my blood with a rush of excitement and alarm, and I crashed off through the branches with my attacker at my heels. We ran together through the woods. I found my own gun-shaped stick and, by the time we heard grown-up voices calling us from the castle, Molly McLeod and I had become firm friends.

As we jogged back up to the castle, Grandma Felicity was outside on the gravel, using her stick to point out something in the flowerbed to her housekeeper. As we approached, she turned round, and her face cracked along its lines into a delighted smile. Mrs McLeod's mouth fell open and her powdered face paled.

"Molly!" She squawked. My new friend hung her head and rubbed her sandaled toes against the stones. "What on earth have you done?" Her mouth opened to chastise her youngest daughter, only Grandma Felicity put her hand on the housekeeper's arm, and took a few wobbling steps towards me.

"Well now, what have we here?" She looked me up and down, chuckling. I glanced down. The knees of my jeans, the ones my mother had bought from a store during her trip to see fashion shows in New York, were green and crusted with mud. My shirt and its matching cashmere jumper were equally dirty, and had bits of leaves and twigs sticking out of the fabric. I looked up at Grandma Felicity, biting my lip, my eyes shining with the tears at the prospect of the expected scolding, but she didn't look cross. In fact she was laughing, her milky grey eyes glistening with delight.

"Have you had a good afternoon getting up to mischief with young Molly? It certainly looks like it."

"Mrs Mackenzie, I'm so sorry," the housekeeper stuttered, her face blazing with colour. "I'll sort Molly out, I promise. It won't happen again."

"Hush Aggie," Grandma Felicity said. "This is just what the boy needs; someone to play with. All this nonsense about spending so much time practicing music and keeping himself clean and tidy; he needs to be out here running wild in the woods, climbing trees and getting into scrapes, not spending hours on end reading about other people having fun. I'll never understand your mother," she said to me, reaching out a craggy, gnarled finger to trace a line of dirt Molly had painted across my face for camouflage. "This is precisely the sort of thing she used to get up to at your age."

I tried very hard, but I couldn't imagine my mother looking like Molly.

As the summer wore on, I think I spent more time with Molly and her family, than I did with Grandma Felicity. To keep my mother happy, Mrs. McLeod gave me some old clothes that belonged to Molly's brothers so I could get as muddy as I liked and it wouldn't matter. Molly and I played in the woods, we had picnics, we went fishing for crabs with her father who laughed when I couldn't get the hang of the fishing tackle and showed me over and over again until I could, we even camped out in a smelly, mouldy old tent, telling each other ghost stories until long after it had gone dark. And my grandmother was right; I felt like one of the characters in my books, getting suntanned and strong, having fun and being free.

We were trying to build a campfire one afternoon when it started to rain. The air had been growing heavy all day, thick and chewy with a threatening storm. At the first rumble of thunder, Molly squealed. We decided to take shelter in the castle, to see if her mother had baked anything good we might sample, and were racing to see who could be the fastest, when I stopped, dread clawing in my stomach. There was a sleek dark green car outside the castle: my mother's car.

Molly was shrieking with laughter, goading me for stopping, but even she fell quiet when she turned to see what I was looking at, and saw the tall figure in a dress towering over my grandmother, waving. I thought about pretending I hadn't seen her and running back into the safety of the woods, but the rain had begun, big fat drops plopping down harder and harder until, with an enormous crash of thunder, I pelted after Molly, charging up into the shelter of the castle.

"You mustn't stay outside in a thunderstorm," my grandmother scolded. "And especially not under the trees." But her words bounced past me. All I could see was my mother's painted mouth stretched wide in a silent screech of horror as her eyes took in my dishevelled, dirty state, her top lip curling with disgust. It had been weeks since I'd seen her. I took a few tentative steps towards her, going in for a hug, but she stepped out of my way, holding her hands up out of my reach.

"Good god, look at the state of him. Mother," she growled, but Grandma Felicity held up her hands.

"Now then Margot, don't get started. He's been having a lot of fun playing with young Molly, haven't you dear? It's just what he needs."

"Just what he needs?" My mother repeated, her hands on her hips, towering over us all. "Just what he needs? I can't believe you've let him run wild when what he needs is to be careful he doesn't break a finger or something. What if he'd hurt one of his hands and couldn't play his cello?" And to me she snapped "get your things. You're coming home with me. Oh and make sure you leave those, those," she looked me up and down, her glare scalding me with shame as she searched for the right word, "revolting clothes behind. And wash your hands, you are a disgrace."

I caught Molly's eye. The rest of my mother's words flowed by my ears unheard, shut out by the delicious idea welling up in my mind. We understood each other so well by this point, that when I charged down the hall towards the kitchen, she followed.

"She's going to take you home," Molly said. "What shall we do, hide? We could camp down on the beach, no one will think of looking for us there."

"I've got a better idea," I whispered. "A much better idea. But we need to go back to your house. Do you still have your wood knife?"

She nodded. Molly's grandfather had given her a knife and taught her to whittle. She had shown me, although my clumsy attempt to copy the robin she'd made out of off cuts from the timber of a beech tree her grandfather had felled on the estate was laughable. The knife was kept in a special tin in her bedroom. We ran there through the rain.

"What are you going to do?" She asked as we shut her bedroom door to fend off her brothers' queries as to what we two weirdos were doing now.

"Did you hear what she said?" I whispered in case anyone was listening at the door. "If I hurt my hand I can't play my cello. Well if I can't play my cello, there's no point her taking me back to Aberdeen. She doesn't like having me around in the holidays because she's got to go to work," I explained. "If I hurt my hand, then I can stay here. It's brilliant."

Molly chewed over my plan, and gave a solemn nod.

"How are you going to hurt your hand? Do you want me to stamp on it?"

"No. It might not work. But if I cut the tips of my fingers," I held up my left hand, "I won't be able to press down the strings, so I won't have to go home. Where's your knife?"

It had seemed like such a brilliant plan. We crouched together on Molly's floor, I took the knife, counted to three, and sliced deep into my middle three fingers, and she groaned in horror. Nothing happened for a moment, but just when I was wondering if I hadn't cut deep enough, crimson blood began welling up and out of the wounds. I watched, enthralled: it was amazing. But I hadn't expected so much blood, and I didn't know what to do. Molly gave another strangled groan, and rolled over onto her side with a thump. I was shouting at her to help, but she didn't move. It wasn't until Fergus, her eldest brother came to investigate that I realised she had fainted.

Fergus marched me back up the castle. My mother took one look at my fingers, turned on her heel and marched out. I heard the wheels of her car spinning, sending the gravel spraying as she left. Hot tears spilled down my face as I looked to Grandma Felicity for support. But she was staring at me, her thin lips pulled tight with reproach.

"Did you do it on purpose?"

"I don't want to go home," I mumbled through my tears, staring down at the white bandages wound round my fingers. Mrs. McLeod said I needed stitches. I imagined a doctor sticking a huge silver needle through my fingers and felt my head swim. "I don't want to play cello, I want to stay here with you, Grandma Felicity."

"Well then," she said, holding my head and making me look right into her eyes. "Let it be a lesson to you, boy. This wasn't the way to ask."

"She doesn't listen," I snivelled through my tears, but by this point Grandma Felicity wasn't listening either, she was wobbling out of the room with her stick.

It was easy for her to say that, I thought, because she didn't know how much my mother wouldn't listen to me. She didn't understand. My mother came back later that afternoon, packed my things, ordered me into the car, and ignored me all the way home. She drove away, refusing to ever speak to my grandmother again. They never made up, and Grandma Felicity died not long after. I still miss her. She loved pottering around her gardens on Skye, pouring over catalogues of seeds and drawing endless diagrams of how she wanted her flowerbeds planted. I wish I could show her around my garden; she would be thrilled to see what I've done.

I break off, shaken. My eyes study the white gauze wrapped around my throbbing fingers, and for a moment, I am so conscious of how much of myself I have exposed, I can't look at Trudy. When I dig deep enough for the courage, I look into her soft brown eyes, and find nothing there other than the gentle glow of understanding. I let out the breath I have been holding.

"That's quite a story," she says, squeezing my hand.

"I've never told anyone before."

"Why not?"

I shake my head. There were a lot of things I don't tell people, things I keep locked away in the dark because they are too frightening for even me to see, and I was there when they happened.

She sighs, and threads her fingers through mine, smoothing my pallid, wrinkling skin as though this has the power to soothe away the hurt. I watch as she lifts my hand to her lips, and presses the gentlest kiss. But I am shaking. I want her to love me, I want her to hold me tight and care for me, to be a safe haven in a cold and uncaring world, but this is getting out of hand. First, I can't keep my distance around her, and then she persuades me to confide in her things I have told no one. I want her, but I'm afraid to have her too close. The real me is a monster, despicable and undeserving. And I know, just like Rebecca, it is only a matter of time before she realises this.

Her eyes glance up at the clock.

"You know, I'm going to have to go in a minute. Are your fingers hurting? Do you have some painkillers?"

I tell her I do, and there's no need to worry. She fusses over me, saying I should have my fingers dressed again tomorrow, that she'll come and do it for me if I want. But as she's talking, I see a beetle scuttle across the draining board behind her head. I try not to look, but she follows my eyes and turns round.

"What is it?"

""I thought I saw a cat at the window," I say the first thing which comes to mind. She turns back and studies me with an appraising eye. I look down at the table.

"A cat, or someone watching you?"

Actually, it was a beetle, I think but don't say. I can hear the scratching and scuffling again, the sound echoing from inside the wall. I bite my lip and look at Trudy, but she seems oblivious. It's probably just as well. I don't want her to think my house is infested.

She says she'd better go, gets up, and slips her coat around her shoulders. I follow her out into the hall, but there is something different about her, something missing.

"Oh, my scarf. I think I've left it on the table."

I pop back into the kitchen, and there it is, a green scarf flecked with pink sequins. Hidden by the door, I bury my nose in its soft fabric, and breathe in the warm, delicious scent of Trudy. I wish she could stay.

In the hallway, she is standing with her back to me, flicking through something on the hall table. Hearing my footsteps, she turns round.

"Ewan, what is this?" She holds up my diary.

"Um, it's private," I say, going to take it out of her hands, but she hides it behind her back. Damn. You know, the whole of one wall in my front room is shelved to house my music collection, why couldn't she have spotted that? We could be talking about something far more interesting, and I could be digging out albums she might like to borrow.

"Oh, is it? So who's this 'Vi', and why are you so worried about her?"

My shoulders tense. I'm still not sure I can trust Trudy. I think she's safe, but I haven't found out a way to tell.

"My neighbour. She's watching me. I think she knows that I know about all the stuff that's going on."

"What stuff?" Trudy asks, and then thinks better of it. "No, what I mean is this seems like a lot for you to deal with. Have you ever thought of showing your diary to anyone, Ewan?" I look up. She is watching me, her dark eyes soft and gentle in her calm face, soothing away my worries with one cool, unflappable glance.

"Like who? I mean, you're reading it. Doesn't that count?"

"No, I just wonder if there's someone you could show it to, someone you trust, that's all. I mean, this is a lot of stuff, a lot of responsibility for you to have to shoulder alone. What about your GP, could he help do you think?

I consider the idea of Dr. Sanderson sitting in his chair, hands clasped beneath his chin, nodding and saying 'go on' while I lay bare everything which has been troubling me for weeks. The last time that happened, Rebecca did all of the talking and I haven't forgotten the way he sat there smiling encouragement while she spilled out her archives of my 'bizarre behaviour', as she put it, smiling and nodding, the whole time his dark eyes probing mine, his gaze worming ever deeper until I felt as though he was peering around in my head himself.

"I know you won't like me saying this," she says, putting the book aside. "But Rod is a friend of mine. Roderick," she explains when I stare back, no idea to whom she's referring, although I startle at the clarification. "I talked to him about what happened yesterday, and he says you can go in and chat to him any time. You could just have a quiet word with him to see if there's anyone he knows who might be able to help you with this. It would be safe," she says, silencing my instant protest by raising her voice. "I know you have mixed feelings about him, but you can trust him."

Trust him? The image of Roderick standing here, standing right here in my hallway, my precious book in his hands, sends a cold shudder rippling down my back. I look at Trudy with fresh eyes. She's mentioned him as a friend from work before. I must try harder to remember this. His intervention is the sort of help I could do without.

Chapter 19

No amount of whisky stops me from me fretting all night about what Trudy's said to Roderick Henderson, and by the time morning drags itself along, one thing is clear. I mustn't have anything more to do with her, and I must tell her as soon as is possible. I rehearse the message I must leave her over and over again, but I'm too afraid to pick up the telephone and before I know it, it is time to go to work.

I steal upstairs and into the office long before Alex or Rebecca arrive, and sit at my desk, my mobile phone in my hand, going over and over the message I've been composing. The room is swaying; I seem more hungover than usual. My fingers are trembling, so it takes me longer than usual to type my message, I keep hitting the wrong key. Trudy, look, think things are getting out of hand, can we just be friends? I read it through, over and over again. It says exactly what I want it to say, and although pressing 'send' has my conscience walking away in disgust, it is a way out of my predicament without the risk of being drawn into any further conversation. I have said enough to Trudy. She's getting too close. It's no good.

Voices approach, Alex and Rebecca. I gulp, and send the message, breaking out into a fresh hot sweat at their imminent arrival. That's another thing I've been rehearsing, although I'd prefer not to make my apology in front of Rebecca. But I am resolved. The weirdness and lack of self-control of the last few weeks is over. Today I am taking charge. The door opens. I shamble to my feet, but stumble and come close to sprawling over the end of the desk.

"Ewan? Are you okay?"

I am about to yell 'why the hell does everyone have to keep asking me that', when I remember I'm supposed to be apologising to Alex, not making everything worse. Taking charge, I remind myself. Staying in control.

"Alex, Rebecca, I've thought long and hard about what happened yesterday, and I'd like to apologise unreservedly for my rudeness. I didn't mean to be rude, but it was like in that film er, what was it called?" I rub my sweating face, my rehearsed speech darting ahead and leaving my tongue flapping in its wake. That's not funny, I shout after it. I'm trying to make everything better here, and you're not helping. Oi, get back here now. Damn it, I can't remember what I was going to say now. "Oh, I can't think. Doesn't matter. I just wanted to say that I never meant to be rude. I didn't mean to cause any sort of offence. I never set out to offend anyone, only I never set out to be in that position in the first place, only I never meant to be rude and, oh damn it, I'm sorry. Do you want a cup of tea?"

It's hard to say whose face is the most shocked, Alex or Rebecca. They're both staring at me, eyes wide and mouths hanging open. I look from face to face, a nervous giggle bubbling up into my mouth.

"What? What is it? What are you looking at me like that for?"

"I'm not being funny mate," Alex says. He puts a hand on my shoulder, leans in close, and sniffs. "Have you been drinking or something?"

"What?" Why on earth would he think that? I look again from face to face, panic rising in my chest at the thought he's making a joke and I don't understand. But neither is laughing.

"Yeah, he's been drinking, haven't you Ewan? You're such a loser. It won't be long now," Rebecca says in my head. She kept saying this over and over again last night, *'it won't be long'* until I lost all control and screamed and screamed at her to stop. It didn't work. I wound up smashing one of my crystal tumblers. Stupid, I know, but I was so desperate to make her stop, I threw it at the wall.

"You're not making a lot of sense," Rebecca says, shaking her head. She's staring at me as she might stare at something particularly nasty, cells infected with bubonic plague multiplying under a microscope. "And you look awful. Are you feeling all right?"

"Why the hell does everyone have to keep on asking me if I'm feeling all right?"

"All right mate. Don't start getting uppity again," Alex says, holding up his hands. He heads behind his desk, edging sideways as though I might attack if he takes his eyes off me for a second.

"I am not getting uppity." This isn't how I planned this conversation; this isn't how it's meant to be going. But it's as though I'm the only one who bothered to read the script. I'm supposed to say sorry, Alex then laughs at the thought I took his being offended so seriously, and Rebecca? Well, she's meant to stand there quietly, rehearsing how she's going to tell me she's decided Thatchington High isn't the school for her, and she's moving on. I'll write her a glowing reference, really I will.

"Look, why don't you sit down, I'll put the kettle on," Rebecca says, still getting it wrong.

"No," I shove her out of the way to get to the kettle. "I'll do it." I'm making the drinks. I know what she's up to. They've told her to drug my tea to bring me back under their control. Well, no one is putting anything in my tea, not while I'm watching. I'm taking charge, staying in control. Damn, but it's so hot in here. I wipe my face on my sleeve. My phone picks this moment to ring, startling me into the air. I try to ignore Alex and Rebecca's repeated exchange of looks, and pull it out of my pocket. It's Trudy. Damn and damn again.

"Trudy, I can't talk now. I'm at work. No, I'll call you later. What do you mean? You'll call me and then we'll what? What do you mean I'm not making sense? Will everyone just stop bloody-well asking me if I'm all right?" I shriek from behind clenched teeth. "I said I'm doing it," I snarl, blocking Rebecca as she tries to sneak past me to doctor my tea. I know what's going on here. They're all in it together.

"That's enough," Alex tries to intervene. "Is that Trudy? Give me the phone." He's so much bigger than me, and stronger, even before I lost weight. He snatches the phone out of my hand as though he were taking a toy off a toddler.

"Trudy? It's Alex. Look, do you have any idea what's going on with him? Yeah, I must admit we're wondering if he's been drinking too. What's that? No, I don't think he's very well either."

"Oh for god's sake, that's it. I've had enough." I take my jacket and storm out of the office. All I wanted to do was apologise, and I have no idea what went wrong. I surge down the stairs, shoving my way through throngs of children piling in off the buses, heading for my classroom. I haven't been in there for more than five minutes before Mrs Phillips appears, alerted by my so-called friends.

She knocks first. It's such a contrast to her normal method of barging in, I'm sniggering as she peers around the door. Sat at my desk, my classroom cool with the windows open, I have composed myself, anticipating this audience. She is all softness and sympathy as she asks me if I'm all right, and I manage not to bristle at the question. I point out I haven't been drinking, I've had something of a misunderstanding with my colleagues, and I'm tired, that's all. My performance must be a good portrayal of 'normal', as she doesn't linger or say anything beyond suggesting perhaps I need an early night. Ah, an early night. If only such a simple thing had the power to make everything better, I'd dedicate the rest of my life to the pursuit of 'early nights'.

The first lesson goes well, and the second. In fact I'm congratulating myself on how well the morning is going, given its dubious start. But unease is never far from my mind, spanner in hand, ready to tighten the tension in my body. One minute everything is in chaos, the next, innocent and calm, and I don't like it. I shiver. The chaos is beginning to lengthen, and it's threatening to take over. Still, the morning wears on, and I manage to keep going. Everything will be all right, I tell myself over and over. I am all right.

And I am all right. Everything holds up well until after lunch. I spend the morning and lunch breaks in my cupboard, with the door locked to deter anyone searching me out. Its order is soothing. It reassures me that no matter how frightening I'm finding the rest of the world, there are no beetles or plots in my cupboard, just me and my shelves. For an hour or so, I am happy.

After lunch, I'm listening to my year seven class performing compositions I'd asked them to prepare in small groups. They've tried hard, although their tuneless efforts vary in degrees of painful discord.

I'm sitting at my desk, my head propped on one elbow, listening. The classroom is very hot, despite my having opened all the windows, much to the chagrin of my pupils. They sit shivering and moaning, but I can't understand what all the fuss is about. I sit, the music drifting through my ears. It's quite cool in the cupboard, now I think about it. I'd like to be in there right now.

Scuffling startles my calm. I keep very still. Movement catches my eye. I half sit up. Three boys are performing, making a squeaking, screeching racket with recorders, but I'm not hearing them. My heart is thumping. Something has just fallen off the ceiling. It's one of the beetles, and the biggest I've seen.

I stare at it. It's not real, I tell myself. I shut my eyes, squeeze them tight shut, but when I open them, it's still there. It landed on the line of desks that face mine, and as I watch, it begins to move. It doesn't scurry, scuttling from dark hiding place to dark hiding place, it saunters, its nasty barbed legs moving, almost hypnotic. I stare. I'm too afraid to breathe. And as I watch, it clambers over the hand of the girl facing me. I don't know how she can bear to sit so still.

"Mr. Davies? Mr. Davies?" I blink. I realise she is almost shouting at me, but I'm still staring at the beetle moving on her hand. How can she possibly have not noticed it? "Mr. Davies, are you all right Sir? You don't look right."

I look at her in horror, wondering why she's not bothered about the beetle, and why she's doing the 'are you all right' thing too. And a voice speaks. I hear it loud and clear.

"God, he is so lame. I wish we had Mrs Cartwright, don't you?"

"Who said that?" I leap up out of my seat, fists clenched at my sides, shaking with the strength of my fury. "Who spoke? Come on."

The whole class cower, heads bowed, bodies sinking down in their chairs, no one daring to meet my eye. I storm up and down the classroom, ready to savage whichever of the little brats it was who spoke, who dared to speak and wish for Rebecca. No one speaks to me like that. No one behaves like that in my classroom. We have discipline and order in here, my version of order, not the touchy-feely hippy nonsense Rebecca's so fond of embracing.

A tiny, quivering voice speaks up, its owner, the girl whose desk faces mine, trembling on the verge of tears.

"You were looking a bit funny like you weren't very well, Mr. Davies. I just asked if you were feeling all right."

I stare at her. But as I stare, it's not a schoolgirl looking back, but Marcia in her flowery, yellow jumpsuit, an insouciant smile loitering on her plump pink lips.

"Hello Ewan."

I clamp my hands over my mouth to smother the scream, and stagger backwards. The door's handle jabs into my spine. I whip round, wrench it open, and rush out. My cupboard: that's where I'm going. It's the only place I feel safe.

I open the door. There's no one in here. I listen, but I can't hear any scuffling, so I slip inside. The safest place is to be tucked up onto a shelf where nothing can get at me. I slide into a space, and press my cheek against the cool wooden shelf. It is safe in here. And no one knows I'm here.

Time loses meaning while I'm curled up on my shelf, hugging my knees in the comforting dark. Then I hear footsteps. The door is thrown open and light contaminates the dark shelves.

"Ewan, are you in here?"

I see Rebecca's feet, a flowery skirt flapping around her legs as she moves. She walks past, and for a moment I think I have succeeded in making myself invisible, only her feet halt, retrace their steps, and the next thing I see is her face peering at me where I'm lying curled up on the shelf.

"Ewan, what the hell are you doing?"

"Nothing," I say, amazed at how my voice is behaving itself so well it sounds almost calm: almost. "I'm just looking for something."

"What?" She squawks, but another raucous volley emits from my classroom smothering anything else she might have to say. I watch her scowl and tut. She gets up, sweeps through to my classroom, and uses that voice even I know not to defy. Silence descends, disturbed only by the sound of her swishing back into the cupboard. You know, she's very good. If I was Fiona Phillips, I'd be thinking about giving her my job too. I swing my legs over the side, and try to sit up. The cupboard shifts and spins, lurching from side to side.

"What the hell is wrong with you?" She's crouching down, glaring into my face, but I can barely find the strength to sit up, never mind meet her eyes. "What are you doing lying on the shelves? I heard you shouting. The kids say you went nuts."

Did I? I'm not really sure. My head has begun to throb, and I rub my forehead with a clammy hand. It comes away wet. I hold it at arm's length and examine its gleaming surface. Strange. I don't feel hot enough any more to be sweaty. And what was I doing? I'm not sure. Maybe I bumped my head or something. I really can't remember.

"You think you bumped your head? I don't think you're very well," Rebecca says, assuming her favourite role by taking charge. "Come on," she takes hold of my arm, and tries to pull me to my feet. "Let's get you out of here, somewhere quiet where you can lie down."

I was somewhere quiet where I could lie down, I try to protest, but I haven't the strength to fight against her. There is a shocked hush as she leads me back past my classroom, as twenty-two young mouths fall open, bearing witness to my downfall. Rebecca barks instructions for them to get on with their work, but no amount of threats can undermine the novelty of seeing me struggling to put one foot past the other, hanging on to my ex-wife as though she alone can save me. At another command from Rebecca, one of them gets up to shut the door. I go to mouth my thanks, but as I look up, it's not one of my pupils holding open the door: it's Marcia.

Rebecca shoos me into the school's sickroom, spins on her heel and goes off in search of the Head, leaving Monica on guard. There is a small bed and a chair, but I am too jittery to sit down. I pace the floor, my teeth chattering at the shock of finding Marcia alive and well in my classroom. Monica watches, chewing gum. She asks if I want a cup of tea, but she must know she is the last person I would trust with such a task. I wind my fingers together, entwining them round and round like Rebecca does, to see if it helps me feel any calmer. It doesn't.

As always, I hear Mrs. Phillips before I see her. She thanks Monica, steps into the room with Rebecca at her heels, and shuts the door. I'm backed into the furthest corner, the walls cool and solid against my back. It isn't until I realise both women are staring that I realise I'm still contorting and twisting my hands. I must keep still. It doesn't look right if I can't keep still. I have to behave as though everything is all right, otherwise they might think they've already won. With my pupils now conspiring against me, it feels as though my position here is pouring away through the gaps between my fingers.

"You're not well, are you Ewan?" Mrs. Phillips says in a soft voice honeyed with concern. "I think you should go home. Nathan can give you a lift. He's not doing anything important at the moment."

"I don't need to go home."

I wrap my arms around my body to hide my trembling hands from their judging eyes. Everything will be all right. I just need a bit of quiet to pull myself together, to gather up the shards of my shattered composure. A cup of tea, maybe with a spoonful of sugar in it: that's what I need. I've got some marking and stuff to do, I can just go and sit quietly in my office and get on with that. Besides, there is no way I'm getting in a car with Nathan at the wheel.

"I think you need a few days off," the Head folds her arms. "We all know how hard you work. And once we move into the Christmas term, you'll be busier still with concerts looming and the exams coming up in January. I'd rather you had time off now and get yourself back on your feet than to be unwell when we really need you."

"I'm not 'unwell'," I say, but I'm not sure who I'm trying to convince, her or me.

"Rebecca can mind the reins, and give you a chance to relax. In any case, it's time you started giving her more things to do."

Oh yeah, she'd like that, wouldn't she?

"I don't need time off," I say from behind clenched teeth, but Mrs Phillips isn't listening. She has turned to Rebecca, who's all smiles and nods, satisfaction her prize is within her grasp a cold clear light gleaming in her eyes. Why won't the Head listen? This always happens to me. I'm trying to be heard, but the women in my life are never listening, so caught up in their own damned forgone conclusions it's as though I am trapped behind soundproofed glass and no matter what I try, I am doomed to be forever ignored.

"It would be good for me to take some of the load off your shoulders, Ewan."

Rebecca's cool tones chill me to the core. Her plans are coming together and there's nothing I can do but watch from behind my glass.

"I keep saying you need to delegate. Del-e-gate," she smiles. "I only want to help."

"And you look tired," the Head says. "I've been saying that all term." She's beaming smiles although I don't know why she's bothering to try and disguise their conniving plans to get rid of me. It's too late for that. I know exactly what's going on. And I'm not taking time off. I'm not giving in and handing them everything they want. What's more, I'll fight them through every bloody tribunal in the land before they force me to give up my job.

Mrs Phillips sighs. She folds her arms ever tighter. Rebecca is staring at me, shaking her head, her mouth hanging open and even her freckles paling.

"That isn't what's going on here," she says, her voice small and calm, a lighthouse flickering amid the tempest of the darkest, most ferocious winter storm.

"No one is trying to force you out of your job." That's strange; Mrs. Phillips is using the same voice too. "But if you aren't well enough to be here, I will have to insist you take time off."

"I am well enough."

"Your class reports you were behaving strangely and you were found hiding in a cupboard," she says, and she cocks one eyebrow. "Need I say any more?"

My mouth opens to deny everything, but as I'm staring at the two women, movement catches my eye. Don't move Ewan; it's my voice now talking in my head. Perhaps it is what they call 'the voice of reason', whatever that means. Just keep very still and calm. I try to pretend it's not there, but the gleaming black beetle skitters up over the surface of Mrs. Phillips's smooth blonde hair, and as I watch, cringing with horror, it burrows down and disappears into her head.

"What's the matter now?"

"It's nothing," I say, not daring to take my eyes off the top of her head. "You know, perhaps you're right. I haven't been feeling too well this afternoon. Perhaps I will go home." It might be safer there.

She's frowning at me, her mouth a thin, straight line, but all I can do is marvel at her self-control. I can't understand how she can be so cool and calm with that thing trying to burrow into her head. But perhaps this is the ultimate proof the beetles and the authorities' plots are connected. She isn't bothered by the beetle because she's one of their agents. It won't bite, won't attack her, because it's me they're after. I shudder. I'm so preoccupied, I don't realise she's started talking to me again until Rebecca speaks up and snares my attention.

"Ewan."

I look at her in surprise. What does she want now, for god's sake?

"I would feel better if I thought you were going to go and have a chat with your GP," the Head says. "Which surgery do you use? Monica can ring and see if we can get you an appointment. I really think it would be for the best."

How dare she? I'm perfectly capable of making myself an appointment, I point out. All this overreaction: being a little tired hasn't rendered me incapable of looking after myself. I will go home because I'm sick of all their insinuations. No, I do not want anyone to ring for a damned taxi. I will walk home because the fresh air will do me good, and I will be back in the morning. Their shoddy show of fabricated concern irritates me into indignation, and I flounce out of the sickroom ready to march home without another moment's delay.

As I walk and the school grows smaller and smaller behind me, something becomes so obvious, I'm blind to any other thoughts and stupefied it hasn't occurred to me before. There is only one way to thwart their plans to get rid of me, and that is to be more in control of myself. I need to sort myself out, and take charge. It's no good the way things have been going on. I know exactly what I need: sleep, something to eat, and to stop drinking so much. Then I will be able to hold my head up, face up to what's happening, and keep them, Vi, Rebecca, Mrs Phillips, at bay. I can do this, I know. I can survive any plot to bring me down. I know this for certain; I know it as well as I know myself.

I've done it before.

Chapter 20

The first problem, I conclude as I walk along the pavement, is my lack of sleep. Nothing would seem so bad if I could only sleep. To have one, just one single night wrapped in the bliss of a whole, uninterrupted sleep, to clamber, sober, into my soft, warm bed and slumber through the darkness, adrift from the tiresome, ceaseless babble of my thoughts, to journey through sleep and to beach at last on the welcoming shores of a gentle, sunlit dawn; is that really too much to ask? I long for this respite with such a hunger, it is as though every cell in my body is crying out with need, hoarse voices joining together, rising, twining round and round and merging into one loud, wild, unworldly shriek 'I need sleep'. I'm tired of this. I'm tired of the voices, the worries blending into sound, endless white noise screaming between the ordinary sounds of the world moving around me. I need to switch it off. I need to take charge.

Trouble sleeping? Giant red letters jump out of my memory. They skitter around, delighted, I'm sure, to be remembered, all gleeful and bright before they settle themselves in order on a white page, on an orange wall surrounded by other posters advising patients about travel immunisations and alcoholism help lines and diabetes and how to have a healthy heart. Trouble sleeping? Talk to your GP.

Hmm. Maybe I should make an appointment.

I see myself sat in the soft, black leather chair, Dr Sanderson nodding as I confide in him, his soft thoughtful eyes leaching soothing sympathy before he hands me a prescription to make everything better. The prospect dangles before me, pouting, smoothing skilled hands over voluptuous hips with a lascivious wink. Yes, that's what I want. All I have to do is make one telephone call and I can bathe in the benign, cool waters of medical expertise. But memory raises its head with a gasp of disbelief, and I banish the good doctor with a gulp.

What am I doing?

In my experience, there is no such thing as 'benign' medical expertise, but it's got me thinking. I wonder if I can buy something to help me sleep; I hadn't thought about it before.

The pharmacy's stiff wooden door has a bell which almost falls off under the force I have to use to shove the door open. It opens suddenly, sending me floundering into the shop under my own momentum. The shop assistant looks up. She is one of my former pupils, a beautiful girl, her enormous eyes widening from behind her mask of makeup. Damn. I wish I hadn't come in.

"Hello Mr. Davies, Sir. How are you?"

Why does everyone keep asking me how I am? It's like they've all got together and decided they must ask me, and ask me again, just in case. No, that's silly. She's just being polite, that's all. She always was a nice girl.

"I'm very well Alicia, thank you. I didn't know you worked in here."

"Been working in here since I left school." She looks around the shop, slowly nodding, as though this is the first time she's seen it and she's trying to decide if she likes it. "I like it, it's a good job. Now, how can I help?"

"Um," I am not discussing my problems with a former pupil. I think about asking for the pharmacist, but they might talk about me after I've gone. My eyes see the selves behind Alicia. "Just some paracetemol please Alicia."

Yes, I am pathetic.

I leave the shop clutching a little packet of chemicals which couldn't begin to fathom the depth of pain I feel inside. As I walk out, the prospect of sleep seeps away, soaking down into the ground as though it never existed.

I carry on down the street. It's all right Ewan. So you couldn't get anything to help you sleep. Probably wouldn't have worked anyway, you know what these things are like, pretty bottles promising the world but they're just a con to steal money from the gullible. But a proper meal, that's something you can do. You can be brave. Yes, so our food is laced with all sorts of unpleasant things, but it's not going to kill you for one night. You're just going to have to forget that for a bit, get yourself back together and nurse your strength. You're going to need to be strong for the battles to come.

A woman darts an uneasy glance at me as she walks past towing a tow-haired toddler, a living doll in matching pink wellies and coat. The child stares at me as though I have some hideous deformity, her mother stepping onto the road to avoid contact with such a mutant. Why are they so wary of me? Wait a minute, was I talking to myself? Ah. I have a nasty feeling this is true.

I pause and look around, taking in the timbered buildings and familiar places, taking notice of my surroundings for the first time. I'm near Market Street. If I cross over, cut down there and onto Higgin's Lane, that'll take me out near the supermarket by the bus station. Fired with purpose, I alter course.

It's a ghastly building, terracotta bricks filming grey with grime belched from the backend of buses kept running on routes which don't pay for replacements. You have to wade through the stink of hot engines to get to the shop's entrance, and through stainless steel and glass doors which smell more of public conveniences than any toilet you've ever used, no matter how unsanitary, and follow grubby footprints across a cream-tiled floor to get inside. It surprises me the supermarket chain tolerate this, it's one of the reasons I don't shop here, but it evidently doesn't deter people. I step through the automatic door and into a seething mass of bodies ramming shopping trolleys here and there, their soulless eyes glazed, their reason left outside. For a moment I think I didn't realise so many people lived in Thatchington, and then I shake myself for being stupid. Of course they don't Ewan. They drive here, or arrive on the bus. Get a grip man. No, don't talk to yourself, not out aloud, there's a good man.

I take a basket. That would be easier if I didn't have my briefcase. I try looping it over my forearm, but this leaves it sticking out at a ridiculous angle and almost decapitates a sticky-faced, red-cheeked infant sat in its exasperated mother's shopping trolley, chewing on a bunch of shiny silver keys. She tuts and glares, and for a moment I stare back, trying to work out if she is another former pupil, her top lip curling with reproach, with a savage disgust she would never have been permitted to express in Thatchington High, but I don't think so. We are not in school now, I remind myself, so even if she were, I am not afforded any particular respect; I am just another piece of flotsam bobbing in this particular cesspit of human creation, 'the supermarket', and must take more care not to cause offence. I apologise, manoeuvre the offending basket into my free hand, and go wandering off, wondering what I want.

My stomach is growling at the thought of being treated to a proper dinner, and as I weigh up the culinary options, my taste buds prickle with anticipation. Don't get excited, I tell them, my stomach too. You know you're only reacting to the smells of food they pump around the shop, and they only spend the energy doing that to dupe us into buying more. We'll have to be careful if we're going to get out of here without succumbing to their devious tricks.

I don't know what I want. The fresh bread smells so good, I can almost taste the warm, slightly salty, crispy crust breaking as I bite into a warm baguette. But I walk past. No, I tell my taste buds. Don't you remember we read somewhere they put so much yeast in the dough, it's very bad for the digestive system? My gut stirs as though in response. What I need is 'good and wholesome', not 'manufactured for effect'. I know: vegetables, salad; that's what I need, lots of leafy greens to make me feel better. But I pore over the shelves remembering you've got to be very careful because fruit and vegetables are filled with pesticides and all the chemicals they use to make the produce look this good so we lemmings buy buy buy, killing ourselves while the supermarkets' shareholders' coffers swell. Organic then, but there isn't much choice, and they charge more, and it's probably not good for me either, and

I don't know what to do.

It's hot in here. I swallow. My throat is constricted by my tightening collar, the heat building up under my clothes. I loosen my tie. No one else seems hot. They're all bustling past while I stand here, growing ever more conspicuous like Alice in bloody Wonderland getting bigger and bigger towering over the shelves until people can't help but bump into me with their trolleys. 'Sorry love' 'oo, sorry mate' they mouth, no one brave enough to say what I can hear their voices roaring in my head, 'what are you standing there for, you fucking idiot?'

Ewan, get something to eat. Just chose something.

I remember where I am, and glance round. I shouldn't talk to myself. It doesn't look as though anyone has noticed. Everyone just hurries by. None of us want to be here.

I step back into the stream of shoppers moving along, and bob along with the current until I find myself in the aisle with ready-made meals. 'Ready-made': I don't need to do anything, just choose one, take it home and heat it up. They go in the microwave, but microwave ovens are very bad for you. Yes, I've read all about it too. They do something weird to the food that causes cancer, and there's no telling what they do to your brain if you stand in a room beside one that is working. Perhaps I won't buy one of these meals after all. Perhaps I should get rid of the microwave in my kitchen. What if it's dangerous even when it's not turned on? After all, if something is contagious or radioactive, it emits whatever it emits all the time. I should definitely throw it out.

What am I going to do?

I know I should eat, but the thought of all this manufactured food full of chemicals is ruining what little appetite I have. The thought of everything they do to make our food look good, to make us want to buy is so sinister, I wonder why there is anyone in here, let alone me. Why doesn't anyone else realise we are being controlled? I look around, my breath quick and shallow. No one realises. No one realises, but me. Perhaps it's up to me to do something, but what? The responsibility is so onerous and so enormous, I feel too small to really make a difference. But I have to do something. Should I jump up onto the shelves and start preaching?

My heart is beating very fast as I look round once more. It wouldn't take much for me to clamber up on top of the nearest row of shelves. There is music playing, but I could raise my teacher's voice loud enough to be heard. I've never understood the need for random acts of altruism towards my fellow man, but this is important. People need to know. When would any mass movement, any uprising, from William Wallace to the Arab Spring, have happened without the actions of one single person brave enough to stand up and shout out 'this is wrong'? I put down my briefcase, and start to climb, hauling myself up past the baked beans, the gasps of milling shoppers echoing from below.

"Fellow shoppers, listen to me," I shout out, admiring how I sound vaguely Shakespearian. "You must listen. Stop buying all this food. You're being controlled, and you don't know it."

I like it up here on top of the shelves. The whole store lies before me, and I feel like a king addressing his domain. Everyone has stopped to look up at me. This is my time, my chance to wake everyone up.

"It's a conspiracy. The government, the authorities, they want to keep us all down in our places, doing as we're told, so the farmers, the food manufacturers and the supermarkets, they all put drugs in our food to control us. We're being poisoned by their chemicals."

There is a wave of tittering, and someone shouts 'I'll have whatever drugs you're on mate', but I press on. If I achieve nothing else today, at least I will know I've tried to alert the good people of Thatchington to the truth.

I'm getting to the core of my theories when I see movement out of the corner of my right eye. Not beetles this time, but two men, one in a suit, the other in the starched white shirt and epaulets of a security guard, running towards me.

"Oi, you. Get down from there."

I swither. Should I let myself be arrested to draw more attention to my cause, or would it be better to make a run for it? Without too much thought, I choose the latter. I haven't been feeling well, and I'd rather go home than play the martyr today. I leap down from the shelf, grab my briefcase, and sprint for the door, weaving in and out of gawping shoppers. A few people make a token effort to grab me on the way out, but most shrink from me as though I were some sort of lunatic. I charge out through the doors and run to the end of the street, doubled up with a stitch I can ignore no longer.

It isn't until I get home I remember I haven't got anything to eat tonight.

Chapter 21

I thought everything would be all right at home, but it isn't. The beetles are everywhere. No sooner have I shut the front door, than I can hear scratching and scuffling. It's very faint at first, and I have to strain to listen. But when I put my ear to the plastered walls, I can hear them moving around, climbing over one another, forcing their round shiny bodies through cracks in the wall, chewing at the timbers, at the very structure of my house. I don't know what to do. Biting my thumbnail, one arm wrapped around my waist, I pace up and down the hall wondering if I should ring some company that specialises in pest control to come and get rid of them. 'Fumigating' is what they call it, I think. But if the beetles are here to keep watch on me, trying to get rid of them might result in me being taken into custody. I don't know what to do. I pace up and down, and up and down, chewing my thumbnail: chewing over my quandary.

The telephone rings. I press myself against the wall, and stare at it, my heart thumping and my palms moist with sweat. Don't answer, I think. But no, I must answer. I mustn't do anything unusual. They will suspect me if I don't answer the telephone.

"Hi Ewan, it's me. Look, the kids are going out for tea with their Dad, do you fancy a quick drink at The Dolphin? We could have a bite to eat if you like. I think we need to chat about what you were talking about earlier, and I wondered if your fingers want re-bandaging."

"Trudy," I wipe my sweating face with my damp, perspiring hands and glance over each shoulder to see if any of the beetles are getting closer. There's one scuttling along the wall at head height. I thump the wall. It disappears.

"Ewan, are you all right?"

"No. I mean yes. There's these beetles," I manage to stammer out the words. But as soon as I've said it, I know I shouldn't have said it. I don't know if I can trust her.

"What beetles?"

"These little black beetles. They're everywhere. I don't know what to do."

She tells me to take a deep breath, and to try and keep calm; she's coming round to help. But the thought of what she really means by that frightens me so much, she winds up shouting down the phone she'll bring some bug spray. Yes, bug spray: that's what I need. I clutch at my fragile senses and listen as she tells me to sit still. She tells me to sit on the stairs and keep talking to her. I hear the sound of her front door slamming, her heels clicking on the flagstones and the car door creak open. She keeps talking to me, asking me where the beetles are now and what they're doing as she drives across town towards me.

Her car pulls up outside. I open the door. She jumps out and runs up the path, her plump cheeks pink with exertion and so out of breath she can barely speak. Her eyes scour the walls as she steps up into the house, but the beetles have gone. They must have known she was coming.

"Come here." She puts her arms around me, and holds me tight. I haven't realised how much I'm shaking until I hold her firm, still body, and I cling to her as though she was an anchor. My eyes close, and for a moment I am safe, until I feel something crawl across my fingers. There is a beetle on her back. I let go and jump back with a scream.

"Where?" Trudy twists this way and that, but she can't see it. I go to flick it off, but it disappears. I think it's crawled up into her hair. They do that, I tell her.

"Ewan, listen to me," she takes hold of my hands. "This is a serious infestation. We have to do something about it."

"I knew you'd listen to me Trudy. I knew you'd understand."

"I do understand Ewan, really I do. You can't stay here. Come with me, I know somewhere that's safe, and I know some people who will be able to help. You trust me, don't you? Come on, let's get you in the car. It will be fine, I promise."

I let her lead me outside, but as soon as I step over the threshold, I claw at the doorframe, struggling to get back indoors.

"What is it?"

"It's Vi. She's watching. She'll guess where we're going."

"No she won't," Trudy says, prising my fingers free. "Trust me, it's safe."

She closes the door, takes my arm and leads me down to the car. It's as though I'm in a bubble, sealed off from the outside world. I see Vi waving, but I can't hear what she's saying. The trees are moving, but I can't feel any wind. The sun is beaming perfect golden sunshine, but I can't feel its warmth. And I'm supposed to be going somewhere, but I don't know where.

"Where are we going?"

"Somewhere safe. Trust me."

I sit in her car, my hands on my knees, as she turns the vehicle round, and pulls back out of my street. Is it a safe house or something, I ask her, wondering if I should hide beneath the backseat so no one knows where I'm going, so I don't blow the refuge's cover by leading the authorities straight to their door. Trudy puts her hand on my shoulder. It will be all right, she promises. Everything is okay now.

And I go on sitting there, believing in Trudy, accepting everything she's saying to me right up until the moment she turns the corner into Thatchington General Hospital. Then I realise it's a trap.

"What the hell are you doing? I thought you said 'somewhere safe'."

"This is safe Ewan. I don't think you're very well, and there are people here who will look after you."

"Stop the car, damn it." I slam both hands down on the dashboard. "How dare you do this to me? I thought we were friends."

"We are friends, and that's why I've brought you here."

"Some friend," I shout, struggling out of my seatbelt.

I fling the door open as she swerves up to the casualty entrance, and leap out. The car's momentum leaves me lurching across the tarmac. I lose balance and fall over, skinning my knees, but I haven't time to worry about that. Trudy is shouting 'stop, Ewan. Somebody please stop him,' but I'm on my feet and running as hard as I can, her voice fading. Fear powers me down the pavement. I charge across the road leaving screeching, swerving drivers cursing in my wake, and run off into a housing estate I know leads down to the river, and a shortcut back to the safety of home.

Chapter 22

I haven't been home for very long before there is a knock at the door. No, it isn't a knock. 'Knock' sounds polite and considerate. This is a thump, an angry, insistent thump thump thump, demanding my attention. I put the bottle of surgical spirit and the cotton wool I'd been using to dab my knees down on the kitchen table, and get up to answer the door, my whole body aching with the effort of the day's exertions. It will be Trudy, I know, and I'm going to tell her I don't want to see her again. We are not friends.

Thump thump thump.

I teeter into the hall, my knees stiff and throbbing. A patch of daylight suddenly appears on my front door, fingers thrusting through the letterbox. Eyes peer into my hall, and fix on me. It isn't Trudy. A familiar Glaswegian drawl paralyses my limbs.

"Hello Ewan, it's me, Roderick. Why don't you open the door eh?"

"Go away."

I don't want this to be happening. Perhaps it isn't, and I'm going to open my eyes in a minute and find myself in bed going 'god, what a weird dream'. Or perhaps if I go and hide somewhere, curl myself up in a little ball and stick my fingers in my ears, everything will go away and none of this will be happening. But it is happening. This is real. And I'm trembling so much, I try leaning against the wall to steady myself.

"Ach, come on," Roderick says. "That's not very nice when I haven't seen you for so long. Come and open the door." And when he sees that I don't move a muscle, he adds "it's a very nice front door, be a shame to get one of these officers to kick it in."

"You've got no right," my cowering voice squeaks, but I know there is no point in saying this.

"It's been reported to us that you might be in danger of causing harm to yourself, so yeah, we do have the right as you well know. So come on Ewan, stop messing around and just open the door." He lets go of the letterbox, and shouts through the door. "I'm gonna count to three, Ewan, and if you haven't opened this door, we'll open it for you."

He's got it all wrong really. When you think about it, Trudy's already opened the damned door. She did it the moment her nurse's eyes took in my scars and remembered she'd seen me before.

"Here love," I hear another voice, Vi's breathless tones. "I've got a key, I have. Is he all right, Mr. Davies? Only he's been behaving queer-like for a while, he has. Mrs Harris next door, she says she hears him shouting at someone, she does, only he lives here all alone, he does."

Her voice fires me out of my stupor. I scoot the length of the hall to fasten the safety chain to the door, praising the day I decided to fit it. The key turns, and as the door opens, I hear Roderick speaking to Vi.

"Thanks love. Now look, if I need any more information, I'll come and talk to you but it's best if you pop back indoors now and leave us to it. Ta.

"Oh that's perfect," he snaps, trying to look at me through the gap. "Ewan! What do you think I am, a contortionist? How am I supposed to take a look at you if you won't open the door properly? Come on, take the chain off please." There are two burly policemen standing behind him, arms folded across their fluorescent jacketed chests, peaked caps stiff with authority. Beyond them, I can see their parked car, and further still, on the other side of the road, Vi and her grandson, and old Mrs Harris from next door, watching the spectacle.

"There's nothing wrong with me. Go away please."

I hear one of the policemen tell Roderick there are cutters in their car to take care of the chain, but he tells them he's confident he can talk me round, the fool. His arrogance has always had the ability to coax out every last scrap of childish petulance lingering in my brain.

"Come on Ewan, all I want is a cup of tea and a chat. Come on, that's not so hard, is it? Just let me in to have a look at you," he says, holding up his hands. "No tricks."

If I'd never met Roderick before, I might have fallen for that one, but I'm not stupid. Damn Trudy. All I wanted was someone to help me, an ally, and instead she's betrayed me and served me up to the chief inquisitor. I've got to get out of here, but how am I supposed to get past not only Roderick, but two whopping big great policemen at the same time? I'm already exhausted from running, and my knees ache. But sometimes you need to feel cornered to have a flash of inspiration.

"Wait a minute," I say to Roderick, marvelling at the ingenuity behind my plan and crossing my fingers it works. "Did you hear that? Something's boiling over on the stove. I'll just go and turn it off."

Roderick protests first I must open the door, and then he'll turn the bloody stove off, but he's too slow. I pound back down the hall. As I pass the side window underneath the stairs, a flash of fluorescent yellow stops me mid-flight. It's one of the policemen charging up the drive, having guessed my intention to escape out of the back door. Well, I suppose it wasn't the brightest idea, but I don't have that many options. Roderick is rattling the front door and yelling to his other accomplice to hurry up with the wire cutters. The back door opens. I shove open the side window and scramble out, remembering to shut it behind me. As I tiptoe round into the back garden, I hear muffled shouts as the officer inside my house discovers he can't find me, but I don't pause to savour this small victory. I hop over the fence between my garden and Mrs Harris's, cross her lawn, and scrabble up and over the wall into the next property.

I carry on this way until at last I'm negotiating the mess of briar rose and brambles marking the edge of the copse at the end of the road, Roderick's shouts fading. And yes, I am vain enough to marvel at how

I've managed to outwit them, although the damage done to my favourite suit, the wool snagging and tearing on gleeful thorns, is a hefty price to pay. I trudge off into the woods, going deeper and deeper, and further into the undergrowth.

My legs are aching, my entire body so heavy and tired, it's as though I'm having to drag myself as I pick my way between the trees, the woodland alien away from the cosseting, comforting familiarity of a well-trod path. Dark fir trees press together, their spiny fronds blocking out the daylight and any hint of a world outside. All I can hear beyond my laboured breathing and rapid heartbeat is the sound of tree boughs swishing and swaying in the wind. The sound is insular and makes the hairs on the back of my neck rise. I could almost imagine Thatchington and the human world, my world, have disappeared, vanished, obliterated in a moment as though they have never even existed. I am vulnerable in here, lost in a wilderness far from my usual domain. Perhaps I am the only human left. What would I do if that were true, I wonder as I plod, hands stuffed deep in pockets. I imagine myself emerging into empty streets never to see another living person again. Would this be heaven or hell? I pause to catch my breath, and lean against a tree trunk. It's starting to rain now, as though I could be any more wretched, the droplets coming down thick and fast. I go to glare up at the sky, but I can see nothing but the trees.

The rain begins trickling through my hair, cold drops slithering down my neck. I have to keep stopping now to wipe my glasses. Nowhere looks familiar. I know I'm lost, but somehow it doesn't matter. At first all I wanted was to get as far away as possible from Roderick and his cronies, but now I've achieved that, and they didn't give much of a chase, I don't know where to go. My feet are squelching in my shoes. I examine my black leather shoes, turning my feet this way and that, ruing the fact they're so wet and muddy. They'll have to be thrown away, the leather ruined. And my poor, favourite suit. I examine my torn sleeves, the material ripped and frayed. Mr. Findlay's skills won't be enough to salvage this. Why did Trudy have to do this to me? I should have known I couldn't trust her.

There is a fallen tree lying, blanketed in thick green moss. I make my way across to it, and slump down, hugging my arms around my body for warmth. The wet moss soaks through the seat of my trousers. Being out here and getting wet like this is a stupid idea, I reflect. Never mind seeing things, I'll probably wind up giving Rebecca everything she wants by catching a cold and needing time off. I start biting down my thumbnail again, savouring the pain. So far this afternoon, I've been too taken up with everything going on around me to confront the one occurrence which has disturbed me the most. Marcia. What was she doing there in my classroom? I don't believe in nonsense such as ghosts. At least, I didn't. If you'd asked me, I would have told you I considered such rubbish to be the product of an overactive, deluded imagination. Right now I'm wondering just what this means about me.

What has happened to me? I quite liked being 'Ewan Davies', an ordinary, unremarkable man with an ordinary, unremarkable life. How the hell have I ended up here, a fugitive hiding out in the woods in the rain when ordinary people the country over are just getting home from work, ready to eat their evening meals and settle down for another boring night in front of the television? I shiver. How on earth have I ended up here? And then another thought comes to me. Is this really happening?

I turn round at the sound of scuffling in the undergrowth near my fallen tree. A twig snaps. I stand up, pulse racing. Damn, I think as I look round for the source of the noise. Fool that I am to think Roderick would give up that easily. But it isn't him. There is a figure walking towards me, swathed on waterproofs, and a white and brown dog, some sort of Spaniel I think, comes bounding up to me. I recoil from its enthusiastic, tail-wagging approach, the ghastly, smelly creature. Its owner calls it away, and clips on a lead, red and patterned with little paw-prints. I expect it's supposed to be 'cute', although I've never understood this infantilising of domesticated animals.

"Sorry," a woman's voice sounds from the weathered face peering out from inside the waterproofs. "He's just a very friendly dog. I say," she looks me up and down with a mixture of disbelief and disgust on her face, and takes a step back. "Are you all right? You look, well, you look a bit," she struggles to find the right word to sum up my dishevelled appearance. "Well, you don't look dressed for such awful weather. Is there something the matter?"

Is there something the matter? I wouldn't know where to begin my answer. In spite of myself, I guffaw and she takes another step backwards, clutching the dog's lead. The question strikes me as so funny, I progress to laughing out aloud, the woods ringing with my mirth long after she's hurried away, dragging the dog and darting glances over her shoulder to make sure I'm not running after her, I don't know, axe in hand or something. Terrible imaginations some people have. I blame the press for generating such hysteria. Still, I think, looking down at myself. I don't look good. If I were to see me walking down the street in this state, I'd probably cross the road. I need to do something. I need to get out of this rain.

My mind tries generating a list of options. I daren't go home, that's for sure. Even if Roderick has gone, Vi will be waiting. What else can I do? I need somewhere warm and dry, but more specifically, safe. My brain rakes through the piles of my friends and acquaintances, picking up each one and discarding most as unsuitable. Trudy? I can't believe I even thought of her. Tessa and Alex? Tricky, I don't want to upset the children if the police are following me. Rebecca? No. I think of having to explain myself to Rick, and throw that idea down as though it burnt me. The only person I can think of, and that's only because I think his profession should make him a safe choice, is Neil.

I follow the dogwalker's path through the copse, and it comes out near the golf course, not far from the vicarage. As I re-emerge back into the human world, into the built-up streets of Thatchington, I slip along the pavement keeping tucked against the buildings, trying to be inconspicuous. Well, as inconspicuous as a wet, muddy man in tattered clothes can look, I should say. Every now and then I stop to look round, to check if I'm being followed, but so far it seems as though I have escaped detection. Occasionally I think I see beetle-ish figures scuttling across the walls, just out of the corner of my eye, but when I turn to look, there is nothing there. My spirits start to balloon. This was the right thing to do.

I turn into the driveway up to the crooked, ivy covered house, light welcoming me from behind latticed windows, hopping onto the lawn rather than have my feet sound noisy and suspicious on the gravel itself. Padding up to the front door, which nestles beneath a tumbling-down porch, its bottle green paint peeling, I check again, but I am still safe. No one is following. I ring the doorbell and it sounds, faint and far-off in some deep corner of the house. Neil's steady footsteps sound heavy as he walks down the long wooden-floored hallway to answer the door.

"Ewan," he opens the door, his round face beaming all-over. But he seems to do a double-take, and seriousness clouds his composure. I wonder what he's seen, and glance over my shoulder, but all seems well. I don't appear to have been followed.

"Whatever's the matter?" He asks, holding the door open wider. "You look awful." For a second I panic, wondering what he means, but then I look down at my rumpled suit, remember the water trickling down my neck, and realise what he means.

"Neil, I need your help, but we mustn't talk out here," I say, putting my finger on my lips. "You never know who might be listening." He gives his head a shake as though trying to make sense of something perplexing, and motions me inside. I squelch indoors, but refuse his offer of a change of clothes. We both know nothing of Neil's will fit me, and no matter how desperate my plight, I will never don one of James's hideous colourful sweaters, irrespective of how cold I feel.

"At least let me make you a cup of tea," he says. "Come through to the kitchen and I'll put the kettle on." He starts to waddle towards the warm, light room at the end of the hallway, but I grab his arm. It's too predictable. They'll guess that's where we've gone.

"Who will guess?" He asks, leaning in and putting his arm around my shoulders.

"There's a chance I might be being followed," I say. "That's why I need to talk to you. There's this plot, you see. I found out about it, and now they're trying to make me disappear. They've tried to take me into hospital so I can't tell people what I've found out, and I keep seeing these horrible beetles everywhere I go, and that's to warn me the authorities know that I know, and I don't know what to do. And I'm frightened, Neil. I just don't know what to do."

Neil ponders this information with a solemn nod, pursing his lips as though he were tasting this information, disassembling it into component parts with a vintner's palate.

"I say, have you been drinking, old chap? I mean, nothing wrong with a bit of an early-evening tipple, I'm rather partial to one myself, but you really aren't making a lot of sense you know."

I grit my teeth as a wave of panic washes through me. They must have got to him first. He's been brainwashed, that's why he doesn't believe me. I haven't been drinking; I have uncovered a terrible plot. I am the only one who has any idea what's going on and it's put me in terrible danger. It's so simple. Why won't anyone listen to me?

"I tell you what," Neil says, patting my arm. "Why don't you go and have a seat in my office. The fire's on in there. I'll go and make us a pot of tea, and then you can start at the beginning and tell me what's been happening. I have the feeling we might have rather a lot to talk about. Go on, no one will know you're in there. It's quite safe. James is out visiting his mother, so it's just you and I. Go on old chap, make yourself comfy."

He ushers me into his enormous study, shelved from floor to ceiling with dark walnut, the most valuable of the Parish's books locked away behind glass. Neil usually says he hates this room with its archaic musty scent, its antique furnishings looking on in disgust if he so much as moves a chair, but there are logs burning in the grate and a half-drunk bottle of wine standing on the enormous desk like a lighthouse presiding over a sea of paper. He leads me over to sit beside the fire, tells me he won't be long, and bustles out to the kitchen.

I could spend weeks in here, I think, as my eyes travel along the shelves, taking in the rare and ancient books, volumes dust-bound and titled in gold. Curious, I get up to take a closer look. Some of these books must be worth a fortune, Latin tomes nestling beside the writings of Christianity's architects, fashioning the word of god to their own ends. My thoughts are remembering a television programme I saw recently about writings they edited out of the bible, when I hear the far-off sound of a phone ring. As I hear Neil answer, I go on looking at the books. Then I catch a few words which send alarm jangling through my body. Suspicion seizes my hand and drags me to the door. I've learned a valuable lesson from Trudy. There's no way of telling who can be trusted.

"That's right," I hear him saying. "At first I thought he was pissed, but he isn't. Least, I don't think so." My breath freezes in my chest. I tiptoe through the door and out into the hallway, pressed against the wall and treading lightly for fear a board should betray me with a creak.

"Alex, I don't know," I hear him protest. "He's spouting all this tosh about being followed. I don't know what to do."

I do. Without a care for stealth, I charge down the hall. As I dive out of the front door, I hear Neil cursing, calling my name and begging me to wait, but I don't stop. I hobble off down the drive, the vicar still yelling after me and hurry away down the darkening streets, keeping to the shadows as I flee for the dubious safety of my own four walls. No one can be trusted: no one. I have to get home.

Chapter 23

As I reach the corner of Orchard road, relief soothes away my fear at the sight of no police car outside of my house. Without my door key, I sneak up the side and try the side window. To my joy, it opens and I clamber back indoors. It strikes me as good sense to leave the lights off so no one will realise I'm home. But I've no sooner got in than the telephone rings. I creep down the hall, and sit on the stairs, shivering with cold. The answering machine kicks in, and I hear Neil's voice telling me to pick up the phone, and ordering me to call him back. Then it rings again, and this time it is Alex saying the same thing. 'Ewan, answer this phone. All right, call me back as soon as you get this message'. And then it rings yet again, and this time it's Trudy, her voice wavering and tearful.

They're using my friends to get to me. I'm in so much trouble I don't know what to do. My heart is fluttering rather than beating properly and I wonder if this is it, I'm having a heart attack. And it's dark. I don't like the dark. And there's the scuffling sound getting louder and louder, and a beetle, a big black beetle coming across the floor towards me. And there's another one. Oh god. And I can hear Vi. Or is it Rebecca? Or Trudy? Or Fiona? I can't tell.

"End of the line, love. We're coming for you."

No. I hug my wet, tattered arms around myself. Go away, I tell the voices. Go away. I have to be strong, I tell myself. I am the only one who knows the true story, the only one who can wake everyone up and stop what is happening to us, and I can't do it by sitting here cowering in the dark. I have to be brave. If I could just feel calm, I would feel more able to cope. There is only one reliable way I know to instil calm into my quaking flesh when I'm feeling this bad, and it's something I haven't done since Marcia died. But I don't have the luxury of time to spend dwelling on what happened to her. I need to take charge of this situation if I am to survive. I need to make myself calm.

I creep, my feet in wet socks making no noise as I make my way into the kitchen. My hands reach for the box on the top shelf on the pantry. It has been so long since I needed it that it's furred with sticky grey dust. I carry it upstairs and into my bedroom, shut the door and the curtains, and look around. No, there are no beetles in here. I am safe. I turn on the bedside light, strip off my wet clothes, and settle myself in the corner of the room, pressed against the reassuring solidity of a three hundred year old wall. My fingers squeeze the lid, and the box opens with a pop.

"You're too late," say the voices. *"That's not going to save you now."*

"Welcome back," says the knife nestling between my fingers.

I focus on the sound of my breath rasping in and out of my nostrils. In and out, in and out, like waves crashing on a shore, a rhythmic beat, the sound of the universe echoing across space. I must be calm. This isn't a night for ice-cubes or elastic bands, or any other of Roderick's stupid strategies. Action is what is required, not soft words spoken down some half-arsed helpline. I know it, and Marcia knew it too. Some nights, more is required than others. 'Sorry Marcia,' I mumble, tears pricking the backs of my eyes at the thought of her pale, bloated body, cold and lifeless in a bath of crimson. I pull up my left sleeve, and draw the knife across my skin.

The relief is instant. A protective blanket woven from calm and perspective wraps itself around me as I watch vivid ruby well up out of the cut. My lips part with a groan of satisfaction. And the knife cuts again and again. The house is still and quiet. There are no voices. I can't hear a single scuffle.

After a while, the blood clots. I am so sated, so satisfied, I am ready to sleep. I clamber onto the bed, work my way under the duvet, and fall headlong into the safety of a deep and dreamless slumber that has evaded me for months.

I sleep so well, that I don't wake until the pale morning sends its fingers fumbling though the curtains to spread through the room. My first thought as I begin to stir, is to wonder why I feel so unwell. Everything aches as though I've been beaten up or run over. My mouth is foul and sticky, and as I shift position, my head thumps in protest. I keep still, trying to remember why, but I don't think I drank anything last night, never mind too much. Ah, wait a minute. Last night. School. The supermarket. Roderick and the police. And I cut myself.

Wincing at my headache, I roll onto my side to inspect my arm. My left arm is scored with a series of crusted red cuts. I flex it, remembering how beautiful the blood had looked spilling out of each slash. When it feels so good, it's a miracle I've managed to abstain for this long, but I suppose that's the measure of how deep I felt Marcia's death. I go to sit up, but my head goes into another spasm of jabbing pain, and I rub my forehead with one hand, berating my own stupidity. I didn't eat or drink anything last night, and then I cut myself. When I used to do it regularly, I always ate something first, and then forced down a sachet of dehydration salts afterwards. It's as though I have forgotten everything I have ever learned. No wonder I feel bad. I lie back down amongst the pillows and stare up at the ceiling. There, in the corner, is a beetle.

I lever myself up, my eyes on the beetle, my peace destroyed. There's no way I can lie here with the damned thing watching me. I throw back the duvet. Colour catches my eye, black against my white sheets. I look down, and launch myself off the bed with a scream. The bed is full of crawling beetles. I have been sleeping in a nest. Sweeping the damned things off my body, I run for the shower.

The water is scalding, but I think it's the only way I can be sure I'll kill the insects. I stand under the water, scrubbing at my hair and body until my skin feels raw before I am content they've gone. My teeth are chattering, clattering with horror. This isn't what I planned for today. I needed to feel calm. I felt calm last night. There weren't any beetles after I cut my arm. Without a second thought, I paddle through to the bedroom for the knife, taking care not to look at the bed, and return to the shower.

One. Oh, that's better. Two. Mmm, better still. Three. Ah. That's a bit deep. Ouch. I shouldn't have done that. Damn. That is deep.

The blood is welling up out of the cut faster than I want to see. I turn off the shower, and step out, fumbling for a towel. The dark blue hand towel will do; I wrap it tight around my forearm to staunch the bleeding. Damn, I've never made such a mistake before; it must be because I'm out of practice. Damn damn damn.

A dark stain spreads across the navy blue. The cut had gaped under the knife, pausing for a moment as though in surprise, before the void began to rush with blood. I need another towel. The cupboard is on the landing. I paddle through, dripping water, my cooling flesh shivering in the early morning chill. Back in my bedroom, the beetles gone, I sit on the edge of my bed and press down on the wound, trying to remember all I've learnt from first aid lessons through the years. Apply pressure and bandage. Should be simple, but the blood keeps soaking through, and it's only pretty to watch when I'm in control. My head spins, my teeth are chattering, and burning bile rises up into the back of my throat.

I grip the edge of the bed as the room lurches, and I glance at the clock. Damn, it's after seven already. There's no way I'm going to be able to sort this out and be at school for my normal time, plus I'm going to need to re-bandage my sore fingers. Damn. I don't want to be late. I mustn't be late. I shuffle my buttocks, desperate to be busy getting ready for work. I can't be late. I get up. It feels better if I pace. I can't have Mrs Phillips and Rebecca thinking they've won. Then my thoughts alight on the memory of Roderick. I'm not sure if it's safe to go outside today. What if they're watching, what if they try to grab me on the way to school? I stop pacing up and down, and wipe my damp face with my free hand. What an idiot I am. I can't believe I got so carried away.

There is a packet of adhesive plastic stitches in the box I took from the kitchen last night. I rummage for it, and find some rolls of bandage. The bleeding seems to have subsided a little, so I decide to take a chance and unwrap the towels. The cut gapes like an angry mouth, all red and scolding, threatening that the slightest move will set it off bleeding once more. My brow furrows as I examine it. I'm not sure the sticky stitches will be enough. But they will have to do, there's no way I'm taking myself to hospital. If I do that, I might as well just report straight to Roderick. No, I tell myself. I will be fine. I can look after myself. So I set about sticking my arm together. But it is a hard task to accomplish one-handed, and I am out of practice. And to complicate matters further, not only are the fingers at the end of my damaged arm still raw from Claire's cello strings, but they won't work properly. It takes several attempts before I can manage to secure the bandage tightly enough, and all the while, it is getting later and later.

Bandaged at last, my arm is hot and has begun a dull, niggling throb that threatens to grow worse as the day wears on. I swallow a couple of painkillers and decide it might be safer to walk to school. Driving might cause the wound to start bleeding afresh, and I'm not sure I'm going to be able to grip the steering wheel properly. I choose a dark navy suit with a fine pin stripe. If the blood soaks through my sleeve, no one will notice. But my hands won't stop shaking, and my fingers still won't work properly, and as I struggle to fasten my tie, I catch a glimpse in the mirror of something black scuttle across the wall behind me. That's it. I had begun to wonder if, and Rebecca be damned, it might be more prudent to call in sick today, but I can't stay here with the beetles. No. I will be okay. I am okay. I know that I'm okay, and it doesn't matter what Trudy and Roderick want to think, damn them. I am okay.

Mind made up, I set off walking. At first this feels like it was the best idea I've had in weeks, and I saunter along enjoying the early morning air, cool and fresh after last night's rain. My bad hand in my pocket, I'm whistling, thinking about the melody from my composition and wondering if I might have it ready for the school's Christmas concert, and it's not until I'm climbing up Belmont Hill towards The George Hotel, I begin to notice how hot and clammy I'm feeling. A cloud of little black dots wavers before my eyes and I sway, putting my hand against a wall to steady myself. I don't feel well at all. My head is swimming, and it's as if I've never manoeuvred, never 'driven' this body before. I try to keep on putting one foot forward, and then the next one, but the effort feels as though I'm struggling through treacle, my muscles aching and protesting after yesterday's exertions. By the time I reach The George, I decide I'd better call a taxi.

The George's receptionist has far more important things to do than telephone a taxi for some stranger off the street, but she takes a second look at my sickly visage, and agrees, probably afraid I'll do something tedious and inconvenient like collapse in a heap on the floor if she doesn't, and make the place look untidy. She calls a waitress to fetch me a glass of water, and for this I am grateful. The foyer is spinning round and round. Sitting down is better than standing up, but I'm beginning to wonder if I shouldn't just go home. I'd like to lie down. Maybe I should get a room here in the hotel. Surely there won't be any beetles in here. No, I tell myself, I will be all right. Just need a cup of tea or something when I get to work, and I'll be fine. I sneak my fingers up my sleeve to check my bandage. It's okay. I let myself breathe again. It feels dry. My face is clammy. I slip off my jacket.

The taxi pulls up outside school at half past eight. I have resigned myself to the fact I'm not going to get those year ten essays marked before class; I'll have to do them later. Or perhaps I should just give them to Rebecca since she's always on about how I don't give her enough to do. What did she say yesterday? Oh yes. 'You need to learn to delegate, Ewan. Del-e-gate.' Well then I shall delegate my marking. That should shut her up.

As I clamber out of the taxi, I see Alex running out of the building towards me. He jogs over, his hands stuffed in his pockets, but stops short, his eyebrows locked in a frown.

"Good god mate, you look bloody awful. Are you okay?" He puts a heavy hand on my shoulder.

"I'm fine," I shrug out of his grasp and go to flounce past. "Why the hell does everyone have to keep on asking me if I'm okay?"

"Because your friends care about you," he says, his sombre voice like a sick dog, so conspicuous is its missing exuberance. Is it my imagination, or is he deliberately blocking my path?

"Well that's very touching, but as you can see, I'm perfectly all right and rather late, so if you'll excuse me," I go to step past, but it isn't my imagination. He mirrors my move and stands in the way. "Damn it Alex, will you get out of my way?"

"Mate, Mrs. Phillips wants to see you in her office. Right away. She says it's urgent."

"Oh so that's what you're doing out here, is it? Loitering around like a good little soldier ready to do what she says. You've got to admit it, that's a change of tune for you, isn't it?" And out of the corner of my eye, I see movement and fluorescent colour coming closer and closer. I glance round. It's a policeman. He's breaking into a run. He's running towards us, towards me. I launch my briefcase and jacket at Alex.

"You bastard, you set me up," I screech as I take to my heels for the third time in twenty-four hours, and run.

I have no idea where I'm going, but I lurch indoors through the school's side door, and stagger up the staircase shouldering bodies out of the way, pupils and staff. There are two policemen after me, bellowing to me to stop, and ordering bystanders out of the way. I run down the corridor past my office, stumbling into walls as though I've been drinking all night. Rebecca and Nathan appear in the doorway as I shamble past. I hear her yelling 'Ewan, what the hell are you doing?' as I barge through the fire doors to the top of the east staircase. Oh and look, here's Alex and smarmy Stu, galloping up the stairs to meet me, having guessed my route. They charge me, but somehow I am more nimble on my feet. I swivel out of their reach and go for the stairs, only the ground vanishes beneath me, and the next thing I realise is that I'm falling and falling, and I go on falling down into nothingness.

Chapter 24

I surface from the groggy, fathomless depths of the deepest sleep I've had in months, wondering why everything is so bright; it's not normally this light in my bedroom. My mouth is furry, gummy, and my tongue twists like a dying, drying slug, searching for moisture, for anything that might promise to restore it to normal. I go to move my limbs, and smack into a wall of white pain. I hurt. Everything hurts. My eyelids struggle open, and I cry out as my eyes burn in the light.

I shut them tight. This isn't my bedroom. My head lolls from side to side as I trawl my senses for a hint of explanation. Where the hell am I? A hint of memory stirs, stutters, trying to illuminate my mind, but fizzles out into darkness. I remember a vague sense of indignation driving my limbs, surging forwards, and a tsunami of fear, of helplessness, my senses reeling as I powered forwards, floundering through the air, down and down into nothingness. That's all I remember.

I must open my eyes. If I do it bit-by-bit, perhaps it won't hurt so much. I must open my eyes. I have to know what's going on.

There is a man standing beside me. I have to squint to make him out, and then recognition bowls me flying with a leaden ball of fear. My instinct to flee from his side fires more pain jolting through my body. I shut my eyes, the nine year old in me hoping that maybe, if I've shut my eyes fast enough, this isn't really happening. But it is. They've caught me.

"All right Ewan, take it easy," Roderick says, his nonchalant tone both comforting and terrifying; comforting in that it's always reassuring to encounter a fellow Scot, yet terrifying since he's not here under the guise of being 'nice'. He speaks as one distracted. I hold my eyes open this time to see he's standing over me studying the contents of a thick, tatty, buff folder, his watery blue eyes darting back and forth behind their gingery lashes, his freckled forehead furrowed in concentration. With a click of his pen, he writes something down, then closes the file and sticks his pen back into his top pocket.

"Good to see you awake. How are you feeling?"

"Where am I?" I ask him, only my slug tongue won't work properly, and the words slur out, incomprehensible even in my ears. Roderick asks me to repeat what I said, and bends in closer to hear, but no matter how hard I try, I cannot get my words out. Panic shortens my breath and sends cold shuddering through my body. What the hell is wrong with me? He's done something to me, he must have. This must be the retaliation for me finding out all their terrible schemes. Oh my god, will someone help me? I'm in terrible danger. Help me please.

"All right Ewan, you're not making a lot of sense," he opens the folder and makes another note. "Perhaps it's better if you try not to talk, just nod to me if you understand. Okay?" He fixes me with an expectant look, like a dog waiting for a titbit. I stare at him, panting through a haze of pain, my heart thumping, and give a reluctant nod.

"Do you know where you are?"

Why the hell is he asking me this? I don't know. Perhaps it's some sort of top secret detention centre. Oh my god, are they going to torture me? I've got to get out of here. I want to go home. What have they done to me? I knew this boy once. They got him. John, I think he was called. They got him, and they tried to kill him. They tried to fry his brain with electrodes, laughing in his face and telling him it would make everything better. Help me god, please. I know I've always doubted you exist, but if you do, please help me now. Please get me out of this, I'm begging you. Please.

I look around trying to make sense of my surroundings, but it hurts too much to move my head. Everything is blurry without my glasses. I guess they've confiscated them, knowing how much I need them. My eyes have always been a weakness.

Roderick watches me looking around, and daylight must illuminate his tiny mind for he produces my glasses, and pushes them down onto my face. I blink, and pale blue curtains come into focus around where I'm lying. A tube emerges from bandages swathed around my left arm and hand, and my right leg looks somehow bigger under a mustard yellow blanket draped over my body. I stare at my unfamiliar form as though somehow it doesn't belong to me. Nothing makes sense.

"You're in Thatchington General Hospital," he says. "You've had an accident. Can you remember what happened?"

I think hard, but apart from the vague sensation of falling, my memory lies cold and still. I shake my head, wincing with regret at the fresh flares of pain igniting in my neck. I keep forgetting how much everything hurts.

"All right," Roderick folds his arms. "You fell down some stairs at work. You've broken your leg and cracked a couple of ribs. Going to have to take it easy for a bit."

I stare at him through widened eyes, cold sweat pouring from my pores as fear goes rampaging through my body. They've broken my bones. I wonder if Vi gave the order. They've tried to make it look like an accident, but I haven't had an accident. This was deliberate. Maybe they're trying to kill me now. Yes, that's it. They're trying to kill me. I'm not safe here. I have to go home.

"Ewan, are you all right?" He clamps a hand down on my shoulder and I cry out at the bolt of pain it sends jarring through my body.

"I have to go home," I mumble.

"I don't think so," he snorts when, after a few attempts, I manage to get my message across. "You're in no fit state. As far as I can tell, you're going to be with us for a while, I'm afraid. Better start getting used to it."

Used to it? I have to go home. It isn't safe here. I'm hot now, my face sweating and burning, and I'm getting hotter, the heat building, unbearable, in my body. And as I'm lying here, the sound returns to my ears. I can hear the beetles scratching and scurrying in the wall behind my bed. Perhaps that's how they're going to torture me; they're going to release the beetles while I can't move. I gulp at the thought of them clambering over my body, scuttling into my ears, their horrible mandibles ready to feast on the very tissue of my brain itself. As I lie here, I can picture the creatures burrowing into my skin. They'll eat me alive, and all because I stumbled across a plot I was never meant to find.

"Ewan, what's the matter?" Roderick puts both hands on my shoulders, his smirk conspicuous in its absence. "You're shaking. Keep calm. Talk to me, what's the matter?"

My teeth are gritted to stop them clattering together, to stop the scream building in my throat as the scratching scrabbles closer and closer. Perhaps if I don't show fear, they won't attack. Roderick lifts his hand to the wall, and I hear a buzzer sound. Terrified he's released the insects, I blank the pain and struggle against his grasp.

"Nurse, get Gerry in here," Roderick barks as someone makes the curtains swish. He has me pinned against the bed. I'm struggling and screeching to be free before the beetles start biting, but he won't let go. Feet come running, and a tall, blonde-haired young man appears over Roderick's shoulder, and helps to hold me down. I lash out in a frenzy, desperate to escape, and I don't see the syringe until Roderick plunges it into my arm.

"No! What the hell are you doing?"

"Calm down Ewan," the blonde nurse says, grinning. How the hell does he know my name? "Keep still. It won't hurt if you keep still." His muscles flex as I struggle, but I'm like a fledgling under a cat's paw. I am pinned. I can shout and struggle, but the day's events have robbed me of my strength. All I can do is watch and curse as he restrains me, and as Roderick discharges the syringe's contents into my blood.

"It'll help you sleep," Roderick says as they release me. "That's going to make you feel better, isn't it?" He throws his head back with a hearty guffaw. At least, I think he's laughing. And the other nurse is laughing too. And as I watch, there are beetles, tiny black beetles cascading out of their mouths. I try to scream, but everything is growing dark and fuzzy, and I'm getting heavier and heavier, and I think I'm drowning in this soft inky darkness pulling me down and down, Roderick's laughter fading as, for the second time today, I fall into oblivion.

Chapter 25

Voices wake me. When I say 'wake', I don't mean 'wake' in the normal sense. It's more a case of becoming aware of a vague noise around me, like the first light of dawn after the darkest night, no instant transformation, but a gradual process, a fumbling, creeping sense of becoming ever more 'awake', a slow ascent from the depths of sleep, and not one I'm making willingly. No, I was warm, relaxed and so at peace in the sleep where I'd been, I didn't want to wake up. But this is the reality of the human mind. No sooner have I heard the noise than my brain identifies it as voices talking. And once I've come this far, I begin to be aware of my surroundings.

I am in bed, I realise, although I've no idea where; I'm obviously not at home. But that doesn't matter too much, I'm warm and comfortable, and thinking I might just slip back into sleep until I make the mistake of stretching my limbs. This innocuous movement sets pain throbbing in my leg, my shoulder, my head, my hip, and with such ferocity, I cry out. As I stare up at the ceiling, willing the pain to subside, I give my memory a sharp kick, hoping this will fire it up to provide an explanation, but it splutters and dies, with nothing forthcoming. I have no idea what's going on. The only thing certain is that everything hurts. And, if that's not bad enough, as if I wasn't already suffering, my body spasms, and I vomit bitter bile over myself, over the bed, and the effort sets fresh pain roaring in my head, and my vision turns red. I cry out again. Somebody please help me. Please.

There is a collective 'ugh' as I lie there groaning, panting in my own vomit. I hear the curtains swish, and a voice stammer you okay buddy? And someone else says better get a nurse and goes off shouting nurse, nurse, their voice fading as another bout of vomiting leaves me whimpering and groaning. I can't see properly. And the pain: the pain thundering in my head. Part of me detaches and wonders if I'm dying. After all, someone went to call a nurse so that must mean I'm in hospital. Am I dying, and is this what it feels like? We spend a lifetime wondering, and this is it?

"It's all right, Ewan," two strong hands reach down through my pain, and take hold of my shoulders. "You're all right, my love." No, I am not all right, but the voice oozes a warm reassurance that softens the edges of my pain. "Everything's all right." The warmth spreads. I plunge my scepticism into its heat and let it wash away my fear. Yes, I'm okay. Someone is helping me. They're going to make it stop. I relax and let the hands soothe my knotted shoulders. My body starts retching again, but the voice says it's okay. I screw my eyes shut, and cling to whoever it is holding me as though they were a lifebelt in a stormy sea.

I don't know how long it is before I feel safe enough to open my eyes, but gradually the nausea subsides, the pain recedes, and calm descends. I'm bundled this way and that as they change the bedding, as they change my robe. Someone even wipes my face, and I think of all the reports I've read about falling hospital standards. These nurses are kindness personified. I want to tell them this. I try to tell them, but the voice tells me I don't have to speak. She says I need to rest. I open my eyes, but I can only see out of one. My left eye is gritty and sore, a curtain of red obscuring my vision. I go to rub it, but someone catches my hand.

"My eye," I protest.

"Try not to touch it."

"Why?"

I try to ask what's wrong with it, but it's as though the link between my brain and my tongue has been severed. The room lurches as though I've spent a heavy afternoon drinking. Actually, is that what I've done? Have I finally fulfilled Rebecca's prediction my scotch habit will be my downfall? I can't remember. All I do know is this is the most frightening hangover I've ever had, and there's something very wrong with my eye. It's as though there's something attached, growing on the surface of my eyeball, like some disgusting tropical parasite burrowing its way in to feed on the matter inside. Like a beetle. I gulp. Perhaps this is what they're going to do, lull me into a false sense of security with kindness, and then release the beasts.

"You burst a blood vessel while being sick. It's very common," the nurse says, I note, with the customary bluster of medical types who see this kind of thing every day. She hunkers down beside me so I can see her face. She has chocolaty skin and braided hair, her eyes as dark as

Trudy's, twinkling in the muted light. Wait a minute. Trudy. Where is she?

I look round, trying to focus, but I can barely see. If I'm in hospital, then perhaps she's here. No, wait a minute, there's something about Trudy that's not safe. Damn, but I can't remember. I can't remember anything.

"What is it? What are you looking for?" The nurse studies my face.

"Trudy?"

"Oh, Trudy," she says, her mouth breaking into a wide, white-toothed smile. "She's been in to see you a few times, only you were fast asleep. I'm not sure if she's still on duty, I think she was going home at six. Do you want me to ring her for you? I'm sure she'll come in and see you if you'd like. Rod said no visitors, but I don't think he meant our Trudy."

Rod? Who the hell is 'Rod'? I try to ask. The nurse tries and tries again to make sense of my slurring, but shakes her head.

"I'm sorry my love," she says. "I just can't make out what you're saying. You've had a lot of drugs today; I think that's the problem. Now come on," she eases me back against the pillows. "Let's try and get you comfortable."

I don't want to 'get comfortable', I want to go home. Perseverance leads to the successful transmission of the word 'home'. I look at the nurse, hope burning in my heart. After all, she's been so kind perhaps she'll help me get out of here.

"What?" She springs away from me as though I've just pinched her soft arm. "Are you serious?"

I am serious. There is nothing I want more than to be at home in my own house, lying in my own bed.

"I think we both know the answer to that my love, don't we?" She unhooks something behind my head, and puts it beside my right hand. "Now, try and go back to sleep. If you need anything, or if you feel sick again, or," she wags her finger as I protest I understand. "If you need something more for the pain, you ring for one of us, understand?"

Resigning myself to my fate with a sigh, I lie there staring up at the ceiling. It's tiled with the same tiles as the ceilings at school, off-white and pockmarked with random patterns of swirling spots. My eyes follow the swirls, looking for sense amid the chaos. There's a face, a Native American adorned with a brace of feathers. There's a car, or maybe it's a train. Or maybe it's not a train at all, but a building. Or perhaps it's not anything at all, just me and my eyes looking to impose order where none can exist.

I find something else to examine, the curtains. They have a diamond pattern, tiny flowers laced together. Or are they sloping squares? And as I stare, the flowers begin to move and swim in front of my eyes. If I stare hard enough, they seem to lift from the fabric and float towards me on the vertical plane. Like that picture Rebecca's mother had in the sitting room. She explained to my untutored eye the cleverness behind the picture, what made it worth so much was its inherent illusion the fruit was floating towards you. Who would ever have imagined that hospital curtains could be also be works of art? I go on staring at the flowers, staring at the spots until, for the third time today, I find myself being drawn down into a fathomless darkness sucking everything from my universe. I sink, unresisting.

Chapter 26

Time wears on. I wonder if I've been asleep, it feels as though I've been lying here for hours. Which I suppose I have. Been here for hours, I mean. How long have I been here? I wonder what time it is. I wonder what day it is. Let me see. It was Tuesday, I think. I went to work and then, oh I remember now. I was being chased. They were trying to get me. They chased me round school and Roderick said I fell down the stairs. Oh my god, Roderick. He's here, isn't he? And I've got a broken leg. They've broke my bones. Oh my god, I'm at their mercy. He injected me with something. Hang on a minute. Is he allowed to do that? I didn't give my permission. And what the hell was it anyway? Perhaps it was poison. After all, they held me down and he laughed in my face. They laughed at me. They're not allowed to do that, are they? I mean, injecting me with chemicals or whatever it was. I've got to tell someone. I have to complain about this. I have to get out of here.

"Nurse!"

Oh no, I'm not supposed to shout, I'm supposed to press this button. Where is the button? It's gone. Oh no, they've taken it away. They must have known I'd try to raise the alarm once I'd worked out what's going on. They must know. Oh god.

My hand is shaking as I go to wipe my sweating face. I'm burning hot, my hospital gown damp with sweat. Roderick is trying to kill me. That's why I was so sick. My body was trying to save me. They've got me here so he can kill me. They've told him I know too much. They've told him to get rid of me. That's how I came to fall down the stairs, they told him to make it look like an accident.

"Nurse!"

Dear God, somebody help me. They're probably all trying to kill me. The people in the other beds, they're probably listening, watching out in case I try to escape. They don't want me to escape, that's why they've done this to my leg. I didn't really fall. None of this is real. They're going to kill me.

"Help!"

Roderick yanks the curtains open and pulls them shut behind him. I scream. I try to get off the bed, but they've got me pinned by my leg. I tug at it, trying to work my leg free of their devilish contraption, but I can't. Roderick advances, syringe in hand, his red mouth brimming with razor sharp black teeth, and he's getting bigger and bigger and sprouting muscled arms covered with fuzzy blonde frizz, and he's looming over me, blocking out the light, and this time he's going to kill me, and I try to scream and scream, but I'm falling, falling back into nothingness.

I open my eyes. There's no one here. I'm still alive. That's funny. I thought. Hmm, what did I think? I'm still here. Where am I? Oh, it's this place. And there's the floaty flowers coming towards me from the curtain. I should probably tell someone about those. And the beetles. I can't believe I thought they were just spots on the ceiling. There's a terrible infestation here too. Someone ought to do something about that. No one must know they're there. I'd better watch them. I'd better keep watch. I mean, what happens if one of them falls off the ceiling? Oh my god, what if they all fall off the ceiling? What if they land on me? They'll crawl all over the bed. They might go up my nose if I fall asleep.

They're going to eat my brain. I mustn't go to sleep. I must watch them. It isn't safe. I have to watch them to keep everyone safe.

The curtains swish open. I open my mouth to tell the nurse about the beetles, but it isn't a nurse, it's Trudy. Trudy, I say, thank god you're here. There are beetles everywhere; you've got to save me. But she's not listening. She's coming closer and closer, grinning all over her face, and as she comes up to my bed the air shimmies and I realise it's not Trudy at all, but an enormous beetle. That's right, it's a giant black beetle, and it's advancing towards me, snapping its jaws. I scream. I try to yank my leg free, but I can't do it. I can't escape and the beetle is coming closer and closer and...

Dear God, could this get any weirder? I wake up to find the whole room pitching and rolling. There's the sound of screaming, nurses running, panic in the air. I try to sit up, and that's when I see what's happening. With each pitch, green liquid is sloshing across the floor. What is it? It doesn't look like the sea. It's getting deeper. I've got to do something. I've got to get out of here. The curtains open. It's Roderick. He's holding a lifebelt. He says 'Ewan, quick, we're sinking,' and he holds out the lifebelt. I reach out take it, but he doesn't let go. I look down and see his arms have turned into tentacles, tentacle after tentacle, and they're winding around me, pulling me down, down into the green, and down into deep dark nothingness.

I have to say I'm beginning to like the nothingness. It's a lot less frightening than reality.

Chapter 27

I open my eyes. The room is dark, but daylight seeps in around the blinds screening the window. I keep very still, but the room seems calm. There's the sound of a world going about its business outside of these four walls, but its quiet in here, and I am alone.

I go to raise my head, but everything shifts and lurches, my vision fuzzes into grey splodges. I stop moving, and shut my eyes. The nausea swills back into calm. I try again. This time I see my glasses in a table beside me. I reach out, and put them on.

This looks like a hospital room. Oh. I catch sight of a twinkling fragment of memory. I don't manage to grab hold of it, but I get a good look. That's right, I remember. I was in hospital. I'm still in hospital. Why am I in hospital? I don't know. I look round, and this time the room doesn't move with me. There's an alarming collection of both orange rubber and clear plastic tubes, and a funnel mounted on the wall behind where I'm lying. I don't want to know what they're for. There's a sink in the corner with lever taps and a wall-mounted tub of industrial hand-wash chemical. Apart from my bed, and the cabinet beside it, I'm happy to observe there's nothing else in here. No monsters, no beetles. I relax back into the pillows, reassured.

But I only manage to lie there for a minute of two before the questions start welling up in my head. I don't really know where I am, and the more I think about it, I really don't feel well. I feel as though my head isn't attached to the rest of me, as though it could spin off and float round and round the room. I'm hot. No, did I say hot? I'm cold. No, I feel as though somehow I've turned to liquid, sloshing around in a body that doesn't feel like mine. Taking deep breaths, I examine my memories, but everything seems hazy, like it doesn't really make sense. I remember, yes I remember. There was an octopus that looked like Roderick Henderson. I haven't seen Roderick in years. Where am I?

I shift from side to side, restless for answers. A pain grumbles in my right leg, and it doesn't move along with the rest of me. Oh yes, that's because I've broken it. Wait a minute. I have seen Roderick. I saw him the other day. But the memory, which had been solidifying, begins to vaporise once more, and slips out of reach. I can hear the sound of my breath labouring in and out. This isn't right. I want to go home. I'm getting hot. It's very hot in here.

I go to wipe the sweat from my face with my left hand, but the movement sends a sharp pain jabbing into the back of my hand. And there, sticking out of the back of my hand, pretending to be innocuous, nestled between virginal white gauze, is a long clear tube twisting away out of sight, up to a pouch suspended behind my left shoulder. Beside it sits a machine mounted on a tall stand and, as I watch, its colourful digital display shifts and changes monitoring, I realise, following the wires which disappear down under my gown, the living mechanics of my body. I am being watched, observed on every level. What the hell are they doing to me?

I have to get out of here. Gritting my teeth against the nausea, I force myself to sit up, but it leaves my head reeling and my body pouring with a horrible sweat. But I must be strong. It will stop when I get out of here. I just have to get out of here.

I hoist my good leg over the side of the bed, and feel my toes touch the floor. It feels good, nice and solid and acts as a counterweight to balance out the washing nausea. All I need to do is wrench off the tubes and wires restraining me in place, and tug the plastered leg over the edge. As I struggle, I realise I have never felt so weak. I don't have the strength to stand up, but I grit my teeth. I must find it if I am to escape with my life. Somehow I get my leg off the bed, but my foot hits the floor with a thump, and I cry out as pain explodes inside the plaster. It takes me a minute or so to gather my composure, but I am upright, and that is a triumph.

I rip off the wires attached to my chest, seize the drip in the back of my hand, and wrench it out. Blood follows it, but I don't have time to care. The monitor starts wailing. It's trying to betray me. I have to get out before they come running. With every scrap of strength I can summon, I lever myself onto my feet.

And collapse in a heap. The floor is hard and cold, streaky greenish linoleum, I don't want to think what traces of medical horror I might have landed in, but it doesn't matter. I can't stop myself from crying out, hot tears welling not from pain, but exasperation. Everything hurts. My leg is alight with white pain shrieking from the marrow out that I need to move it, but I'm too weak. There is blood pouring from the back of my hand, and I think I'm going to be sick again. And if none of this was bad enough, as if I could even imagine it any worse, I feel cold air chilling my skin, making hair rise on my legs, my buttocks and my back. Yes, that's right, I realise, giving the grotesque joke of which I am literally the butt, a wry acknowledgement of its victory. I am wearing a hospital gown, and, as we all know when we're not trying to make an escape from a medical facility, the damned things are only fastened at the back, meaning that I've managed to not only wind up in a helpless, bleeding mess on the floor, but a naked, helpless, bleeding mess. It isn't my finest hour.

I'm not left floundering for long. The machine has raised the alarm, not so much betraying as rescuing me. Feet come running as a nursing cavalry charges to my aid. I'm mouthing apologies as they take hold of my limbs, lift me up on the count of three and untwisting my leg, the pain subsiding as I am laid back down onto what could pass for a legendary feather bed, my dignity restored under warm blankets. There is a fleeting jab in my arm before I let go and feel myself falling, floating back down into sleep's soft, dark maws. My last thought, before the nothingness draws me back into its dark embrace, is I've been put back exactly where I started, my attempted escape nothing more than a waste of effort.

The next time I wake, my memory decides it's time it did some work. So as I surface, it reminds me it's not worth moving just to see what still hurts. I open my eyes, and look around the room. Beside the door, a nurse in a pin-striped mauve tunic sits reading. I examine her braided hair, her plump face, thinking I'm sure it's the nurse who was kind to me when I was being sick, but I'm not sure. Was I sick? It all seems like a very long time ago, as though it was a film I watched, something that wasn't real, something that didn't actually happen to me at all. As I watch, she seems to grow aware of my scrutiny. I see her rub her face, run her hand over the back of her neck before she looks up and sees I'm awake.

Her face breaks into a wide smile. She puts her book down, and the chair creaks as she levers her ample body up onto her feet. Her gait is stiff as she waddles towards me, yawning and stretching as though she's been sat there reading for a long time. She puts her hands in her pockets, and cocks her head to one side as she studies my face.

"Aha! You're awake. Welcome back, sleeping beauty. How are you feeling?"

"I'm not sure."

I try to raise myself on my elbows, but the movement sets off a thumping and churning in my head, and for a moment, everything spins. She puts one arm on my shoulder, and tells me to take it easy. I hold my breath, close my eyes and keep still, and this restores everything to its rightful place. She sits down on the bed beside me and takes my hand. As calm settles back into place, I open my eyes to find her beaming from ear to ear.

"You okay?"

"I think so," I say, my tongue working, but sticky and sour in my mouth. I swallow, pulling a face at the taste. "I'm thirsty. Could I have a cup of tea or something?"

"A cup of tea," she says, smiling even wider. I try to place her accent. It sounds vaguely Jamaican, but she's probably from Hackney. "I'd say you must be feeling better if you fancy a cup of tea, Ewan. It's about time."

The bed twangs as she gets up, and she laughs as though this is the best joke she's heard all day. She stretches across the bed, and presses a button on the wall. I twist round to see what she's doing, and she flashes me a dazzling smile. She tilts her head to one side, studying my face, and her podgy fingers reach out to touch. I read the name tag pinned to her uniform: Sandra.

"You got some colourful bruising, that's for sure."

"I have?" My left hand is sore, swollen and puffing out from under white gauze, so I touch my face with my right fingers. It doesn't feel right. My fingers explore and find lips cracked and swollen, my skin not only tender, but hot, puffy and stretched tight like a drum. "What's happened to my face?"

"Well," Sandra says, arching her eyebrows. "First you fell down some stairs, and then at one point you decided to try and discharge yourself from hospital, and fell out of bed. At least, we think that's what you were doing," she says, beaming. "And then you've been on a lot of medication, and that might have caused some swelling. Don't worry, it will soon get back to normal. Ah," she says as the door opens and a tall nurse with gingery hair and dark-rimmed glasses steps into the room. "Look Daphne, Ewan's awake. And not only that, but he says he'd like a cup of tea."

"Wow," Daphne's smile shows big, crooked teeth. "You must be feeling better Ewan. I think we'd better try him on water first though," she says to Sandra, as though I'm not really here, my input as to what might be good for me dismissed as inconsequential. "It's been such a long time since he had anything to eat or drink. We don't want him being sick again. You stay here and keep an eye on him, I'll page Rod."

Rod? The only 'Rod' I know is Roderick-bloody-Henderson, whom I think I've seen a few times since I've been here, only so much of what I can remember seems unreal, I'm not sure what is, and what isn't true. I hope that's not who she means, because I certainly don't want to see him now. Sandra offers to adjust my bed so I can sit up. She starts messing around behind me, but all I can focus upon is how awful I feel. I'm so dizzy, and I feel as though I have less strength than a newborn lamb wobbling on twiggy legs. I'm so absorbed in gritting my teeth, the only thing I can hang on to while waves of nausea crash against me, I don't realise she's finished until I feel her hands on my shoulders, easing me back amongst a nest of white pillows. She touches my sweating forehead with cool, reassuring fingers, and we both startle as the door creaks open.

"Ewan," Daphne is grinning. I wonder why she's never had those teeth straightened. "Guess what?"

Unless she's going to say 'you can go home', there is nothing in this world that could coax a reciprocal excitement from me.

"You've got a visitor!"

Her head withdraws, and in its place appears dark bobbing curls, Trudy's wide, sensuous mouth grinning with an irrepressible smile. She sidles around the door, Sandra mouthing platitudes about what a nice surprise this must be. My nerves jangle in a slight breeze, a sudden whiff of something ill between us, but it is gone again before any detail forms clear enough for me to grasp. I realise then the one thing that has eluded me since I woke up this time. Physical aches aside, I feel nothing other than flat, smooth calm; no pleasure, no fear, nothing, just the flat line on a monitor of a heart stopped beating: emotionally dead. I feel nothing.

"Ewan." Trudy rushes to me, and as she throws her arms around my shoulders, I catch a glint of tears glistening in her eyes. She hugs me tight, crooning over me as though I were a small boy she's just scooped up after a fall in the playground. Her embrace is soft and warm. I bury my nose against her neck and breathe in the sweet musky scent of her skin.

"Oh Ewan," she says, drawing back and brushing my hair from my face with fingers which linger, caressing my skin. "I've been so worried about you. You've been so unwell."

"I can't remember." I think hard, scanning for the slightest clue to explain what she means, but I can find nothing remarkable amongst the smooth narrow walls housing my mind. "I want to go home though. Can I go home now Trudy? I think I'd feel better at home. You've come to take me home, haven't you? I knew you would."

"No, I don't think that would be a very good idea." Her fingers fall from my face, and I see her exchange fleeting looks with Sandra sat back on her chair. Unease wafts a shiver across the hairs on the back of my neck but, as before, it's gone before I can pick up so much as a crumb of understanding. My eyes flitter around the room, as though there is something in here that will point out what it is that I'm missing.

"You're going to find it hard to manage at home with your leg," Trudy says, smoothing the back of my right hand with her finger.

My leg. Memory rushes in through the hole in my brain, plugging the breach with an onslaught of recollections. I grab Trudy's hand, my heart thumping, and drop my voice to a hoarse whisper. Sandra has sat down again with her book, but I'm not convinced she isn't eavesdropping.

"I've just remembered why I'm here. They've broken my leg. You've got to help me Trudy. I've got to get out of here."

"No Ewan," she shakes her head. "No one broke your leg. You fell down some stairs while Alex was trying to help you. He's been in bits about it. It'll be good to tell him you seem much better."

"Alex was trying to help me?" I lean in closer to Trudy. Again I see her exchanging glances with Sandra, but I'm too frantic to worry. "Does he know they're trying to kill me? You'll have to warn him Trudy. If they think he's trying to help me, they might try to kill him too. They'll stop at nothing Trudy. You've got to help me get out of here. Please Trudy, please."

"Ewan," she is shaking her head, her brow furrowed as though I'm speaking a strange language she doesn't understand. "No one is trying to kill you. Listen to me," she puts her hands on my shoulders and leans in, forcing me to look into her eyes. "No one is trying to kill you. You're in hospital. It's safe here. Everyone is trying to help you get better. That's why I tried to bring you in here the day before your accident. Everyone understands, and they just want to help you to get better."

She did. I remember it now. She tried to bring me here. I snatch my hand out of hers and recoil, clutching at the sheets as though they have the strength to shield me from her malevolent intent.

"You're in this with them." Her betrayal stings through the smooth, balanced walls, warping and twisting them into more familiar territory. "Get away from me. Go away."

"Ewan no," Trudy is shaking her head. "I'm not plotting against you. I care about you. I just want to see you get better."

"Go away."

The door creaks open. She gets up off the bed and steps backwards, hurt accusing from her face as though I've just slapped her. Movement catches my eye, and I look past her to see a tall woman in a fluttering white coat march into the room, validating all of my conclusions. I manage to stifle my scream. I mustn't show fear.

The door opens again, snaring my attention away from the doctor, but the sight of Roderick Henderson's tall, pony-tailed figure in his pale blue nursing uniform only concentrates my panic. Trudy makes to come back to my side, but I yell at her to go away. She walks past the white-coated woman, heading for the door.

"You okay Trudy?" I hear Roderick say. He's watching me, his arms folded tight across his chest. "Stay if you like. It might make things easier."

"Thanks Rod," she glances back at me as she puts her hand on the door. "But I think my presence here is only making everything worse."

Roderick turns to her as though to hide what he's saying, but I'm not deaf.

"Don't be attached to anything he says at the moment," he tells her. "It's either the psychosis or the drugs talking. He needs you."

I am torn between shouting I don't need anyone and demanding just what the hell he thinks he's talking about, when I realise the woman in the white coat is standing at the foot of my bed rummaging through a file of paperwork. She looks up and her painted mouth pulls into a warm smile, but I am not fooled. The door closes as Trudy leaves. She leaves me alone with my captors.

Chapter 28

The doctor approaches, her hips swaying with predatory stealth. I try to scrabble further up the bed, but I'm pinned by my useless, plastered leg.

"Mr. Davies, Ewan, I'm Dr. Lockhart." Her heels tap as she strides round to my side, looking as though she's going to try and shake my hand, only I'm clutching even tighter at the bedclothes, my limbs trembling. Instead, she folds her arms and cocks her head to one side, her lips pursed and calculating. She has long, manicured nails which match the burgundy colour of the smartly tailored blouse under her open coat. "How are you feeling?"

She doesn't wait for my response, but sits down on the chair Sandra has brought over from her post beside the door, crossing one slim leg over the other. Taking a pen from her top pocket, she reaches for the file lying at the bottom of my bed.

"I'm a consultant psychiatrist here in the 'Woodlands Unit', and I believe you already know my colleague and senior nurse, Roderick."

"Not really," I mutter. I wouldn't say we 'know' each other as such. If you say you 'know' someone, it suggests a degree of reciprocal familiarity that goes beyond being forced to bare your soul in front a bunch of strangers, all in the name of 'therapy'.

"Ach, Come off it Ewan. What has it been, eight years or so, hasn't it?"

"Eight years," Dr. Lockhart muses, tapping the pen against her mouth. I've been so preoccupied mulling over Roderick's conceit that he 'knows' me, I'm only just realising how she introduced herself. 'A Psychiatrist'? A chill shudders through my flesh, and sets my anxiety quivering all the way down into its cold, fathomless depths deep in my gut. I try to pull the blankets even further up, but they are tucked around my heavy, plastered leg, and won't oblige. And 'The Woodlands Unit'? She says it as though I should know what it means. I don't, but I mustn't show them I don't know. I mustn't let them see I'm shaking.

"Ewan," Dr. Lockhart says. I hate the way doctors do that, use your name as though you are great friends. She has a long, horsy face with a large dark brown mole on her top lip which, now I've noticed it, is going to hog my attention, no matter how much I try to avoid looking at it. I wonder if, being a psychiatrist, that's her secret test of a patient's sanity, whether they talk to her or the mole. Maybe it talks itself. No, I mustn't think about it. I don't want it to come true.

"Do you have any idea how long you've been in hospital?"

"Um," no I don't. Every time I think I've managed to get hold of my will-o-the-wisp memory, it vanishes again leaving me grasping at thin air. "Not really."

"Two weeks," says Roderick. He's leaning against the window. The daylight shows he has a sickly green and purple bruise around his left eye. One of his nutters must have punched him: I understand the compulsion. "You were admitted two weeks ago on Tuesday the 9th of October. It's now the 23rd."

My mouth falls open as my brain scrabbles around the ramifications of having been missing from my life for two weeks. How will they have managed without me at work? Rebecca might like to think she could do my job, but I tense at the thought of what won't have been done in my absence. It'll take weeks to sort out the mess. No, wait a minute; it's been the half term break, hasn't it? Or has it? My memory holds its hands up and shrugs. It can't remember. I look at Roderick, at Dr. Lockhart, shock swilling round and round in my gut. I can't have been in here for two weeks, two whole weeks. It's impossible.

"It's true," the doctor says, using the same kind-and-concerned voice employed by all the medical staff. It must be in their training. "Two weeks. You haven't been at all well, and we've had to keep you sedated for a large proportion of the time, both to try and lessen the hallucinations, and to limit further damage to your leg and ribs."

"What hallucinations?"

"That's something we'd like you to tell us," she smiles, fingers toying with a tiny diamond suspended from a delicate gold chain around her neck. "But for now, let's just see how much you can remember. For instance, what can you tell me about why you were admitted, or what has happened since you arrived here?"

Although I'm busy wondering what she means by 'hallucinations' I notice Dr. Lockhart sharpens her focus as though she's examining me spread-eagled under a microscope. I feel my cheeks beginning to burn, and wish for the ability of a sea anemone to retract, to draw myself inside, safe from the glare of the doctor's gaze. That's the problem, you see. I know she can make all sorts of deductions from the tiniest nuance of reaction in my face. I don't understand why a psychiatrist wants to talk to me, and there's so much I don't want her to see. Who would willingly open themselves up to be examined in this way, to have every aspect of their mind, every quirk and hang-up probed and dissected by a such knowledgeable, judging mind. I gulp. My throat is sandpaper dry, so this hurts.

And what do I remember? I think hard, and bits float by. Everyone constantly on at me, asking me over and over again 'are you all right Ewan?' until I wanted to scream. Trudy teasing me with ripe strawberries as I lay in her bed. The fingers on my left hand hurting. And running, running because I was so afraid of being caught, terrified of what they'd do to me, and yet here I am. I could run, but there was nowhere to hide.

"I fell," I say to Dr. Lockhart, my voice wavering. She nods.

"And after you were admitted?"

"I can't really remember." It's very hazy. And I don't want to talk about beetles, the monsters and the water.

Dr. Lockhart gives a gentle smile, and turns in her chair. It's as though they've rehearsed this conversation, and this is Roderick's cue. He ambles over, and plonks himself down on the foot of my bed.

"Your memory might return in fits and starts, or it might not at all," he says. "I saw you not long after you were admitted. Do you remember talking to me?"

"You tried to kill me." I'm not going to forget that. I swallow back the panic rising in my throat. "You held me down. You and that nurse."

"Bingo," says Roderick, and he and the doctor exchange looks. "Ewan, why do you think I was trying to kill you? I'd like you to try and explain."

My face is burning with colour. I've said too much now. I mustn't talk, I mustn't tell them how much I know, or then I will be expendable for sure. Again, there is an exchange of glances, an unspoken dialogue in which I am the subject, but not a participant. This time it's Dr. Lockhart who speaks.

"Ewan, you were admitted to hospital following a fall at work, but we believe you were also suffering what we call a 'psychotic episode', the terminology you might be more familiar with is a 'nervous breakdown'. You're in 'The Woodlands Unit', the psychiatric wing of Thatchington General. This is a room on the ward for patients requiring more acute medical care."

"What?" I squeak, the cocktail of outrage, disbelief, and fear this is another weird dream conspiring to strangle the voice that sounds like mine. I clutch at the blankets, trying to pull them up as a shield around me to save me from the doctor's diagnostic proclamation. My eyes even turn to Roderick, praying for the comfort of dissent on his face, but he's nodding.

"It's true," Roderick says, stroking the gingery blonde fuzz covering his chin. "I've known you for a long time Ewan, and I've never seen you in the state you've been in, not only after you were admitted, but on and off over the last two weeks. It's taken longer than we would have expected to stabilise you with medication, but the fact we're having this conversation means we've got it right at last." The expressions he and Dr Lockhart are exchanging speak of exasperation melting into quiet, triumphant relief. I'd like to slash through their air of self-congratulation with a honed, cutting remark, but it's as though I have never possessed the wit to formulate anything original to say.

Instead, I try to think. If I could only remember, I wouldn't be scrabbling around on the starting line while they romp ahead unchallenged. I ignore them both, and try very hard, but there is nothing there, not even an interesting shape waiting to be investigated in my mind. I have no idea what he means by 'the state I've been in'. He told me that I'd fallen, that I'd broken my leg: I remember those things. And I see now why people speak of 'solid facts', I can almost feel them in my hands. My mind conjures scenarios of being taken into hospital, but I cannot summon one that involves me. And I can find nothing to explain what he means about my needing to be 'stabilised'. There is nothing in my memory but wispy holes.

"You had to be restrained and sedated before the ambulance crew could get you into their vehicle," the doctor explains. "You were fighting everyone who was trying to help you."

The image of me fighting is so ridiculous, I laugh. But Roderick and Dr Lockhart aren't smiling. And if it is true, then it isn't funny. But it can't be true. It isn't true.

"That's ridiculous."

They don't flinch. My fleeting humour ices into hard and serious.

"You know, I've heard enough of this. I don't know what you're doing, but it isn't funny. You're saying I've had a mental breakdown? Well I'm saying this is a made-up pack of lies. You have no right to keep me here drugged and sedated so I can't complain. I am going to complain. As soon as I get out of here, I'm going to take this as far as I can."

"Ewan, calm yourself." Roderick's voice is composed, but even in my self-righteous pique, I see how its sound suspends in mid-air, glistening with threat. I ignore it, I must speak out. I must stop what they've been doing to me.

"You've obviously got my notes mixed up with someone else's. And you don't know me," I say to Roderick. "You don't know me at all. Now if you don't mind, I've had enough wild accusations. I'm going home, and I'm going to discharge myself right now."

"I have all the details here," Dr Lockhart says, lifting the file from her knees. She glances at me as she flicks through it. "Ambulance crew report, accident and emergency room report, ward observations," she looks at Roderick. "Everything you have said and done, it's all recorded in here."

"I don't care what your file says. You can get a parrot to say whatever you want if you keep at it long enough."

"Not to mention statements made by friends and colleagues who've all informed us that, in their opinions, you have been behaving oddly for some time," Roderick says. He is staring without blinking, so intense is his scrutiny. It's making my skin crawl, and I can't hold his gaze. "You became so violent whilst they were trying to administer first aid, you broke Mr Garvie's nose."

Alex? And then I remember the surge of emotion, of wild, white, untameable anger, and it was Nathan I'd been trying to hit. Good god, what wouldn't I have done for the satisfaction of embedding my bony fist in his pink, podgy face? My spirits find themselves knee deep in a cold puddle of regret. I won't get another chance to do that again.

Roderick's eyes tell me he's seen the memory flicker in mine. I feel a fresh flush of colour stewing in my face, advertising my guilt. He snorts, and points at the bruising around his eye.

"I'm glad to say you missed my nose. Don't worry, I didn't take it personally." And he enjoys a hearty guffaw, having a good laugh at my expense.

I hit Roderick and I don't even remember? Dr. Lockhart is studying me even closer than before. She has taken something out of the file and is shuffling the pages. I can't look at her. The thought of what she sees in me sets me trembling even harder. I don't want to hear any more. If I close my eyes, perhaps this will just be another dream, another nightmare. But when I open them once more, she is still staring at me, and Roderick has his arms folded once more. They are waiting for something, and they remind me of a pair of cats sat by a hole, waiting for the hapless mouse to reappear.

"I'm going home. I'm going to discharge myself, you can't stop me." And if my body wasn't being so damned weak and useless, I'd be up off the bed and streaming out of that door.

"Ewan, I have to inform you that you are being detained under section two of the Mental Health Act for your own protection while you undergo both ongoing assessment and treatment of your psychological condition."

"What psychological condition?" My voice is a dry husk of its usual self. "There's nothing wrong with me. This is all lies. Did she tell you all this, eh? Trudy? She's obsessed with the thought I'm unwell. There's nothing wrong with me, I'm telling you. There's nothing wrong."

"All right Ewan, calm down." Roderick puts a hand on my shoulder.

"Get off me," I twist out of his grasp. "You have no right to treat me like this. There's nothing wrong with me. Get off."

"We'll be the judge of that," Dr. Lockhart says, her eyes wide and serious. "And yes, we do have the right. Section two requires you to stay in hospital for twenty-eight days, although even at this point I think it likely we will seek to detain you under section three for a further six months, unless you agree to become a voluntary patient. Being sectioned requires you to cooperate with a care plan that includes medication and a package of therapies until we are satisfied you are well enough to be discharged."

"Agree?" The words snarl from the back of my throat. "Agree be damned. I do not agree. I want out of this wretched hospital this instant." My chest is tightening, so tight I can hardly breathe, my vision narrowing until all I can see is the doctor in her white coat announcing her verdict, destroying my world as though she were just describing the weather.

"I am the clinician in charge of your case, while Roderick is responsible for your day-to-day care. You do have the right to appeal your section, although I think it unlikely you would be successful. Do you have any questions?"

I stare at her, no, I gawp. I sit there on the bed gawping at this woman whom I've never met before as she tells me, as she condemns me into a world beyond my control. They've got me, I think. They knew I was onto them, and now they've got me. Every story I've ever heard, every film I'm ever seen, every notion I have of being imprisoned in an asylum, the deprivation, abuse and torture opens a wide, leering mouth, ready to swallow me whole. And as I go on staring, Dr Lockhart's mole grows barbed legs and goes scuttling off across her face. She covers her ears as I start to scream.

Chapter 29

The next time I awake I am visited by two more doctors, one to fuss over my leg, and the other to talk about what he did to my arm. I sliced through tendons with the deepest cut, the one, I am thinking, which precipitated my downfall. But it's all right, the doctor assures me with an enthusiastic haw-haw, he managed to repair the damage. I study his youthful face with its big brown eyes and oversized features. He doesn't look much like a surgeon to me. I can imagine long, floppy ears and a lolling pink tongue, so if I were to take my arm off and throw it across the room, he'd go bounding after it on all fours. Must Make Arm Better. 'Thanks' I say.

The leg doctor thinks I should be moving around by now, so after he's gone, Sandra and Daphne make me get up. But my body has got so used to being horizontal it is as though I have never been upright. My head is heavy and my neck buckles under its weight, sending the room and my vision swaying. All I want is to lie down again, but my helpers encourage me, and bit by bit things stop moving. When I do get onto my feet, the nurses supporting me on both sides, I'm not sure I have ever negotiated moving this thing, this body. Not only do I lack the strength to move a step forward, but the coordination too. By the time I have shuffled the three feet or so from my bed to the chair, I want to collapse with exhaustion. But the nurses are ecstatic. You've done it now, they say, the first steps are the hardest. It seems it is me who is the clever dog in their eyes.

Sandra comes back with a tray. She plonks it down on a table, and wheels it over to me. The smell punches my fragile senses, and I recoil with disgust.

"Take it away." I try to push the table, but Sandra has her foot anchoring it in place.

"Ew-an," she scolds. "You've got to eat."

"I don't want it."

"You've got to try," she says, hands clamping to her ample hips. "You've got to eat. Let's see you try a few mouthfuls at least. It's scrambled egg, just the thing to be gentle on your stomach when you haven't had anything for so long."

It's scrambled egg? I eye the greyish mounds sitting on the plate, little congealed islands in a yellowy millpond sea, but I can't see anything to confirm her assertion.

"Two mouthfuls," she says. "Come on, I want to be able to tell Roderick you've had something to eat. You want me to help you?" She goes to pick up the fork, a thick plastic yellow creation I would have thought more appropriate in a nursery.

"I don't want it." I turn my head in case she tries to ram a forkful between my lips.

"Listen to me," she leans closer, her voice lowered as though she were revealing some grand secret. I can't resist, and turn to look. Her brown eyes are wide and speak not of intrigue and dastardly plans, but sincerity and concern. "You're under section. If you won't take your medicine, we make you take it. If you don't eat, Ewan, we'll make you eat. You don't have a choice. Better to eat by yourself than be force-fed."

"You can't make me eat." I fold my arms, proud of my defiance. They can't take everything from me, I think, congratulating myself on my inner strength, my core of steel. But Sandra is not impressed.

"Yes we can, and we will. And believe me Ewan, we'll only have to do it once and you'll be so afraid of it happening again, you'll go outside and eat soil if we say so." I want to laugh at the idea, but she goes on staring at me through those big, warm eyes, and I realise she is being serious.

I turn to the plate. The 'egg', if indeed that's what it is, lurks as repulsive and unappetising as when she first unveiled it. I've read terrible things about the supplements they feed chicken to maximise egg production. And that's to say nothing about the genetic breeding programs that created the birds themselves. We are being poisoned, and I can no more eat this than inject myself full of venom. In fact the latter option is the more tempting. Sandra sits down, watching my struggle.

"Two mouthfuls, that's all." When I shake my head, she sighs "why not?"

"It isn't safe," I glance around the room, wondering if it's bugged as she presses me to explain. She's been so nice to me, the very least I can do is explain. Knowledge is power; if she knows what is being done to our food, she can choose to protect herself. She listens as I run through my theories but, just as when I tried to explain to Alex, I can see my message is lost.

"This is why you're so thin, isn't it? How long have you been worried about all this, Ewan?"

I can't remember when I read the article about the salmon; I think it was during the summer. Up until then I just had a vague sense of unease, like something brewing, bubbling under the surface. I think it was my body realising something was wrong, but until I read that article, I couldn't quite explain. It was as if that piece of writing gave me the vocabulary to articulate a truth I felt but couldn't describe.

"What is the worse thing that could happen to you if you ate normally?"

I reel off a list of cancers and brain damage, sensory impairment and psychological problems, enjoying the chance to talk about my pet subject with an enthusiastic listener, but Sandra counters every fact with the neutralising lotion of medical fact, making my theories look thinner than a voile curtain fluttering in a summer breeze. And it's strange. I've been so afraid of eating, but sitting here talking to the nurse, it's as though my fears have been smoothed over, coated in something gelatinous, sealing off the voice of panic which once shrieked with a madman's wail until it has become only the slightest of murmurs, something easily ignored.

"So now we've covered the likelihood of every life-threatening illness you could possibly contract from eating scrambled egg," she says, unfolding her arms. "Let's see you eat those two mouthfuls."

"It might be easier if you gave me proper cutlery." I huff, chasing the egg around the plate. It takes a great deal of concentration to spear a lump of egg with the stupid plastic fork. There are, I realise, entire generations of children growing up out there whose parents' think they are being stubborn or mischievous, when in fact it is almost impossible to eat properly with these thick, rainbow coloured tools. "Why can't I have proper cutlery?"

"Ew-an," she huffs and points at my sleeve. Oh, I see. Now, I'd hoped she wouldn't have noticed the way I try to keep the gown arranged over my arms to hide the cuts from medical eyes trained to draw their own conclusions, but I was being naive. I'm about to point out a round-bladed dinner knife would only be the weapon of choice for a masochist, when what's left of my sense suggests she might not appreciate the information. She may seem friendly, but she is a nurse after all, and there's no need for me to give them any more ammunition to aim at my head. Instead I make myself smile, as she tells me she's going to make a cup of tea.

I put a piece of lukewarm, eggy rubber in my mouth, and gag. It takes an enormous effort of will not to spit it out. My nausea swirls, but Sandra's words come back to me. I must eat this; I must eat. But by the time I manage a second mouthful, primal need takes over. My body is so desperate for food, it overrides my disgust and suspicions, and I cannot shovel the egg down my throat fast enough. When Sandra returns, the plate is not only empty, but I want more. "Now that's more like it," she says as she goes back to kitchen to see what's left.

By the time I've demolished two plates of scrambled egg, toast and tea, I feel as though I'm radiating contented wholesomeness, and better than I can remember since before my accident. Sandra sits down, and takes out my file. There are a few things we need to sort out, she says. I need some clothes. And even in here, I need money to buy myself a newspaper, or a tube of toothpaste. She suggests asking Trudy, but I decline. Trudy can't be trusted. It's her fault I'm in this mess.

There must be someone, Sandra says, amongst my friends who could bring things in for me, and goes flick-flicking through the pages until she finds the sheet she's looking for. It is a record of people who have rang the hospital to enquire after me. Alex, Tessa, Neil, even Mrs Phillips has rung a couple of times, probably covering her back with some damned protocol that insists she make enquiries.

"I can't think who you could ask," I say. Once upon a time I'd have asked Alex and Tessa, but that was before I broke Alex's nose. My face colours and I cringe at the thought. I need to apologise to him. What did the doctor call it, 'a psychotic episode'? Yeah, sorry about your nose Alex, but I was having a psychotic episode. Oh well mate, I try to picture him saying. That makes everything all right.

She leaves me with a newspaper. It isn't the broadsheet I would favour, but a sensational splash of sex, sensation and salacious tittle-tattle. Given that I've missed two weeks of the world, I think I should read it, but I'm tired, and I flick through it with listless interest. It's full of the usual rubbish about assorted acting types of whom, I'm proud to say, I've never heard. There is still enough hatred to secure another generation of bloodshed in the Middle East, there is still fear being fanned into life as union bosses flex withered muscles to prove decades of hostile policies have not really rendered them impotent, and still allegations of fraud and corruption from people one would consider rich enough to know better. Blah-de-blah-de-blah. The world is still turning, human affairs dragging round and round with its orbit, and my absence means nothing. It is of no consequence to anyone but me.

I fold the paper up, lay it down on the table, and glare at it. My arms ache and I can't be bothered to read any more. I have been out of touch with the world for two whole weeks. Surely something interesting should have happened in that time, something to mark my time here, something about which I will always sigh and say 'oh I missed that, it happened during the time I was locked up in hospital. 'Locked up', it sounds so final, the ultimate threat. I think about how I have been 'locked up' to prevent me from drawing attention to the truth of what is really going on. As I think, I wonder if there are other people like me being held captive for the same reason. I eye the newspaper. Perhaps I should read it again, this time looking for clues I am not alone.

I've read it three times and found nothing, when the door opens. The thing is, I've never had any compulsion towards detective work of any kind, and I can't bear television dramas around the clever, socially inept copper who can fashion truth from the most haphazard of circumstances, so I'm not sure what I'm looking for. Sandra speaks to me three times before I realise her beaming face is even there, bending around the door to look at me.

"Ew-an," she looks like a little kid waiting to go downstairs on Christmas morning to see if Santa Claus has left any presents. "You know we were talking about someone getting you some things? Well, lo-ok." She holds up an expensive-looking brown leather holdall, and my brain gives a little jolt of recognition. I have one the same. "Look what Trudy's brought for you."

Trudy. I shiver.

Sandra puts the bag down on the bed, opens it, and takes out a pair of stripy pyjamas that look a whole lot like the ones I have at home. I gawp, and it takes me a minute to realise this is my bag, these are my clothes. The smell of my own house, of my own things rushes up my nose, and wraps arms around me, hugging me tight with the insistence, the confirmation, there is life outside of this hospital, and I am who I think I am, not this fugitive locked up in this ward. I wrestle the pyjama top out of her hands, and bury my face in it, breathing in the scent of my home, of my life, of me. And yet still, something jars. Why has Trudy done this for me? She must be up to something. I'm not safe.

"Are you all right?"

Sandra's voice makes me jump. I look up. She's watching me, her brow creasing with a slight frown, making observations I know she'll record in the file at the end of my bed. I swallow, afraid of what she thinks she's seeing. It's already occurred to me that I'm going to have to be very careful what I do and say if I'm ever going to get out of here. I can't trust anyone.

"I'm fine, thank you." Hmm, I sound rather convincing, if I do say-so myself.

"How about a bath then? And then you can put your own clothes on. That'll make you feel a lot better, won't it?"

I sit up smiling. It's the nicest thing anyone has said to me since I got here.

Chapter 30

The sight that awaits me in the bathroom mirror is not comforting, but a nightmarish creature conjured from a dark and twisted mind. I don't think Sandra meant to leave me face to face with this apparition while she and Daphne readied the bath, but that's where they parked my wheelchair. I leant forward, examining my bruised face. With one eye bloodshot, both dark ringed and my cheeks sucked hollow and gaunt, it seemed to me I look as mad as they say I'm supposed to be. I looked a little better after I'd shaved off the greying stubble, my hand shaking under the nurses' watchful eyes, but it was only a minor improvement.

And my whole body is covered in mottled, purple bruises. I sat turning my arms over and over, and examined the extent of the marks on my chest and hips, forgetting to be embarrassed at being stripped and bathed by two strangers.

Back in bed, I spend the day slipping in and out of sleep, the passing of time marked by the changing light and the colour of the sky through my window. Late afternoon brings a magnificent sunset with apricot clouds edged with pink streaked across the sky darkening to indigo as Venus appears above the sliver of a silver crescent moon. I watch pigeons strutting on the ledge outside, envying their freedom as, on a whim, they take to the wing and go flapping away across the metal roofs of the hospital buildings, flying from this institutionalised hell and on to the town that lies beyond.

The sound of the door opening distracts me from the pigeons. I look up and startle as Roderick steps into the room. The contentment, if you can call it that, I'd found dozing after my bath and watching the pigeons, takes flight. He's carrying two mugs, and puts one down beside me on the bedside cabinet. I don't look at him or the mug, but fold my arms across my chest. The pigeons are more interesting; they don't talk.

"Brought you a cup of tea," he explains since, apparently, in his world 'psychotic' must be interchangeable with the word 'stupid'. "How are you? You certainly look better for a bath and a shave. And Sandra tells me you managed to eat. How do you feel?"

"Oh yeah, I'm just great." Tight-lipped, I fold my arms even closer to my chest. "Never been better."

He titters, plonks himself down on my bed, and reaches for the file that so fascinates every member of staff who comes to talk to me. Broken leg or not, the next time I get a bit of privacy, I'm going to have to manoeuvre down the bed to look at it myself.

"Do you have to sit there?"

It can't be very professional of him to sit on my bed, but it seems standards amongst medical staff fluctuate. He laughs. I wish I could remember punching him the first time around. Nothing could be more satisfying.

"Come on, why should you have the best seat? Anyway, good to see you more like your usual grumpy self, although that isn't something I thought I'd ever say. Now," he pauses to take a sip of his tea. "To say there are a few things we need to talk about is something of an understatement, to say the least."

I arch my eyebrows. He can talk as much as he likes, I've got nothing to say to him. Well, nothing polite anyway. And thank goodness I can't hear his thoughts. That would be a torment too far. I turn my head to the window to resume watching the pigeons.

Roderick slurps his tea. I grit my teeth and clench the fingers of my good hand. Two spots of heat ignite, one on either side of my face.

"Come on then. Where shall we start?"

"I've got nothing to say."

I hit back, aiming my shot deep into his half in the hope my hostility will land it way beyond his reach. But one way or another, we've played this before, and he knows my game plan as surely as I know his. I will try to block his every move with a sarcastic rebuff, he will deflect mine with his own snide version of humour, and we will circle each other, snarling and posturing until eventually, and experience whispers it's usually me, one of us relents. For he is a special kind of vulture, and he won't relinquish until he's torn away every layer of pretence, until I am laid bare, my defences eaten away by his trained beak. I gulp, my mouth dry, and look round for the tea. There isn't a part of me that wants to do this. The pigeons don't know how lucky they are.

"Well, we can start with what's been happening now, or we can go back ten years to Marcia. It's your call."

He arches his pale eyebrows. I stare at them, and at how he still wears his greasy ginger hair slicked back into that ridiculous, scraggy pony-tail. I'd like to cut it off, sawing at it with a pair of blunt scissors. I can feel them cold and rusty between my fingers. Does he think it makes him look wise, like the all-knowing guru his ego prides itself on being, or does he think it makes him look young enough to appeal to the teenagers he tries to save. Yeah, I bet that's it. He's probably read somewhere that teenaged girls respond to the unwashed rebellious look. I wonder what Marcia thought. I should have asked her. But it's too late now.

"I don't want to talk."

"Come on Ewan," he drawls. "Oh, okay, well come on then, let's try a different tack, shall we?" He makes a huge show of leafing through the file, clicks his pen, and clears his throat.

"According to a number of your friends and colleagues, you are convinced you are being targeted for having discovered a plot to control the general population through the use of chemical agents in food, to the extent you can barely eat, and you are equally convinced your house is infested with," he peers closer to the page. "Black beetles, hence your friend Trudy, who happens to be a nurse here, tried to bring you in for medical attention, only you ran off."

He pauses, peers over the top of the notes to scrutinise me, the look in his eyes proclaiming he's already drawn his own goddamned conclusions. The heat from the two spots on my cheeks is spreading its horrid flush across my face, creeping down my neck.

"You did the same when I called round to have a chat with you about how you were feeling, and again at work the next morning, which was how you came to fall downstairs. Glad it was your chums from school who were trying to catch you at that point," he says, taking another sip of tea. "Unbelievable amount of paperwork that stunt would have generated here. Now, if you'd come into the head's office like you were supposed to, we could have dealt with it all in a civilised manner and you wouldn't have broken limbs on top of everything else."

"On top of what else?"

"How you've been feeling. Come on Ewan. We know each other well enough not to have to play games. How would you describe how you've been feeling lately?"

"I'm fine."

"Well, what can you tell me about the things your friends have told us? Your colleague Mrs Cartwright told me she found you hiding on a shelf in a cupboard."

"I don't want to talk about it." Fending him off is easy, he's out of practice.

He sighs, closes the file, and puts it back in its place at the foot of my bed. His eyes are weary as he looks at me, exasperation emphasising the lines around his eyes.

"Okay, so I guess it was unrealistic of me to expect you to cooperate just like that. I thought you might actually have mellowed since I saw you last, like that was ever going to happen," he mutters.

"The thing is, whether you want to face it or not, you haven't been well. Now, we can control how you feel by keeping you pumped full of drugs, for the rest of your life if that's how you want it. But given your aversion to chemicals, I would have thought you'd be keen to explore other options. I can help you with that, but if you won't open up and let me, then all I can do is keep prescribing you more medicine. Now, before I go," he says, getting up off the bed. "There's something I want you to think about."

I arch one eyebrow, tired of his prattling lecture. The sky has gone dark now, hung with tiny stars, and my eyes are heavy, sleep calling me back into her fuzzy embrace.

"John Davidson. What can you tell me about John Davidson?"

"Who?" I shrug.

"Who is he?"

"I don't know," I say. "One of my pupils? What is this, 'the random name game'? Haven't you got something else you could go and do? I'm tired."

I close my eyes. He lets out a long sigh, and the door opens and closes, indicating he's accepted defeat, for now. But it isn't a victory to celebrate. I closed my eyes, trying to close the book on a chapter I'd rather not revisit, although if Roderick's read it, I won't have peace for long. Damn. Despite my fatigue, sleep eludes my grasp.

Chapter 31

As I get used to being up and out of bed, I have a visit from a
physiotherapist, who introduces me to a pair of silver grey crutches. It's
always seemed to me they must be uncomfortable things to use. I
remember watching Chloe Sanderson, a pupil from a few years back who
could have been quite an accomplished flautist if only I'd been able to
persuade her to summon the self-belief, struggling down the corridor,
back at school after a disastrous family skiing holiday during the Easter
break. I held a door open for her, and I remember both the knotted fury
twisting her plucked eyebrows, and the pain she wouldn't admit as she
hobbled along, unable to keep up with her friends' attempts to walk
slowly. She'd muttered thanks, her sullen voice at odds with the cheerful
girl who trilled like a garden bird claiming its territory in choir practice.

Now I know how she felt. And not only do I have to endure the growing
discomfort of having to bear my weight upon an inadequately padded
prop thrust under each armpit, but the effort required to move the
damned things the same way at the same time makes me want to throw
them across the room. Several times I come close to doing just that. But
I persevere, and after a few more attempts, I can make it around my
room, out into the corridor, down as far as the locked door, and back.
And now I'm mobile, Sandra informs me, there is no need for me to stay
on the acute medical care ward, I can move down into the residential unit
'with the other patients'. This news reduces me to cold, sweating jelly.
I'm trembling so hard, as I try to swing the crutches they refuse to
cooperate in a coordinated manner, and I have to keep stopping to regain
my balance.

Sandra unlocks another door and leads the way past a reception desk,
through more locking doors, and down a scraped orange corridor. I try
not to look at the marks and gouges, nor imagine myself being dragged
down here, kicking and screaming. Instead I reflect on the quiet irony
that here I am, as unwilling as anyone to be here, yet limping along as
dignified as is possible to be on a torturous pair of stainless steel
crutches. What is this quiet acceptance that has replaced my fighting
spirit? I don't recognise myself any more. And I think this must be
deliberate. The reason they make me swallow all these drugs is to ensure
my compliance.

At the bottom of the corridor is another set of doors, and as we approach,
Roderick appears and holds open the door. I don't want him to witness

how much effort this is costing me, so I grit my teeth to eclipse the pain, and give the crutches a more masterful swing.

"Come on," he says. "Upwardly mobile. There'll be no stopping you now." He tips back his head to laugh at his own joke. It's heartening to see Sandra's look of disgust. She catches my eye, raises her brows and we swap smirks. "Welcome to 'The Woodlands'."

I wonder if it's possible to clip his leg as I pass, but the crutch only swipes at thin air. The intentional injuring of irritating bystanders is, it seems, beyond my current prowess.

'The Woodlands' as Roderick puts it, sounds nice. It conjures an idyllic, sylvan scene of happy people picnicking under the dappled shade of an ancient oak woodland canopy, the floor soft with a litter of moss and old leaves, while fluffy red squirrels and cute little field mice scamper around red and white fairy-ring toadstools, maybe the occasional enigmatic unicorn stepping in and out of view. Whereas the only real connection to woodland 'The Woodlands Unit' has is a flaky mural painted not by a ten year old, as first inspection would seem apparent, but by a former resident. I take the use of the word 'former' to suggest he must have died, since his artwork doesn't vouch for sufficient enough a recovery to have released him from these walls. I shudder, and hobble past.

Sandra and Roderick lead me through another set of locking doors, just in case, I imagine, I have somehow managed to miss the 'secure' element of this wretched place. It opens out into an open plan area, glazed down one side and looking out onto a pitiful enclosed garden full of gravel, weeds and cigarette ends, hardly an inspiring scene. There is a kitchen where, I'm told, I can make myself a cup of tea any time I like. Ah, well, that's fantastic, isn't it? Next to it is a lounge furnished with a mix of institutional vinyl chairs and shabby sofas arranged around an enormous television. Three men and a woman sit watching, all slumped, their bored eyes give me a brief glance, but I am not interesting, just another nutter come to join the fun. There is the smell of food in the air, reminiscent of the overcooked aromas of the school canteen. Sandra points that out it's nearly lunchtime, and my spirits sink further still. More doors, and then we arrive at ward four. The nurse opens the door, and I follow her inside.

There are eight beds, four down either side of the room. I stop dead, weakened by the force of the protest which engulfs me. Sandra plonks my bag down on the third bed on the left. My mouth opens and closes, but for the moment, I am too overwhelmed to speak. Instead I stare at my surroundings, at the hospital beds, at the white bars on the window, at the pockmarked walls painted at head height with a thick band of lime green, and I wonder what horrors these walls have witnessed. They might have been painted over, but I imagine their stories creeping through the paintwork like mould blooming across a damp wall, whispering their horrid tales in the dead of the night. I look again at the window, and my mouth tightens.

"Bars on the window," I hiss. "Is that really necessary?"

"Yes," Roderick stands leaning on one arm against the door, watching me, watching my reactions. "For some patients, they are necessary."

I look round, and round again. A frown settles on my forehead, and a yawning sense of disbelief stretches wider and wider. I know this isn't a five star luxury hotel, but really?

"You are not seriously suggesting I have to share?" With the other nutters, is what I want to say, but don't. Surely I can't be expected to sleep in a room with other people. I thought the aim of the exercise was to make me better, no add fuel to my fire.

But I do. I have to share everything as it turns out. Until they decide otherwise, I can't even take a damned shower in private, just in case I seize the opportunity for 'a little self harming moment' as Roderick puts it, stroking his scruffy stubble, arm folded across his chest, watching me as I feel my face turning redder and redder. And, for the time being, I'm not allowed to enjoy peace and quiet alone in the empty ward, I must stay in the lounge with the other residents unless I'm given permission to do something else.

"It's for your own good, Ewan," Sandra says, her hands stuck deep in her pockets, her eyes fixed on mine, watching, in case I had forgotten amid the warmth of her seeming friendship, she is watching me too. "We just want you to get better."

"How the hell is any of this supposed to make me better, for heaven's sake?" I shout, petulant energy firing my limbs. If you'd suggested to me I could behave like this, I would have thought you the one who is insane, but being powerless reduces me to a tantrum. I lose myself in a savagery of protest, every fibre shrieking and clawing at the unfairness of my imprisonment. My fury is so strong, I don't even see the soft dark numbness rushing up to greet me, to enfold me in its comforting arms and, for the moment at least, soothe the turmoil from my mind.

I come round on the bed, the bleary walls coming into focus in slow motion, along with a pair of pale blue trouser legs folded one over the other and ending in a pair of those weird cream clog things the staff all seem to wear. My eyes follow the legs upwards until they reach Roderick's name badge. Damn. All I want is to be left alone. I think of the four calm walls of my bedroom at home, the crumbling brick chimney breast travelling from floor to ceiling from the lounge below, onwards and up on its way to the sky, extruding warmth and comfort through the winter when the fire is lit, and a sense of reassurance the rest of the year that I am safe and protected lying in my bed, and wish myself there. Every time they sedate me, every time I fall asleep, I still wake up hoping this has all been a bizarre dream. And then the truth hits, thumping away hope with a club forged from pure, harsh reality.

"Can you hear me Ewan? How are you feeling?"

"I'm not deaf," I mumble, and close my eyes. If I can manage to fall back to sleep, he will leave me alone. Sleep is a safe haven where I can rest unobserved, untroubled by having to worry about who is interpreting what from my behaviour, I want to be there, I want to claim sanctuary. But Roderick gets too much of a kick from his role as my chief tormentor to let me escape.

"I'd like you to try and tell me what happened this time. And I'm particularly interested in whether or not there were any insects involved."

I know what he's talking about, just as I knew exactly what Dr. Lockhart was talking about when she referred to my 'hallucinations'. Even that word sets my teeth on edge. I don't care what anyone says, when I see a black shape scuttling, it is real, and I wonder why they're trying to tell me it isn't. Since I've been here, I don't feel so afraid the authorities are trying to control me, but the suggestion there are no beetles sets doubts germinating. He's mocking me.

"Go away. Leave me alone."

I turn my head so I'm staring past the next bed and at the wall at the end of the room, praying this will work, although I know it won't. Roderick snorts and clicks his pen. The thought of him sitting there, proud in his cloak of knowledge, scribing more damning notes on what he interprets as the state of my mind overrides the drugs and re-opens the gates to my anger.

"Sorry Ewan, you know it doesn't work like that. So, try and tell me what happened."

"What do you expect?" I go from lying down to sitting upright in a flash of energy, my anger sparking through the air like invisible cords ready to scorch my interrogator. "You lock me up and treat me like a child. What, do you think I'm going to be nice because you say so?"

Roderick's fiddling with his pen and going 'interesting', but I'm listening to the anger crackling through me, through my veins, in my head, a primal rush of strength I could never begin to control, and I remember, as though I'm being sucked back through time to the moments after I fell down the stairs at work, and I can hear Alex pleading, his voice straining with annoyance, but tempered by the socially imposed bonds of acceptable behaviour, something which now I've been removed from polite society, seem pointless, and not only beyond my grasp, but outside of the periphery of what I even want.

Alex is going, 'Jeez Ewan, you're really bleeding. You must have cut your arm on the step or something.' I see him looking up, looking for something to confirm this theory, and I seize this moment to wrench my arm out of his hands. But everything is whirling and going fuzzy and sparkly, fuzzy and sparkly, little lights popping and fizzing in front of my eyes. And someone's got hold of my shoulders. Mrs Phillips is telling me to calm down. Alex has hold of my arm again, and why will no one listen? There's a wave of biting black beetles washing down the stairs towards me. Why is no one listening? Leave me alone. I roar with every scrap of energy I can summon, but no one is listening.

"Listen Ewan mate, I've got to stop this bleeding. Jeez, will you just stop bloody struggling? You're making it worse."

There's no point in trying to fight us. You will do as we say.

More hands are trying to restrain me. Nathan's ghastly curls appear in front of my face. He seizes my arm. Damn, but he's strong. There is nothing I can do but watch as Alex begins to cut away my bloodied shirt with the first aid kit's gleaming surgical scissors. Snip snip snip. I feel air on my skin.

There is a collective gasp. Nathan pulls back, and I can see the dressing has dislodged. The cut is gaping, a ruby fissure, unstuck plastic stitches curling up and quivering like eyelashes wide with surprise. Noise erupts, everyone jabbering at once while I lie there staring at the traitorous cut. But one voice cuts through the maelstrom.

"Oh for god's sake."

Rebecca turns on her heel and walks away. I lift my head and watch her ankles, the elegant sweep of her skirt as she walks away, and I see how the crowd part, how the wave of beetles parts, to let her through as she walks away from me again. I cry after her, but it does no good. She doesn't pause.

"I've always said he's a nutter," Nathan says to Alex as though I can't hear.

I read somewhere once the only thing no one can take from a man is his dignity, but let me tell you now, it isn't true. As I lay there, the world guffawing at my weaknesses, I had not a crumb left. Everything that I thought defined me and singled me out as Ewan Davies, the man I had taken such effort to construct, had vanished. The rules and conventions which govern us, and to which I had been devoted, none of these mattered any more. I lay there as though I was naked, stripped bare of everything I had ever held dear. And that's when I discovered there was something in me building. When I think about it, as I have, I sort-of knew it was there all along, it just hadn't occurred to me before. In fact, we all have it, not just me. And I suppose what defines us as sane or insane is whether or not we choose to control it.

As I lay there, I began to feel a white hot strength building. It didn't just flow through my body; it surged from some unknown core. I felt as though the old me was being cracked apart and this new one, the real me was being released. And this me didn't care for social niceties, for playing silly games. This me was wild and untamed, a destroyer of worlds. I felt magnificent. I was omnipotent. And I lashed out because

I was sick of being imprisoned, sick of being held down and forced to stay in place like a butterfly specimen in a museum collection stuck on a board with pins fabricated from other peoples' rules. I wanted to be free at last. And you know what? Now I've found this me, no amount of drugs is going to hide him. Even now I can feel the white strength surging through my limbs. This is in all of us. People don't realise. They tiptoe around going 'I'm a nice person, I'd never do that'. And to think I'm the one who's pronounced insane. I'm laughing so hard, my eyes are filling with tears. Damn, but it's funny.

I notice Roderick isn't laughing, but that's because he doesn't realise he could choose to be free either. And he's the one who's supposed to be helping me. He's such an idiot.

"Ewan, stop it."

He's trying to sound serious, but even that's funny.

"Ewan, take a deep breath, and calm down."

So funny.

"Ewan, if you won't calm down, I will have no choice but to restrain you."

You know what? I don't care. I haven't laughed like this for years. My sides are aching and I'm a bit light-headed because I can't breathe properly, but that's funny too. I'm still laughing when they drag me off to a small room furnished, literally, with padded walls, shove me inside, and lock the door.

My head is groggy from the sedative Roderick gave me before. As my laughter subsides, I curl up in a ball on the floor, and close my eyes, the swirling soft drug-induced darkness still waiting to welcome me back. Come back Ewan. Come back to sleep now. I drift off, chuckling.

But the peace doesn't last. Someone keeps saying my name and shaking my shoulder. I half-open one eye. It's Roderick. Damn. What does he want this time?

"Good to see you've managed to calm down."

"Go away," I yawn. "I just want to go back to sleep." It's surprisingly comfortable down here on the padded floor. I could sleep here all day.

"No," he says. "You need to get up." He stands over me, stopping me from getting comfortable, his feet planted against my body. "You'd lost control again, that's why you were put in here. Do you understand?"

"Yeah." I really don't care.

"Good. Now you're coming out of here to settle in with the other residents," he says. "And I don't want any more nonsense. Now get up on your feet." He takes my arm, drags me upright, and hands me my crutches. His hand on the door, he goes to open it, only something crosses his mind. He turns to me, his head cocked.

"That reminds me. Have you thought any more about our conversation the other day?"

"Which one?" I say making my eyes wide with feigned innocence. You have to admit, I have being evasive down to a fine art.

"You were going to have a think about whether you could remember anything about John Davidson."

"Still doesn't ring any bells," I mumble, avoiding his eyes as I swing out of the door.

Chapter 32

Most of the next few weeks vanish in a drug-induced haze, for which I am truly grateful. Incarcerated, imprisoned, the only thing I can do to make myself heard is to let go of Ewan Davies, the one who taught music at Thatchington High, ran the church choir and drank pints with his friends in 'The Dolphin' on a Friday night, and become Ewan Davies, the psychotic inmate who won't do as he's told. I even get a couple of cheers from other patients for refusing to take the new tablets Dr. Lockhart decided I should take, although my bravado evaporates at the speed of light when I discover the nurses have no qualms about enforcing the requirement of my section to take prescribed medicine. As I think back through my hazy memories of those days, I am ashamed to admit I behaved so abominably, snarling and swearing at Dr. Lockhart, but in my defence, the Woodlands Unit would drive the sanest man mad.

Deprived of my freedom and stripped of my dignity, I have nothing other than the constant reminder that someone, some boffin, no doubt holed up in a gleaming laboratory far from the real world, poring over epic tomes and devising new hypothesis into the intricacies of the human mind, has decreed my particular idiosyncrasies so deviant from the 'norm', whatever the hell that might be, no doubt the subject perplexing another boffin in another shiny laboratory with a different set of books, that I am considered to have a mental illness. And if that wasn't enough, Dr. Lockhart informs me I am labelled, classed as suffering from what she calls 'Schizophrenic Spectrum Disorder'. That's nice. So it's not enough that I've been locked up, I also have to be recast from 'unremarkable man' to 'dangerous lunatic', and for what reason? Oh yes, I had an accident, fell down some stairs, and got a bit upset, only the 'upset' part, rather than a normal reaction to an unpleasant situation, is classified as psychotic. I suppose you might say I've fallen from grace.

"Welcome to the club Teach, we're all bloody lunatics in here," one of my listeners quips. I am holding court in the lounge, my voice raised to be heard above the television blaring away in the corner. He sits back in his chair, one leg crossed high over the other, fidgeting the whole time, scratching his stubble, his nose, his ears, fingers missing the security of having a cigarette to hold. There is a tattoo of a tiger sprawling across one side of his closely cropped head, and he is exactly the sort of person who, had you asked me beforehand, I would expect to find in a place like this. His name is Benny, and I have given up trying to correct him to use my proper name. He started calling me 'Teach' thanks to Roderick's unhelpful suggestion I solve the quandary of having nothing to do by teaching him to read. It appears to have stuck.

Maisy joins in laughing, although I'm not sure if she knows what Benny finds so funny. Of all the residents, she seems the maddest, or 'the most unwell', I suppose, if you prefer to play the 'politically correct' card. She wanders the corridors wailing. Sometimes it's a pensive moan, other times a haunted howl. I think the nurses have given up trying to make her stop. The only time she is quiet is when we're all watching 'Coronation Street'. Despite the cumbersome crutches, I try to move seats if she plonks herself down next to me. She huddles behind lanky mousey locks, and reeks of menthol, of the muscle ointment my grandmother used to use. Any attempt to engage her in conversation results in a fresh bout of wails, so I don't try. I learned to avoid that on my first day.

"I am not schizophrenic."

"She didn't say you are, did she?" Benny folds his hands behind his head, smug that he knows more than the older man who might have normally looked down on him out in the street. "She said you got 'schizophrenic spectrum disorder'. It ain't the same thing. Now, Rocky over there," he nods in the direction of a portly man, his milky skin luminous above the curling black hair of his beard, sitting rocking backwards and forwards in a chair. I have yet to work out if his name really is 'Rocky' or whether this is just a cruel joke. He doesn't answer questions. "He's a true schizo, hears voices and stuff, says it's god talking to him. He's your typical nutcase. But you and me, we're the same."

He leans towards me in camaraderie, and I draw back, repulsed both by his blocked drain breath and his assertion we are in any way 'the same', although I am just as willing as anyone here to point the finger at how another's idiosyncrasies make their condition 'worse' than mine. Actually, I haven't heard anyone's voice talking in my head for a while. I've wondered if it's the drugs, interfering with my ability. I've managed to resist mentioning it to anyone. They wouldn't understand it makes me special. I'd be lumped in the same boat as Rocky.

"We're not like him. No, what she means is they don't really know what's wrong with us, we just ain't right."

"Thank you so much for the clarification." I am surrounded not only by lunatics, but idiots too.

"You're welcome Teach." Pleased with himself, he grins from ear to ear. I shake my head and turn away. I have no idea how someone can be so impervious to sarcasm, but Benny manages it without any apparent effort.

Muffled snorts sound from the chairs in front. Ruth turns round. She's sitting with Will, one of the older residents, and she's drawing a swirling pattern of stars and whorls in biro down the side of a magazine page. Her straight hair fascinates me. It's been cut in a manner designed to have it fall back into place every time she moves her head, a gleaming glossy curtain which she takes pride in continually arranging and rearranging, horrified, no doubt, into action by Maisy's unkempt looks.

I'm sure this is the case, because Maisy's problems with personal hygiene have made me take more care over my appearance. At first I protested at my lack of privacy by refusing to shower or shave, no matter how much I detest the itchy greying stubble which sprouts across my face. Sandra and Roderick could tut-tut as much as they liked, it was Maisy who persuaded me to resume my normal habits. Hers is a slippery slope I would rather avoid. It takes at least four members of staff to force her under the shower, so they only do it once or twice a week. Sometimes I wonder if she is actually some sort of decoy, paid to act the extreme to keep the rest of us in line. Until she starts howling, and then her distress is too real to be fake. When that happens, even Rocky stops moving and begs her to stop.

"Ewan, you aren't locked in the psychiatric ward of a hospital because there's nothing wrong with you," Ruth says, shredding the credibility of my sanity with a smirk. "You're a nut, and one of the biggest in here." She exchanges grins with Will, who gives a knowing laugh, his thoughtful grey eyes watching me over the top of his silver reading glasses. I think he's heard it all before. He's told me he's been in and out of hospital with bipolar disorder since his teens.

She and Will have been in 'The Woodlands' the longest, so they are classed as 'senior patients' and given the dubious honour of organising the rest of us into work rotas and therapy groups. There isn't a minute in the day that isn't covered by some pointless discussion group or organised activity, and we're all obliged to get together morning and night to discuss any 'issues' we have with either the staff or each other. And, as I quickly discovered on my arrival, there is no opting out. Both Will and Ruth take their positions very seriously. I hope I don't stay here long enough to be so absorbed into the system I'll do everything to uphold it. The day that happens I will be truly lost. The slightest dissent is met with Will's sombre eyes peering into your soul from over his glasses as he strokes his chin and muses, 'really, now what do you think that's telling you about yourself'. He can twist any complaint into a reflection of the complainer's personal inadequacy. It's impossible to win. The best course, as I've realised, is to play along and keep your opinions to yourself, a good little robot doing exactly as you're told. That doesn't mean I don't take exception to being called a nut.

"I beg your pardon?"

Ruth's smirk takes what might have been a pretty face, screws it up, and tramples it underfoot. She is every reason I prefer my own company rolled up into one.

"Ah come off it, don't get all hoity-toity with me," she says, her cattish green eyes gleaming with satisfaction at my discomfort. "How many times has Roderick had to sedate you this week?"

I purse my lips. I can't actually remember. She takes my silence for defeat.

"You've been done more times than the rest of us put together. 'Nothing wrong with you', my arse. Oh hello," she breaks into a wide smile one could be forgiven for interpreting as infatuation, only I'm not sure Ruth is capable of harbouring a passion for anyone other than herself. "Talking of whom, here he comes."

Roderick's lanky frame is strolling down the corridor towards us, a hefty file tucked under one arm, and a determined look on his face. I sink down in my chair, but it is my eyes he seeks out, me with whom he's intending to make contact. It doesn't matter if I pretend I haven't seen him, or how hard I try to ignore him, I cannot postpone the inevitable.

"Morning Roderick," Ruth simpers, gazing at him, her pen poised between her fingers. I try to fathom just how much she's taking the piss, I'm sure Benny said she was 'one of them lesbians' as he put it, but I can't work her out. But whatever she's doing, her doe-eyes have the desired effect, because Roderick's mouth lapses into a goofy smile.

"How are you Ruth?" He sinks his hands into the pockets of his uniform. I bet he wears it at home, sleeps in it he's so proud of himself. In fact, I wonder why he's not insisted they fashion a matching cape just for him. And a superhero mask. Maybe we should have a whip-round and buy him one.

"Me? Oh yeah, I'm great," she grins, winding a lock of smooth hair around her finger. Then she looks at me, and I startle. "Ewan was just telling us how there's nothing wrong with him, isn't that right Ewan?"

My face erupts into a fiery blush, and Benny guffaws. "You're a total numpty."

"That's enough," Roderick says and looks at me. "Ewan's doing just fine, aren't you Ewan?" I shuffle in my chair, cursing the damned medicine they've got me taking. It has numbed my brain. Sure, I can hold my own with Benny, but Ruth runs rings around me fired on by her youthful arty arrogance. I plod along in her wake and no insult I can throw moves fast enough to hit her.

"It's you I need to see," he says to me, shuffling the folder under his arm. "Come with me please."

"Aw," Ruth pouts. "I thought it was my turn." She reminds me of one of my more insubordinate pupils, brazen, blazing with rebellion, and I can picture her, face painted with a teenaged girl's overzealous hand, lip curling in a perpetual sneer while she swings back on a chair's hind legs, mouth full of gum, daring me to rise to her challenge. Roderick refuses by folding his arms, one eyebrow cocked, and she laughs: a thin, hard, cruel laugh. I glare, but she's laughing at me too. My face burns hotter.

Roderick waits as I fumble with my crutches, as I heave myself upright, and wobble while I find my balance. I follow with as much dignity as I can muster, but as I hobble away, I hear Ruth and Benny's sniggers as they swap odds on the likelihood of me winding up being sedated yet again. Their laughter follows me down the corridor, and echoes, taunting my ears for the rest of the day.

"Good to see you with the other residents," he says as I follow him into the office. I mutter that I don't exactly have a choice, but he pretends not to hear. As I go to follow him into the office, I see Sandra approaching with two mugs of tea. She flashes me her widest smile as she walks in and puts the drinks down on the desk. Like the good pre-programmed robot I've become, I sit down in front of the desk. Roderick takes up his post, opens my file, clicks his pen, and we're off again. He runs through Sandra's notes for the last few days, goes through the usual 'how are you todays', and just as I'm thinking how pleased I am to disappoint Ruth and Benny, he puts down his pen, plants his elbows on his desk, and fixes me with the look I know so well. I sigh and look at the clock. This is going to take a long time.

Chapter 33

He waits until Sandra leaves the room. That's something else I hate about this place, the way everything has been discussed, delegated beforehand. I will say this, you will say that, and then I will do this: a great big machine clanking away, shiny pistons going up and down, up and down, cogs going round and round, round and round, here comes another patient in and out, and in and out. He waits until she shuts the door, then he produces another file from a drawer. It's old, with faded handwritten labels. I try to read it upside down, but he covers it with his hands.

"John Davidson."

I hate the way he does this too, picking up a conversation exactly where it left off, no matter how many days it's been since we had it. I suppose he records it in his notes, he writes constantly filling page after page with illegible blue scrawl which I can't decipher, no matter how hard to try to sneak a look.

He arches his eyebrows and leans forward with an expectant look in his watery blue eyes as though this alone has the power to prise open my shell. They're an interesting shade of blue. Very interesting. I wonder if they'd look so blue if his uniform was a different colour, if it was green or something.

"I'd like you to tell me about John Davidson. You've had plenty of time to think about it, and now it's time for your version of the story. It's going to take a long time if I have to unearth it piece by piece."

"What story?"

Roderick has wrestled something unpleasant out of the shadows which follow me around. How he found it is beyond me, but now he knows too much. I gulp at the ramifications of this, watching them growing, twisting and coiling on and on out of sight into a gaping infinity. It's too big. I will have to think about it later. Mind you, the time he's known me, you think he would have worked it all out before.

"Well, what can you tell me?"

I knew this was coming, so I should have been devising a strategy, working out how to pick my way between the landmines and craters littering this perilous terrain, but I haven't. That's the problem with these drugs they've got me taking. Everything is smooth and flat, and there are these fluffy little holes in what used to be my memory, reason, logic, or whatever it was I had before I wound up in here. I think of what they keep telling us in the relaxation sessions, take a deep breath, and keep calm. This is dangerous ground, and I must pick my way with care.

"John. Davidson."

I can only meet Roderick's eyes for a moment before I have to look away. My eyes alight on the tea sitting on the desk, and I reach forward, thread my fingers around my mug and lift it to my mouth. It's still on the hot side, so I blow on it and sip. The whole time, Roderick goes on staring at me, but I can't look at him. I have no idea how to answer the question, never mind whether I should at all. And as to where in my jumbled brain there might be a point at which to begin, I don't even want to look. Roderick leans back in his chair, and clasps his hands behind the back of his head. He puffs out both cheeks, and then expels the air as far as he can. I carry on sipping my tea, wondering how long I can make it last. The wall clock ticks.

Roderick sits up and opens the elderly file. He leafs through the pages and takes something out, which he tosses across the desk to me. It's a photograph. I don't want to look, but my curiosity can't resist. It's rather faded, curling around the edges, the photographic paper yellowing with age. I didn't expect it to look like something that's been lost for a very long time, mouldering deep in the archives. I don't think I'm so old.

My teenaged self glares up at me from the picture, his accusing eyes asking why, how have you got us back into this mess when you were the one who was supposed to sort it out? I tried, I tell him. But this isn't the answer he wanted to hear. He goes on glaring.

"Perhaps you could start by explaining to me why you haven't been entirely honest about your mental health history," Roderick says, deciding life isn't long enough to indulge in a stand-off to which I've already devoted a quarter of a century.

"I don't know what you mean."

I think I've just seen John huff and roll his eyes in the picture. Okay, I tell him. Maybe I could have done better, but I tried, I really tried.

"Every healthcare worker you've been in contact with since your referral for self-harming nine years ago, from your GP to my good self, has asked you the same question. Do you have a history of mental health problems, to which you've repeatedly answered"

"No. No I don't." I bang my empty mug down onto the desk. "There was nothing wrong with me."

"Hmm, interesting you should say that, given you won't accept the diagnosis we've made based on our observations of your behaviour. But seventeen years old and detained under the mental health act of the day until," he turns over the paper in his hand and reads "you absconded three months later. That doesn't qualify as 'not having a history' or 'having nothing wrong with you'. Why didn't you tell me? I want to know why it was so important to you to hide it, you changed your name."

There speaks a man who's never been on the receiving end of his own professional scrutiny. I stare at him, astonished he could be numb enough to need an explanation as to why anyone, let alone me, might want to flee from the condemnation of mental illness, to hide from the shame, the bewilderment that comes from being told a part of you is so wrong, so deviant, it must be drugged, shocked into line. Imagine being told your leg is a 'bad' leg, because it's just not quite like everyone else's legs. To you, it's just your leg; it's always been that way, it's not remarkable. Why should the mind be any different? I am who I am, and who are you to tell me I shouldn't be so? Can't he at least imagine how hard it is to stand up under such a spotlight?

"There was nothing wrong with me."

"It says here you were diagnosed with paranoid schizophrenia."

"There was nothing wrong with me." I perch on the edge of my seat, my teeth barred, my fists clenched, the strength building in me again. It's not that I'm losing control, but I've had to live with this stuff, whereas Roderick thinks he knows it all by merely perusing the lies they recorded.

"Ewan, sit down."

It is the voice of reason. I must sit down. If I let go again, I'm pouring petrol on my own pyre. I'm going to have to explain if there is any hope of making him see it was all a mistake, a misunderstanding: misunderstanding after misunderstanding, doctors refusing to listen, misinterpreting the stammering words of terrified teenage boy. They will listen to me now that I am a man, a teacher, a respectable part of society. Or at least I was, until I wound up in this dump.

"There was nothing wrong with me, Roderick. You have to believe me."

Slight as I was, it took four of them to take me away that day. I should have known what was coming, I'd been warned what would happen if I didn't take the drugs they'd prescribed, but until you've experienced it, you can't grasp what horrors lurk beneath the façade of society. You have no way of knowing there are other worlds within the one with which most people are familiar, the one 'normal' people inhabit. It's not until you slip off the narrow line that defines normality that you discover there are deeper and darker places than imagination alone can conjure. I was naïve enough to think that no matter how dysfunctional my relationship with my mother, even she would not have condemned me to such a fate. On days when I feel forgiving, I think perhaps she just didn't know. But most of the time, I know she did.

I was seventeen. I was just a kid. Sometimes I look at the older children at school, sixteen, going on seventeen, and my horror grows when I behold their fresh-faced youth and think once that was me, starry-eyed with a universe of possibilities and no idea of the hell that awaited me. I am beginning to tremble, but this isn't the start of another 'psychotic episode', it is fear, and sadness, and wishing, wishing none of it had happened to me.

"Then tell me what happened," Roderick says, thinking this time he's cracked the nut.

I sigh. For a moment I bury my head in my hands, but I know I'm going to have to go through it all, over and over, dissecting every last little detail for Roderick's analysis until the effort leaves me so drained I won't care how far away they throw the key

My parents longed for a child, my mother for a daughter. She tried everything. She ate the right foods, drank weird herbal concoctions and made love under the moon, but for years it looked as though her beloved boutique would be her only baby. Then at last she fell pregnant. But as you know, I've always been an awkward sod, so I couldn't be a girl. My bedroom stayed pink until I was old enough to paint it myself. If that's not an ominous start, then I don't know what is.

"It's not exactly uncommon," Roderick scoffs. "I'm assuming your mother talked about it. Was she angry? Did she suffer from depression?"

"No, nothing like that."

She talked about it, yes, but by the time I was old enough to understand, I'd more than compensated by being good with music. My earliest memory is banging my hands up and down on the piano while my mother laughed and clapped, her eyes sparkling because I was so clever. She used to make me play to everyone who came to the house. From relatives to her friends, they'd have to stand there nodding and smiling while I performed. I guess with hindsight, I must have been insufferable, and Roderick laughs at this, but it made my mother happy, and that was all that mattered to me.

"Go on."

She had great plans for me. All her life she'd wanted to be an artist, only she was such a perfectionist, she'd never managed to complete a picture. She'd fly into a fury if something went wrong. I take a deep breath, remembering the sound of screeching, the splintering of wood and canvas as she smashed the latest picture against the wall, my father going 'please Margot, please calm down' over and over as I huddled in my bed, scared I suppose, because she was upset, and if my mother was upset, nothing in the world was right.

"Why was that?" Roderick muses, stroking his stubble with his pen. "That's a few times you've mentioned how important it was to keep your mother happy. Why did you feel you had to do that?"

Did I? I sit back in my chair and study the scene, frowning as I try to view it through Roderick's eyes, as an outsider looking in. It was just the way our family worked. If my mother was happy, the house echoed with laughter and music, she dancing round the kitchen with my father while I played waltzes on the piano. But if she was upset, nothing he or I could do would change it. She could sulk for days, slamming doors and refusing to talk. But that was nothing to her fury when my teenaged self kicked up his heels and refused to go along with her plans for me to become a virtuoso, a soloist with my beloved cello.

I sigh, and lean back in my chair. The sun is streaming in through the office window, little flecks of dust dancing in its beam. Outside is a perfect autumn day. It's a quarter to eleven. I should be winding up my lesson ahead of the morning break, and later pottering around the garden sweeping up leaves and cutting back dying plants killed off by the first frosts. I must ask Trudy to check if the heating system is working at home. The last thing I want is frozen pipes when it looks as though I'll be locked in this dump all winter. What a mess. How did I get myself into this? I should have known better than to let it come to this. Last time I was lucky. I was afraid I'd be incarcerated forever, only I managed to escape. Here, there's no way out.

"Nah, let's slow down there," Roderick says, a frown creasing his forehead. "We'll talk about your stay in hospital later. I just want to get one thing straight. You went to great lengths to create a false identity so your mother wouldn't find you. Am I right?"

"She gave me no choice."

"What do you mean? Why couldn't you just tell her you didn't want to do what she said, and left it at that?"

"Because she tried to kill me."

"You thought your mother was trying to kill you," he says, flicking through John's file. "That's what it says in here. You've accused me of the same. Why did you think she was trying to do that?"

"She was," I say, sitting up in earnest, my plastered leg giving a twinge in protest. "She kept trying to poison me. I was sick, really sick, and I was constantly tired. It took me a long time to realise what was going on. It was because I wouldn't do as she said, you see. She wanted me to go and study at the Conservatoire in Paris. I didn't want to. I wanted to join an orchestra, any orchestra just to get away, but she wouldn't have it, she wouldn't listen. She never listened." I'm panting with the strength of my outburst, the words tumbling from my mouth, revelling in being released after years of being restrained. Roderick watches me, his fingers resting against his cheek as he listens, listening as no one has ever listened before, a witness to my pain.

"The Conservatoire? Now I don't know much about music, but it seems to me you'd have to be pretty good to get in there. Was that the problem, she couldn't accept you weren't good enough?"

I'm so indignant at this suggestion that when I go to speak, the words get jumbled up, scrambled in their haste to set him straight, I wind up spluttering. He pours me a glass of water from the bottle on his desk.

"Not good enough? I could have had my pick of places to study if that's what I'd wanted." Well, apart from Cambridge where I'd met Rebecca. They'd been impressed with my playing, but I didn't want to study, I wanted to perform, and we'd discussed this during my interview, agreeing the university wasn't the place for me.

"I was tired of my mother telling me what to do. I didn't want more school, more tuition. I wasn't so arrogant I didn't think I needed more," I say, arching one eyebrow before he meanders off down another diagnostic path. "I'd just had enough. I wanted to join an orchestra. She wouldn't have it. 'All the money I've spent on your musical education' she used to say. She wanted a return on her investment. Yes, that's what I was to her," I muse, this hasn't occurred to me before. "An investment. She had her shops, and she had me. I should have made her a fortune, only I'd had enough of doing what I was told.

"I spent my entire childhood minding I didn't hurt my hands, minding I do my practice," I say, mimicking my mother's voice. "I wasn't allowed a day off. And it wasn't that I didn't love to play." I think of Claire Patrick's cello vibrating between my knees, hungry to feel it once more. "I just wanted a normal life," I break off.

You know, people are growing up right now in war-zones, in countries crippled by starvation. People live through all sorts of horrors, but I managed to develop spectrums of angst because my mother forced me to practice classical music when all I wanted to do was play out with my friends and do normal stuff like any normal child would do. It marks me out as petty, pathetic. I am too ashamed to own it. That's why it's John's stuff, not mine. I drop my eyes to the floor, afraid what judgement might lurk on Roderick's face. 'You're nothing but selfish, John', I can hear my mother screeching up the stairs, her voice cutting through the wood of my locked door. 'It's all 'me me me'; that's all you care about. You disgust me.'

I disgusted her, disappointing her in so many ways, and that's to say nothing of the revulsion on her face when she caught me cutting my arm with the thick chunk of glass I'd found in the garden. Hugging my arms to my body, I avoid looking at Roderick, and bite the skin down the side of my thumbnail. I'd like a sharp knife to cut myself right now, to release some of the discomfort crawling through my veins at being forced to do all this picking through the rotten remains of my past. It's beginning to get very hot in here, as though the air is being sucked out and replaced with heat. My fingers reach up to loosen my collar, but I forget it isn't fastened. I'm not allowed to wear a tie, although let me tell you now, it isn't myself I'd be using it to strangle. My chest feels tight, every breath an effort. They're doing this on purpose. There must be a vent or something in here they're using to mess with the air. I look round, trying to spot it.

"Are you all right Ewan?" Roderick says, and I nearly startle out of the chair at the sound of his voice. No, no, I must keep calm. I mustn't let them think they can beat me.

"Just a bit hot," I say. I want to get out of here so much, it's getting hard to sit still.

"I think we've gone far enough for one day. We've been talking for ages." The muscles in his arms flex as he stretches them above his head with a yawn. He glances up at the clock. "We've missed lunch. I hope they've saved some for us."

He picks up his pen and goes back to writing. But as I watch, something catches my eye. A round black beetle falls from the ceiling, down behind Roderick's back. I gasp. It must have landed on him, but he doesn't seem to have noticed. Must be the heat drawing them out.

"What is it?"

"Nothing." I want to tell him there's a beetle on his back, but I can't tell him unless I'm completely sure because he might think I'm having another one of my, what does he call it, ah yes, 'episodes'. I try to crane my neck, hoping he won't notice, to see if I can spot it.

Another one falls. It startles me, and I clamp my hand over my mouth to stifle the scream. Where are the damned things coming from? Someone should do something about the infestation. I can't believe I'm the only person in this damned hospital who knows about it. Ah, that'll be another cover-up too. Let the psychiatric patients think they're seeing things, that'll keep the nutters in line.

"Let me guess, insects?" He says, getting up from behind the desk.

I nod, wondering how he can be so nonchalant when they're crawling on his back.

"All right Ewan, try to keep calm. Take some deep breaths." He strides to the door, and calls for Sandra. They exchange words, but I can't hear what they're saying, I'm so busy concentrating on breathing in and out, my lungs ready to burst with the effort of trying to be calm, trying to resist the urge to get up and run screaming from the room. I don't realise Sandra is by my side until she takes my hand, and curls my fingers around a small plastic cup. Assuming she's handing me a glass of water, I go to drink, and realise the liquid is purple. She still has a hold of the cup, which stops me from following my impulse to hurl it across the room.

"What the hell is this?"

"Think of it was purple pest control," Roderick says, folding his arms. "Drink up."

Another sedative. As I swallow it down, I know Ruth's will be the smuggest grin.

Chapter 34

Roderick comes to find me at breakfast the next morning. I am sitting, toying with a red plastic bowl, chasing a tiny amount of tinned grapefruit round and round with a spoon, while a nurse huffs at my side. This morning it's Gerry, 'coining in', as he puts it, the overtime by working a dayshift. He is so bored, he is busy doing the crossword in his newspaper as I fiddle with my breakfast, pulled apart in a three-way battle between the fiendish hunger Ruth relishes telling me is a side-effect of the 'anti-psychotic' drugs I'm obliged to swallow, my own fears as to what exactly they've sneaked into my food to control me, and the unit's own rule 'thou must eat'. From time to time he reads out a clue to me, and I roll my eyes that he is too feeble-minded to solve it. The state of the education system today, I sigh, gazing across the empty tables to where the others have settled down to the morning residents' meeting.

"Bollocks to this," he says, tossing the half-done crossword across the table. He leans back, fidgeting, his tall frame never designed to be crammed into such a tiny chair, his youthful energy never intended to be restrained in one place, in one situation for this length of time. I smile to myself at his discomfort. Experience has taught me it's only a matter of time before he gives in. He has less willpower than the others, and I can make breakfast last all morning if I have to. "Ewan, two words. For fuck's sake. Just. Eat."

"I make that five, actually," I say, counting the words aloud on my fingers for his dim-witted benefit. If nothing else, at least I will have the satisfaction of knowing I've tried to address the issue of his inadequate education whilst being stuck in here.

He huffs, and folds his hands behind his head. We're in the home strait now, I think. Gerry's repertoire of stern encouragement, cajoling and empty threats have all beached on my stubborn shores. Any minute now, he's going to admit defeat and I can go. I study the pale yellow segments floating in the bowl while I wait for his surrender, each one formed from tiny, tear shaped pockets of juice. The individual tears fascinate me, and sets me off meandering down a path which really could last from now until lunchtime. Does each segment contain the same number of tears, or are there no two segments alike, just as there are no two human brains which are the same, and thus there is no such thing as 'insanity' or 'normality', just a universe, an infinity of shades of difference. I hadn't expected to find such philosophy in my breakfast. As Gerry gives what must be one of his final sighs, I dart a sly glance at his angular, arrogant face, triumph sailing out behind the clouds.

"Oh, look Ewan. Now you can explain to Roderick why you won't eat anything this morning. This'll be good."

Just as I was about to streak over the finishing line, Gerry shoves past, snatching the victory from my hands. I look up, and sure enough, Roderick is strolling towards us, his hands stuffed in his pockets. Gerry sniggers and folds his arms across his chest, settling back to enjoy the show, letting his legs and feet jiggle up and down as his grin stretches from ear to ear, watching my face as Roderick approaches.

"We won't eat anything?" Roderick raises his eyebrows, and exchanges a knowing snort with Gerry. "Now that's not like you, Ewan. What have you got there? Grapefruit? I don't think that's what Dr. Lockhart had in mind when she suggested you eat more substantial meals."

The psychiatrist seems to think that now I'm doped up to my eyeballs, I will forget my fears about the chemicals polluting my food, and gorge myself at mealtimes. I'm also supposed to be concerned because she has an opinion that I am too thin, but I know this is just another trick, this time to worry me into eating. Yes, I am alarmed by the gaunt man in the mirror, whose eyes seem to be sinking further and further into their sockets, but I am strong enough to resist. Trudy tries to cajole me by bringing in packets of food labelled 'organic', but that doesn't work either. I eat a little, enough to avoid being force-fed, but I'm not going to give in. I'm not going to forget and submit.

"I'm not hungry. And as I've said, repeatedly, I don't normally eat breakfast, and I don't see why I should have to now just because I'm stuck here in this wretched dump."

"Ah," says Roderick, folding his arms. "It's going to be 'one of those days' is it? And I see you're managing to avoid the residents' meeting."

He glances over to where the others are sitting, the bickering audible even from here. Last night it was my turn to be on the receiving end. Ruth started it, sitting with her arms folded, malice radiating from her green eyes.

"I don't see why it's fair that Ewan gets to spend time in private with his girlfriend, just because she's a nurse. The rest of us have to see our visitors in the dayroom."

My face had fired with colour. Trudy comes to see me every day, and the short time, maybe twenty minutes at the most, Sandra lets me spend with her alone, is the only thing that gives me any sort of perspective on what's happening to me in this place. She puts her arms around me. Sometimes we talk, and sometimes we just sit in silence. I don't think I could stomach another day in here without those precious minutes of contact with someone who isn't trying to double-guess the motives behind my words, analyse my behaviour, or pick holes in my character. Her visits are like an ointment, cool and calming. It's got nothing to do with the rest of them, least of all Ruth.

"Much as I adore your company Ruth," I said. "Why shouldn't I have a bit of peace with someone who's a proper friend?"

But no, it is favouritism, the mob decreed. So when Trudy comes to see me today, I have to sit with her in front of everyone else. I didn't set out to avoid attending the meeting this morning, but for once Roderick's company is the more palatable. Still, I can't resist the chance for a little light goading.

"I tell you what," I say. "I shouldn't miss the meeting. I'll leave this and go and join them, shall I?"

Roderick slaps his hand down on the table, making both Gerry and I jump.

"You know the rules," his civility is straining at the sides. "Everyone has to eat. There are no excuses. And you know this."

Gerry flexes his arms and cracks his fingers, trying to catch my eye with his victor's grin, but I refuse to give him the satisfaction, and go on staring at Roderick.

"You promised Dr. Lockhart you would eat at every mealtime and," he leans across the table, the merriment gone from his eyes. "You know what will happen if you don't."

I do. Dr. Lockhart was blunt. She produced the tube they will force up my nose from the pocket of her white coat. I stared at it, the familiar hot, sweaty nausea that assails me over any medical practise, even the dentist, set the room spinning around me. As Gerry makes the bones in his fingers give another audible crack, I try not to think of the relish he'd employ in ramming the tube down my throat. And what rubbish would he force down into my stomach? I gulp and turn back to my bowl. Suddenly, whatever was employed in the grapefruit's cultivation, fertilisers, growth hormones, pesticides and all, don't seem so threatening after all.

"Actually, I've got a better idea," Roderick says, pulling out a seat and sitting down at the table as I take a deep breath and shovel a small piece of grapefruit into my reluctant mouth. "Gerry, go and make him a piece of toast. No, tell you what, you haven't had your break yet, have you? Why don't you make us all a piece of toast and a cup of tea, and we'll have breakfast together. Bit more sociable if we all eat together, isn't it?" he says to me as Gerry gathers his limbs up out of the chair and goes slouching off. I stare, wide-eyed at Gerry's retreating back.

"What's the matter now? You know you can manage a piece of toast, you did yesterday."

"It's not that," I say, shuffling in my chair. "It's just, um." I don't know how to put this across without airing pettiness I don't consider becoming to a man of my age. He sits up and leans across the table so there's no need for me to raise my voice, so whatever I say will just be between we two. Yeah, and my case notes. I'm not stupid.

"Come on Ewan, why do we always have this battle? What can I do to make it easier for you to tell me what's on your mind?"

I take a deep breath. He's got the scent of my reluctance. I know nothing will throw him off the trail, and this is a conversation I don't want to have in front of his fair-haired colleague.

"Look, this isn't paranoia, it's a fact," I say, my voice a half-whisper so he has to lean in closer. "It's Gerry. He doesn't like me. I wish you hadn't asked him to make the toast. I don't trust him not to spit in my tea. I'm not being paranoid. I just know he doesn't like me."

"Okay, well why don't you go and make the tea? That way you'll know he hasn't done anything to it, and you can be sure he won't mess with your toast in front of you. Go on then, oh, and two sugars in mine, thanks."

"Two sugars?" I raise my eyebrows. "That's disgusting. Haven't you heard of dental health or diabetes?"

"Once a builder, always a builder. Well go on then," he says, glancing up from my file, clicking his pen as I stare at him. He digs a notebook out of a pocket, and starts writing. I shuffle off, glancing at him over my shoulder, struggling, and failing, to reconcile the idea of my freckled, pony-tailed therapist with a brawny builder.

He's still writing when Gerry and I return with breakfast. I try to read his spiky blue script upside down as I put the mugs down on the table, but I've never managed to decipher it yet. He realises I'm trying to see what he's writing, clicks his pen, and sweeps the notebook back into his pocket. Gerry hands round the toast, and we all sit down to eat. I pick up the toast, determined to eat quickly before the doubts come flooding back in, before I have to endure my companions' menacing scrutiny.

"Were you really a builder?" I ask between mouthfuls, wondering if he was somehow making a joke I haven't understood.

"What?" Gerry squawks. "A builder? Rod?"

"Aye," Roderick says, chewing. "A good one too. Still do bits and pieces. I'm helping a pal of mine renovate a house in Cambridge at the moment. Keeps me busy on my days off. See here. I'll show you."

He produces his mobile phone, and scrolls through a variety of pictures featuring a dilapidated house, its interior peeled back to bare brick walls, and photographed as the renovations proceed, picture by tedious picture. Roderick's eyes are shining with enthusiasm as he points out the bits he takes a particular pride in having completed. Gerry lets him indulge his passion by asking lots of questions and enthusing over his craftsmanship. I sit quietly, sipping my tea. Roderick might well be describing restoring his friend's house, but it sounds as though he could be talking about treating any one of the patients here in 'The Woodlands', myself included, broken down to be put back together piece by painful piece, our case notes the photographs for the doctors to admire. Nurse, builder: in so far as Roderick is concerned, these are the same thing.

"If you love building so much," I say. "What made you decide to go into this line of work?" I indicate the hospital with a wave of my hand.

"I like fixing things," Roderick says, a wide grin stretching across his face, his words validating my own conclusions. "People, houses: you'd be surprised how similar they are.

"Anyway, that's enough of that," he says, putting his phone away. "Have you finished your tea? Right, come on then. I think it's time we got to work."

My reluctant sigh could propel a yacht halfway across the Atlantic, but he pretends not to notice. I lever myself up out of my chair, grab my crutches, and shuffle off after him as he leads the way back into his office, ready for another session of knocking down and rebuilding. Despite what he's said, I can't picture him doing anything as useful as renovating a house with his bare hands, but he seems to take a particular relish in deconstructing me.

Chapter 35

As I swing myself into the office, I realise something is different, there is something out of place. Not something, I note, but someone. Dr. Lockhart looks up from Roderick's desk as we walk in. She does that eyebrow thing with Roderick, and then she and the mole greet me with a smile that crinkles the skin around her eyes. I ignore the mole and look beyond her welcome to see that she is sitting perusing my notes, pen cocked at the ready, and I wonder again what Roderick has found so much to write about. I'm not allowed to read them for myself, so I've been informed, and my nerves twang, plucked by unease at what lies lie recorded on each page.

Roderick waves me to my customary seat. Dr. Lockhart moves aside so Roderick can sit down, and he takes his own pen out of his top pocket, clickety-click, and sits poised to write.

"And how are you feeling, Ewan?" asks the doctor.

It's all about 'how are you feeling, Ewan'. I fold my arms, expecting this is the prelude to another tirade concerning my refusal to talk at any length in the group therapy sessions. Roderick can tell them to prod as hard as they like, but I learned my lessons about 'therapy groups' a long time ago. It's one thing to talk in private to him, and don't get me wrong, that isn't something I enjoy, but I'll be damned if I'm going to pick my sores in public. I'm not even comfortable with Dr. Lockhart being here, but at least it won't be long before her pager bleeps and she goes rushing out of here, white coat flapping in her wake. I say I'm fine. What a word. 'Fine' is a small, but formidable shield with the power to deflect even the most inquisitive enquirer.

"And how's the eating coming along after we talked about it?"

"That's fine too," I say, ignoring Roderick, whose eyebrows are so raised, they could make a break for it and leap off into his hair. Fine, fine, everything is fine. Now let's just get on with it, shall we?

"Okay," Roderick says, hands clasped together on the desktop. "Well, if you remember, we spent a lot of time yesterday talking through different parts from your childhood and teenaged years. I'd like us to pick up from there. There are a few things Dr. Lockhart and I would like to clarify, and a few things I think we still need to talk about. What do you think?"

A sweat breaks out in my palms. My right leg starts bobbing up and down, my foot flexing against the floor, and I can feel hot colour rising in my face. No way am I doing this in front of Dr. Lockhart. I don't want to, I'm not going to. The silence is growing larger and larger, filling the air in the room until I can barely breathe, barely keep sitting in my chair for the compulsion of instinct shrieking at me to run screaming for the door.

"Well?" Roderick says, spreading his fingers, his eyes fixed on mine.

"I don't want to," I say, the words bubbling up and out of my mouth. "I don't want to talk about it. I don't want to talk about anything today. I don't. I want you to leave me alone today. I want you to leave me alone."

Roderick doesn't even blink. He goes on looking at me. Dr. Lockhart's gaze is equally inscrutable. Part of me wonders if that's another thing they're trained to do, the use of the stare as a psychological tool, like one of those sharp picks you use to prise a cooked snail out from the shell in which it thought it would be safe. My thoughts flit back to something Benny said last night about Maisy wailing on purpose "to piss 'em off". I examine my options. But when I'm upset, I'm overwhelmed by my feelings and lose control of my actions. This isn't something I have any idea how to reproduce convincingly enough to get out of this. I file that idea back in the box.

"It's your relationship with your mother which intrigues me the most, Ewan," Dr. Lockhart says, resting her chin on her hand. "I'd like to explore why you felt such a need to please her to the extent that when you went against her wishes, you had to run away and hide yourself for all these years." She cocks one eyebrow, underlining her challenge.

"She was trying to kill me," I try to bat away the question, but it isn't so much one question as a barrage of questions firing from a canon on the doctor's side of the net.

"We'll come to that. I'd like to look back into your earlier years. You told Roderick yesterday everything was all right so long as your mother was happy. I'd like you to explain to me just what you meant."

I look down at the floor. The same wiry brown carpet extends throughout the entire wing. I wonder why the hospital chose it, but I suppose it's hardwearing and easy to clean, and they probably got an enormous discount for ordering so much. If I was shrunk as small as an ant, I could probably get lost in it. I wonder what that would feel like, whether it would be easy to push my way through the nylon undergrowth, or if it would be impenetrable.

Roderick breaks the stalemate with a heavy sigh. I look up from the carpet, having lost myself amid its thicket long enough to have forgotten the question. They're both still staring, daring me to answer, but what is there to say?

"Your mother," Dr. Lockhart says. "Why, as a small child, did you feel it was your responsibility to please her?"

She must know how much I don't want to talk about this. Roderick shone his torch on it yesterday, the gigantic slumbering beast I've spent a lifetime tiptoeing around in the dark, keeping it dark for fear it should wake up. But it's too late. Dr. Lockhart has given it another kick, just as Roderick did yesterday, and it opens one fiery orange eye and stares at me, unblinking, in the dark. I like to pretend it doesn't exist, but here it is. In fact, I should think it's tired. It's been taunting me ever since Roderick woke it yesterday. I eye the door, weighing up my options for escape, but the creature housing my fears and self-loathing is lumbering to its feet, and I know there is no way out.

It circles me, its black body blocking out the light, its foul breath hot against my face. I can't hear what the doctor or Roderick are saying any more because I'm nine years old again, sitting on the floor, my knees hugged to my chest, my cut fingers throbbing while she paces backwards and forwards, her high heels tap-tap-tapping against the polished wooden floor, telling me I'm useless, ungrateful, oh, and by the way, Grandma Felicity's dead. Yeah, that was my fault too. The shock winds me, just as it did then. She had a heart attack just after my mother dragged me back to Aberdeen. I never got the chance to tell her how sorry I was to have caused so much trouble.

"And all because," my mother stopped pacing and hunkered down in front of me to the sound of fabric tearing. "The only thing you care about, Ewan is yourself. And now look what you've made me do." She examined her skirt, discovering the damage with a gasp. The side seam was gaping in protest, having never been designed to stretch so far. "Ruined!" She flung her hands up in the air, turned on her heel, and marched from the room, slamming the door in her wake. I hugged my knees as hard as I could, and ground my eyes against my bony kneecaps. The pain was good. It was a few more years before I discovered how much cutting myself could make me feel better.

It's pathetic, isn't it, that I should have been so in awe of my mother that even now I still plunge into a cringing cold dread at the thought of letting her down, disappointing her yet, as she would say, again. I realise I am clenching my teeth as I sit here, my body rigid as I try to resist the trembling fear, the metamorphosis from grown man to errant child withering in the scorching heat of her displeasure. The more I thought about it through the long, sleepless night, feigning sleep each time the nurses did their rounds, for fear of drawing attention to my disintegrating mind, I began to see what I suspect has been obvious to everyone but me. I hear them laughing, the doctors, Rebecca, Trudy, my boss Mrs Phillips and my mother herself, laughing at me because I've spent my life trying to please the women in my life as though they are replacement mothers, as though pleasing them would be the ultimate redemption, but my efforts always doomed to fail, just as I failed right from the start.

"Why do you think that makes you 'pathetic'?"

I startle as Dr. Lockhart shoves the box of tissues under my nose, but I don't look up. In my mind I can see her and Roderick, arms folded tight across their chests, in some sort of competition as to who can pull the most disapproving look, just as my parents did when I'd been caught playing with bath toys, under the guise of a trip to the toilet, when I was supposed to be practicing my cello. Or the umpteen times I didn't win first place in a music festival. Or the time I asked if I could have karate lessons instead of music. Or now, as I sit here, a grown man reduced to snivelling over his past by the precise incisions of a psychiatrist's questions. I take a handful of tissues, and blow my streaming nose. John wasn't allowed to be a child. Ewan, who was supposed to be the superior version, has been reduced to one. I can't win.

"The 'superior version', what's that supposed to mean?"

"I was supposed to be the strong one, the smart one. But look at me," I give my nose another blow. "I'm caught up in the same mess, while you damned doctors sit there and make up your lies about what you consider to be the state of my mind."

"We make up our lies? So you still don't want to accept our assessment of your illness," Dr. Lockhart sighs as though somehow this is news to her. She leans on the desk, one fist thrust up under her cheekbone to support her head. "And that's in spite of the fact we have reached the same verdict as your doctors did twenty-something years ago."

"There was nothing wrong with me."

"So you've said. 'Repeatedly' as you would put it. Do you understand what the diagnosis meant?"

I shrug. It has nothing to do with me, so of course I don't know what it means. I don't care. The diagnosis has nothing more to do with me than a severed hand found washed up on some far-flung beach: it isn't mine.

"It means the doctors found, as we have, that you were suffering from delusions in which you were convinced you were being persecuted, whilst all the evidence pointed to the contrary."

"There was nothing wrong with me," I thump my fist against my knee, frustrated I can't get her to listen. It's so easy for her to breeze in, read a few notes, watch me suffer and deliver her learned conclusions, but she wasn't there. She doesn't really know, and she most certainly is not trying to understand. "I was telling the truth. It's easy for you to sit there all smug and cocky because you think you know it all, but you know nothing."

"Ever since you were admitted to this hospital," she counters, "you've been telling anyone who will listen how you've been targeted and imprisoned here by the authorities for discovering a plot to control the general population through contaminated foodstuffs. This frightens you so much, you won't eat and haven't eaten to the extent you are seriously underweight. Similarly, the notes from your previous section tell of how you were convinced your mother hated you so much she was trying to kill you, and that you were convinced you could hear her murderous thoughts in your head. Aged seventeen, you were diagnosed with paranoid schizophrenia, and in my opinion, it's something of a miracle it's taken this long for you to need medical care."

"That wasn't me. That was him," I say, wound up so tight, my whole body is shaking, thoughts, explanations, and images charging round in my head, bumping against the sides, against each other and going round and round and round at such a dizzying speed, no single one will keep still long enough to be processed into coherent speech.

"That was who?" Roderick asks, his voice probing with the surprising dexterity of a chimpanzee dipping a twig into a termite mound in search of food.

"Him. John. They said he was ill, not me, but he wasn't. There was nothing wrong with him. No one knew what was really going on." The image of our beautiful old three storey house on Queen's Road in Aberdeen fills my head, a vision of silver grey, sat serene like an old dowager, majestic and representing old-fashioned values such as decency, respectability, never a hint of the howling, painted demon who lived inside and whose voice is whooping right now in this office, in my head going

"John, John: who are they going to believe, huh? The Aberdeen Commerce Association's businesswoman of the year, or the idiot boy who likes to take a knife and cut his skinny arm for fun, huh?"

"He wasn't ill. And I'm not either."

Fresh tears well, a child's tears in the face of adults who refuse to listen. I put my face in my hands, and press my fingers into my eyes. John was bound so tight by all the lies, he couldn't escape. That was why he had to become me, because Ewan was all right. Ewan knew what to do. Ewan wasn't worn down to a fragile shell by all the dreadful things *she* said, because he couldn't hear her voice in his head going on and on, pouring venom into every cell. He knew how to run away, and how to take care of himself, and besides, he had Rebecca, the beautiful girl he'd met in Cambridge. She'd said to him 'any time', but how her jaw had dropped when he turned up on her doorstep, dishevelled and without even as much as a change of clothes. But she hadn't asked questions. She'd opened the door, and taken him in. And if only she were here, if she hadn't died, she could speak up for me, for Ewan, and tell them what really happened.

"What did you say?" Dr. Lockhart's grim voice asks, but I can't answer. All I can do is shake my head. "If only Rebecca hadn't died?"

"Yes," I say between sobs. "She could tell you."

"Ewan," Roderick brings in his 'don't mess with me voice. "Rebecca isn't dead. I've spoken to her recently. You know that, don't you?"

"Not that Rebecca. My Rebecca."

"There are two Rebeccas?"

It's like trying to explain to someone who can't speak the same language. Without words, you are left with gestures and expressions which would be fine for concrete, simple things, but for abstract ideas, concepts, I don't think there can be a way to communicate these without words. I could draw you a picture, but how you and I might interpret my artwork may be two different things. So I see them both, Roderick and Dr. Lockhart leap to the wrong conclusion while I, well, what was I trying to say? Oh yes, Rebecca. She would have testified that I was completely normal, before they did something to her that morphed her into shouty Rebecca, the one who stuck her hands on her hips, huffing and yelling You Need Help. My Rebecca, the real Rebecca wouldn't have left me. She made everything all right. But it wasn't my Rebecca who walked into my classroom at the beginning of term. It was the other one.

"Two versions of Rebecca and two versions of you," Dr. Lockhart rests her chin on both hands, her elbows resting on the desk, the pen forgotten. "So everything is boxed up into neat compartments, this life, that life, this version, that version. It's an interesting approach, although I'm not sure that's how life works."

But it did work, and that's the point. It worked perfectly until the other Rebecca decided to climb out of her box and back into the present day. And now nothing is ordered, everything is in chaos, and my mother's voice is out of its cage and flying round and round the room squawking and shrieking *"thing is John, you're not right in the head. And do you know what I told them, huh? You never have been."* And her fuchsia lips stretch wide and open and she's going *"a-hahahahaha"* as though she's just heard the best joke ever, but her eyes, that's what gives her away. I steel myself and look into her eyes. They are the same colour as mine, olive green and flecked with hazel, only hers are wanton with naked intent, and I know, I just know she's planning to kill me, only no one will listen. But I'm not seventeen any more, I'm forty-three, and still no one will listen.

Chapter 36

Quiet has descended on the dayroom. The Woodlands Unit is usually a noisy place, a constant stream of nurses scurrying, while we patients wander, too dazed to tread a regular path like our caged brethren in every zoo. There is usually a hubbub of conversations, the sound of telephones ringing, the buzzer announcing some innocent is waiting on the other side of the locked door, and the television's constant onslaught of histrionic drama, grating music, and irritating adverts featuring colourful, smiley people twirling around in a colourful, smiley world, happy because they eat a certain brand of frozen pea. Or because they use a certain label of toothpaste. Or because they have a certain sort of car.

I sat here last night watching us watching the telly, sitting here in this dingy room. We have been sucked into some sort of parallel universe from which we can only watch as the rest of the world goes whirling about its business. I don't even really know where we are, I have no idea where 'The Woodlands Unit' is in relation to the hospital, to Thatchington itself, or even my home. It seemed as though Sandra and I passed through miles of labyrinth corridors, with only occasional glimpses through reinforced windows, of a world outside reduced to enclosed courtyards with scraggy plants, vigorous weeds and a lot of gravel. This place could be in another town, could be on another planet for all I know.

But this morning it's quiet. Lucinda is here. She arrived just after breakfast, her elfin face beaming with its other-worldly smile, her blonde curls bouncing with joie-de-vivre, radiating the fresh sparkling energy of one from the outside world who knows she's going back out there as soon as this morning is over. Ruth and Rocky helped drag out tables and chairs, and now the others are all busy with their weekly painting session. As usual Lucinda came over to me, her head cocked on one side. I love to watch her move. She doesn't walk; she bobs along on her toes as though every move was a dance step. But she talks to me with a sing-song nursery teacher's voice, so, as usual, I have told her what she can do with her 'art therapy'. It may well be 'ever so good for you, Ewan', I'm not playing.

I'm sitting reading a book. Well, what I mean is I'm making it look as though I'm reading a book, but if Gerry was really watching me instead of eyeing Lucinda, he'd know I haven't turned a page in hours. Since yesterday, Roderick has insisted one of them stay with me at all times. He knows what I want to do, and I want to do it so badly, I can think of nothing else. The only way I can have peace from my mother's voice is to cut myself. And I'd welcome being sedated; it would mean a break from the howling torment crashing around inside me, making me feel as though I should claw my skin to let it out. For once my so-called 'care' team can see what is happening, so they've changed my medication to see if it helps. It hasn't. On top of everything else, my head is aching and the room spins every time I move.

On a whim, I put the book down, shuffle to the edge of my seat, and heave myself upright with my crutches. I sway, there is no point in fighting the vertigo, and hear Gerry going 'where the fuck are you going this time, Ewan?' but I don't respond. There is no answer. I don't know where I'm going, only that I can't sit here any longer.

I lurch off down a corridor which is pitching and rolling as though I were adrift in a small boat on a wild sea. Actually, that's quite a good analogy for how I feel, because I can imagine myself as tiny little fragments of driftwood being dashed again and again, disintegrating against unforgiving, solid rocks. I have spent years powering away from my past, thinking the oceans were wide enough, their tides strong enough to keep me safe. But the sea has led me back, hurled me against the cliffs where I started, and shattered the little escape boat I'd carved from hope.

There is nothing left for me to cling to. I thought I was beyond the reach of these dangerous shores, and I had no idea just how mistaken I was.

I hit a large wave, and go reeling, crashing against the wall. Gerry tries to grab me, but he's too late. My balance is tipped, and I wind up in a heap on the floor. Both the wall and the floor feel nice, their solidity is reassuring. And just a bit further on, there is a corner. If I can reach it, I think, I can press myself against two solid walls and feel safe. I shrug off Gerry's attempts to pull me up, and scrabble towards my goal.

It's perfect. I hug my good leg to my chest, and press my forehead into my knee. Gerry is going 'Ewan get up' over and over, but I'm not moving. An idea sparks, and I start to sing, anything to drown him out, to drown everything out. I sing random notes at first, and then I recognise the melody. It is the tune I was composing at the beginning of term. I sing it over and over again. C, A♯, G. An old friend, it wraps itself around me, and hugs me tight. Ah, dear friend, if only we were sat at my piano instead of trapped in here then I could let go and watch you fill with colour, with beauty and see you shimmering through the air as I play you notes over and over, stroking the ivory and ebony keys, watching you dance.

"Ew-an, now, what are you doing?"

Sandra's voice interrupts. Her heavy hand lands on my shoulder, and then there is rustling and a thump as her body flumps down beside me. She stretches out her short, round legs and waggles her feet. I shut my eyes and sing louder. She squeezes my shoulder.

"Now it's not that I don't like your singing, you have a wonderful voice, but that's not what's really going on here now, is it?" She gives me a nudge, but I manage to ignore her. Then I feel her hand between my shoulders, smoothing down my jagged scales. How did she know that would feel so good? I stop singing and peep at her from behind my knee.

"It's all right, Ewan." She soothes, her hand firm, working the knots in my muscles. But a bitter taste springs in my mouth and I snort.

"No it isn't. I am not all right."

"Not at the moment perhaps, but you are all right. Everything will work out, you'll see."

"How can you say that?" I raise my head from my knee, my teeth clenched so hard it hurts. "Don't talk to me as though I'm a damned child. I am not all right. And don't forget, I'm a schizophrenic nutter."

She laughs and cracks one of her wide smiles, her white teeth gleaming.

"Just remember those are your words, not mine."

"You're not just a nutter John; you're a worthless piece of shit."

"Did you hear that?"

I crane my neck, and look up and down the corridor. The voice was so loud, it's as though I heard it here in the hospital, echoing down to greet me. An icy fist slams into my gut. Is she here? Tell me they haven't brought her here to confront me, to try and prove everything I've said about my loving mother was a lie. After all, it wouldn't be the first time the doctors have tried it.

"Hear what?" Sandra looks round, following my searching eyes.

"It was my mother," I say, dropping my voice to a whisper. "I don't want her to see me. I don't want her here."

"Ewan, honey, listen to me," she says, grabbing my hand and holding it tightly between hers. "Your mother isn't here. Everything's all right."

"God, you are so pathetic. You should never have been born."

"Can't you hear her?"

I stare in disbelief as Sandra gives her head a slight shake, her eyes serious and unblinking. It's not me disintegrating, it's time. Time has shattered, and here I am, caught in the constricting grip of the biggest monster from my past. I can't control it, the voice won't go away. It had stopped. It had stopped when I became Ewan Davies, when I ran away from John Davidson and everything he represented. I haven't heard my mother in years, but now everything is breaking down. I've been forced to look John in the eye and acknowledge him as real, and as a result everything that tormented him is torturing me. All I want is a way to make it stop. I clasp my hands over my ears, and begin to howl.

With one huge wrench, everything breaks loose and gets sucked into my twisting vortex. Feet come, running feet, people gathering, voices arguing as the nurses bicker over what to do, and who should do what, and telling Rocky and Ruth to go and sit down goddamnit, because Roderick's dealing with it. And all the while Sandra sits beside me, her body the only thing real in this world. I hear her tell them to back off in her quiet, calm way, and they ebb away, hissing threats about what will happen if she doesn't 'get him under control', but they do go.

I become aware of her hand again, smoothing and soothing, caressing my shoulders. The noise I've been making fades away, its passion spent. Bit by bit, I let her prise my fingers from my ears. I'm trembling, exhausted, as though I've been running for weeks. I listen, but I can't hear anything beside the laboured sound of my own breathing going in and out, in and out.

"You okay?"

"Yes. No." My voice is cracked, my throat stripped raw by my vocal exertions. I fish a handful of tissues out of my pocket, and wipe my face. The trembling intensifies, and my teeth begin to chatter, but I cling to the feel of her hand working backwards and forwards across my back. Gerry must be standing nearby, she raises her voice and tells him to go and make us both a cup of tea. The resulting harrumph makes me smile through my tears.

"Time he had something worthwhile to do," she says. "Anyway, I'm not built for sitting down like this any more than you are with your bad leg. What Gerry doesn't realise is that we're both going to need a hoist to get us up when we're done." She shifts her weight from one side the other, and grimaces at the pain. "Now you could have chosen somewhere more comfortable to sit, Ewan, that's for sure."

"I'm so queasy, I hoped the feel of the two solid walls might stop everywhere moving." I rub my face with my fingers, pressing against my temples in the hope this will ease the ache thumping in my skull. My hands are shaking. It won't stop. She goes on massaging my shoulders. I want her to go on doing it forever.

"Can you really not hear my mother talking to me?"

"No. What is she saying, Ewan? Can you tell me?"

"She says I'm the biggest mistake she ever made," I hug my good knee to my chest, trying to stop shaking. "She's saying I was bound to wind up like this, I'm not right in the head. I've never been right in the head. "I'm not right, am I Sandra? I'll never get out of here."

"Is that true Ewan? Think what Roderick would say. Is that really true?"

"I'll never get out of here," I sob.

"Now, you listen to me, Ewan Davies, there's something I want you to hear. Whatever you remember from the past and whatever you hear that voice saying, you are not that person. You are the man who taught my friend's daughter and inspired her to go and study music at university. You aren't well at the moment, yes, but that's just one side of you. You are going to get better. Since you've been here, you've made so much progress, everyone thinks so. And the last few days, I think you've done the bravest thing ever. You've looked into your past, and confronted what was there. Most people go through life pretending, hiding behind masks and playing games, too afraid to look inside themselves for fear of what they might find. It doesn't matter what that voice says, you know who you are."

I know who I am? Right now, all I can see are broken pieces, fragments of who I thought I was, who I tried to be, and who I wanted to avoid. I've spent years hiding my true nature, years trying to be everyone else's version of who I should be. I don't have any idea who I really am. I say this to Sandra, but she just laughs and squeezes my shoulders.

"The pieces will all fall into place," she tells me. "Just you wait and see."

I shake my head, and go back to pressing my forehead against my bony kneecap. Her simple faith is endearing, but as you know, I've never been much of a believer.

Chapter 37

My turmoil subsides as the day wears on, the drugs working hard to smooth the waves back down to medicated, oily millpond calm. Excused from normal work duties cleaning up around the unit, I read a tedious novel, something released to great acclaim last year which Trudy has borrowed from the library thinking it would amuse me. Exhausted from my earlier upset, it sends me to sleep. I doze in my chair like a dribbling geriatric. In fact I miss most of the afternoon until Will comes to wake me in time for tea. He chuckles as I sit up yawning, rubbing the sleep from my eyes, bleary and disorientated after missing the last few hours. There is an enticing smell of food in the air, and my stomach grumbles. Now I'm awake, I am famished, a chemically induced appetite I cannot ignore.

Much to everyone's amazement, I'm so ravenous I not only clear my plate in record time, but I'm still hungry. We're eating one of Rocky's signature meals, sausages in onion gravy, but tonight I don't care about what he might have done to it with his grubby, madman's hands, or what the sausages really contain. I want more. Daphne puts down her knife and fork, ready to leave her meal to fetch me another helping, but I protest. It's only a short distance to the kitchen. I can manage on one crutch.

I ladle more food onto my plate, whistling. Whatever Doctor Lockhart has prescribed for me this time, it is powerful stuff. I feel warm and light, a contented peace radiating through my body. On a whim, I spoon another couple of potatoes onto my plate, thinking Trudy will be proud of me, and that's when I notice the black-handled kitchen knife left lying on the worktop.

It shouldn't have been left there. Someone's going to be in a lot of trouble. The knives are counted in and out of a locked drawer. Someone should have put it away properly. How sloppy. Luckily, I know exactly what to do with it. It slips down inside my leg cast like a sort of sgian-dubh.

Everyone marvels as I polish off my second plateful. Eyes widen as I compliment Rocky on his culinary prowess, unable to suppress my smiles. Glances are exchanged as I sit back in my seat, savouring my feeling of well-being. I can't remember the last time I felt this good, but there's nothing quite like the thrill of anticipation to shore up my spirits.

Without being asked, I make myself useful helping to tidy the kitchen. Will is so surprised by this unfamiliar, cooperative me, he says he'll have a word with the good doctor to see if she'll give him the same prescription. Everyone seems in a good mood this evening, laughing and bantering. Even Ruth isn't being annoying. And when I say to Will in passing that I'm just nipping to the toilet, neither he nor the staff question me.

My hands are shaking with excitement as I shut the cubicle door. I can't quite believe I've got away with this. To be quite truthful, I've lost the hunger I had earlier to cut myself, but there's no way I'm going to waste this opportunity. I take the knife out of my cast and test it against my thumb. Its sharp serrated edge gleams with promise. I pull up my sleeve, and grit my teeth. One tiny cut, that's all I must allow myself. I must be careful. One little cut, not to deep, just deep enough. Ah, that feels better.

I lean against the wall as blood fills the line of skin parted by the blade. It's a mystery to me why I bothered to deny myself this pleasure for so many years after Marcia died. Pretending I didn't want to do it is on a par with suppressing my desire, my need to play my cello. It's as much part of me as the need to breathe.

The blood congeals. I pull down my sleeve, and examine the knife. If I was at home, I'd probably cut a bit more, but I can't take the chance in here. I look around. There must be somewhere to hide it. After all, it's not always the act of cutting that calms me when I'm feeling desperate. Sometimes just knowing I could if I wanted to is all the reassurance I need. There must be somewhere I can put it where no one will find it. My eye falls on the toilet cistern. No one's going to suspect it's in there. I'm a genius.

Will is leaning against the kitchen doorway when I get back, one leg crossed over the other, his arms folded. He studies me over the top of his glasses with his look of the all-seeing-eye. I avoid his gaze, and go to walk past. Nothing has happened. Everything is calm. I don't need to look guilty.

"Where have you been?"

"What? I told you, I went to the toilet."

In the kitchen, Roderick, Daphne and Gerry are rummaging through the drawers. Ruth and Rocky are looking on, their faces strained and anxious. I swallow, alarm strumming the nerves stretching taut in my stomach. But any one of the nutters could have taken the knife. We don't have to assume it was me.

"You went to the toilet at least ten minutes ago," Will's gaze is unwavering.

"Oh so you're timing me now, is that it?"

"There's a knife missing."

"So?"

Rocky is swaying from one foot to the other. He's started to hum, a sure sign his agitation is growing. My luck's in tonight. When he loses control it's always spectacular. A Rocky meltdown is going to take everyone's mind off the missing knife.

"I'm really sorry Roderick," Ruth keeps saying. "I just don't know where it's gone."

"I bet I do," Will says, grinning, his eyes still locked on my face. His air of smugness is glowing like a growing aura around him. "What have you done with it Ewan?"

Everyone turns round to stare at me. I let my mouth fall open in shock.

"Are you accusing me, Will?" I take a step towards him, my fists clenched at my side. He stands his ground, and goes on looking at me with those eyes that can read even the most guarded, reluctant mind. It's a wonder he's not on the payroll. I'm not convinced he isn't.

"Ewan?" Roderick appears at Will's side, his hands on his hips. "Have you taken it?"

"Oh what, I'm the nutter with the self-harm issues, therefore I must have taken it? Is that it? If Will's so keen to go pointing the finger, how do we know he hasn't taken it himself, eh?"

"And why would I do that?" Will raises his eyebrows, a self-satisfied smile loitering at the corners of his mouth

"Well there's one easy way for you to prove you haven't taken it Ewan," Roderick's weary drawl interrupts my standoff with Will. "Pull up your sleeves."

"I beg your pardon?" I hiss from behind clenched teeth.

Yes, if I'm going to be honest, I didn't think I'd really get away with it, but I also didn't see this one coming. I look from his face to Will, who's started to laugh, and my skin breaks out in a cold sweat. Why didn't I wait until later? I should have hidden the knife, and enjoyed using it later after all the fuss had died down.

"I'm not showing off my scars in front of everyone," I say, stepping up onto a soapbox fashioned from self-righteous indignation, hoping this might place me out of reach.

"You'd only be showing them to me and Will," Roderick says, going from folding his arms tight across his chest to planting his hands on his hips. "I've seen them before, and I hardly think they're the worst Will has ever seen. Besides, if you've got nothing to hide, surely you want the pleasure of having Will apologise to you in front of everyone at the resident's meeting tonight. Now, show me your arms."

I don't move. I stare at him, my mouth opening and closing as I try to think of a way out, but before anything comes to mind, Gerry materialises at my side. He seizes my arm. There is no point resisting as he yanks up my sleeve to reveal the fresh cut quivering, all bloody and raw, for their inspection. Roderick huffs, Will scoffs.

"Go and get the knife," Roderick's jaw twitches with the effort of controlling the anger flashing in his eyes. "No, wait. Gerry, go with him. We don't want any more stupid stunts."

'A stupid stunt' is a neat way of summing it up, I reflect the next morning when I wake to a ferocious headache, the legacy of having been sedated for the umpteenth time, this time for breaking what Roderick calls 'cardinal rule number one', namely no self-harming on the unit. I wake to the certainty there must be something, an elephant maybe, sitting on my head, such is the nature of the pain not only squeezing my head, but wringing its way down my neck and across my shoulders. Eyes open, eyes closed, nothing helps. I can't get up and for once they leave me to lie in bed and mull over the last few days.

Chapter 38

They leave me alone for a few days. Slowly, my body re-adjusts and the delicious flat calm returns. The last echoes of my mother sneering in my head dissipate as though nothing ever happened, and after making a public apology for my misdemeanour with the knife, I relax back into the unit, its pointless routines and planned activities. I even manage to have a conversation with Ruth about some of her artwork without wanting to slap her, so these are very good drugs indeed. Even Trudy comments I seem calmer than ever.

When I next see Roderick, he says he has a surprise for me. And I am more than merely 'surprised' when he and Gerry lead me out of the Woodlands, and into the main body of the hospital. Unaccustomed to the noise and vast expanse of open space, I stick close to Gerry without so much as even a twinge of embarrassment. The commotion of so many people jostling and milling in the corridors begins to ruffle my calm. My chaperones hurry me along. Near the chapel, Roderick takes out a key, and unlocks a plain, unremarkable door. He ushers me inside.

My mouth falls open. The room is empty, save for a piano. I look at Roderick, my eyes narrowing. He's up to something, I know it.

"Dr. Lockhart and I are of the opinion that denying you the opportunity to play music is counter-productive to your recovery process," Roderick says, folding his arms. "Hospital funds won't stretch to a cello, so this will have to do."

"What makes you think I'd want to play this old joanna?" I sniff, but I can't resist. My fingers are twitching, reaching for the keys with a life of their own. Propping my crutches against the piano, I lift the lid and try the cool, ivory keys. To my surprise, it doesn't sound as bad as I expected. I sink down onto the stool and my fingers waltz off into one of our favourite medleys.

"Just a hunch," Roderick says, but I'm too engrossed to be rattled by his self-congratulating smile. "We are willing to let you come here every afternoon, but there is one condition."

"What?" I look up as my fingers play on.

"No self-harm, or this stops. You understand me, Ewan?"

I nod, but I'll agree to anything at this moment, every cell in my body dancing along to my fingers' tune.

So every day after lunch, I am accompanied to the music room so I can spend time playing on the piano. My escort will settle on a chair by the door and listen to me play. It depends who it is. Sandra likes to sit near me and request her favourite pieces of music, clapping her hands together in delight that I can play almost anything she suggests. Some afternoons she leaves me alone in here with Trudy. As I play, Trudy sits beside me and puts her head on my shoulder. It's like the night we met. These are my favourite afternoons. I can close my eyes, kiss Trudy's soft warm mouth, and pretend I'm anywhere but here.

This afternoon though, it's Gerry's turn. He sits down with a sigh, and produces a music player and pair of earphones. My music doesn't appeal to his pedestrian tastes. I lift the piano lid, and settle down to play.

But I'm not in the mood today. I tinker away through what is normally a reliable repertoire, but nothing serves to set my soul soaring. My left forearm hurts all the way down to my fingers when I play. Some days are worse than others, but it feels tight and uncomfortable this afternoon. With a huff, I try my errant composition to see if the missing section has invented itself in my absence, but there's nothing there. I don't want to play today. I want a cup of tea.

"I've had enough, Gerry," I sigh, and pull the lid down. There is no answer, but he probably can't hear me with his earphones plugged into his ears. I turn round. The chair is empty. There's no one here but me.

"Gerry?" I raise my voice. He must have gone out to talk to someone. My voice boomerangs round the room, but there is no response. I tut, reach for the stick they've given me to replace my crutches and clamber to my feet, my right leg making its customary complaints at having lingered too long in one position. It's nearly three. There will be tea and cake being served back in the unit. I'm looking forward to the chance to read for a bit before teatime. If I remember rightly, I'm on kitchen duties with Will tonight, although I'm still not permitted to handle a knife. I push open the door, and step out into the corridor, expecting Gerry to be leaning against the wall gabbing to some pretty nurse, but he isn't there.

I crane my neck, and look up and down the corridor, trying to spot his shiny blonde hair bobbing above the heads of people thronging along the passageway. People are hurrying up and down the corridor, but I can't see him anywhere. There are so many people. It is visiting time, I suppose. Over in The Woodlands Unit, we never see this volume of people coming and going. I press back against the door to the room with the piano, my heart beating in alarm. It's a little like being back in school, currents of chattering pupils gushing past my office, immersed in their own worlds and oblivious to mine. No one looks at me, Ewan Davies, the schizoid nutter. I am invisible, the outcast lurking beyond the fringe of everyday life.

This time I strain on tiptoe to look for Gerry, but there still is no sign of him. I sigh, exasperated, and wonder if I should report him when we get back for abandoning his post, for leaving me. Tightening my grip on my walking stick, I am about to set off back to the unit by myself, when inspiration cracks a hole in the dull grey monotony of my humdrum life here in hospital, and sears my brain with its brilliant light. No one is watching me. I look round, a thousand butterflies fluttering excited wings inside my chest. The main entrance is that way. I can walk out. I can go home.

With one last look to make sure Gerry hasn't spotted me, I plunge into the torrent of people, hobbling as fast as I can for the entrance. At first the distance seems insurmountable, but I press on. I keep looking round to check if I am being followed, but it is as though I am invisible. People keep bumping into me. I wonder if they're doing it intentionally to hamper my progress and stop me escaping, but I struggle on. Sandra's voice is in my ears. Breathe Ewan, keep calm. But with every step my agitation grows. It's as though the crowds of people are closing in on me, my ears assaulted by their cacophonous chattering. Keep a grip Ewan, I tell myself through gritted teeth. You can do this. You can get out of here. My prize beckons, the outside world luring me to the hospital's wide entrance doors, past the volunteers' post, past the WRVS coffee stand, until at last, I step out into a cool, bright day.

I stand in the entrance, marvelling at the simplest thing, the feel of the wind on my face. How can I never have been so amazed by it before? It rushes over my skin, cold and refreshing, cleansing me of the taint of hospital life, of everything I've been through. I am free. I want to shout and throw my arms up in the air.

"Oi, you, get out of the fucking way."

A man with a mottled red face and greasy combed-over hair is bristling with pent-up frustration and snarling at me, his hands shaking as they grip the handles of a wheelchair bearing a silver-haired, white-faced woman who stares at me from her throne with reproach that one such as I should dare to block her path. I mouth an apology, and step out of the way, only to find myself in the path of a pram.

"Hey! Watch where you're going."

I move, but I tread on someone else's foot, and another person tuts, and a pair of hands shove me, and I turn round, I'm floundering in panic and I'm in someone else's way, and I trip and someone else tuts and stands staring at me like they can see I really am a nutter with whom they must avoid actual physical contact, and I step off the pavement and there is a screeching sound and I see something shiny and red bearing down on me and I go to twist to the side, and it brushes hard and solid against my leg and the driver jumps out and he yells at me to watch where I'm fucking going too, and I don't know what to do I'm so confused, I don't know which way to turn.

And then I spot the trees, beckoning like an oasis from across the hospital's grassy grounds.

They are beautiful, this line of horse chestnut trees. Canopies spread so wide, their leaves rusting with the autumnal chill lurking in the air, they offer me a sanctuary from this bright, noisy, insane world into which I have emerged. I sit down, and press my back against a solid trunk, wondering how old this particular tree is, and thinking about a magazine article I read about how they could tell not only the age of a tree, but the climatic and planetary conditions through which the tree had lived, and I sit there wondering what they could tell about me and what I've endured were they to take a slice of my brain.

The ground beneath the trees is littered with the debris of years of fallen leaves. It is soft and dry, and crumbles between my fingers. I pick up handfuls, watching it disintegrate and letting it scatter, blowing away by the wind stirring the branches above me. I can hear the waves of human activity breaking and receding around the hospital, hear the drone of traffic that encircles us, hear sirens coming and going, and planes passing overhead, but it is nothing to us, the trees and I. We sit together, in one fixed point in the universe, as a chaotic world swirls around us. I was going to go home, I remember, but it feels like too much effort now. I just want to go on sitting under here, sitting, safe with the tree.

Movement catches my eye, a thin figure striding across the grass towards my oasis. As it grows closer, its head bowed as though in contemplation, I realise its hair is slicked back into a ponytail. I sigh and nestle back against the tree. Someone really ought to tell Roderick to get a haircut. He must have no idea how much it would improve his image. People might even take him seriously.

"You think so?" He says as he plonks himself down next to me, leans against the tree, and stretches out his legs with a long sigh. "I take 'me' very seriously as it happens."

He fumbles in his pocket, produces a packet of cigarettes, takes one, and offers them to me. I let my withering glare answer.

"Ach, come on Ewan, live a little."

My gut clenches. That's what Marcia said to me the night she died. I haven't thought about her since that day she appeared in my classroom. A chill breeze blows around my neck and I shiver.

"I can't believe you're offering me a cigarette," I say, shrugging off my unease as he flicks the lighter and smoke puffs around his face. My lip curls.

"You like a drink, I like a smoke," he says, blowing a white plume upwards. "Talking of which, you'll have to watch that when you leave here. Alcohol and anti-psychotics don't mix. I can put you in touch with a very good counsellor who can help you with that. We'll talk about it nearer the time."

I sit very still, barely daring to breathe. I'm not going to give him the satisfaction of asking how he knows about my drinking habits. Trudy again, I expect.

"And cigarette in hand, there you go again, preaching to the rest of us about self-harm."

He guffaws, spluttering on his smoke.

"But that's what makes me so good Ewan," he says, jabbing the air with his cigarette with every word. "If I do 'preach', it's because I've been there. I know how it feels. Anyone can read a book and paraphrase the writer's pain, but they'll never truly understand, not like I do." He sits grinning at what I imagine he thinks is his own genius. I sigh, and go on staring up in to the canopy.

"Something I don't understand though," he says after a few minutes. "Why are you still here in the hospital grounds? When I heard Gerry had lost you, I thought 'that's it', you'd be long gone. What, are you getting soft in your old age?"

"Lost me? What, like an old glove?"

The image of Gerry scouring the corridor, trying to spot me lying lost on the floor makes us both laugh. I think about the brilliance of the idea to walk out, how it shone down on me as I stood there, and my disbelief that I could have wasted so much time up until that point looking for Gerry when I could have been making my escape. Yes, I had thought of going home, but when I examine the notion now, I think I was only really interested in seeing how far I could get before I was detected. Sitting here with Roderick, I wish I'd just gone to find Trudy. We could have had a cup of tea together, that would have been nice.

"When I first noticed Gerry wasn't there, I thought I'd go home. I don't know why, now. It just seemed like a really good idea. I was curious to see how far I'd get. But everything was so noisy and confusing once I got outside, it was frightening. I might have gone back inside, but I couldn't think of the way back to the unit, and it looked safe over here under the trees." The enormity of what I've just said hits me with a winding punch. "Does that mean I'll never go home?"

"You will eventually," he says, stubbing his cigarette out in the deep leaf litter. "But you won't just be walking out on a whim one afternoon. You can't go from a secure unit like The Woodlands to back outside just like that. It's going to be overwhelming, and we need to know how it's going to affect you. We have to build up to it slowly. I'm not just going to sign papers, open the door and tell you to go. You'd be back with us before you know it. Anyway," he crosses one leg over the other. "We still have much more work to do with you. The one thing we've yet to discuss is Marcia."

Marcia. I can imagine her sitting here beside us under the tree, cigarette dangling between her pouty lips, telling me to 'loosen up' and Roderick to 'drop the bullshit' while she fidgets, playing with her long hair and fiddling with her bracelets. It's been almost ten years. I wonder what would have happened in ten years. She'd be married by now, for sure, and I imagine her with children, the picture of her sitting here smoking shifting to include two grubby-faced children, a small girl with her mother's dark hair and insolent eyes refusing to do as she was told while her brother is busy digging in the soil. Marcia would be a contradiction, savage in her impatience, fierce in her protectiveness. But it will never be. I gulp, a lump in my throat.

"You have to let her go," he says, his voice missing its usual bluster.

"I saw her in my classroom the day before my accident."

"Interesting. You didn't tell me that. Why do you think you've found it hard to get over her death?"

"What can I do?" A chill sweeps through my veins as I see her floating anew in her bloody bath. "It can't be undone."

"Can you tell me why you feel responsible for Marcia's death?"

"Aw, come on Ewan, live a little," she said, pressing the lit cigarette into my hand. "One puff isn't going to kill you." We were sitting side-by-side in the open doorway, looking out into my back garden. It was going dark and the air was full of the smell of night-scented stock and the twittering sound of bats zithering here and there through the air. She'd come round to see me because I'd asked her to, because I'd been afraid I was going to cut myself, because she was my 'buddy' the one I called

when I felt bad. We sat there drinking tea, she laughing at me because I was such an old fart, because drinking tea was something her mother did. Then, after I took a drag on her cigarette, she looked at me as though she could look right into my soul, and she kissed me. No warning, she just pressed those full lips against mine and kissed me. And it wasn't like anything I'd experienced before, not like being with Rebecca. But I looked into her eyes, and wiped a tear from their edge with my thumb. I can't, I whispered, my lips mumbling against hers. You're a beautiful, young woman, but you're just a child. I'm much too old. It wouldn't be right.

I pause, caught in the memory's burning pain. She had looked at me as though I'd slapped her, or called her a name, or done something unspeakable and inappropriate. But she was the same age as most of my pupils, and I was, although Rebecca and I had separated, still a married man. I couldn't bring myself to do what she wanted: I'd never thought of her that way; I didn't want to think of her that way; it wouldn't have been right. I didn't realise how badly she must have been hurting beneath her youthful swagger, too caught up in the soap opera of my own life to reach out to her, to realise she was asking me for help. Marcia shrank from me as though I had caused her great harm. She picked up her bag, and slipped away into the night. I would never have let her go had I realised she was going home to kill herself.

"She didn't go home to kill herself," Roderick says. "She came to see me." He takes another cigarette out of the packet and lights it, and for a moment, I think I see his hand shake.

"It was nearly half-past ten when my doorbell rang. I'd gone to bed. I didn't hear it, but my wife did. She woke me up. We lay there hoping whoever it was would go away, but they didn't. In the end I went downstairs to see who it was, and it was Marcia.

"She'd been drinking. I could smell it on her breath as she pushed past. She sat on my stairs, and said she'd been thinking about me all day, and decided it was time she came to see me. She said she knew I had a thing for her, and would I like to take it further. I might have been able to get her out of the house at that point, only Cathy, that's my wife, came to see what was going on.

"When she saw Cathy at the top of the stairs, Marcia went nuts, accusing me of cheating on her, and so on. I thought I was going to have to restrain her, but I thought if I could get her talking, calm her down, it would be all right. But it wasn't, I couldn't get near her, she was screaming and throwing anything she could lay her hands on, and in the end, one of our neighbours arrived at the door shouting he'd rung the police.

"That was it. She bolted out of the house, and no matter how hard me and the neighbour ran, we couldn't catch her. We must have chased her half-way through Thatchington before we lost her down by the river. I sent the police round to her flat, and rang the hospital to let them know she'd be coming in, but they never found her. She'd gone round to her boyfriend, he was a dealer of course, shot herself full of smack, and taken a knife into the bath. No one will ever know if she meant to kill herself. You and me, we might have been what the police would call 'contributing circumstances', but what happened is no one's fault. Marcia Hammond had a history of mental health problems and a drug habit to match. You can't blame yourself. It was probably only a matter of time before something like that happened, whether you or I for that matter, slept with her is beside the point. She was a disaster waiting to happen."

'A disaster waiting to happen'. I am staring at the human activity swirling to and from the hospital, but everything seems muted. The colours have changed from remarkable to monochrome, individual noises have blended into a single dirge as everything, the whole world, courses a predestined path into inevitability, the process scooped up and placed in a glass case to be gawped at, revealed in all its ugliness by his damning indictment.

"Is that what I was, 'a disaster waiting to happen'? Is that how you saw all of us in the group?" I say, turning to look at him, the betrayal draining the pleasure of sitting here under the trees. Ever since I met him I've watched him working with his patients as though he were advising chess moves across an imaginary board of psychological rights and wrongs. He made us feel as though we could all win. All we had to do to checkmate our demons was to master our vices, overcome our individual flaws, and everything would be all right. The thought that he knew all along which of us didn't stand a chance of succeeding reveals his approach as nothing other than a sham, a pretence of caring. And he hid it all under the disguise of 'you can trust me, I'm one of you'. I don't want one of his cigarettes, but I could use a large scotch.

"No," he shrugs. "That's not true. And besides, you kept so much to your chest, no one would ever have known. But Marcia's death brought home to me how little I really knew about mental illness. I mean, I thought I knew." He spreads his fingers wide, his eyes staring at some point beyond his feet, and I catch a fleeting warble in his voice as he stares his own demons in the face. "I thought I knew everything. 'Come to me and I'll help you'. What didn't I know? I had years of psychiatric nursing, of caring for my mother with her dementia, dealing with my own stuff and all. I thought I knew everything. But I couldn't save Marcia. I went over and over that night, dug over everything in the weeks leading up to it, but all I could find was my own ignorance staring at me from every turn. So I did more studying, got a degree, and here we are. I still don't know everything, but," he breaks the spell with a flash of his smug grin. "I am good."

I glare at him, my eyes narrowed at the thought that despite what he knows of the workings of the human mind, he can be so puffed full of his own inflated self-opinion.

"Don't look at me like that, you know I'm right," he snorts, and stubs out the second cigarette. "Come on," he says, glancing at his watch. "Much as it's pleasant sitting out here under the trees, I have work to do, and it's nearly teatime. Let's get you back indoors."

He holds out his hand, and helps me up. Together, we walk back inside. And despite the extent to which Roderick's company annoys me, for the first time since Marcia died, I feel at peace with my conscience. A burden has lifted from my shoulders. It wasn't my fault.

Six months later

Chapter 39

The car surges on, speeding through a landscape rendered featureless by the darkness, my discomfort gnawing deeper with every road sign directing the way to places I had pretended to forget, but whose names come back to my tongue as though it were only yesterday I last saw them. Fettercairn. Laurencekirk. Inverbervie. Durris. As the miles slip by, so too do the years. I am seventeen again. I never left.

I stir in my seat, shuffling limbs which have been bored into stiffness by the sheer longevity of the journey. Trudy glances over from the driver's seat, but I go on staring out of the window watching the signs go by, pretending I haven't noticed. I made her promise she won't keep asking me how I'm feeling before I agreed to this trip, but the words hang thick in the air between us. And am I all right? I might be, if I were anywhere but here.

Roderick and Trudy have cooked this up between them, and I'm the only one nursing reservations. One minute I'm agreeing it would be nice to spend a weekend away with Trudy to celebrate having been released from hospital, the next I'm embroiled in a conversation with Roderick about how constructive it would be for me to go back to Aberdeen and, if only for a few minutes, confront my past by visiting my parents. I think it's a ridiculous idea, but he became so evangelical about how much he thinks it will help with my recovery, I was afraid he would insist upon coming with us. It's one thing to have a drink with him in The Dolphin, something we did in the run-up to my release, but I'm not sharing a room with him on holiday.

We'd silenced every conversation in the pub that evening when we'd walked in. I'd bought us a drink, beer for him, lemonade for me, only to find him introducing himself to Jeremy Fotheringham as a consultant psychiatric officer after the latter asked if my being there that evening was what amounted to 'care in the fucking community'. We sat down at a table in the Dolphin, by the window. I'd sank down into cool relief at being rendered inconspicuous and unworthy of the attention my appearance had precipitated, by ducking below eye level of those assembled at the bar. Even Nigel's eyes skittered in their sockets, betraying nerves at having a dangerous lunatic under his roof. There was an obvious shrinking from my presence, hence the reason we ever found a seat in the first place. I sipped my lemonade, and raised one eyebrow.

"A consultant psychiatric officer? Is there such a thing?"

"Ha," Roderick leant back in his chair, his eyes dancing with admiration at what he still, regrettably, thinks of as his clever wit. "Now then Ewan, haven't you learnt anything from me? Cardinal rule number one is counter bullshit with bullshit.

"I thought cardinal rule number one was 'do as I say'?"

"Ach, you're good," he laughed, picking up his glass. "But you're not good enough. Different context, see? That doesn't apply when you're dealing with dickheads who think mental illness is something that only happens to other people. I love it when the high-and-mighty fall. It makes my day. You know all about it now," he said, dropping his voice to a whisper and thumbing over his shoulder to where Jeremy was holding court, yet continuing to throw me apprehensive glances. "The higher a man spins his web of pretence, the further he has to fall and the bigger the mess to sort out. So you see he can be as snide as he likes, scoffing at 'care in the fucking community', as he put it, but your friendly community practitioner here will be waiting for him when it happens."

"If it happens," I muttered. "Mental illness isn't that prevalent you can predict who will and won't suffer. And he's the sort of jammy sod who will sail through life unscathed. They always do."

"Ah, don't be so sure," he mused. "You've no idea what goes on behind closed doors, and you've got to ask yourself why, out of all the people in here, he was the one to make the comment."

"Because he is, as you said, a dickhead?"

"Yes, but in my experience," he says, lifting one eyebrow. "The ones who point the finger and shout the loudest usually have the most to hide."

I hoped he'd forget about the whole Aberdeen thing, but it seemed the more he thought about it, the more inspired an idea it seemed. It didn't help me that Trudy was as excited about it as he. She even suggested writing to my mother.

"I can't see the point," I'd huffed, face down and gripping the sides of the table as Roderick fiddled around with the syringe full of my medicine. I have to report to him for this once a fortnight, but he says he'll wean me off the anti-psychotics if I can prove to him I'm learning to control my schizophrenic symptoms by myself. He expects me to keep not just a diary, but some sort of journal detailing any thoughts or worries I have about being watched or what he calls 'anything unusual' I start to notice, including strange insects.

"Accepting who you are has been the key to your whole illness," he said. "Now, no one's suggesting you forget everything that happened and throw yourself headlong into some sort of loving reunion with your family, but if you could just make some sort of peace with your mother in particular, I think that would be an enormous step."

I harrumphed by way of a response, hoping he'd drop the subject.

"I'm sure she'd love to see you," Trudy said. She was sat in a chair by Roderick's desk, waiting while I lay on the padded table behind the screen, trousers undone and hoping he'd employ less force that I've learnt he's capable of using to plunge the syringe into my bare buttocks,. "I don't know why you're so sure she wouldn't be proud of you, you're the head of music at one of the best schools in the country."

"Was," I corrected, gritting my teeth as the needle pricked into my skin. The week I left hospital I went to see Mrs. Phillips to hand in my resignation. I saw it as a pre-emptive move, solving the problem of how to dismiss me. It couldn't have come as much of a surprise.

"I won't lie to you Ewan, I'm glad you've made this decision," she'd said, folding my letter between her fingers. "It's good to see you feeling better, but it would have been difficult to integrate you back into school life in view of what's happened to you. I can see you've recovered, but it might have been a little awkward with some of the parents."

"I didn't think there would be a job for me to come back to anyway," I said, shrugging my shoulders. Alex had already told me Rebecca had taken over. They even had the awful Miss Harris back, an easy replacement since she supposedly already knew the ropes. Once upon a time I would have been aghast at the probable drop in standards, but thankfully the drugs work too well for me to be so easily upset. However, I knew at that point I could never go back, whether they'd wanted me or not. If I couldn't summon the need to care about what was being done in my absence, my heart wasn't in it any more and I'd never find the energy and enthusiasm to step back into my previous role.

"Why didn't you tell me about the history between yourself and Rebecca? I would never have put you in the position of working with her, had I known. It must have been intolerable."

I shrugged again. Why did I do it? Out of a sense of duty, a hope to recapture something long gone, or perhaps because, sub-consciously, I was all ready hell-bent on self-destruction? All of these things, and yet none of these things hold the answer.

"She needed a job. I thought I could handle it."

Silence brooded as she considered my words, and I lost myself in wondering whether Rebecca precipitated my unravelling, or was merely another symptom of the process in motion. I'm not sure I will ever know. I'm not sure it matters.

"There is one thing," Mrs. Phillips said, leaning across the desk. "Would you consider instrument tuition?"

"I thought you said the parents wouldn't like it."

"Yes, that is true," she said as I shuffled in my seat. "But you are a brilliant teacher. Alex tells me you're teaching his children to play. I don't want to lose you, and I think the students miss you. Working with just a few pupils on a one-to-one basis as you'd be, I can't see why your health issues would be a problem."

'I don't want to lose you'? Never could I have imagined hearing her say that to me. I don't think she had any idea how much of a gift she gave me that day beyond the offer of a job, something I had imagined forever out of reach now I had a reputation as a certifiable lunatic. The idea that she valued me and held my small contribution to the school in some regard wove protective layers around the shattered fragments of my ruptured self-esteem Trudy was helping to repair. What could I say? I promised to think about it. I still haven't said 'yes'. But I will.

Trudy sighs, stretches her arms up to the top of the steering wheel, and shifts in her seat, her foot still pressed to the floor as we fly past other cars dawdling along the road. There have been a lot of speed cameras, sentinels lurking along the road from Dundee, and I'm afraid she might expect a ticket from each one. The thought doesn't trouble her.

"You know the one thing I'm looking forward to the most when we get there?" She takes one hand off the steering wheel, and props up her head with her elbow resting on the door.

"Would that be apart from me taking my clothes off?"

"A bath," she grins and her teeth gleam in the light from her instrument panel. "And you taking your clothes off, of course."

"And dinner," I say, my stomach growling, lunch a distant memory.

"Perhaps we should have room service, and combine all three. Oh wow!" She exclaims, sitting up in her seat and leaning forward. You never told me it was so beautiful."

Just when it seemed as though Aberdeen was some figment of the imagination, travellers doomed to drive through the darkness for ever, the road falls away and there lies the city waiting, sprawling as though on a couch, a seductive, twinkling vision of fairy streetlights stretched out in front of us. As Trudy is gasping, I'm back to glowering, the twenty-five intervening years blanked out in a blink.

"Welcome home," the endless rose beds whisper.

"Are those rose bushes? Wow, they're everywhere. I bet it's magnificent when they're all in bloom. I never imagined it would be like this."

"You are back," the familiar street names sigh.

"Look, that sign says 'Hazelhead'; isn't that a lovely name?"

"Did you think we'd forgotten you?" Memories mutter, lurking in the shadows of tree-lined streets.

"Gosh, look at the buildings. Is it straight on here, Ewan?"

"No, turn right."

She glances at me, concern gelling once more in the air between us. I hadn't meant to sound so gruff, but if I hadn't made her change direction, we'd be driving past my parents' house on Queen's Road, and I'm not ready for that yet. We're doing it tomorrow, she's told me, tomorrow at ten. I concentrate on taking deep breaths, thinking how best to counter the awkward silence filling the car. She's put so much thought into trying to arrange a nice weekend, family reunions aside, I don't want to spoil things for her.

"Sorry," I reach across and slide my fingers across her soft, warm thigh. "I didn't mean to be short. I'm just tired, that's all, and being here, well, it's a bit unsettling. I mean, it's one thing to talk about it, and another thing entirely to be here. I'm sorry."

"Apology noted," she says as my fingers rove up and under her skirt. "I'll let you make it up to me as soon as you've taken your clothes off."

She's booked a room for us at The Caledonian Hotel, right in the centre of town. When I was younger, it was a hellish vision of tartan carpets and kilted staff, but the modern version is one of opulence, of thick, velvet drapes, gleaming chandeliers, gold and marble. Trudy giggles as she hands over her keys to an immaculate concierge who offers to park her car. I find him obsequious, but she is blushing, flattered by his polished patter. She giggles too as the receptionist refers to me as 'Mr. Smith'.

"Mr. and Mrs. Smith," she says, slipping her arm through mine as we wait for a porter to show us to our room. "I never thought about that when I booked it. They probably think I'm your secretary or something."

Our room is right at the front of the building so its majestic windows, veiled with voile, overlook the leafy trees of Union Street gardens. Trudy appears at my side as I look out, and I put my arm around her body as I point out landmarks: the theatre, the art gallery, the university buildings, and the hall where I had to perform at countless music festival competitions throughout my childhood. She presses against me, her eyes blazing with the yellowy gold of the streetlights, her face tilted to me and a smile, the certainty this was a good idea of hers after all, playing around her lips. I let the curtain fall, and cup her face in my hands. Her skin is warm and soft against mine. She closes her eyes as I lean in for a kiss.

We are interrupted by a knock, by a waitress bringing the tray of tea we'd ordered by way of a prelude to our evening, the chance to relax after our arduous journey, and, hopefully, relieve some of my growing anxiety. But I don't need tea for that, not while I have Trudy.

She slides her hands down my chest, her fingers unbuttoning my shirt. The sweep of her hands across my bare flesh leaves a tingling trail, nerve endings trembling under her touch as she eases the fabric from my shoulders. My lips trace a line of kisses along the line of her jaw and down across the shy, soft skin under her ear, which makes her shiver and gasp, pressing herself harder against me, her hips moving against mine, her yielding curvy flesh beckoning me in until nothing, nothing matters than to lose myself in the here and now, to make love to her, and she to me, while whole universes revolves around us. She takes my hand, and leads me to bed.

Chapter 40

The next morning dawns grey and sodden with driving rain. I lie listening to the city alive and throbbing with the roar of traffic swishing through wet streets, the clip-clopping feet of bodies coming and going about their daily business while Trudy slumbers beside me, and I fret over the day to come. There is a heavy, sick feeling in the pit of my stomach, and before Trudy wakes, in my head I have sneaked out and escaped many times over.

She yawns and stretches amid the bedclothes like a sleepy cat, then her eyes open and she sees me, my nerves stretched so tight, I think if she touches me, my body will literally twang with jarring sound.

"Are you all right?" Her voice is quiet, she is afraid to ask.

"No." I'm clutching the bedclothes, clinging to them as though they could shield me from what is to come. Part of me wishes Roderick was here. One look at me and I'm sure he'd write the whole thing off as a bad idea. It is a bad idea. Maybe it was a test, to see how far I'd go along with their plans. Maybe I don't really need to do this after all, maybe they never expected me to.

"It's going to be all right," Trudy's hand appears from under the blankets and alights on mine. I startle. She holds on, her warm fingers smoothing my skin. "We don't have to stay for long, and then it will be all over. And you're going to take me to see that castle afterwards, aren't you? I've asked the hotel to pack a picnic."

Another of Roderick's bright ideas, have something lined up for afterwards, both as a treat, and so we can make our excuses if things don't go well. Trudy doesn't realise we will have to leave the city, the castle lies to the south, and I'm hoping I can persuade her to just keep on driving, back the way we came.

Trudy orders breakfast. I can't even stomach the sight of her eating, so I disappear into the bathroom to shower and shave. When I'm done, I put on my favourite shirt and trousers, worrying what my mother will make of my taste, worrying what she will make of Trudy's taste, what she will make of Trudy at all, and, oh god, I think I'm going to be sick.

At half-past nine, we get into the car, and set off.

Number three hundred and seventy five Queens Road has been in my father's family for generations. As Trudy pulls up outside the black, wrought iron railings which barricade the garden from the dirty, noisy street, I dare to look up at the building, and notice how little it has changed. On a sodden, grey day like this when everything is running with rainwater, the faint glimmer of light from its grand bay windows, hung with ruby red drapes, do nothing to soften its austerity. I gulp. There is nothing welcoming in this granite edifice. For a moment, I think about leading Trudy round the side, through the wooden gate in the garden wall and across the gravel to the less imposing back door, just as I would have done as a child. But it's been so long since I've been here, it doesn't seem appropriate. I take a deep breath as she swings open the gate.

Trudy takes my arm as we start up the path. My heart is thumping, my feet faltering. There is no need to do this. I don't want to do this. I stop. Trudy squeezes my arm.

"It's okay Ewan. I'm here. We don't have to stay long. It will be all right, I promise."

I don't know how she can make that promise, but I can't argue because I don't trust myself to speak. My feet begin to move again, chivvied along by her momentum.

We reach the bottom of the steps that lead up to the front door. Again, my feet falter, resolve getting too weak to resist the temptation for flight, but at that moment, the heavy wooden door with its gleaming brass knocker creaks. It grinds open. And there in the doorway appears a figure which is both familiar and unrecognisable, such has it aged. It is my mother, and a single word issues from her painted mouth.

"John."

We gawp at each other. She seems smaller somehow, diminished by time. Her dark wavy hair is still dark and wavy, and her face is as artfully made-up as ever, but they don't sell anything to disguise her weathered skin, as wrinkled as an old leather bag. Her shoulders droop, and I notice she is leaning, the bony knuckles of her shaking, skeletal hand gleaming, on an ivory-topped walking stick. The years, it would seem, have not been kind.

"Good morning Mrs. Davidson, I'm Trudy." She trots up the steps, her hand extended, but my mother is too busy staring at me to notice. We go on staring at each other, the air thick with recriminations unspoken. "Is it all right if we come in?"

"Yes, yes of course," my mother says, the warm, buttery familiarity of her voice setting off a throb of nostalgia in my gut which threatens to overwhelm what little poise I have. I didn't have a bad childhood, far from it, and the simple sound of her voice pitches me headfirst into warm memories I had hidden along with the ones I chose to forget. She opens the door wider. "Would you like to come in, John?"

No, not really, but I walk up the steps. I reach the top, and we, my mother and I, we look at each other, unsure what to do. Should I hug her? Her eyes are bright with tears, but she holds her composure, pride keeping emotion in check. Ever since Trudy first mentioned visiting I've wondered what I would say to my mother. Now I'm here, I still have no idea.

I walk past her, and into the dark hall with its bottle green walls, and look round. Everything is as I remember it, from the Turkish runners leading down the hallway, to the teak table with its crystal vase of cloying, scented white lilies. Nothing has changed, and yet everything is altered. My mother shuts the door. I startle, trapped, and look to Trudy. We shouldn't have come, I knew it.

"Would you like a cup of tea?"

"That would be lovely, thank you," Trudy says, taking my arm.

"Come through to the sitting room," my mother says, wobbling on her stick. Then she pauses, and turns to me. "You remember the way?"

"I don't think I could forget," I say, trying to decipher a second meaning.

"In here," she says, shoving the dark door open with her stick, light spilling out into the hall.

"I'll come and help you make the tea," Trudy insists. "Ewan, er, John, I mean," she winks. "You go and sit down, and I'll help your mum."

I walk into the bright sitting room which overlooks the back garden. This was always my favourite room, although with its cream carpet and beige settees, I was seldom allowed in here as a child. Its huge bay windows are as fussily draped with swathes of fabric as the front, but with a lighter fabric which compliments rather than detracts from the world outside. I cross the floor and look out across the garden. At this time of year both the ancient apple tree and the enormous beech at the foot of the garden are adorned with spring's zingy, lime-green foliage, and as I watch, a squirrel hops across the lawn.

I turn, and look around the room. Everything still looks the same in here too. It is as though I just popped out for the afternoon. On top of a walnut sideboard, nestling in between a set of fancy glass tumblers arranged around a matching decanter filled, I know, with Glenmorange, my father's preferred tipple, are pictures of me.

In some of the faded pictures, I'm so young I don't remember the day they were taken. Others show me dressed up in a suit, posing with my cello. I loosen my collar, remembering that suit, it was hot, nylon and uncomfortable. There is a picture of me with Grandma Felicity standing in the doorway to her castle. I pick it up to study it closer, plonking it back down when the door opens and my mother shuffles into the room, Trudy following with the tea tray. She catches my eye and winks. I wonder what on earth they've been talking about.

"Sit down John," my mother says, waving me to a seat. "Thank you dear," she says, as Trudy puts the tray down and sets about handing round the cups. So long as Trudy keeps bustling, the silence isn't too onerous, but once she sits down, having run out of things to do, it flexes its muscles and leers at us sitting there. My mother clasps her bony hands on her lap.

"I must say dear, it was a surprise when your letter arrived," my mother tells Trudy, her eyes watching me. "It had been so long, I didn't even know if John was still alive." She shifts position in her chair. "What made you decide to get in touch? Why has it taken so long?"

"I don't know," I say, my voice barely a whisper. "But you know why I left. I didn't think I'd ever come back."

"Do I?" She lifts her saucer, the cup rattling.

"What matters is that you're here now, Ewan," Trudy says. "Sorry, I mean 'John'."

"What, did you change your name as well? Even that wasn't good enough for you, eh? I'm glad your father decided he couldn't face seeing you. Would have broken his heart, that."

"That's not fair," Trudy says, flexing in her role as peacemaker.

"How would you feel if either of your two boys vanished without even so much as one word to say they were all right, eh? Don't tell me you'd stand for it. One word," she turns back to me. "Just one word, a postcard or something to let us know you were all right. Such a small thing. Why couldn't you have done it?"

I should have come with some sort of recorder hidden in my pocket so I could play this to Roderick, right before I wring his scrawny neck for suggesting this was a good idea. Trudy is shaking her head. I hope she's satisfied too, but instead she speaks up, and hers is the voice of sense, of calm in this malevolent maelstrom.

"You know I wouldn't stand for it," she says. "But if that's what happened, I would be too relieved to find out they were alive and well to bear a grudge. John's here now, and he hasn't been well. Surely you can put your differences aside."

"Haven't been well, eh?" Her green eyes make a sweeping appraisal. "Is that why you're so thin? Of course, you weren't well when you went missing. Is that why you've been gone all these years, because of the schizophrenia?"

"Yes, I suppose some of it was," I say, surprised because this hasn't occurred to me before. Perhaps this is what Roderick was driving at. I left because she wouldn't listen, because I was convinced she was trying to kill me in revenge for refusing to audition for the conservatoire, and when that failed, that's when she had me sectioned. But perhaps both none and all of this are true, states of mind created, yes, by my schizophrenia. I look at Trudy. She nods and smiles.

I see my mother's demeanour soften, as though a brittle mask, her protection has slid away. She shuffles once more in her seat, nods and drops her head.

"I'm sorry if I seem sharp, but it hasn't been easy and I do think you could have made an effort to keep in touch." She lifts her head, and this time the tears are glistening, wavering on the edges of her lids. "I would have liked to have known you were still alive. You've no idea how much I dreaded every phone call, every knock at the door, fearing it was the police to say they'd found your body. That's why Graham's not here," she says to Trudy. "He couldn't cope with John having a mental illness, and in the end, it was easier for him to think he was dead."

"Well, at least you've had the chance to see each other now," Trudy says. "I think it's been brave of you both, but we will have to go soon. At least it won't be so difficult the next time."

'The next time'? I didn't sign up to anything other than one visit. My mother might have charmed Trudy, but not everything that happened can be explained away by schizophrenia. Some of it was very real.

"So soon?" My mother's relief is palpable. She reaches for her stick, and seems to creak to her feet. I stand up. We stare at each other across the room before she speaks. "There's something of yours here I thought you might like. Come and see."

She leads the way back down the hallway towards the front door, but turns into the room on the right hand side; my old music room. I follow her in, my feet hesitant, wondering what I might find. As in the rest of the house, it is as though everything is suspended in time, the only difference in here being that the red letters I daubed across the wall, 'help me, she's trying to kill me' have gone. I wonder if they washed off, or are merely imprisoned between layers of powder blue, waiting to tell their story if ever the paint should come to be peeled back by the hands of a skilled archaeologist. Perhaps this is why I was so drawn to Rebecca. I hoped she would be the one to unearth the truth for me, never realising it could only ever be told by me myself.

The dark mahogany piano stands as polished as ever. I go to it, drawn by its sleek dark looks. The lid lifts, and I cannot resist but run my fingers over the keys. It sounds as marvellous as ever.

"I keep it tuned," I hear my mother's voice crack as she talks to Trudy. "I've always kept it tuned in case he came back."

I turn. Trudy has her arms around my mother, who's nestling, sobbing against her shoulder like a small child.

"Why don't you play something?" Trudy says. "I think she'd like it."

I shrug. I sit down. My fingers tinker here and there, moving from tune to tune as I play when I'm trying to impress my pupils with the sounds a piano can really make. I was never interested in becoming a concert pianist because I like messing around and breaking the rules too much. My fingers fly up and down the keys, I lose myself in the beautiful tinkling sound, and something occurs to me. What am I playing, but the missing section from my composition, pouring up and out of my soul as though I've never had any difficulty expressing it. I play and play triumphant in the knowledge I am not going to forget this. All I have to do is listen to the quiet music in my head.

"That was beautiful," my mother says, blowing her nose as I pull the lid back down over the keyboard. "He always had such a talent, didn't he Graham?"

278

I turn round. A tall, skeletal figure with straight white hair and glasses just like mine is standing in the doorway, staring as though he's seem a ghost, as though I might fly across the room and attack him, as though I might taint him with my madness, but he nods, swallowing hard.

"That he did Margot. That he did." He turns on his heel, and disappears down the hall.

Trudy helps my mother up. I'm shuffling my feet and looking at the floor. We've stayed much longer than I expected, and now I'm exhausted, ready to leave. My mother hobbles across the room.

"I don't know if you want it, of course you can leave it here if you'd prefer, but it's been waiting for you all these years," she says, and she runs her hand over my cello's smooth black case. "It's yours. Take it if you want it."

I hadn't noticed it when I walked into the room, my attention focussed on the piano. But now I see it, it calls to me with a siren's voice. Do I want my cello? I ache to feel it between my legs, to feel its strings vibrating under my fingers, to hold its bow. Claire Patrick's instrument was a nag compared to this thoroughbred. I want to take it out of its case and lose the rest of the day making it sing. I look at my mother, and this time, it is my eyes blurry with tears.

"It's yours," she rasps. "Take it."

We don't go to Dunotter Castle. From the second my eyes saw my cello sitting there, trapped in its case for all this time, there was no way I was ever going anywhere than back to the hotel, to anywhere I could release it and let it tell its story for the first time in years. Trudy doesn't argue. And she waits patiently, playing roulette with the city's traffic department by parking across double yellow lines on Union Street while I sprint into the music shop where I spent so much time in my youth to buy reams of blank manuscript paper. We take it, and our picnic, back to our room.

Trudy unpacks lunch, and sets about making a pot of tea. She curls up on the bed knowing, I think, she has lost me for the time being. I sit at the dressing table, her cosmetics shoved out of my way, my pen flying across the staves, recording the notes which have eluded me for so long. And when I've finished, the umpteen cups of tea gone cold, Trudy fallen asleep and my lunch untouched, I prise open the stiffened clasps of the cello's case.

She is overjoyed to see me. I help her out, and she leans into my arms for the first time in years. My fingers strum her strings, and she hums as I adjust her into tune. I sit down with the pages of my composition, but I don't need them. As I begin to play, she sings the notes with such intonation, such feeling, I wonder how I could have been so blind, so stupid as to think I could have written this or written anything without her.

I play until my fingers are so sore I can't press them hard enough against the strings to produce a clean sound. Putting the bow down, I examine my treacherous hand in the half-light of streetlamps shining into the unlit room.

"That was beautiful."

I swing round. Trudy is smiling at me from the bed, her sleepy eyes gleaming in the light from the windows. I had forgotten she was even here.

I lay my cello back in her case, my joints stiff and creaking after sitting for so long. Trudy shoves the remains of lunch aside so I can lie down beside her.

"You haven't eaten anything."

"I didn't notice I was hungry," I say. She catches my fingers, and studies them with her nurse's eyes.

"These look painful."

"They'll toughen up in a few weeks."

She smiles. Her fingers brush the side of my face, and catch hold of my chin. I am lost to the irresistible draw of her melting chocolate eyes, her inviting mouth.

"You're happy," she whispers. "I've never seen you seem so light and bubbly. It's as though everything that's been troubling you has suddenly disappeared."

It's true. Roderick's going to be insufferable in his smugness. But I've found a piece of me, a chunk that had been missing for so long, I had forgotten it was gone at all.

"Ewan Davies, I love you," she holds my face between her hands. "Sane and insane, I love all of you, every last bit." And she presses her smiling mouth to mine in the gentlest of kisses.

I thought I loved Rebecca, but it wasn't like this. Our showy passion had everything to do with me hiding myself behind my red-haired firebrand as though she was some sort of sticking plaster with the power to hold together the crumbling edges of my psyche as it did everything it could to avoid the black hole sucking at its centre. And just like all my efforts to hide from myself, it was destined to fail.

Afterwards

The air in the church is alive, buzzing with the buzz of hushed conversations. I draw back the vestry's thick red velvet curtain just far enough to let me see out. Thick creamy candles are burning in every window, but it's not these I'm looking at but the swarms of heads bobbing on the pews. I swallow, and loosen my collar. It is hot in here, and my hands are sweating. My eyes scan the church and see Alex with Tessa, Vi and her friend Agnes. There's a woman with straight black hair chatting to Roderick, I wonder if it's his wife.

There is a rustling behind me. I swing round, my heart thumping. It's Trudy. She has poured herself into this beautiful, rusty-red taffeta dress which wraps around her curves. Her eyes are bright, her lips painted red, and in this moment, there is nothing I'd rather do than take her home and unwrap her. She walks towards me, her hips swaying, and slides her arm around me as she takes her place at my side.

"You have a house-full," she says, craning her neck to follow my gaze around the curtain. "Neil's gone to find some more chairs."

"So many people," I sigh. I can't see her, but I know my mother is somewhere in the church. Trudy insisted on inviting her, she insisted on coming.

"Are you nervous?"

"No, not really. I just wasn't sure many people would come. Neil's going to be chuffed anyway." I can see him flapping up and down the aisle, and I chuckle. "Although I bet he's in a tizz over health and safety regulations."

Trudy giggles, winds her arm tighter around my waist, and presses her head against my shoulder. I'm just about the kiss her, when a door opens behind us, and Della, the organist, scurries into the room.

"Mrs. Davies, you really ought to go and find your seat," she says to Trudy. "They're almost ready to start. How are you Ewan? Not too nervous, I hope. I've never seen the church so packed," she stands up on tiptoes and peers over my shoulder.

"I'll see you afterward," my wife says, kissing my cheek. "Good luck. I would say 'break a leg' that's what you're supposed to say before a performance, isn't it?" She grins at Della. "But frankly, after the last time, I'd rather you didn't."

"Don't worry. I'm not in a hurry to repeat that experience." It still feels stiff, and it aches when rain is coming. The consultant says it's to be expected at my age, the damned cheek.

Trudy pulls a black lace shawl around her shoulders, bustles out, and shuts the door. Della smiles, and begins pacing. I turn to the black case leaning against the wall and open it to reveal the polished body of my cello, 'the other Mrs. Davies' as Trudy puts it. I lift her out, and check her strings, but she is perfectly in tune, we've been practicing all day.

Neil's face appears around the door to announce it's time.

Applause breaks out as I follow Della out onto the dais. She sits at the piano. I settle myself on a stool and ready the cello between my knees. Hushed anticipation hovers in the air, but I'm too busy concentrating to find it unnerving. Someone coughs. Della sits with her hands poised. I raise my head, meet her waiting eyes, and nod. We begin.

I sweep through several of my favourite pieces, my bow really an extension of my arm, the mellow sound it makes against the strings filling the air, setting it vibrating all the way up to the ancient rafters high above our heads. Della plays well once her nerves settle. When I first asked her if she'd be my accompanist, she sat wringing her hands, lodged in refusal. She has struggled to find herself since Henry died, so fixed in the mindset of 'we' it has almost been impossible for her to embrace 'I'. Tonight is as much about her teetering along a road of recovery as me, an important step for her too.

Our audience applaud, but I don't notice. I have one last piece to play. Della slips out from behind the piano, and goes to sit down beside Neil. The church is so still, it's as though everyone is holding their breath. I close my eyes, and summon the music, the composition I have spent my life creating, the notes which come together to sing the story of my life. And as I play, there is no one there but me and my cello, singing our song to the stars, to the cosmos, to all the far-flung places, and the worlds in-between. Our music sighs and sorrows, it twirls on pointed toes and goes tippety-tapping, it's feet getting louder and louder until at last, with one final crescendo, it vaults the realms of possibility and echoes back from the space, the potential, before landing back into now, the moment, the only place to truly be.

The applause is deafening. My audience get to their feet, clapping. My face explodes with fiery colour, and I shrink, mortified at the attention. I don't know what to do. This part is unknown and unrehearsed. Playing, performing, yes, these are things I understand. How do I react to their reception? I've no idea.

Neil steps up to try and save me. He takes my arm and pulls me to my feet. The applause becomes louder. I bow.

The Women's Institute have excelled themselves with the spread laid on for afterwards. Trestle tables groan under the weight of sandwiches and every manner of cake. Vi's pouring tea from an enormous enamel pot. She sees me looking over, gives an enormous grin and waves. I wave back. Everyone wants to shake my hand. I move through the mass of people as though I'm in a bubble, looking out, watching as someone who looks like me goes through the motions of smiling, shaking hands, gratefully receiving compliments and cracking jokes with his friends. Even the hubbub of conversation is muted, shut out by my bubble until somebody slips their arm through mine. I turn. It's Trudy, smiling.

"Happy?" She hands me a cup and saucer.

"I feel a bit like I'm dreaming, like I'm going to wake up in a minute and discover none of this is real."

"Would you like me to pinch you really hard?" She says, her hand snaking around my waist. I laugh, and twist out of her way before she gets the chance to fulfil the threat. And as I move, something catches my eye. I freeze, dread strumming taut nerves.

"What is it?" Her eyes harden, scrutinising me for a clue, but I am a polished performer and I give nothing away. A sip of tea smoothes away the ruffles in my composure, and I've never found it hard to force a smile. To me, mine is a very ordinary madness, and I'm more than used to it by now.

"It's nothing,"

I'll tell her later I saw a beetle in her hair.

The end

Acknowledgements

A huge thank you to my wonderful first readers: Maureen, Sue R, Michelle, Sue J and Katrine. If it wasn't for all your help, kind words and encouragement I would never dared to see this project all the way through into print.

Lots of love to you all,

Sam.

5457614R00159

Printed in Great Britain
by Amazon.co.uk, Ltd.,
Marston Gate.